THE SLAVE SCHEME

THE SLAVE SCHEME

a novel

Eric Krantz

Epigraph Books
Rhinebeck, New York

Paperback ISBN: 978-1-951937-15-7
Library of Congress Control Number: 2020902486

Book design by Colin Rolfe

Epigraph Books
22 East Market St., Suite 304
Rhinebeck, NY 12572
(845) 876-4861
www.epigraphps.com

For my wife Jane
and my brother Jed.

Who made this book, and so many other things, possible.

CONTENTS

Book Two

PROLOGUE

THE DIE IS CAST

Dawn broke in February 1847 on a picturesque road in Buena Vista, Mexico. The road ran below the beautiful Sierra Madre Oriental mountains. The high peaks were covered in snow, which created a beautiful effect juxtaposed against the rosy winter sky. Features of the landscape were illuminated by the rising sun and stood out in a wide array of colors. The color that stood out best was the red color, which reflected off the crisp white snow. The scenery lived up to its name, Sierra Madre, the mother mountain and the main mountain system of Mexico in every way.

Lieutenant Josh Lawrence led his company of Indiana soldiers down the road on foot, headed toward where the fighting had been going on the day before. He cut an imposing figure of six foot two inches in height. He wore a sky blue uniform, which had nine silver buttons, and he had a pair of binoculars around his neck. A blue forage cap and all the blue colors seemed to accentuate his deep blue eyes.

The fighting had been going on about two miles further down the road. His men were to be held in reserve in case they were needed in this part of the battle. They had been part of General Taylor's victorious army, which had marched all the way there from Corpus Christi, Texas, winning battle after battle. When the soldiers started out that morning, the birds were singing gaily, but as they marched along, the noise they made seemed to extinguish all of the sounds of nature.

Josh stared down the road for a long time, carefully scanning the distant vista. He saw something moving a mile or two down the straight road in front of him. He took out his binoculars to get a better view of what appeared to be a cloud of dust in the distance. Was it the beginning of a Mexican cavalry charge, or a small tornado? Many different thoughts raced through his mind. By carefully focusing the lens of his instrument he was able to make out what appeared to be his regimental mail wagon rushing toward him, the horses at a full gallop. In the distance he could clearly hear a sound from the mountains, a bugle blowing the call *in battery*–a preparation for firing the cannons.

He also saw what appeared to be Mexican soldiers standing in the road in line of battle, shooting at the wagon as it rushed away. The wagon pulled away from the fracas with the Mexican soldiers and appeared to be in the clear, getting closer and closer to Josh's position. The battery of US Howitzers on a nearby hill had taken careful note of the dust cloud. They had been expecting a Mexican cavalry charge at dawn and had been firing test shots at a barn next to the road the evening before to zero in all the guns so that they all had the proper range. He then heard the bugle call *commence firing*.

They opened fire on the US Mail wagon, thinking that because it came from enemy lines it must be the enemy cavalry charge. The dust from the road hid the marking *US Mail*, and the orientation of the hill in the sunlight did not help the soldiers distinguish details. Josh and his men heard a boom in the distance followed by three more, then a sound like a loud tearing of four big sheets of paper. The first shell had a shorter fuse and exploded about fifty feet above the wagon and slightly to the right, showering it with shrapnel. The next two shells exploded on either side of the road, missing the wagon by a wide margin but sending up columns of dirt. The fourth shell hit the back of the wagon squarely, scattering mail all over the road. The two drivers were unhurt, stopped the wagon, and sought shelter in a ditch on the side of the road. The artillery gunners on the hill were now able to see that their target was a US Mail wagon and stopped shooting.

Josh and his company made their way to the wagon, which was still smoking, and got to the two soldiers in the ditch. One was still shaking as he spit out the words. "Boy, ah sure thought ah was a goner two tahms!"

The other soldier, traumatized by the experience he had just been through, had trouble getting out the words, "So did ah, Joe!"

"What were you doing behind Mexican lines?" Josh said.

"We'all got lost! Them Mexicans almost got us—and then our own guys just missed us! What a day!" Since they were being held as reserves and might not be called upon for some time, if at all, Josh helped the mailmen pick up the mail that was not destroyed. Much of it was heavily damaged, burnt, or shredded.

While they were working, the colonel in charge of his sector came down the road, saw what was going on, and said, "There's not going to be much fighting today in this sector, but tomorrow is a different story. Your company can stand down for the day. I would suggest you help those poor, unfortunate men who were delivering the mail. Help them sort out the undamaged letters, and maybe some of them can still be identified and delivered."

Eager to render service to the mailmen and aware of the fact that many of the packages contained goodies from home which might not be deliverable and could be eaten by them legitimately, the soldiers eagerly went to work. They picked up what they could, identifying some of the burnt or shredded packages and letters, and retrieved eating and drinking contents from others that were not identifiable. The whole company worked assiduously for about an hour. It was around breakfast time when they finished the job. Some of them appeared to be somewhat intoxicated from the contents of some of the packages that had no decipherable markings. Some of the men were singing, "Lord preserve us and protect us, we've been drinking whiskey afor breakfast."

At the end of their work there were still five or six packages left with partial markings or letters that might, with considerable work, be traceable to someone either on the battlefield or at home. Josh picked up a package with most of its address obliterated, but found the beginning of an address spelling *Col*, then at the end of the written line–*Davis*. It came from Mississippi and was stamped at the Vicksburg post office. It also had a long letter enclosed, talking about the management of a plantation and how he treated the Negro slaves.

Reading the letter was a strange experience for Josh. First of all, he felt he was violating someone's confidence by reading a letter not intended for him. He was able to partially rationalize his act by the fact that he was going to return the package to its rightful owner. The "mailmen" had given up on this package and were about to put it in the unidentified pile when Josh said, "Look, we were tenting next to a regiment of the Mississippi Rifles. I bet we can trace this down and return it to its rightful owner."

The mailman responded, "If y'all want to try your luck, y'all go ahead, since we would probably throw it out. But ifn you can't find the owner, bring it to regimental headquarters for us."

Since the fighting was done for the day, Josh carried the package and led his men back to the clearing, a short distance from where the mail wagon was attacked. He went over to the Mississippi Rifles camp, just next door, and asked if he could speak to Colonel Davis.

"Whah-shoa, Captain, ahl be most glad to take you to his tent. Y'all jest follow me." They walked over to a large tent where two officers, a colonel and a captain, were cooking several chickens over an open fire. They were both dressed in sky blue uniforms. The Colonel had thin fine features, an intense look, and piercing eyes which seemed to look right through Josh.

Josh took a chance and asked, "Are you Colonel Davis?"

"I am," he answered, "Jefferson Davis from the Mississippi Rifles."

Josh introduced himself to the Colonel, and said, "I believe this package belongs to you. We picked it up on the road after those howitzers on the hill shelled the mail wagon and blew off the back."

"Oh boy—we got some heavy fighting tomorrow. Ah do hope they acquit themselves better tomorrow, or we are in for trouble," the Colonel replied.

"Yes, Colonel—I hope they take the time to identify what they're shooting at. They better, if they know what's good for them," said the other officer, a thin, gaunt-looking officer with a narrow face.

Davis said, "This is Captain Braxton Bragg. He is in charge of all the artillery in this sector." They shook hands, and Davis added humorously, "Captain Bragg runs his artillery unit with an iron hand. He will get to the bottom of what happened." Then he added, "Picking up all that mail must have worked up a mighty good appetite. Why don't you stay here with us and have dinner? It's the least I can do for you after you saved my mail from home. We'all were lucky enough to steal these chickens from a farmer—otherwise we would be eating slop like everyone else. I wouldn't refuse this meal if I were you, since this might be your last chance to eat well before the big battle tomorrow. Santa Anna has moved a large army here, and we're going to be up against it tomorrow!"

With that introduction Josh found it impossible to refuse

Jefferson's invitation. The chicken was delicious, and it was washed down by an excellent bottle of French wine, which Colonel Davis had hidden in a corner of his tent. The conversation turned to the disposition of the troops for tomorrow's battle, and Josh became privy to some important information.

The United States army had only about five thousand troops in and around Buena Vista, and reconnaissance had picked up a much larger army of Mexicans moving in to attack them under General Santa Anna. They figured he had at least twenty thousand troops. Davis and Bragg were given the order to move their men and artillery into the mountain passes so that they could be well entrenched in good defensive positions.

"I hope we don't wind up like Leonides at Thermopylae," said Davis, making reference to the Greco-Persian War in which all the defenders died in a heroic attempt to keep the Persians out of ancient Greece. Except here, Josh knew, the roles were reversed because the Americans were instead the invaders, as the Persians had been, but were lucky enough to hold the mountain pass.

After some further discussion of tactics on how to stop Santa Anna, Josh took a tour of the Mississippi Rifles camp at the request of Davis and Bragg. Colonel Davis had one question to ask Josh. "You know, Captain, you have a distinct New England accent for someone leading a company of men from Indiana. How did you get to lead this group of men?"

"Well, Colonel, I was living in Indiana at the time. I wanted to see if I could make a living apart from my family. My father owned a large mill, and I wanted to try out another business, but it did not work out. Things came apart just at the time war broke out with Mexico, and I was the only person with West Point training in my community, so the governor offered me the commission. Since the governor offered it to me, I felt I should go." He did not tell Davis that he had had severe misgivings about whether he should go and had resolved in favor of going when he heard and believed that US troops were fired upon.

They took a tour of the camp nestled in a little valley, juxtaposed against the tall Sierra Madre Mountains, several of which were shrouded in clouds. Bright sunlight illuminated the lines of tents, giving them a white gleam from the reflected sun. Captain Lawrence noticed that the camp was laid out in a very orderly military way, with lots of guards and pickets who repeatedly challenged the group as they moved about the encampment. Everything was well-ordered until they came to a large group of soldiers gathered about a soldier who was moaning and holding his stomach.

Josh asked, "What is going on?"

One of the soldiers answered, "Whayl, Captain sir, he'all has got taken eell from eatin' the food and drinkin' the water. We'all got several soldiers who done got sick the same way, and we done got this Mexican, called a *curandero* or something like that, to cure them."

"What is a curandero?" asked Josh.

"It's a kind of witch-doctor who cures natives from their illnesses," the soldier said. "It done worked for the last three soldiers, so we wants to try it on Corporal Jones here. We got people getting sick here, so we figured maybe these local people know how to cure this thing better. It sure has worked well so far."

Behind the crowd stood a man half naked covered with feathers. The tall, youthful curandero, swathed in scanty decorative belts and flaps of exotic cloth with a bare chest and four-foot headpiece of peacock feathers, circled Corporal Jones, who had his uniform off and was dressed only in pants and an undershirt. He stopped holding his stomach and stood up so the curandero could work on him. Bending over low to the ground, his ankles circled with rows of flowers, the curandero grabbed two bundles of fresh herbs in either hand from a pile of medicines next to him. The medicines gave off a strange, pungent odor which permeated Josh's nasal passages. This exotic, pungent odor reminded Josh of the smell of the hold of a ship in Boston Harbor that had come from the Amazon in South America. The hold contained some South American poisonous snakes, which the crew promptly threw overboard. The snakes proceeded to swim around the harbor until they drowned.

The curandero held the herb bundles to Corporal Jones's stomach and then swathed down the soldier from his stomach to his neck. Then he rubbed a white powder in his hair and all over his body. This same unforgettable odor emanated strongly from Jones's body and filled the air around the group, as there was only a gentle breeze to dissipate it.

The curandero then grabbed a smoking urn, and he danced and sprayed Corporal Jones's stomach with a strange liquid. He then pounded on his arms and his back. Corporal Jones was still standing straight and tall, and the curandero eagerly tugged on both the soldier's hands in an effort to give him balance. He shook all over, and his long peacock feathers rustled as he danced around the Corporal. He then put a white powder in Jones's mouth and gave him a liquid to drink. Jones's lips curled in a twisted grimace as he tasted the bitter powder, and he looked like he was going to throw up the liquid, but it went down and stayed down. Josh heard one of the soldiers say, "That's jest what he done with the three other guys. If it works the same way, he'll be all cured by morning."

But this time the curandero motioned for the interpreter, Private Sanchez, who had lived in Mexico and was familiar with Aztec expressions. When Sanchez stepped up next to the curandero, he was dwarfed by his size. Almost immediately, the man began to speak, mixing Spanish and Aztec phrases that Sanchez began to translate.

"For the last week I have been helping all you men, and this young man will recover his health as well, but I have to tell you all something. Our protecting spirit Quezalcoatl is very displeased with your mission, so I won't be able to help you any further. Our spirit has told us that you are here to conquer this territory to enslave other human beings. This is totally unacceptable to him because it breaks the harmony of the stars and the firmament. Quezalcoatl wants you to know that, for every force applied in the world, there is an equal and opposite counterforce. Our country contains a poisonous seed, which if taken in by your country can cause great calamity to you. If you steal this country from our people, you will be destroyed by a worse war, which will pit your brothers against each other."

At this point, overwhelmed by a torrent of ancient Aztec words, Sanchez began to cough, causing the curandero to slow down. Sanchez looked up at the sky for a moment, then resumed. "This may take ten or fifteen years to happen, but nothing is more certain than that it will come pass. Take my warning and leave this land now, for you will set a whirlwind in motion that will have great consequences for your country's future. There will be no future in enslaving your fellow man."

After the curandero finished, the group of soldiers began to discuss his warning speech. "Do you'all think what he don'all said could really happen? Ah spek so, it could, but ah doubts it, we'all live in the United States. We is above that sorta heathen thing!"

Another soldier added, "We live in a free world of free people—we have a Constitution."

Josh thought to himself, "Do we?" Then Josh, knowing a lot about the politics that led to the war, began to feel that the curandero's prediction could indeed turn out to be true.

Book One

CHAPTER 1

ABOLITIONIST MEETING

One afternoon in Lowell, Massachusetts in 1858, a group of four young blacks, two men and two women, strolled over to an old, abandoned stone-built mill that had once been used to manufacture fabric for clothing. Now, after a financial crisis, there were no more orders for new fabrics, and the mill had finally shut down. They were on their way to attend an abolitionist meeting.

Observing the state of the structure from a distance, Nate Washington, a tall, thin young Negro halted abruptly and frowned at the others. "Wait. Stop! Is this the right place?"

Wilma, a mulatto woman slightly taller than Nate, stared past the mill to the early evening mists on the Merrimack River and nodded to reassure him. "Yes, we were told the meeting would be here."

The building—once a herald of a new industrial age—looked empty, neglected, and in much need of repair. The four gazed up at the vacant, dirty windows that had moss sliding down the glass.

Jackson Greene, a handsome, imposingly tall black man with a broad nose and dimples on his cheeks, put his hand on his friend Nate's shoulder and said, "Let's get in there then, pal."

Approaching the front door, he let out a sudden whoop. "Hey, Nate, look at this sign!" A large outdoor sign outside the building announced, SOCIETY FOR THE FUTURE DEVELOPMENT OF BASEBALL IN LOWELL. Nate and Jackson were on the same baseball team.

Joan Dubois, a sensitive looking brunette, whispered ironically to Wilma, "No baseball going to be played this evening for Nate and Jackson."

Inside, the four moved hastily across the noisy wood floor and up a narrow staircase, where they entered an empty room with wooden chairs and large, pillared stone walls. The room was used for meetings of the abolitionists. People were just beginning to gather.

"Welcome," said Josh Lawrence to the four young Negros as they entered. "Have a seat."

The newcomers sat down behind Josh. Josh's wealthy New England family owned this mill, and they owned a giant mill complex in Methuen, Massachusetts as well. Josh's mother was a socially prominent woman, active in many social causes. His family had always been against slavery, but recent moves by Congress had further inflamed their passions against the slavocracy.

Joan Dubois, a thin, sensitive black woman with high cheekbones, sat down on a wooden chair next to Nate, directly behind Josh—along with the other two blacks. She knew Nate, Jackson, and Wilma would have a lot to discuss when this meeting was over. They gazed around, wide-eyed with anticipation.

Josh Laurence was dressed in a light-blue, three-piece suit with a double-breasted vest that matched his blue eyes. He had brown hair and an expressive face. He wore a white starched shirt with a small, black ribbon bow tie.

At that same moment, Emily Bradford, a young, attractive, blond-haired white woman, one of the newly indoctrinated abolitionist members, entered the building. She had joined recently. Entering the mill, she lifted up her long green silk taffeta dress from the bottom so that she could climb the stairs quickly. She hastily moved on the creaky wood floor and up the narrow staircase to get to the meeting on time.

When she entered the meeting room, the brilliance of her blond Grecian hairstyle and the shimmering green taffeta fabric stood out against the bland grey stone walls and cobwebbed windows.

Josh noticed her and immediately offered her a seat next to him. She sat right down and said, "Thank you."

Color came into his face as he took note of her vivid dress. He felt more than pleased that she was there for the meeting and whispered, "Glad you could make it here."

Emily stared over at Josh and smiled a greeting at him. "I am with you on this—glad to be here," her determined smile seemed to say.

"He looks so handsome," Emily thought in a rush of admiration. Slender, with long thighs—Josh sat cross-legged in his blue suit with blue eyes flashing. She wondered if he was going to attend the same wedding event she was invited to right after the meeting.

Josh stood up and called the meeting to order with the natural ease of a military officer who had carefully thought out strategy and tactics for a coming campaign.

"I would like to start the meeting by introducing Ben Taylor, who escaped from the famous politician Robert Toombs in Georgia. He was married and had two children and had worked as a waiter in a hotel in New York City. Four years later he was kidnapped from Manhattan without any judicial process and returned to slavery back at Toombs plantation. I want you to hear from him what happened when he returned to slavery."

Mr. Taylor, a small, thin black man, came up to the front of the room and held his hat in his quivering hand while he spoke.

He removed a bandage from his forehead and stood under the light. A big frightening R stood out on his forehead.

"See dis mark on my forehead? Dis is de letter R for runaway. Master Toombs was away when da overseer got me back. Dis is not the work of Master Toombs. He was away. But da overseer, he heated up da iron and put it on my head."

Everyone in the room said *oh* in a low voice of sympathy. Someone yelled out, "He had a right to run away!"

"When dey brought me back to da plantation," Taylor went on, "I was powerful angry, and I missed my wife and daughters something terrible. Dey did not give me my old job back right away. At first, I did dirty jobs, but after a while I gots my old job back. Dats when I began talking to everyone about da life up north, and how important readin' was."

Nate Washington, sitting directly behind Josh, nodded adamantly. He felt this was very significant because he had only learned to read books later in life.

"I telled everyone ways to escape," Ben Taylor went on, "and how to contact da people up north. Ober da next year twenty slaves done escaped, and none of dem came back. I figured I'd paid master Toombs back twenty times for kidnappin' me. Den I got my chance and escaped again. My wife and chilin den done moved to Boston. It's too dangerous to stay in New York City wid kidnappin'. My chilin could be kidnapped too, as they wuz born to a mudder who wuz a slave. I met dem in Boston, and we have lived dare since."

Ben received a round of cheers from the group, and the four young blacks stood up and applauded loudly. "It is so important to read," Nate murmured to Jackson.

"Yep" he said, applauding as fast as his hands could clap.

Then Josh got up and said, "It is very important for us to remember what Ben did. We need to discuss the fugitive slave law today. But first we want to introduce our four newcomers," he added and glanced back at the four young blacks. He knew the abolitionists would want to get to know them because older members had become very mistrustful and suspicious since some slave catchers had sought to infiltrate and join other abolitionist groups nearby.

Josh first turned to Wilma with a courteous smile. "Ladies first. Wilma, tell us about yourself."

Wilma, a muscular young woman of imposing height and hair in tresses, stood up and introduced herself. "My name is Wilma Turner. My father owned a cotton plantation in South Carolina," she began, "and I remember well how things went there." She turned her face down for a moment and went on.

"My father had a liaison with his light-complexioned housekeeper, my mother, who became his common law wife. He freed my mother in South Carolina and was able to marry her in Pennsylvania. Then he adopted me as his daughter. When I was young, I loved riding train cars, and my father took me to plays in Washington, DC. I've always liked books and culture. I also enjoy outdoor physical work, animals, and horseback riding."

The abolitionists looked up at her with interest.

"I was raised close to my mother," she continued, "because my father was always too busy working on the plantation. My father did not like slavery, but he felt that to abolish it suddenly and completely might destroy us economically. He was always worried about who would marry me—an intelligent mulatto woman. What would my future bring? My mother was always there for me when I was growing up."

She cast her eyes down again. "I guess you could say I had a happy enough childhood."

But then she looked up forcefully and with defiance. "I have always hated slavery. If I meet anyone who supports slavery, I get so angry I lose my temper right away. I don't know what I'd do, but I hate slavery!"

Wilma sat adamantly back down in her chair.

The group smiled with appreciation and applauded, as did her three black friends who nodded to her in support.

"Thank you, Wilma. Now Joan?" Josh asked her to rise and face the group.

Joan stood up. Thin, with high cheekbones, and a slim physique with delicate features, her hair was stylishly cut in curly brown ringlets. "My name is Joan Dubois. I was born in New Orleans, before we came north," Joan began. "I was born to a wealthy free Negro family. Even though my family made its fortune in the cotton business, they have always been committed to abolishing slavery.

"I was educated in Switzerland and can speak several languages. My father has always stressed the importance of education. He wanted me to grow to be the best person I could be.

"I enjoy sports, such as swimming, hiking, fishing, and horseback riding," Joan went on. "And I like drama. I can easily revert to speaking like a poor Negro field hand, and pretend that I am one," she added.

The group smiled with appreciation and applauded, and Josh added, "That might be very helpful, Joan."

"After the Mexican War," Joan went on, "my father was so disgusted at the South's attempt to expand slavery to the captured territories. He freed all his slaves, took his profits, and moved up north here to open woolen and cotton mills in New England. Right now, my father is a partner at the Kirkwood Mill in Methuen."

Proudly, Joan sat back down.

Josh glanced over at Nate and nodded.

Nate stood up, looking down his long face and, at first, murmuring a bit shyly. "I am Nate Washington. I first want to thank some of you for giving me some college books and novels to read. It has been very helpful. For many years, all I read was cooking recipes, and these books have helped my reading skills a lot.

"I grew up in Virginia with two brothers and two sisters. My parents died of consumption. My master, who was a well-known French chef, taught me how to cook at an early age. I've spent my whole life cooking. My master began by doing all the cooking, but as he got older, he taught me to do more. He thought that it would greatly benefit my cooking skills. He cooked as a hobby, and then he turned the cooking in the plantation over to me. He took me to Paris twice to learn cooking from French chefs and taught me how to read recipes in English and French. Then he sent me to a restaurant on the Virginia coast to work in a tavern where I learned to cook in a more stressful environment.

"My master was a good man," Nate went on. "He didn't believe in slavery, but he wanted me to stay close and cook for him. He wanted to free me but never had the chance. Then he died from Bright's disease and too much drinking.

"My new master who took over was horrible," Nate said with his face turned down. "He wanted me to cook for him too. Other Negroes I knew were whipped, beaten, and even murdered. That was when I knew I had to escape, or I might possibly lose my life. I finally escaped on the Underground Railroad and ended up back north here. All I can say is, something has got to be done, and *now*. I think we need to attack the slave system in the South instead of confining most of our work to only just helping slaves escape."

Nate sat down, and the abolitionists once again applauded. Joan, seated two seats away, looked over at Nate supportively. "Good job," she seemed to be saying.

Next, Jackson stood up, seeming to gauge his audience for a moment before a smile reached his deep-set eyes.

"My name is Jackson Greene. Cooking is Nate's trade, and blacksmithing is mine. My master taught me blacksmithing and farrier work. I enjoy treating sick animals, especially curing horses. I also enjoy pitching on the local baseball team here.

"I was born in North Carolina." Jackson's dark eyes flashed. "My first master taught me how to read. I grew up reading the bible, and he had me memorize chapter and verse. He eventually had to sell me due to financial problems, and it was to a meaner master, so I knew I would have to escape. So I did. I encourage my people in our church to read the scriptures in the bible. I believe it can help them with their problems. I often explain these scriptures to members of the church to help them solve the problems they run into in life."

Several abolitionists nodded affirmatively.

After the introductions, Josh brought up the Fugitive Slave Law to the group for discussion. It required that all escaped slaves, upon capture, be returned to their masters—and that officials and citizens of free states had to cooperate with this law or suffer severe sanctions if they did not. "We have discussed these laws many times before, but recently things are getting worse for all Negro slaves and free Negros as well."

Emily gestured to Josh that she would like to speak. "Emily, I understand you have something to say on the subject," Josh said.

Emily got up from her chair and in her forceful, energetic way she said, "This law has sometimes been extended to free blacks that are forbidden to explain their free status because they are presumed to be slaves and are forbidden to speak in their own defense. Now is this right?" she asked the group.

"This law has been around for several years, but the last two presidents have been so biased toward the South that is being more strictly enforced every day. Officers of the court have told me that all a white man has to do is produce an affidavit stating that the slave is his to begin the deportation hearings. They told me many Negroes are sent south on very weak evidence."

There were jeers against the villainous law.

Joan, sitting behind Emily, motioned that she would like to speak. Emily turned the floor over to Joan.

"Just imagine yourself walking along the street on a beautiful summer day," she began. "All of a sudden you are picked up by the police, manhandled, and thrown in jail—and you can't get a lawyer to represent you because a determination is made that you are another person's property.

"Next you are brought up before a court where the deck is completely stacked against you. The magistrate makes more money if you are sent down south than if you are freed and allowed to resume your life. The police are given economic bonuses by the slaveholders. They also get rewards from their bosses for making an arrest. Please picture this image in your mind."

"It has been happening more and more, recently," said Josh, amplifying Emily's and Joan's comments.

There were more groans against the inhuman application of this law.

"We have one more item on the agenda. I'm going to ask Bill Washburn, who came here tonight, to speak about an issue that developed in his Suffolk County group."

Washburn, a tall, thin, wiry-looking man with a long nose who was seated nearby rose to tell his story. He coughed several times to clear his throat and began. "A man started coming to our vigilance committee meetings. He said he was from New York, and he had a New York accent. He was unusually tall, well over six feet—and quite portly. He was a real giant of a man. You couldn't miss him because of his size.

"He said his name was Henry Delamorte. During the meetings he was always coming up with the most aggressive ways to fight slavery, but most of them made no sense at all. After coming to our meetings for several months, he made sure he got the names and addresses of all our members."

The abolitionists stirred in their seats and someone called out, "Oh no!"

"Over the course of the last month some of our members

were assaulted by criminals and thugs," Washburn went on. "We thought it was just a local crime wave, although it was suspicious that so many of our members were being attacked over a short period of time. Then one of the members of the Vigilance Committee saw him in a tavern out on the Cape, sitting at a table with well-known slave agents."

The whole crowd began to get more and more agitated as Washburn went on.

"Henry Delamorte has since disappeared from our meetings. Although this is not a brand new issue, we want to warn all the groups in the area to be suspicious of strangers. Do not give them any real information until you know them better. Our little experience with Delamorte cost us dearly, and it even caused trouble in nearby groups where he was able to obtain people's names."

At that point Josh spoke up. "Remember friends, if we're trying to destroy their slave system, they are also trying to destroy us. Because of hard times up north, the South still has plenty of money compared to us these days, and they are using it to try and destroy our abolitionist groups. That is why we have a baseball sign out front."

"*De la mort* means 'from the dead,' but it's also used in the Caribbean to mean 'the kiss of death,'" said Joan. "They are signaling clearly what they want to do to abolitionists."

On that note the group finished its business, and some of the members filed out with agitated looks on their faces.

As the abolitionists were leaving the building, Josh walking quickly to catch up with Emily, who was just ahead of him. He liked the way she dressed and carried herself and had been keeping an eye on her at recent meetings.

He now felt a thrill run through his body when he decided to talk with her. The thrill was quickly followed by a pang of anxiety, as his direct and straightforward manner with women hadn't always gotten him where he wanted to be. He began his quest in a more conservative way than was usual for him.

"Emily, I liked the way you explained the ramifications of the fugitive slave law," he said as they walked along together. "That was very well-investigated. Especially how it's been extended to free blacks who were forbidden to present evidence to show their status."

Emily, anticipating Josh's interest in her said, "Josh, did you really want to discuss this with me now?"

"Actually, I just wanted a chance to talk to you, since we rarely get a chance for person-to-person interaction," Josh said earnestly, "and I would like a chance to talk with you personally."

"Why is that?" Emily asked him.

"Well, because I like what you have to say, and I want to get to know you better," Josh told her, looking right into her eyes with his heart pounding.

Emily brushed back her blond hair, smiled up at him, and said, "That is most agreeable to me, too, as I feel the same way about you."

The four young blacks trailed somewhat behind Emily and Josh, past the stone pillars and moss-laden windows. Out of the murky building and into the fresh air, they crunched their way over a gravel path to depart.

"I think we need to be down south if we want to destroy slavery," Jackson murmured. "We're sprinkling water on top of the flames, instead of getting to the fire." The other three nodded.

"Go down south," asked Joan? "Wilma, are you ready to pick up and just move down south?"

Wilma hesitated and said, glancing at Joan, "I don't know."

Little did they know that they were about to embark on a journey so profound and life-altering that their four young lives would be irrevocably changed forever.

CHAPTER 2

FRIENDS AND FOES

The solid beginning between Emily and Josh soon developed into their keeping company with one another. Josh was drawn to Emily's quick and accurate perceptions and judgment on many subjects, and together they shared long talks and discussions.

One evening they went ballroom dancing. Emily, attired in a long, blue hooped-style dress with a white bodice was overjoyed as Josh proudly led her out on the dance floor. Gazing up at him with a flushed face, she said, "Josh, you can take me dancing anytime, anywhere—I love this!"

Leaving the dance that night in a glow of contentment, Josh escorted Emily back home in a horse and buggy. With the gaiety of the evening behind and the dark country road before them, their mood seemed all at once to become more serious, and conversation dwindled.

Josh was the first to speak up. "All this finery is most pleasant, most specially in your company. Yet since the war, Emily, I have felt with even greater conviction that my life's work should be to destroy slavery. I can no longer keep myself from thinking that any detour from that path has become somehow empty and worthless. I feel as my family does, that slavery is a poison seeping into all the things we enjoy most."

Emily nodded affirmatively.

As the buggy bounced up and down the rocky road back to her home, Josh explained further. "Before the Mexican War, I felt that slavery would die out in the South after slave trade was made illegal, but it never did. Even though I served in that campaign, I have always felt that the Mexican War was immoral, and that we had stolen thousands of miles of territory from them. And what's more, the South is fighting over it because they want to turn much of it into slave states. As a curandero told me in Buena Vista, the situation in the country is but payback for an evil deed."

"I completely agree, Josh," Emily said looking into his eyes.

One evening later on in the courtship, Josh came calling at Emily's house to meet her father, Jordan Bradford. Emily's mother had died of consumption several years before. Seated in the living room, Mr. Bradford offered Josh a drink and explained why they had initially left South Carolina and moved up north.

"I was a tugboat captain. I had made a decent living using a fleet of steam-powered tugboats to move ships around and haul freight on barges in the Charleston, South Carolina harbor. Included in the freight traffic were barges carrying slaves up and down the coast for auctions. Although the treatment of slaves was indeed far better on the coastal barges than on the slave ships that came across the Atlantic, I became sickened by slave trade altogether. So I let my wife talk me into selling this lucrative business, and the three of us headed north, even though I knew I could no longer make the kind of living I could make down south.

"I guess you could say I went from being a big fish in a small pond, to being a small fish in a bigger pond that was Boston Harbor, where there was extensive competition. So, life became a bit harder for us, but at least I did not have to feel I was part of the institution of slavery."

"You did the right thing father," said Emily, looking at him proudly.

Josh told Mr. Bradford that he had an uncle in South Carolina whom he often visited, and that he had even lived there with him for two years. He spoke familiarly of life in the South, but stressed that his family, too, was very much against slavery.

Will Bradford nodded, enjoying the prospect of another man in the family to talk to.

After a relatively brief courtship, Emily and Josh decided to be married in a simple ceremony by an abolitionist minister—a friend of the family. They both felt strongly that a large, luxurious wedding just didn't feel right at a time when slaves were toiling in bondage in other parts of the country.

Their marriage plans were quickly accepted by both families, understanding as they did the depth of the couple's sense of commitment. The newlyweds then took up temporary residence in the large colonial home of Josh's parents, Katie and Will Lawrence.

CHAPTER 3

DANGER LURKS

The simplicity of their marriage gave Emily and Josh a kind of moral leadership within the abolitionist group. Several weeks after their marriage, one of the abolitionist meetings gave evidence of a marked turn towards a more aggressive attack on slavery. It was obvious to everyone that congress and the president were on the wrong side of the slavery issue.

The group met in the abandoned drawing room of the old mill, where they were seated at several large tables. The evening's discussion soon turned towards how ineffective their work had been toward an impact on the slaves down south.

"Nothing has really worked well, other than the underground railway," said Bill Snow, a local abolitionist with a long grey beard in a brown coat with a wide velvet collar. He drummed his large, gnarled hands on the table as he slowly spoke.

"We tried mailing notices and literature, but nothing is reaching the slaves. If it does reach them, most of them can't read, so it has to be explained to them by a sympathetic person.

"The slavocracy there is onto us now. It's not like it was a few years ago. We tried carrying pamphlets down there. We either posted them around the countryside or gave them to sympathetic individuals. All this literature quickly disappears as fast as it is put up. Hired people are roaming the countryside, taking down our stuff and destroying it or burning it. It is illegal now to incite the slaves to run away or revolt. If anyone gets caught disseminating information to do this, it is doubtful that it would even get to the courts. The slave owners would take the law into their own hands."

"You are absolutely right, Mr. Snow," said Emily, rising up from her chair to speak. Josh looked over at her proudly. "There is no due process of law regarding these issues, and even if there were, the planters would take care of you quickly. You would probably be found hanging from a tree."

Many nodded in affirmation at what Emily was saying.

"The whole thing is very discouraging. These days hired guns, private detectives, and people impersonating abolitionists have been infiltrating abolitionist meetings. If they are successful, they are feeding our ideas right back to the slavocracy. We are going to have to change tactics."

"As a follow up on last week's issue in Suffolk County, I asked Bill Haverstraw to come here and tell us about the occurrences at his Connecticut group in the last few weeks. After what happened with Delamorte in Washburn's group, I think you have to be very careful. Go ahead Bill, and tell us what happened," said Josh

Bill, a well-dressed businessman, walked up front to face the group.

"This fellow," he began, "who said his name was Jeremy Purmort, has started coming to our meetings for a couple of weeks. He always speaks in an angry way about slavery. Last week he told us that his family owned a print shop and that he could take care of getting leaflets printed up at a nominal cost if we all could chip in money. He is expecting our contributions next week."

"Wait a second!" said Joan. "What did this guy look like?"

"A real big fellow—very tall and heavyset," said Haverstraw.

"*Pur mort* means 'pure death' or 'plain death'—and remember from that meeting a while ago, *de la mort* can mean 'kiss of death,'" Joan continued. "I would lay you odds that Purmort and Delamorte are the same man. The whole thing is mighty suspicious."

The audience began to hiss and jeer. "Well, what are you going to do about it?" other members of the group asked.

"If you give him any money you might as well kiss it goodbye. And if he gets names of abolitionists, people will wind up beaten up or dead," said Bill Snow.

"I know how we can take care of this," said Haverstraw.

"What are you going to do?" asked Wilma.

"Don't ask" said Haverstraw. "It will be taken care of. I will first meet with Washburn to see if he or anyone in the group can identify Purmort as Delamorte."

Loud groans came from the audience at these words.

"Look, we have to be very careful," said Josh. "Remember what I said at the last meeting. If we are plotting to destroy their system, we have to be aware that they are plotting to destroy our system as well. As Isaac Newton said, 'For every action there is an equal and opposite reaction.'"

Bill Snow, his face red with anger, slammed his fist down on a table with a crash to set the tone for the evening. "I have had enough of this garbage. I'm for arming the slaves, getting them rifles so that they can march north and escape from slavery."

Bob Chamberlain, pastor of one of the local churches, countered, "But they'll be breaking laws and maybe committing murder."

Snow continued. "They're being held against their will. They have a right to break out and escape as the Jews did in Egypt. If people try to hold them in bondage, it's morally wrong. These slave agents are hiring thugs to beat up and kill our people. We have to fight back. If they are coming up here, we could go down there."

"What about Dred Scott? What about the laws of the land

today?" Chamberlain asked. "Look what the Supreme Court did! And congress passed the Kansas Nebraska Act. We will be hanged for this!"

Some abolitionists yelled out yays and nays. The group was evenly split on the use of violence to attack slavery, and neither side gave any ground.

The discussion became very hot and heavy until Josh stood up. "Look here! I'm a military man. I fought in Mexico for the annexation of those western lands, which has pushed our country into chaos. Liberating a large number of black slaves with no plan and no military background is suicide and anarchy."

Emily stood up next to Josh, rushing to his defense, and declared, "Women like me want to do something, but we are not ready or equipped for open warfare!"

"The revolting slaves won't even know how to use the weapons," Josh declared powerfully. "They'll be an easy mark for militias or US troops."

"So, what!" said Bill Snow "They'll make their mark and show the South!"

Josh rang out in response, his face also reddening. "Show them what? We want something to succeed, not fail and cause even more suffering. I have an idea. Hear me out!

"A group of us go down south. We could forge bills of sale. I have a cousin who works for the state offices in South Carolina, and she hates slavery. I may be able to get a phony South Carolina bill of sale for several slaves. It would be almost impossible to verify them."

"We get the bills of sale, bring in slaves, start up a phony plantation as a front for our activities–even purchase some more slaves–and then and there start educating and training the slaves to fight back. Eventually,"–Josh banged his fist on the table–"we'll have a powerful group that can plant the seeds to destroy this abomination. Education and training are the keys to solving this problem. Remember what Ben Taylor did to Robert Toombs's plantation. What he did worked! What we can do will work also!"

There was an uncommon silence in the room as abolitionists considered what he had said. No one seemed to have any immediate objection to this idea.

"Please," Josh went on, "let's think this over until we get together next Thursday. We'll discuss the idea further and see what we can come up with." With everyone agreeing, the meeting was closed for the evening for further discussion at the next meeting.

As everyone filed out of the building, Emily and Josh left the mill, walking arm in arm. They quickly fell in step with two of the newer members, Nate and Jackson. Jackson, broad of shoulder and a head taller than Josh, with dark brown eyes set in deep molasses-hued features, flashed a smile and said, "You know, we could do what you're talking about doing. We'll be your slaves. If you get us titles, no one will know."

"Except for us, of course!" said Nate, a little less enthusiastically. He was a young man of slighter stature and light color. His long, but finely chiseled, forehead and cheekbones tilted back as he looked up at the other two men. "But we need more people," he said in an animated voice.

"What about some women who could connect with some women down south there," Emily said, staring up at Jackson. "What about your friends Wilma and Joan? They seem highly intelligent and do seem to feel the same way we do about slavery."

"We know this is dangerous if we get caught. But those slave holders down there are a bunch of fools," Nate said.

Josh quickly fired back, "Don't underestimate your enemy—it's the first step to disaster. If we are careful, we can pull this off or at least start it up. But we need to have some military training as a backup plan if things get nasty."

Jackson looked at Josh, questioning him, "How are we going to do that?"

"Me. I'll do it. I trained recruits for the Mexican War. I can train all of us. But you have to listen to me on this," said Josh. "If we bring women, we'll have to train them too."

"They may not like that. Women don't like guns and violence. It scares them," Nate answered. "Come to think of it, I don't like guns and violence either."

"I'm willing to be trained," said Emily. "Oppression of the slaves is a violent act."

"That this is what we have to do scares me too," replied Josh. "But I'm willing to do it to destroy slavery."

CHAPTER 4

THE LION'S JAWS

There was a buzz of chatter and a good turnout at the next abolitionist meeting at the mill. One of the larger rooms chosen for the event was crowded with select local townspeople. Women in long, flowing dresses and men in three-quarter-length coats with tall, black top hats came in. People were standing in groups, and some were sitting. They were all talking fervently among themselves. Josh, who was seated at a large, old wooden table with Emily at his side, stood up to begin as the first speaker.

"We read an article in a magazine about a plantation near Vicksburg, Mississippi, called *Davis Bend*, named after a bend in the Mississippi River. Jefferson Davis, a politician and the Secretary of War, and his brother Joseph Davis set up a society. Slaves live there on a kind of commune after a model set up by a British man, Robert Owen. They don't really have freedom there, but they have more freedom than other slaves.

"If we set up our organization in this area, we can make slaves more aware of their status, and we can teach them to read. The way I see it, we work with slaves in the area near Davis Bend. Then, if and when this works out, we get bigger and bigger."

Emily's eyes were glued on Josh, who seemed to have grown into the mantle of a natural leader. She knew how intently he had researched all aspects of his idea. He had spent days reading encyclopedias of knowledge. Everything was read with an eye to putting his proposal into practice.

Josh did not reveal at this time in the meeting that, while serving in the Mexican War, he had intercepted a letter meant for Jefferson Davis from Davis's brother Joseph. He retrieved it from the friendly fire incident with the mail wagon in Buena Vista. The letter described the plantations they both owned, the slaves who worked on them, and some rudiments of Robert Owen's theories. From this letter he was able to infer the workings of the Davis Bend plantation and understand its construction.

Emily watched Josh's eyes very carefully while he spoke. She knew he was thinking that this is something he could deal with, even though her own mind strayed to self-doubts and concerns about what could happen to them both if something went wrong.

But right away, people in the audience of the meeting began to voice the same objections that Emily was thinking. "You sound very confident," they said to Josh. "Suppose something goes wrong. What will happen to all of you? We don't want to support an enterprise where all of you get strung up."

Josh came right back. "I know this will work out. All we have to do is raise awareness and maybe teach the slaves how to read. That will slowly strangle slavery from the inside out. Even a little teaching will go a long way. We can't really fail here if we get involved."

The biggest opposition came from Jack Thornebush, a man whom Josh viewed as a big blowhard. "I don't want to put my money behind a harebrained scheme. This could take years to work! I want to do something that works now."

Josh replied, "What do you want to do—arm the slaves? Jack, we talked about this last week when you were not here. This would be chaos! They haven't any military training;

militias would make short work of them. This will make things much worse for all the slaves in the area. After Nat Turner's revolt many slaves were injured and killed because their masters were terrified of the blacks. An armed rebellion will get the slave owners angry, maybe bring in the army, cause anarchy, and result in many slaves being killed. The method we're talking about is slower I admit, but it will eat away at the core of slavery from the inside outward. I feel it's worth the effort. If it works, it could make a tremendous difference. The slave owners won't realize what hit them."

Josh glanced over at Nate, Joan, Jackson, and Wilma, who were standing close by him. They seemed very excited by the discussion. Josh continued, "You four expressed interest in participating in this mission. You know, for all intents and purposes, you will be slaves during this period. You will have to act like one in every circumstance. If you're caught out, your legal status will be that of a slave. As terrible as that would be, it won't be as bad as the fate Emily and I will face if we are all caught. I'd still rather have to work in the fields than get lynched from an oak tree."

The discussion went back and forth for two hours. At the close of the meeting Jack said, "It's your necks in the noose, but if you are set on doing this, we'll help. Whatever this comes to, at least I'll feel we're doing *something* about the problem."

The meeting broke up at 11:00 p.m. A vote was taken, and the abolitionists finally resolved to go ahead and provide funding. Josh mentioned that his parents would make up whatever was not provided for in their budget. This embryonic plan would still require research and planning to begin to put it into practice.

Walking home together after the meeting, Nate's and Jackson's usual friendly banter was overshadowed by the growing realization of finding themselves down south with their heads in the lion's jaws.

As close friends, they discussed how this future move might affect them.

"Hey, buddy," Jackson said, "We are going to be completely controlled by white men. Can we trust them with our lives?"

"It's their lives too. They are risking as much as we are," Nate answered. "I guess that's going to be the end of our playing on the town baseball team. I really enjoyed playing on the team, and we're both so good at it!"

"It's too bad, but we got bigger fish to fry. This is a chance to do something important with our lives," Jackson told him.

CHAPTER 5

ON STAGE

The front door of the substantial two-story house opened. Framed between the freestanding columns supporting the Greek revival portico were Nate, Jackson, Wilma, and Joan. Not having been informed of their coming, the middle-aged housekeeper looked back and forth quizzically at the four. Joan stepped forward with assurance.

She announced with some formality that Mr. and Mrs. Lawrence were indeed expecting them.

At that moment a cheerful woman's voice rang out from halfway up the main staircase. "It's all right Marion, these are Josh's friends, and they are most welcome."

The voice belonged to a silver-haired woman of matronly age but still light of step and almost girlish in figure. She immediately introduced herself as Katie Lawrence. "I'm the other Mrs. Lawrence," she said, nodding to each of them, fixing each one firmly in her slate-grey eyes. Her look spoke more than words of her knowledge of their visit.

After helping them off with their coats, she handed them to Marion. She then escorted the group to a spacious parlor with several leather armchairs and a large sofa facing a fireplace with a warm crackling fire. The glow coming from it highlighted the golden chintz wall covering.

"Josh and Emily will be down shortly."

As she turned to leave, she looked back at them and added, "Of course, it's none of my affair, but I know you are here on business, and I believe it's of the most important kind. Let me just say that my husband and I wish you well in your future endeavors. If you ever require our aid, we will do all in our power to help you, just as we'd do for Josh and Emily."

The four stared straight-ahead, deep in thought. Almost immediately, Josh and Emily entered the room. On her way out, Katie flashed them a welcoming look and promptly waved goodbye to everyone as she left—waves they immediately returned.

"Josh, your mother is a very godly woman," Jackson said.

Wilma intoned, "Amen."

"Well," Josh replied, "she's been my anchor in many storms and has always held fast." Looking across at Emily and smiling he added, "Of course she's no longer my only anchor. From here on we're going to have to look at each other as family, and not just as members of a tight-knit group. We must be an extended family, because our lives will depend upon it. Okay, now that I've said my piece, let's get down to business."

Josh began by telling the group some of this thoughts and plans. "My father has been corresponding with Robert Owen, a famous British socialist and industrialist who owns mills both in Britain and here in the United States. His son has been taking over a lot of his work as he has been getting too old to work.

"Owen has a big following in this country, including some plantation owners down in the South. One of those plantation owners was the former Secretary of War, Jefferson Davis. I met Jefferson Davis in Mexico when we both fought together at Buena Vista."

"What do you know of him," Joan asked, curious.

"Well, my father met with both Jefferson Davis and Davis's brother, Joseph. They were part of a Robert Owen group he attended. Joseph gave my father Will ideas for his mill that worked out successfully. I've also learned a great deal about the layout of their plantations."

"How did you find this out?" asked Nate, flashing him an inquisitive look.

"Well, quite by chance. Let me explain," said Josh.

"During the battle of Buena Vista, a mail wagon was delivering mail, when an explosive shell from one of our howitzers flew into the wheels and axle, smashing them to bits. It scattered the mail all over the road. My company picked up most of it. The mail was so badly damaged that we had to open it all to see whose it was.

"I found this one long letter, which appeared to say *Davis* on the front, so I opened it to figure out whom it belonged to. I went to the regiment paymaster who was able to piece together who the recipient was, and then it was returned to Jefferson Davis, the Secretary of War who was then a colonel."

"Did you read the letter?" asked Joan.

"I did. I'll never forget the contents of that long letter. I confess I read much more than I should have. It laid out the whole framework of their plantations in a way that was very easy to understand. From what I learned I was later able to formulate today's plans for how we should organize our infiltration activity down south.

"I'm quite sure my father can give me a letter of introduction to either Jefferson Davis or his brother, Joseph Davis. I've got a lot in common with Jefferson, since we both got wounded in the battle at Buena Vista."

"Maybe you can get together and rehash the battle over a glass of wine or have him over for some dinner," said Nate, already thinking ahead to his potential culinary contribution and smiling.

"Right," replied Josh. "We both went to West Point, although many years apart. He does not know I'm an abolitionist, and on this issue we part company. Mill managers who are abolitionists have to be very careful not to arouse the ire of the South because they are the major supplier of cotton to our mills. Without their cotton we could all go bankrupt. We need our meetings to be held in secrecy. That is why we have our baseball sign out front to lead them in a different direction," he went on.

Jackson curled his lip in a grimace.

"Jefferson has championed many principles of socialism but does not believe in granting equality to Negro slaves. From what I can tell, he sees them as an inferior race. But I'm not completely sure how he stands on all of this.

"Anyway, I will be able to connect with Jefferson Davis and Joseph Davis through my father."

Josh next turned to his wife, "Emily, can you hobnob with the crème de la crème of southern society? You'll have to act the role."

"I really don't know," she said thoughtfully.

"I'll have to teach you then," Josh replied. "This is going to be very exciting and stimulating, provided we don't get caught. Since we both lived down south before, we should be able to talk the accent pretty well. I think–with your charm you should have no problem at all."

"I once acted the role of a southern belle in a play," Emily mused. "Y'all have ah nahce day, yah heeear."

Joan turned to her and retorted with a mischievous gleam in her eyes. "I like to act too. I can pretend and talk like a poor Negro field hand any day. But having to dress like a poor peasant and telling people I came up from the fields ..."

"You are surely having a hard time convincing us of that, Joan!" Jackson broke in, looking her up and down appraisingly and smirking amid the guffaws of the others.

CHAPTER 6

BASEBALL RULES

Jackson Greene was an outstanding player on the Lowell baseball team, particularly in his role as a pitcher. His friend Nate was his catcher during many of the games, although his job as a chef in Boston's Parker Hotel would at times limit his availability.

As much as Nate was dedicated to that job, he always hated to have to miss a game. These two young black men were two of the reasons why the Lowell town baseball team had become one of the best in the state. Not only were they very fast and clever hitters, but they also had great throwing arms, an indispensable asset in the version of baseball they played, called the Massachusetts Game.

A player who was deliberately hit by a thrown ball during a play was automatically out. Because each team was allowed only one out per inning, throwing accuracy was of the utmost defensive importance.

The local mills were the big sponsors of the team, and its success was a great source of pride for the town. That afternoon was the occasion for a big game with Natick, their archrivals. The mills, where most of the players worked, gave team members the afternoon off. Of course, the team's performance was also important for the mills, as the management would usually place a wager on the outcome of the game.

The Natick team arrived early, and some of the team members took the opportunity to whet their whistle in the tavern next to the large common where the game was to take place. As they left the tavern in their game uniforms, they were easily spotted by Nate and Jackson, also in uniform, approaching the common from the other side of the street.

"You black bastards are going to take a terrible thrashing," called out one of the Natick players from across the street.

"And just who's going to do that?" demanded Jackson, stopping in his tracks and giving them a piercing glance.

"We are!" answered the three in unison.

Nate whispered to Jackson, "They're just trying to razz us and get us worked up so we take our eye off the ball during the game."

"Let's see if you can deliver what you all are preaching. Talk is cheap." yelled Jackson at the Natick boys and then set off for the common.

Almost the whole town turned out for the game as workers were let off their shifts.

Many of these were women, reflecting their great numbers in the working population of the mills. This was a social occasion for them to be seen in their most fetching attire.

Joan, Wilma, and Emily were sitting together watching the game in seating set up by the mill workers made up of old church pews under an awning. The pews came from the Unitarian Church in town. The women were discussing the fact that Josh's father, Will, had talked other mill owners amenable to Robert Owen's ideas on worker treatment into sponsoring these events. They would let the workers off their shifts early for these types of games.

"I'm glad," said Emily, "that my father-in-law Will was able to help set up this system in the area so that the workers can play ball. Most of the other mill owners, who don't believe in Robert Owens's ideas, will never let their workers off. They run real sweatshops. The workers work from dawn to dusk with no relief in sight, and their kids work right alongside them. Is that any way to run a country?"

"When people can't even make a living wage and support their families," said Joan, "sooner or later they are going to turn mean and bitter toward everyone. I know a worker from the Allen Tannery mill in Haverhill. When he got older, he had to go to the bathroom more often to pee, and they wound up firing him for that. I saw him begging for money on the street."

"Yeah I heard about that," piped up Wilma. "Hadn't he been one of their top workers when he was young?"

"A lot they care about the fact that he spent his entire life in that sweatshop," replied Joan. "For them he has simply outlived his usefulness."

"That's not all that's wrong with that Allen mill," said Emily with a disgusted look on her face. "They have a company store where all the mill workers buy things on credit against their wages. They charge higher prices than all the other stores, and if the workers are late in paying, they charge usurious interest rates. Some of the workers owe hundreds of dollars just in interest. This binds the worker to them. They can't quit without going into bankruptcy and losing the few possessions they have. In any case, the mill will not give them a good reference, so they can't get another job easily. My father-in-law Will told me all about it. The net effect is similar to slavery."

"The more people that know about that tannery mill, the better. Everyone should shun that place," said Joan.

"The problem," Emily replied with a serious look on her face, "is that in hard times people will take any work so as not to starve. They tell themselves it will only be for now, a short time–but, once they start buying from the company store, they get locked in and can't get out easily. I wish all the mills and factories were like the ones that Will has negotiated with, but sadly they are not."

"Wait a minute," interrupted Joan. "Isn't Mr. Allen one of the supporters of our abolition group?"

"Oh yes, but not for the same reasons *we* are in the group," Emily replied.

"What do you mean?" said Wilma, staring at Emily with a perplexed look.

"He gives speeches to his workers at least once a month, frightening them with statements that the mills in the North will be unable to compete with merchandise manufactured by the slave labor in the South, and workers here will all lose their jobs.

Since he tans hides, he does not have to rely on the cotton industry down south the way the textile mills do. He is actually a competitor, as his hides are used to make leather clothing. He has been going around all the towns stirring up the workers who are getting terrified of the South—all out of his fear of his industry being wiped out by slave laborers in the South."

"I'm terrified of the South too," said Wilma, "but maybe not for the same reasons."

"So am I," agreed Emily. "If the times were not so hard, people might not take him so seriously. At first, we thought Mr. Allen would help our cause by making workers more aware of conditions down south. But over time we found out he really does not care about the plight of the slaves at all. All he cares about is his business. What he is saying is stirring up the workers to the point that they want to make war on the South."

"That is terrible, but maybe it would end slavery," answered Joan thoughtfully. "Now that times have turned hard for the mills, aren't there a lot of business owners who feel the same way as Mr. Allen?"

"Oh yes, there surely are," said Emily, "but anyone tied up with the textile industry is afraid of aggravating the situation in the South and cutting off our supply of cotton. Look," she said, changing the subject, "we are here to have a good time today. Let's forget about the injustices in the world and have a special day."

The game finally started, and Jackson began pitching. He had great skill in putting different kinds of little effects on the ball as he pitched it overhand, often with considerable speed. Opposing batters had great difficulty reading where and how he was going to throw it. A couple of them even had the additional handicap of coming directly from New York-style baseball, where underhand pitching was the rule.

Fueled by his righteous anger at the insults he had already endured, Jackson was anxious to prove himself, and his throwing only increased in speed as the game went on.

At the end of the thirteenth inning—as the Lowell team came up to bat Nate could be seen on the sidelines, speaking to one of the mill hands. When he returned, he was wearing a work glove on his right hand.

One of his teammates took the occasion to tease him. "Hey catcher, we don't play baseball with gloves! They're for mill work, or maybe for society ladies going to the opera," the last words uttered in a mock falsetto voice.

Nate fired back, "Sorry, but I have to go to work tomorrow. I catch mostly with my right hand, but I need both hands when I work in the kitchen. Anyway, if it really matters to you, why don't you go out there and try catching the smoke that Jackson's throwing? I'd love to play second base and have a chance to run around a bit more." His teammate answered with a grudging smile and briskly shook his head.

When Lowell took the field again, however, the taunts from the Natick players were anything but good-natured. Torrents of insults and abuse flew from their bench. "Come on, you black bastard, you're gonna crack up! Go back to Africa! You're not fit to play here."

"What a curve," said the second baseman, who had an excellent view of the pitch.

"Stee–rike three! You're out!" cried the umpire.

The more they yelled, the better he pitched. When it was clear that Natick was probably going to lose the game, one of the Natick players threw a rock at Jackson, which he deftly ducked. At that point the umpire stopped the game. He warned Natick that anything more like that would cause them to forfeit the game for bad sportsmanship. He also threw the rock-throwing player out of the game.

This quieted them down for the remainder of the contest. Under Massachusetts rules, the first team to reach one hundred runs was declared the winner, and as the final run came in, the Lowell team gathered around Jackson and gave him a hero's victory celebration.

Jackson and Nate, sweaty but exuberant, walked home together after the game. They were both very pleased, even though they could not put the darker thoughts out of their minds. The rest of the team followed them at a respectable distance to make sure no Natick players came after them.

"Oh boy!" Nate exhaled. "Things are rough up here also. Why do you think those guys from Springfield are so vicious to us? There is no slavery up here anymore. What is bothering them?"

"I really don't know, but I imagine maybe they are worried that we have come up to steal their jobs, because free blacks have been known to work for less money," said Jackson. "Many black men just don't have the confidence that whites have, particularly when it comes to asking for more money. Most of the guys from Natick are from Irish families that came over here during the potato famine, and their kids still think like starving people. They think that the black men are just going to take away the little bit of money that they have been able to set aside.

But it's not just us. They also hate the French people who come down from Quebec for the same reason."

"So, we're going back down south—out of the frying pan and into the fire," Nate commented.

"I don't know which is worse," Jackson replied. Then he shrugged and continued with more determination, "Oh well, if it comes to it, it's much worse down south for sure. At least if we don't like it here, we can go somewhere else. The slaves don't have that luxury down there."

CHAPTER 7

SIGHTS ON DAVIS BEND

"Where will we live and put our plantation?" asked a drowsy Emily just before they went to bed. They were back at Josh's home with Will and Katie Lawrence.

"I'm thinking about it," Josh replied.

As he gently slid the blanket over Emily, who was nodding off to sleep, Josh stayed up with many questions flitting through his mind. "How," he wondered, "will I train black men and women down south? I never did this before. Can I get enough money from the abolitionists to start a phony plantation? Will the locals accept us? Where will we live and put our plantation?"

Then his thoughts turned to Joan and Wilma. Joan was more naturally sociable and bubbly, yet Emily had felt that Wilma possessed a quiet inner strength that could be of great value in trying situations. Some additional concerns were Emily's growing uneasiness at feeling directly responsible for other people's lives.

At last, when even the desire for sleep deserted him, he got up stealthily and sat down in an armchair next to the window. He might have dozed off for a moment—for the next thing he knew, his eyes were open and the full moon was rising. A single, clear thought flashed through his mind, becoming an audible whisper. It has got to be Davis Bend!

His reawakening consciousness now began to put together information like pieces of a puzzle. He remembered the letter he had read during the battle of Buena Vista from Joseph to Jefferson Davis, mentioning Jefferson Davis's secretary. His name was Benjamin Montgomery, and Josh suspected from the context of the letter that he was a black slave. Another aspect of the letter that was firmly held in Josh's mind was that Joseph Davis seemed ambivalent towards slavery, even though he was a huge slave owner. It almost seemed that the two brothers had some intellectual sympathy but not support for the principles of abolition. It was, after all, the Davis brothers' only means for making a living.

Having come to a decision as to their destination, Josh shut his eyes, He would reassure Emily in the morning that his father knew the families of both Joan and Wilma and had worked with them in the abolitionist movement. When he awoke later, he was startled to see that the sun had replaced the moon.

"Good morning, Josh," said Emily, who was standing in front of him.

Coming down to breakfast later than was his habit, Josh found his father at the end of the long dining table finishing a cup of coffee while reading the day's news. Dressed in a stylishly long frock coat, striped vest, and cravat–Will Lawrence glanced at the grandfather clock in the corner of the room and gently chided his son's tardiness.

"In the military, it always pays to steal a march on your enemy. In business, that means getting up before your competitors. Do you know where you are going down south? You don't have any land or a plantation."

Josh, who was overtired, appeared a bit annoyed over his father's meddling. "I was going to go down and try and buy some land near Joe Davis's plantation—that is, if I can get an introduction from you!"

Will, looking over his reading spectacles, noted his son's irritation, laid down his newspaper, and leaned closer to him.

"Let me help you. Joe Davis is a friend of mine. I can write to him and tell him you're interested in starting a plantation using Owen's methods. This will be a much smoother approach, since he and I have had a working relationship. I have publicly hidden my views regarding abolition, and I'm certain he has no idea of how I feel on the subject. Nobody does, except our abolition group. I can ask Joe if he has any land to sell, or if he knows anyone nearby who wants to sell land."

Josh thought this was not a bad idea, and Emily seemed to like it also.

"We'll think about it," Josh told his father.

Josh and Emily processed the idea and continued discussion over breakfast. They resolved to let his father go ahead and contact Joe Davis, which he promptly did.

About two weeks later, Josh's father received a reply. Joseph told Will in a letter that he did not have any land for sale, but that his brother Jefferson was becoming more and more involved in politics, so he would be very content to run a smaller plantation in the near future. Jefferson Davis was not going to use all of his land and intended to give some of it back to his brother Joseph.

"Since Joseph Davis will be getting a substantial amount of land back from Jefferson, he will let you use a portion of that land for your proposed plantation," Will told Josh.

At that point Josh brightened up and looked at his father intently, sensing the fruition of some of his plans.

Will went on, "Joseph has advised me that he does not give title to any land that he has given out to anyone, not even his brother Jefferson or his own family, so there will be no bill of sale. It will just be a written understanding between the two of you. But if you are able to successfully work the land for a number of years, he will find a way to give the land to you eventually."

Will added, "Joseph also told me not everyone is cut out for this type of work. You will know pretty quickly whether this is for you or not. The only stipulation would be that if you did not want to continue to work the land, nobody else could be brought in to do it unless Joseph Davis accepts that person to do the work."

Josh's irritation and fatigue seemed to vanish, and in an eager voice he cut his father off and said, "This is very exciting. Looks like we are going into the cotton business! How did you get him to do it?"

"You know, we are both students of Robert Owen. That is the cement that binds us together. I share industrial ideas with him, and we see our work as joint experiments. We are only too happy to help each other out if we can. I would be willing to help him out more directly if he needed industrial help, but I don't see any way that his system of slave labor could be made to work up north.

"Let me spell out what he wants from you: All agricultural supplies are to be paid for by you, Josh. Twenty-five percent of the crops' profits are to go to Joe Davis. You will have to agree to use the same factoring house in New Orleans that work with Joseph and Jefferson Davis for the sale of all crops. Most importantly, the cotton crop must constitute the majority of the production."

After two days of further discussion with Emily, Josh decided to go with his father's plan. Speaking with both his parents at dinner, they concluded the agreement.

"Okay, Dad—Emily and I talked it over. If you are both still willing to help us, we would like to go ahead with your plan to get the plantation from Joe Davis." Josh added, "It looks like hard work, but it fits well with our plan to attack slavery. Also, we're not trying to make any real money, as it is blood money."

"True enough, but remember this," his father countered, "you will have to try to be successful in the enterprise in order to provide a cover for your secret operation, which means you will probably have to show a profit to keep the enterprise going."

That evening Josh accompanied his father to a Congregational church in Lawrence, Massachusetts to meet with some conductors of the Underground Railroad who were part of the Boston Vigilance Committee. Josh's father had been providing support for the Underground Railroad, as did many of the wealthy mill owners in his congregation. This support came through middlemen so that no one could blame them directly for circumventing United States law.

It was a stormy night, and rain beat down on the church roof. Lightning illuminated the stained-glass windows. The atmosphere portended distress for Josh's upcoming trip down south. What they would learn that evening would put much more of a damper on his newborn enthusiasm.

Josh began by talking to two conductors who began to question him. One was black and one was white. The black conductor was gaunt and had obviously been through some unspeakable hardships, which showed on his face. He had the cadaverous appearance of the grim reaper himself.

"You wants to go to Mississippi? You sho goin' far! Ain't many houses or people to help you down dare if you gets into trouble down dare! Closest place we know of is in Memphis."

The white conductor, a tall man with regular features, chimed in, "The one and only person who has ever helped us in the past in Mississippi is a German man who we think came from a revolution in Germany."

CHAPTER 8

LOOKING AHEAD

After a sleepless night, Will Laurence felt concern over the future safety of his children, not knowing much of the living and working conditions down south. It weighed on his conscience now that he bore a great responsibility in making the perilous enterprise of Josh and Emily possible.

Sitting stiffly by the old colonial fireplace in her long dress, Katie Laurence could hardly control her emotions. Her eyes welling up with tears, she blurted out, "Do you really know enough about these four people to stake your lives on them?"

At his mother's emotion, Josh felt a knot in his stomach and felt the tension increasing rapidly. Sitting on the edge of his chair, he exchanged a glance with Emily, who then took the lead. Patting her mother-in-law's arm, she said in a soothing voice, "Katie, you've already met them here, and you know them all from meetings and as employees. Are you familiar with the Kirkwood Mill in Methuen? Joan Dubois's father is a partner there. He has been very successful in that place and has made a lot of money there. Joan is a wonderful, honest, moral person with good values. And her father freed his slaves and moved up north to open the woolen and cotton mills right here in New England."

"I trust your judgment, dears. We've already spoken with her at meetings. We like her. We're just a bit scared. You read all this stuff from Kansas—it's scary," Katie replied.

"I know you have had a lot of experience working with Wilma Turner," Emily went on. "She's a fine woman with great inner strength and as strong as most men. She is not afraid of physical labor."

"Yes, we have, that's true," added Katie. "She's a very smart woman."

Josh didn't mention Wilma's wicked temper when crossed as he did not want to upset his parents further, and he felt her temper could be managed with good communication.

"And Nate Washington," Josh went on, "you know, he's one of the best cooks in town, a very formidable chef. He'll be able to cook fine meals for all of us. And Jackson—he not only treats sick animals and horses, but he has memorized the bible in an effort to help others."

"Well, I don't mind other people cooking for me, healing my sick pets, and even reading from the bible if it comes to it," Katie countered, "but I don't see how these skills in particular fit in with your larger plans."

Josh began to explain his vision of their potential roles. "We plan to have both an agronomic business and a living space for us all," he explained adamantly.

"The day-to-day administrative and social activities will take place in the main house. The fields, the warehouse, and the stables will be tended to as well. Jackson will do well to tend to the horses, wagons, and their attendants—and to transport goods, merchandise, and provisions. It's the logistic part of the business. And our chef Nate will purchase and maintain our food to feed us all. He will ensure our ability to entertain and gather the community around us."

Kate nodded, listening intently.

"And Wilma and Joan will manage the other slaves, serve and

entertain at social functions, and—most importantly—promote our credibility among them," Josh went on.

Josh turned to his father. "We should plan a trip to Mississippi soon to check out the plantation and finalize all our plans with Joseph Davis."

Will nodded and said, "I'd like to do a little more research about current conditions down south before we leave. I'm thinking of contacting Nathanial Dubois, Joan's father. He's been part of the Underground Railroad network."

"That's fine," said Josh.

Emily nodded her head and said, "Joan and her father are very close."

"I'd like to leave soon for Mississippi. Will this be all right with you?" Josh asked Emily.

"Yes, I have to complete a class that I'm teaching in bible study, which will take the rest of this month. Maybe you two should go, and Katie and I should stay here." Katie quickly nodded her head to Emily in agreement.

CHAPTER 9

THE KIRKWOOD MILL

The next day, Will Lawrence, who was anxious to move the plan forward, sent a telegram to Nathaniel Dubois. He hoped to get a current perspective on living and working conditions down south. The telegram read, "Need to meet with you on most urgent business."

Two days later he found himself at the Kirkwood Mill and was surprised to find it cleaner than most, well-lit, and properly ventilated. He reached Mr. Dubois's office by a stairway that led to a much smaller, annexed building with thickly carpeted corridors and wood-paneled walls. Announcing himself at the reception desk, a young male clerk looked up from his study of an invoice to direct him to a wood and glass door at the end of the corridor. It seemed that he barely had time to knock on the door before it was opened by Nathanial Dubois, a thin, wiry man of olive complexion who offered his hand with a dignified smile.

"Welcome to the Kirkwood Mill, Mr. Lawrence," he said with a glint in his eye. "I imagine you've had a chance to look around a bit?"

"Just enough to tell you that I'm impressed by the working conditions here,"

Will replied.

"Well, to be frank, I'm glad you noticed that. Yes, these benefits cost money to provide, but I've always insisted on it to my partners. Worker health and morale is important to us. I know you are very familiar with these principles from your work with Mr. Owen."

"Of course. I agree with you," said Will with enthusiasm.

"As important as working conditions are, I don't think that was what you were referring to in your telegram as urgent business," Mr. Dubois said as his affable demeanor turned to a more piercing look.

"All right, I'll get to the point right away," said Will. "But I must first ask for your indulgence in a matter of secrecy."

"As long as it doesn't concern my partner's interests, you may count on my discretion. But if I'm thinking correctly, your visit has little to do with our professional relationship."

Will nodded.

"I rather believe it has to do with our respective children. Before you go any further, let me tell you that my daughter Joan and I are very close. She has spoken a great deal to me of the plan they are hatching."

"Yes, this is why I've come," said Will.

"I just want to say I am proud of what Joan has chosen to do, just as I'm sure you are of your children," Dubois said.

After a few hours of discussion, Will was satisfied that he had a good perspective on current living and working conditions in the South. There was nothing in Dubois's perceptions that contradicted his own view of what was going on there.

CHAPTER 10

WEAPON'S TRAINING

In a sand pit behind one of the historic buildings in the mill complex that Josh's father owned, sporadic gunshots rang out. Before leaving, Josh felt it was imperative for everyone to learn weapons training. Over a two-week period he trained all five participants in the use of, assembly, and cleaning of firearms—as well as the use of explosives, sabers, and knives.

Everyone agreed to the training, and they carried it out in late afternoons and early evenings to attract a minimum of attention.

Emily complained about the handguns. "They are only made for one thing, shooting people."

"We're not talking about offensive strategy for shooting people," Josh replied. "We're talking about defending yourself if you ever get in a tight situation. We may need to defend others—and our overall plan. The most important thing about handguns is to know when *not* to use them."

Emily nodded and then applied herself well to the shooting.

The three women all turned out to be good shots with a pistol.

Nate, being quite methodical in everything he did, tested well. On the other hand, Jackson was no better than fair in the use of firearms.

"A man who could throw a baseball through a hat at sixty paces should be able to do better than you did with the gun," said Nate with a quick grin.

"It's just that every time I shoot, I imagine some poor creature that I am shooting at, and it throws my aim off," replied Jackson.

"We're going to a very dangerous place," Josh said in a more serious tone. "Almost everything we do could be judged illegal if we get caught on the wrong side of the law. Remember, I want everyone to practice with the tiny Philadelphia derringer pistol until you all can use it well. I want you to be able to load it and clean it. Hopefully, we will never have to use it." Josh said fervently.

CHAPTER 11

ARRIVAL AT DAVIS BEND, MISSISSIPPI

In April, Josh and his father Will traveled down to Mississippi for a brief stay. They took a coastal steamer to New Orleans and then a fast packet up the river to Davis Bend. It had taken almost two months to finalize the land deal. The April weather was beautiful, unlike New England, which when they left was cold and snowy. It was warm and dry with winds blowing pleasant river smells across the land. The smell of the fresh plowed land was very soothing, and Josh felt a strong attraction to the land he was to acquire. The crops had just been put in, so he did not have to worry about planting.

After Will's preliminary discussion with Joe Davis, they planned to hire Joe's old overseer's son, Karl. He was a warm, intelligent man with a thorough knowledge of crops and cotton. Josh immediately reflected that perhaps Karl wouldn't be so warm, friendly, and helping if he knew what they were up to.

A most memorable part of the trip was two brief rides on a riverboat, going up from New Orleans to Davis Bend plantation and back down again. The boat that brought them upriver had to fight the current all the way, while the return voyage, with the aid of the current, was accomplished more swiftly.

There was an extra pilot on board going upriver. His name was Mr. Bixby. Standing near the bow of the boat, Josh struck up a conversation with him. "Travelling on this river is sure a beautiful thing, but you get to do it every day don't you?"

Bixby looked Josh over, trying to take the measure of who he was in the scheme of people he knew locally. Then he spit some tobacco juice into the river. "Ayah, I do, but it ain't always easy! Look out there in the middle. Sometimes there's trees or parts of trees in the river big enough to turn this boat around, or turn us over. I don't want to scare you, but there are sandbars jest waiting to trap the boat."

"I don't scare easily," Josh replied.

"If these things don't get you, once in a while the boilers blow up, but that has never happened to me," said Bixby. "We don't rush and put too much steam in them. We go a little slower!"

"How fast can this boat go?" asked Josh. The scenery on the shore passed slowly as they came upriver fighting the current.

"If we push the boilers hard, we could get ten knots out of this boat, plus or minus the current. Right now, the current is pushing five knots. Would you like a chaw of baccy?" He offered Josh a big piece of chewing tobacco. Josh politely declined. Bixby then looked over the side and spit a wad into the river, which was quickly demolished by the chunking side paddles.

"You know a lot of those problems with steam boilers are caused by young, inexperienced captains who are in too much of a rush," Bixby said, his shock of red hair disheveled wildly by the air rushing over the deck of the boat. "Mostly, when you go upriver when the current is strong you've got to hug the bank like we is doin' now. If there are no obstacles around, this way you don't need as much steam! The current is much slower here closer to the bank. You can't get too close. A boat could get grounded—or worse, you could turn over!"

Josh rolled his eyes and said, "I didn't realize it was that dangerous."

"We don't want to scare the passengers, but this is how we earn our money. We've all been working on this river for ages. It can be very unforgiving if you don't know what you are doing. These young guys want to run the ship like a bull in a china closet. They pile on the coal for steam and power and over-charge the boiler. Next thing you know–*boom*!"

Josh looked carefully at both pilots and the captain. He felt in good hands–as though they saw their role in navigating the river as if it was their highest calling. Not only did they love their job, but they also cared deeply about the passengers they were carrying.

From talking to these men, Josh began to feel a respect for the river as well. As they moved upriver fighting the current, Josh watched every bend and meander of the river. He saw how to take best advantage of the current and maintain a steady speed. After a while he found himself anticipating the turns and began to talk to himself–giving imaginary orders to the helmsmen. The talk with the pilot had initiated him into a whole new world of nature and the river.

Josh changed the subject to a lighter note when he approached the pilot for some more information later on in the trip. "The weather here sure is beautiful," he said.

Bixby looked up at the sky and then turned to face Josh. "Ayah. But you should see it in about two months. Every day mostly hot and wet enough to drench you. Some of the houses by the river are cooler, and some of the plantations have big fans run by steam engines to cool the owners off. Summer is long here–it don't cool off much until October."

During the last few hours on the river cruise, Josh's thoughts turned towards his destination. He took the time to discuss with his father some perceptions he had felt at some of the abolitionist meetings he had recently attended.

"Dad, I've been noticing some of the mill owners who are attending the meetings and providing financial support to our cause. They don't really seem to care for the plight of the Negro slaves the way we do."

"You better believe that that is true, son."

"Then why do they come and give us money?"

"They are terrified that the system of slave labor will get out of hand, become applied to industrial activities up north, and wipe us out. The planters, on the other hand, are making fun of our northern system—claiming we don't take care of our workers in sickness and in old age. There is a kind of war going on between our two systems," said Will. "It has not been a really hot war, but rather a cold type war, except in Kansas."

"We used to laugh at the planters' claims because we were making money hand over fist until recently. Since the financial panic and depression that started in Ohio, our free labor system is not doing that well, and many people have been thrown out of work. At the same time, the South has been selling cotton all over the world and has continued to make money hand over fist."

"I know," said Josh. "We have all been hearing them gloat about these successes in speeches. And they appear to have control in political power."

"That's the essence of what is going on," said Will. "Some business owners are giving us money, but not because they care about the Negro in slavery. They want to destroy the slave labor system because they are terrified it will take over our factories that exist now, along with ones that are started in the new slave territories. They are afraid this throwback to the Middle Ages will bury us economically now that they have obtained a modicum of success."

"Is that really possible, Dad?" Josh asked.

"It's not that likely," replied Will. "What is more likely is that if the South gets all these slave states, there will be no place for people from the North to go to. We will be closed out of these territories by slavery. Then they can bargain with congress for a more favorable position regarding the expansion of slavery."

"Another concern is people like Mr. Allen frightening workers by telling them their jobs will be lost to slaves and slave labor. By telling them this hogwash he is getting them to work harder and never complain about their working conditions because there is always the specter of slaves taking over their factories and throwing them out of work.

"As far as political power from the South, it is a wonder to behold. Anyone related to the textile industry is terrified to talk against the South in public. That's a lot of businesses directly involved or indirectly related to textiles. Look at all the businesses in New York. It's staggering!"

Josh groaned. "This sure affects you, Dad!"

"That's why I have to lead a double life," he whispered. "My abolitionist side can't come out in public, or the long tentacles of the South would surely strangle me as they have done to others. Other abolitionists can attend public events and bake sales. I can't do any of that. Everything I do has to be hidden from the South."

As they approached the Davis Bend landing Josh began to notice the muscles in his neck were tight. He also felt a bit lightheaded and wobbly on his feet. His father looked him in the eyes. "Josh, you look tense and uncomfortable. Are you worried about your plan?"

"I don't know these people," Josh replied, "even though I want to carry out this plan more than anything. I feel like a sharpie about to put something over on them–like a snake-oil salesman. But I'm sure I'm up to the job. I used to get feeling like this before the battles in Mexico."

CHAPTER 12

MEETING THE DAVIS FAMILY

As the boat came up to the landing Josh spied a well-dressed, prosperous-looking, middle-aged couple waiting for the boat to land. "Dad," he asked, "is that Joseph and Eliza?"

"It sure is, son," Will replied.

As they descended the gangplank, the couple approached them. "Nice to see you again, Will. Is this the son I've been hearing good things about?"

Joseph shook hands with both Josh and his father. His face was long and gaunt with deep lines, and he had a thick white beard. "This here's mah wife, Eliza." Eliza appeared to be a kind-looking older woman with wide eyes and long brown hair. Both Josh and Will took off their hats as a sign of respect for her.

Eliza smiled and spoke. "Y'all been doin' a lot of travelin'. We'll get y'all situated in the carriage house, where you can relax and get cleaned up for the rest of this afternoon. Then I hope you can join us for dinner at six o'clock."

Josh's queasy feelings quickly vanished in a sea of southern hospitality. From that moment on, Josh and his father's business dealings with Joseph Davis were to go smoothly.

During the next few days, Joseph gave them documents stating his plan to let them work the land and pay for supplies, which they all signed. He asked for twenty-five percent of the profits. He also made an addendum, which included Jefferson Davis's signature for agreeing with the plan.

Joseph had them stay at the Hurricane Garden Cottage next to the plantation, which was an imposing building with multiple Greek columns—more elegant than the most lavish houses in Haverhill or Lawrence, Massachusetts.

They took their meals in the Davis's household along with their family. They were treated with the utmost courtesy throughout their stay.

Eliza in particular quickly warmed up to them both. Not long after their arrival she said to Josh, "When you come down, you bring your wife Emily to visit me, and I'll help her get adjusted to life down here. It's quite a good life, except it gets very hot in the summer. Sometimes it can breed diseases like malaria, but we know how to deal with that."

"What do you do?" Josh asked with a concerned look.

"We leave for the summer months," Joseph said. "We have some great places to go—either to the mountains or to the beaches up north—or we go the city of Atlanta. It rarely gets as hot in Atlanta compared to here. We have good people running the plantation. We'll teach you! After you get used to it, you won't want to go back up north!"

During one of the meals, Joseph's cousin Dee Ann came over to visit. She was a tall, attractive, vivacious, blond woman—very stylishly dressed.

Eliza introduced her. "Dee Ann is our family abolitionist. She hates slavery, as we all do—but she wants to end it right now. Luckily, she can hold her tongue with neighbors and in Vicksburg when we go to town! Joseph has tried to explain that if we end slavery now, we could have hundreds of thousands of Negroes running around with no way to earn a living, and it would destroy our economic system down here."

Then she looked at Josh and his father and shook her finger "It is the most frightful thing you could talk about. If anyone mentions abolition, folks get real scared around these parts. Then they turn mean. When you all come down here, don't you dare mention abolition, even if you think it, unless you want real trouble. Don't forget this! Some folks from up north have done it, and it got them in a heap of trouble."

Josh inquired. "What do you mean—a heap of trouble?"

Dee Ann quickly turned around and entered the conversation, looking straight at him. She said boldly, "There was a Jewish druggist who came from New York. He opened a pharmacy. He told a plantation owner that slavery was not a good thing, and it ought to be abolished. He was talking about the future, not now—but some folks took it the wrong way. One morning they found him tied to a tree all beat up. Please, no matter what you think, don't say anything to anyone about abolition. It scares folks, and they go crazy! We have to warn all northerners coming down here about that. Remember, abolition represents the destruction of their life as they know it, even though they might not like slavery."

One evening, Joseph and Eliza invited Josh and his father to a soiree at the main house music room. Joseph announced, "Dee Ann is going to sing some of the songs by that new songwriter, Stephen Foster. If you haven't heard them, they are quite beautiful. She also likes to sing Schubert songs in German."

The musical entertainment began at 8:00 p.m. that evening, and was quite memorable. Dee Ann sang and Eliza accompanied her on the piano. From Foster she sang "Old Folks at Home," "Camptown Races," and "Jeannie with the Light Brown Hair." Then she sang two beautiful Schubert songs and finished with "My Old Kentucky Home."

This song was still going 'round in Josh's head when they

adjourned for the evening. He felt the beautiful Dee Ann certainly gave off a powerful, romantic gravitational force. Whether or not it was deliberately directed towards him, he was unable to decide. But it certainly had some effect on Josh, without Emily around to stabilize him.

When all the business was completed, Josh and his father headed back up north. Joseph and Eliza took them to the landing to see them off. They both felt a glow from the warmth and hospitality they had encountered. The cotton fields silhouetted against the rising sun and the alluring Mississippi River were etched firmly in their minds.

As they sat on the deck of the riverboat heading to New Orleans to pick up a coastal steamer to head home, they talked about their experience staying with the Davis's. "You know, Dad, I have some mixed feelings about this place," Josh said to Will. "If this place wasn't built around and mixed with slavery, it would be an awfully nice place. The people are friendly, and they have better hospitality then up north. It feels like they go out of their way to make you feel more comfortable, and it's an easier pace of life provided you're not a slave."

Will said, "Sure, life is a lot easier for some people if they live off the backs of slavery. We can't really measure what life would be like because these are not real people. Their slaves protect them from feeling the full measure of the slings of outrageous fortune."

"But, Dad," Josh stared up from the river toward his father, "they still have to manage their slaves. That's a full-time job that someone without slaves doesn't have to do. I think this reminds me of all the wealthy people back home in New England. They have servants to protect them too, but they don't seem very happy."

On his way home every night Josh dreamt of the river. He could smell the water, the freshly plowed fields in the distance, the alluvial sands, and trees and branches carried by the river.

He also remembered the concert by the beautiful Dee Ann. "My Old Kentucky Home" seemed a stand-in for the Davis plantation. The lure of the plantation had a gravitational pull which was hard to resist.

They stopped at the port of Charleston, South Carolina, on the way home to talk with Josh's cousin Charlotte. They discussed obtaining proper bills of sale for the four "slaves" that Josh wanted to take with him down south. Cousin Charlotte was very amenable to Josh's plan, but her lip curled in a distinct look of disgust as she revealed some of her feelings on working in the Deep South.

"I don't know how long I can continue to live and work here because this state is full of fire eaters who want secession and war with the North. I'm so disgusted with this whole place that I want out very soon. I have some bills of sale that have been used to sell slaves recently."

"I also have some blank bills of sale as well, so you can fill in the demographic information they require. If you give me this basic information, the vital statistics, and the place where the sale took place (who was selling and who was buying)—we'll be all set."

After Josh provided her with the data, Charlotte felt that the bills would look better if they had some fictitious slaveholders as the sellers and Josh as the purchaser. She used slave merchants who were either deceased or had become inactive in recent times.

Josh and his father had to stay overnight while she had the bills printed up, filed, and given the state seal of South Carolina. Charlotte said, "This bill of sale looks like the real thing, because it *is* the real thing."

Will thanked Charlotte for her assistance and said, "When you get fed up and need to come north, we will always have a job for you in personnel at our mill."

All their business completed, Josh and Will sailed for home.

When they got back to Massachusetts the weather was damp and cold, a tremendous change from the mild, balmy weather down south.

As Josh and his father entered their home, Emily greeted them at the door. She rushed towards Josh to throw her arms around him on his arrival, all dolled up like a southern belle. "Welcome home," she said joyfully, hugging him tightly. Nate and Jackson, who stood alongside her smiling, were dressed up in suits–just the way housemen in the plantation region would dress.

"I'm so glad you're back," Emily said. She turned to Jackson and ordered, "Jackson, do bring me a glass of water."

"Don' you worry, Miss Emily. Jackson will get it for you. Does you want anything with it, Miss Emily?"

"No Jackson, that's all. Nate, take this book and put it on the shelf. It grows heavy in my hand."

"Yes'm, Miss Emily."

Wilma was dressed like a cook, and Joan like a maid.

"Wilma, what are we havin' for dinner?" Emily asked.

"Why Miss Emily, you knowed we is havin' roast chicken. Does you still want it?"

"Joan, make up the bedroom for the guests and clean that bathroom."

"Miss Emily, does you want me to use duh new sheets you done jess bought?" replied Joan.

Josh and his parents smiled broadly and applauded the little show with a standing ovation.

Later that evening Josh talked for hours with Emily about his findings on the trip, and his feelings about being down south. Not only was he impressed with the start-up plan for the plantation, but so was Will. Their joint approval made a powerful impression on Emily, who highly regarded her father-in-law's judgment.

"I can't wait to carry out the plan now, Emily," Josh told her when they were alone. "Joseph Davis and his wife Eliza were most cordial and welcoming. You will enjoy meeting them. I don't think the family is really too hot on slavery, even though it is the primary way they make their living."

Emily listened eagerly and nodded, excited about their upcoming trip down south. "Isn't it fashionable in intelligent circles to talk down slavery, while on the other hand do nothing to get rid of it?" she asked. "Some people can rationalize that slavery will be destroyed in the future, when society is ready to get rid of it, and they do nothing in the present to get rid of it."

"That's true," said Josh. But in spite of his concerns over slavery and the dangers of being down south, that night he had pleasant dreams about plantation life.

During the next two weeks the group prepared for departure to the Deep South. Josh, Emily, Jackson, Nate, Joan, and Wilma spent many hours a day role-playing as master and slave until they got their act down pat.

When they had rehearsed it to the point of perfection, they put on a show for Mr. and Mrs. Lawrence. "Be careful," Katie Lawrence said, "you've got to live these roles." Mr. Lawrence said, "You slip up, and it could be very dangerous for you."

The Lawrences hugged them all and wished them well.

CHAPTER 13

DEPARTURE FOR MISSISSIPPI

The prospective family of six left two weeks later, heading for Vicksburg, Mississippi, and the Joseph Davis Plantation. Josh—now a handsome, well-dressed young man with a fake beard and moustache—escorted his beautiful wife, Emily, who was wearing a wig. The couple was well-attended by their hired help, who were told to play a low-key role until they crossed the Mason-Dixon Line. The traveling party took a coach to Hartford, Connecticut to avoid being recognized at any of the Massachusetts train stations.

"We have to be very careful, even in the Northeast, as there are slave agents everywhere looking for escaped slaves and taking note of all occurrences in train stations and public places. Don't lay on the slave-master role too heavily till we cross the Mason-Dixon line," Josh admonished the group.

The black servants were impeccable in their appearance. Jackson, who was six foot six and powerfully built, stood out at the station dressed in a blue suit and cravat. His woman Joan, right next to him, had a striking appearance as well, dressed in a full skirt with ruffles from the knees down. Her waist was form-fitting tight to show off her hourglass figure. Her dress was cut low in the front to show off her ample bosom. The dress had ruffles around the shoulders with puff sleeves. She wore a red sash, which called attention to her narrow waist. This was gauged to be perfectly normal for a house slave of the South, as they were often allowed to dress more elaborately than their white masters. It was a useful custom for traveling.

Nate was stylishly dressed in a white shirt and olive-colored vest with black pants and shiny leather shoes. He cut a very handsome appearance. Wilma appeared very tall and stately, of heroic proportions. She wore a calico dress, which accentuated her shapely figure. Her head was covered with a scarf.

The six travelers drew a fair amount of attention at the Hartford train station due to their well-dressed appearance. Josh felt that these customs and dress would not stand out when down south and would create no problems at all, especially when they crossed the Mason-Dixon Line.

As they boarded the train, the women felt many eyes on them. One woman-traveler took it harshly when her husband appeared to stare longingly at Joan.

"We got to start acting like hired servants right away!" Josh mumbled under his breath. "There are slavers everywhere looking for escaped slaves and kidnappers looking for free blacks to spirit away down south to be slaves!" Everyone quickly shifted to his or her roles.

"Let me clean yo-ah boots, dey looks dirty!" Jackson said to Josh.

Joan began to help Emily carry a bag. "Shoa is a nahce day, Miss Emily."

As they got more obsequious, Josh began to feel contemptuous glances from other passengers. Joan overheard the comment "Look at that idiot couple. Those could be slaves. It makes me sick!"

Josh whispered to the others to tone down their slave talk.

Despite their attempts to play down the master and slave

role, the group had miscalculated. The way they were dressed and looked, and their sheer number–four blacks and two whites traveling together–led some of the passengers and black porters to identify the blacks as slaves accompanying and taking care of their two masters.

The first test of their plan took place in New York City where they had to change trains for their trip down south. Despite Josh's admonition, it was apparent that this was a master traveling with his slaves. Josh, Emily, and their four slaves were sitting alone in an empty railroad car when two well-dressed men with top hats came up to them.

"Well friend, aren't you taking a chance bringing your Negroes up north where they could run away?" one man said to Josh. "Friend, don't you know about the repeal of the nine-month rule that Governor Seward signed into law quite a while ago? Any slave brought here by his master is now free in New York."

The other man added, "Outside of New York City, nobody would help you get them back!"

Josh glanced at his four Negroes and said, "They won't run because we take good care of them." But when he looked up, he saw that he was staring at the barrels of two guns.

"Well friend, we aim to free your slaves. We need to get them out of New York quickly, so we have tickets for them to go somewhere where you can't lay your hands on them. We are also going to give them ten dollars each so they can make it in freedom."

The two men looked at the four slaves and said, "We will take you to a safe-house where you can begin your freedom."

They took four ten-dollar gold pieces out of their pockets and were about to make off with the foursome when Nate spoke up. "Please, masa. We don' want to run off–our chillin is back on de plantation. If we done run off we'll never see our chillin again. Please masa, don't make us go!"

The other three members of the group continued to entreat the men not to take them.

"We is never going to see de chillin again–please, masa–leave us be."

"You could work and raise money to buy your children," one of the men said.

"Please, master– let us be. We is not ready for dis. Our chillun is not ready for dis."

Looking crestfallen, the men walked out of the car and quickly disappeared. Joan thought she heard one say. "Boy, you never know what you're going to run into! I guess old Governor Seward can't help us here!"

"That was a close call," said Josh after the men left. "You guys were great!"

"What about the forty dollars we just passed up," said Jackson with a deadpan expression. "We could have had a lot of fun with that," he said smiling. "But seriously, you can see how quickly the best plans could go bad in an instant."

When they reached Baltimore, they began to feel a change in the air; other people came over to talk to Josh and Emily. They felt people warming up to them. One traveler came over to them. "I'm a goin' back to my tobacco plantation, we sure had a good growin' year. Ah wish ah had slaves that looked as good as yourn! Ahl bet they could cut tobacco rail fast."

"Hey, friend," Josh shot back with a phony southern accent, "theys not for worken in the fields. Theys for worken round the house. But lord knows, theys good workers at anything they does! Can't you see they ain't no field hands?" They were all enjoying riding in the railroad cars, and as they got further south the earth began to turn more orange from the iron in the soil. Emily began to make note of all the stations as they passed by–Richmond, Lynchburg, Knoxville, Chattanooga, Decatur, Corinth, Meridian, Jackson–until Vicksburg, the last stop.

There were some long, straight runs in Tennessee when the

engineer piled on the coal and built up the steam. The choo choos came faster and faster, like a metronome picking up the tempo—*choo choo choo choochooooo*—until they were almost continuous. The chimney on the engine had a spark catcher, but at high speed there was still a shower of sparks coming out of the chimney, albeit a smaller shower then without the catcher.

The whole train began to shake faster and faster. Emily began to get anxious about the jarring and the high rate of speed. She held tight to Josh's hand. As the train lurched back and forth, Josh felt as though his hand was being squeezed in a vise.

He asked the conductor walking by, "How long to Decatur?"

"About an hour," the conductor replied. "We're sure makin' great time. The engineer told me that we hit almost 70 mph on this stretch every day. Y'all know, that's faster than one mile every minute!"

To Emily, seeing her anxiety, the conductor said, "Don't you fear, little lady. We does this every day. You gets used to it, and it becomes fun."

The train's whistle was blowing with a high-pitched screech as they went through little towns. The vents and windows were open. When the wind was not blowing the smell of burning coal into the passenger compartment, one could smell the pleasant aroma of fresh plowed earth.

As they got further and further south, the smells that Josh remembered began to come back to him. "Emily, can you smell the land? What a grand smell!"

When they got near Vicksburg the smell changed to the Mississippi River, that mélange of plowed fields, fresh water, and alluvium carried by the river. This glorious smell was so memorable that all of the party was talking about it.

Nate and Wilma were trying to communicate but had to fall back on slave talk to keep from arousing suspicion.

"Show is beautiful country. Lordy, smell dat land," Nate said enthusiastically.

"Why you no 'count man, you isn't gawn run off on me," Wilma replied.

"No honey-chile, I sure isn't! You is jess too beautiful! I wouldn't have nobody den," said Nate.

Not to be outdone, Joan and Jackson began their own dialogue.

"When ah gets home, ah is goin' to give you a big present," said Jackson.

"What you mean–big present? You is not goin' to give me nottin ah wants! You iz a no 'count man too."

Some of the fancily dressed white passengers seemed to be enjoying the black dialogue. Josh relaxed even more. He felt Nate and Wilma could ham it up like real actors, and nobody would ever know.

They had five main stops in Mississippi, Corinth, Meridian, Jackson–and, finally, Vicksburg. The city of Vicksburg was laid out on high bluffs over the Mississippi River. A large courthouse building dominated the highest point of the city with a tall steeple. All the other buildings, such as St. Paul's Church, were fairly substantial in size and were arrayed around it–but well below. It seemed to Josh that with its high citadel the city resembled a kind of southern Quebec City. However, Vicksburg was overlooking the Mississippi instead of the St. Lawrence River.

Not having time for a grand tour of the city, they picked up the steamboat *Lacey*, which made the last twenty miles of their journey to the Davis Bend plantation.

As they got underway riding the steamboat on the Mississippi, Josh was in his glory. He began talking to the crew as they rounded the second bend in the river. It was shoaling up. The boat had slowed down, the paddle wheel had stopped turning, and two crewmen were on the front deck with a plumb line and lead weight to measure water depth. They were calling out the depth: "*Mark four! Mark four! Mark four!*"

At that point Josh asked one of them, "Are we in shallow water?"

"Not jest yet, but there be a sunken tree near here, and we jest don't want to hit it!"

More readings came in—"*Mark three! Mark three! Mark twain!*"

The pilot called out, "All ahead–slow!" The great paddle wheel began to turn as the boat inched forward. "*Mark twain! Mark three! Mark four!*" came the readings as the depth increased. The captain gave the order ahead, one third, and the wheel turned faster and faster, and began to chunk, as the boat picked up speed. Emily could sense Josh's excitement at the procedure he had just witnessed.

"Would you like to be a pilot on this river?" she asked Josh.

"You better believe it! But I can't really do this for a living. I'd just like to try it a few times if they'd let me!"

Josh had telegraphed ahead from their stop at Jackson to the Vicksburg Telegraph Office to advise his approximate time of arrival. The message was carried down river from Vicksburg by a fast packet ship earlier in the day because there was no telegraph line to Davis Bend. So, when the *Lacey* blew its whistle to announce its arrival, Joseph and Eliza Davis were at the landing to meet the party.

CHAPTER 14

ADJUSTING TO PLANTATION LIFE

Eliza, wide-eyed and smiling, greeted Emily and Josh warmly, like old friends, as did Joseph Davis. "Welcome! Y'all must've had a long hard trip," said Eliza. "We've set up the guesthouse for you." The four "slaves" stood quietly by, knowing it was not their place to speak but nevertheless taking it all in.

Eliza led them to the Hurricane Garden Cottage, a large, elegant building next to the plantation with tall Greek Columns on the façade. It was to be their new home. As they approached their new residence, Eliza took Emily's arm and said, "Come, I'll show you around the cottage." Joan and Wilma followed close behind them, not speaking—but their glowing eyes indicated they were indeed impressed with the surroundings.

Joe Davis was renting them the guest cottage at a very fair price of fifty dollars a month. This was until they built their own main house. The cottage was huge! It had eight bedrooms, four bathrooms, an enormous kitchen, and other rooms that could be used for all sorts of things, including meetings. It had a large fan run by a steam engine and pulleys to cool off the house in the summer. The house appeared to be able to keep its inhabitants reasonably comfortable, provided it did not get too hot in the summer.

"Y'all rest up and take a hot bath. We're having dinner at seven. Y'all come over when you are rested up," Eliza said.

"Wow," said Nate to Joan after Eliza left. "Did you see that kitchen?"

"I know," said Joan. "But this is going to be a formidable place to keep clean."

Wilma and Joan went upstairs together and started to unpack their belongings.

The next morning Joe Davis came by to walk Josh around the land and give him a tour of the plantation. As they were walking around the fields, Joe explained, "Ah consider your father a real good friend of mine, and so ah am going to treat you like family. Your father tells me you're a real hard worker. So, I'm going to help you get started. If this works well, even though you are giving me a twenty-five percent cut of your profit on your cotton crop, there should be plenty of profit for you. I want you to keep a journal so that we can present our findings to Robert Owen's group. You know he died last year, but we want to keep up the work he started.

"Now, provided the weather will cooperate and there aren't too many natural disasters to take up our time, we all are planning to render you quite a bit of assistance. As you've seen, we've got a nice place for you and your family to live in, along with your servants.

"Jefferson's slave secretary, Ben Montgomery, runs a store here where you can buy most local supplies that you need," Joseph went on. "He is a very smart, skilled Negro, who Jefferson taught to read and write. Ben can help get you any supplies that you need. He is one amazing slave. Ben has been trying to get a patent on a type of propeller for riverboats, but the patent office keeps turning him down because he is a slave."

At Joseph's warmth and offer of assistance and his

comprehension of the Negro's extraordinary abilities, Josh began to feel pangs of guilt at the fact that he was going to perpetrate a fraud on Joseph and his family.

He was, however, able to banish these thoughts by a combination of rationalizations. "Deep down, Joseph does not really seem to like slavery. He holds his niece, who has abolitionist thinking in very high regard. Although it is still slavery, what's being practiced here seems like a distinct departure from the type of slavery that we have been fighting against."

Joseph then took Josh over to the slave quarters and told him of some of their conditions for the slaves' employment. The slaves' quarters were small buildings with three rooms with a hearth for cooking. The buildings had a loft above for children to sleep in. While the accommodations were simple and plain, they were bigger and better than most of the slave accommodations he had seen on other plantations throughout the South. Some of the bedrooms had beds, others had straw mattresses. While it was difficult to make direct comparisons with workers' housing up north, Josh found that these particular slave quarters were not that much worse than many workers' housings that he had seen in various mills throughout the northeast. Some of the slaves' quarters seemed to reflect a higher standard of living than others. This was in keeping with the Davis's adherence to Owen's methods of positive reinforcement for hard work.

Joseph explained that all slaves got their medical and dental care at the plantation's expense by high quality white doctors. He told Josh these slaves could make extra money by working on their own free time at the end of a workday. Except for times during a harvest, his plantations normally had a ten-hour workday, but it could be twelve hours or more during an emergency or during a harvest. The slaves got an hour for lunch and got one day off, mostly Sundays, to practice religion.

If the slaves choose to work on their day off or after hours, they could earn extra money to buy animals or other things they might want. They could also get all the food they wanted or needed.

Then Joseph added a caveat, "Only plantations in this area do things like this. The working conditions in many other parts of the South aren't anywhere near as good, and some might be awful."

The slaves seemed to have most of their human needs met, but they were not free to leave without the owner's permission. Slaves were encouraged to marry, but their marriages were not legally recognized in courts—and, ultimately, they were still slaves. They did, however, get some better benefits then some of the workmen in the mills in Massachusetts.

Joseph explained to Josh that his brother Jefferson had a Negro slave who was the overseer of his plantation workers. "He is kind, and the slaves feel he understands them better than we do. If I found a man like him, I would make him overseer of my plantation as well."

Joseph then offered to lease Josh some of his own slaves. He offered slaves who had good expertise in cotton growing. But he would only lease them to Josh on the condition that he treat them with the same methods the Davis family employed.

After two weeks, Josh, Emily, and their extended family of "slaves" began to adjust to their environment. One night they got together in the living room when they were alone to brainstorm and plan their initial strategy.

Sprawled out on the living room couch, Nate said, "I don't think we should trust anyone, even other slaves. We don't really know any of these people yet."

Jackson looked up and responded, "I agree. If we take them into our confidence, we increase their danger as well as our own.

"Why don't you rent out two of us after a while to some of the other neighbors, if they are willing." Jackson said. "We can get a better view of things from the inside out. Four people are enough to keep this house running well enough. Right now, we have a lot of free time on our hands."

Joan added, "I heard it's illegal for whites to teach Negros to read."

"My master who taught me to cook, died," Nate said. "I could explain to authorities, if I had to, that he taught me to read recipes in cookery books, and that's how I learned how to read."

"You're right," Josh added. "In some states it is illegal to teach Negros to read. This rule came after the slave revolts, but it's not really too well enforced. Some people want their Negroes to follow shopping lists. It makes life easier if a Negro can read and follow simple directions.

"So, if we rent you out," Josh continued thoughtfully, "you can't reveal you can read anything until we know the various slaves better. You have to choose very carefully whom you teach what to. First, we need to know these people real well."

After pondering this issue a bit further, Josh felt it was too early to rent people out. "We need to get to know this place a little better before we can even think of renting any of you out," he said protectively.

CHAPTER 15

A SPECIAL CHEF COOKS DINNER

Two weeks after Josh, Emily, and their slaves arrived, Joseph Davis got up early one morning and found his wife Eliza sitting in the drawing room fingering her cameo necklace and staring into space. "Is something bothering you, Eliza? You look kinda concerned over something."

"No, Joseph," she sighed, "I'm just waking up." She yawned, looked straight ahead—and her lip came down in a kind of pout.

"Come on Eliza, I know you better than that," Joseph said.

"Well you know, Joseph, I've been thinking—I really like Josh and Emily a lot. They are such a good example of what young people should be like. I believe they are going to fit in here, but what I'm thinking about is their slaves. Those four that they brought with them—they look after their masters like they are family. That is fine and good, but there is something different about them compared to the slaves around here."

Joseph rolled his eyes and then blurted out, "What exactly do you mean, Eliza, when you say 'different'?"

"That Jackson, for example. He looks mighty confident for a slave. The only slave confident like him was Buck Richard, who killed his master. Y'all remember that trial before they hanged him? Before he was tried, his face always looked earnest, sincere—and he would look folks right in the eye when talking. He was also real big and strong, like Jackson."

"Eliza! Big strong folks sometimes appear real confident. I think it's the same with blacks as white folks. And Buck Richards's master, Sam Belcher, was a blackguard.

"Eliza," Joseph went on, "Belcher treated his slaves like dirt! You know how I feel about this. You got to take care of your slaves like children in your family. It's a heavy responsibility. Some folks aren't up to it, they got too many problems of their own."

Joseph's jaw tightened with anger. "Sam Belcher—that wasn't his problem at all. He was just plain mean, and he had to control everything, otherwise he wasn't happy!"

"Yes, he was a terrible person," Eliza agreed.

"Remember, I loaned him one of my slaves, Grover, to help him with his harvest—and Sam whipped him bad! When I saw Grover's bloody back, I wanted to kill Sam myself! He had scars there for the rest of his life, and some folks thought I did it. You know that Sam and I had words, and I had nothing more to do with him. I'm glad he is dead. Good riddance to bad rubbish."

Eliza cocked her head and corrected Joseph, "Please don't talk ill of the dead. It's not a very Christian thing to do."

Josh and Emily's slaves," Joseph continued, "have been exposed to life up north in Maryland and Virginia. Slaves from those parts are going to be different. They don't seem angry or surly. I'll wager they'll fit in over time, once they get used to life down here."

Eliza's face took on a worked pout. "My only concern is how our slaves are going to react to them. What happens if our slaves become surly and start demanding more things then we can give them? We could have a revolt on our hands!

"Joseph," she continued, "we have almost five hundred slaves on our hands now. We have to think about their welfare too."

Joseph then rose to the occasion, looking intently into

Eliza's eyes. "Ah think your blowing this out of proportion. There's no way those four nice slaves are going to cause a revolt. The best insurance against a revolt is good and fair treatment of all slaves under our control. Eliza, don't forget, we have a court system for slaves to redress their grievances—and it works!"

"I know," Eliza said in a slightly irritated tone, "and I also know they get the same medical care we get, and it doesn't cost them any money, but there are still revolts happening on some plantations."

"Our servants get free housing," Joseph continued. "Most of the workers up north don't get that. Why, we take care of everything for them, and we do it in a nice way. Eliza, I've spent my whole life setting up this system. If this system fails, there must be something wrong with me or the system I set up."

Joseph looked her boldly in the eye. "You know what, Eliza. If this system can fall apart that easily—let it! I welcome the challenge. Those are good people, I'm not afraid of them."

Eliza then sighed, her eyes turned down, and she said, "Okay, Joseph—you're the boss of the plantation. If this is how you feel, I'll go along with what you believe. You asked me what's bothering me. This is it, but ah feel a lot better now that I talked about things ah was upset over."

Joseph and Eliza then decided to communicate more with Josh and Emily. Eliza planned to bring over a pie that she had baked and see if she could get them all to socialize. Eliza and Joseph agreed to invite them all over to the main house now that the newcomers were beginning to adjust to their new environment.

The next day Eliza came by the guesthouse carrying a pie and knocked on the door. Jackson answered the door, towering over the diminutive Eliza. "Shore is a nahce day, miz Eliza. Ah gets miz Emily for you. Y'all waits in here. Does you want a nahce cool drink while you waits?"

Eliza smiled, and her pretty face lit up the room, showing

off her perfect set of even white teeth. "Thank you, Jackson. I'd like that." Jackson's obsequious behavior had gone a long way to calming some of her inner turmoil. While she waited, she put her palm under her chin, deep in thought.

"Maybe Joseph is right," she thought. "These slaves are not from these parts. Maybe I just need to get used to them."

By the time Emily arrived, Jackson's kindly, solicitous manner had greatly improved Eliza's mood.

After a quick discussion of niceties and the weather, Emily turned to the pie.

"You know Eliza, its tea time. We had lunch just a while ago, but we never had dessert. I can have Jackson serve us some tea, and we can taste some of that wonderful-looking pie."

The pie had a golden crust and was still warm from the oven, giving off an enticing aroma. Even though she had eaten some dessert not long before coming, Eliza concurred in the interest of facilitating communication with Emily.

Tea and the pie were served by Jackson, catering very carefully to the two ladies. The pie tasted delicious and provoked further discussion on cooking.

"Did your cook Nellie bake this pie? It sure is exquisite."

"No dear," said Eliza. "I baked it myself."

"What a great job you did. It's the best peach pie I ever had," Emily said enthusiastically.

"I'm glad you like it." Eliza smiled back. "Those are fresh Georgia peaches in the pie. It's hard to make a mistake when you have wonderful fresh ingredients like that. Joseph tells me your man, Nate, was trained by a French chef who was his master. Is that so?"

"His master studied in Paris under one of the chefs who was world-renowned."

Eliza was quick to pounce on that statement. "Oh Emily, you must get him to cook a meal for us!"

"Let me talk with Josh about a date when we can get together,

Eliza. Josh has scheduled some work for Nate to do, so I need to clear it with him."

"Well I guess we'll be in touch then, dear," Eliza said warmly.

Upon finishing the dessert, Eliza rose cordially and said, "I do have to get back and finish some work for Joseph."

CHAPTER 16

IN THE HURRICANE GARDEN COTTAGE KITCHEN

The kitchen in the Hurricane Garden Cottage was a large room with a wood floor and a brick fireplace with an attached brick oven on the side. There was also a wood-burning stove with a separate oven, which was used for baking and roasting. The top of the stove and the kettle hanging from a cast iron hook in the fireplace were used for boiling food. Both ovens were used for baking and roasting. A large farm table graced the middle of the room, on top of a a painted oilcloth on the wood floor. There were oil lamps on the tables. Pantry cupboards and a pie safe lined one side of the room.

After Eliza left, Jackson walked into the kitchen where Nate was putting some baked bread into the brick hearth fireplace.

"Well, Nate–looks like you're going to be on the spot soon. I heard Emily is cooking up a plan. You're going to cook for a lot of people. What do you think about that?"

Nate brightened up immediately. "I welcome it. I like to cook for big groups. It makes me feel good when they like my food, and most people like my food. These two ovens, the brick hearth oven and the woodstove oven, are big enough to cook for a very large group."

"I sure like your food," said Jackson.

Nate stood up and put his hands on the large wooden farm table.

"Oh Jacks, by the way, I couldn't help seeing you looking at Joan out of the corner of your eye. Do you like her?"

"She sure is pretty, and I like to look at her, but if you want to know whom I'm most attracted to, it's Wilma. She really gets me worked up."

"Does she know that you like her?"

"Not really. To tell you the truth, I'm afraid to tell her. I'm a bit scared of her because I'm attracted to her."

"You've got to tell her—if you like her, Jacks. Tell you what. Let's make a bargain. You know I like Joan, and you like Wilma. So I will help you do the right things to get Wilma, and you leave Joan to me. That way I won't be upset if I see you sneakin' a peek at Joan."

"You help me get Wilma, and you won't ever see me sneaking any looks at Joan," promised Jackson.

"Just one more thing," said Nate. "I want to tell you about women, Jacks. I have done a lot of thinking about how woman operate, and I'm pretty sure of this. I've worked around a lot of woman in the kitchen and listened to them talk. Women love romance and romantic gestures. This means you need to do a lot of romantic talk to show her you are interested in her—give her special presents, candlelight dinners, and tell her she is special. You do these kinds of things, and you can't go wrong! Think about this stuff and put it into practice."

That afternoon when Josh returned home from his work in the fields, Emily brought up the day's events, including her prospective invitation to the Davis family and other planters. Josh and Emily decided to bring everyone in to discuss the coming plan. They all got together in the dining room, pulling up chairs to the old oak table that had been left for them at the cottage.

The meeting had much of the appearance of a board of directors meeting, except it contained an unlikely group—Josh and Emily, and their four Negro friends—all trying to develop their plans. The six partners in the enterprise cut an impressive appearance as they spread out around the table.

"So, they want me to cook them a gourmet French meal." Nate smiled and spoke out in his rich baritone voice. "I will be glad to oblige them. I will go over my menus to plan out a really memorable feast."

"Nate," Josh began, "I don't want to pressure you too much, but this meal is important. If it works out well, maybe we can persuade Joseph and some of the other planters to let you and your kitchen staff teach the other cooks to make fabulous meals.

"It would require reading recipes, which is technically against the law for slaves to do because it involves reading," Josh went on. "But some planters ignore these laws, because it makes life easier for them."

Emily added a grace note. "What planter wouldn't want his cook to be able to cook like a Paris chef!" she said, smiling over at Nate.

Jackson added his comments as well. "As your assistants, maybe we can get in on some of the action too. I've done some cooking before—but never at your level, and the women have also."

At that point the women joined in the discussion. "Nate, why don't you start your cooking classes with us," Wilma coaxingly added. "This could be our way into the other planters' houses."

Then Joan chimed in, "Why don't we invite several other planter friends of Joseph and Eliza's to the meal. If the meal is a success, we can teach the other servants who are cooks, how to read recipes."

"Sounds like a good idea," Jackson said.

Everyone was excited about the concept, and plans were made to go ahead with a grand meal.

Back in the kitchen, Jackson started thinking about the two women he and Nate had been discussing. He had always been drawn to women with strong mannish-type strength, and they had to be physically attractive as well. He sometimes wondered why he was attracted to this type, as many of them wound up hurting him. They were not nurturing and would not make good mothers. They had poor social skills and were not easily accepted by other women.

Wilma was unusual as she had the physical strength and power of a man but still had a feminine side and was very nurturing to children. Her physical appearance had a powerful impact on Jackson. He felt quite ready to pursue her but usually was at a loss for words when he was around her. He was always eager to make a good impression on her.

After his discussion with Nate, Jackson resolved to make a greater effort to woo Wilma. He decided to get some help from Nate to cope with his shyness in her presence. He thought more about the upcoming meal they were planning to cook. He decided that if he worked more with Wilma in preparation, either in the kitchen or in setting up the house for a banquet, he might have a good chance to get closer to her.

Most of the chores he had done so far were fixing things around the house. Shoeing horses and other tasks which were traditionally men's work did not give him much opportunity to spend any time with Wilma. He often gravitated to that type of work so that he would not have to feel excess anxiety when he was around her because he felt extremely awkward in her presence. When he was around her, he would often end up doing things he thought were stupid, because he was so self-conscious. After the talk with Nate, he resolved to move forward—even if it meant making a fool of himself.

CHAPTER 17

QUESTIONING SLAVERY

That very same day, two ministers dressed in long black frock coats with high stovetop hats carefully headed towards the main plantation house to meet with Joseph and Eliza Davis. They were the Reverend Joseph Sloan and the Reverend Jebediah Stewart, and they had come to solicit money for the construction of a new rectory at a nearby Episcopal church.

They were shown into the sitting room by the Davis's butler, and Eliza and Joseph were called in to receive their guests. Any casual observer who knew Eliza well could tell that she was not too comfortable with these two ministers. She did not offer the usual goodies that she made available to most visitors, and she had a tense, hard look as she stared at them.

It was obvious to Joseph that his wife had taken a dislike to both of them, but he went on with the conversation that began with small talk and then progressed to the issue of the rectory.

Eliza looked boldly into the faces of both Reverends and abruptly changed the direction of the conversation by asking, "What do you two think about that decision by the Supreme Court on the case in which a slave was adjudicated as property and had no rights whatsoever. It said that he had no rights to due process under the legal system."

Both men looked thoughtful. The Reverend Sloan answered first. "I follow Paul's first epistle to Timothy from the Bible:

"Let as many servants as are under the yoke count their own masters worthy of all honour, that the name of God and *his* doctrine be not blasphemed. And they that have believing masters, let them not despise *them*, because they are brethren; but rather do *them* service, because they are faithful and beloved, partakers of the benefit. These things teach and exhort. If any man teach otherwise, and consent not to wholesome words, even the words of our lord Jesus Christ, and to the doctrine which is according to godliness..."

The Reverend Stewart then chimed in to add, "This means slavery is an honorable profession. To go against it is to go against the teachings of God–and according to the Bible is blasphemy! This slave should accept his fate and go back to his master. This is the right and moral thing. To flee from his toil is morally wrong and ungodly. To file suit against the institution of slavery is immoral and ungodly, according to the Bible. I therefore think the Supreme Court did the right thing in following the teaching of the Bible."

Eliza turned away briefly, and appeared deep in thought. This doctrine, she worried, appears to be at variance to the way we run our plantation. We have a court system for redress of grievances. Joseph has spent the better part of his life developing it. He has been using the principles of the constitution to help the slaves. He can't be wrong here. Everything he has done cannot be in vain. Maybe I had better keep my mouth shut on this point, as we don't want his practice to be seen as at odds with church teachings.

Joseph was glad at that point that Eliza had turned away because she had a look on her face that appeared like the angry snarl of a wild cat. He then fought to quickly modulate the discussion back to calmer waters.

He said almost rhetorically, "The Reverend has quite a command of the scriptures—doesn't he, Eliza?"

Eliza nodded politely with a tight look on her face.

"I've got to have it. I'm doing the Lord's work," the Reverend Sloan answered. They then got back to discussing the rectory, and Joseph gave the Reverends a nice contribution for the building fund.

After they left, Eliza sat down forcefully on their colonial sofa, looking distraught.

"Joseph, did you hear that blowhard Sloan quoting from Timothy in the Bible to justify slavery? There is no justifying it! It can't be done! What about Jefferson's man, Ben Montgomery? He can't patent his invention of the propeller because he is a slave.

"The Supreme Court said slaves have no rights. We are slaveholders, yet we know it's fundamentally and morally wrong! I will keep my mouth shut so that your methods are not seen as at variance with church teachings."

Joseph smiled at her words and nodded his head.

"I believe" she went on, "these ministers are the ones who are morally wrong. Your work and experiments with the slaves, Joseph, are an attempt to make slavery more humane. In spite of what these ministers are saying, I hope that the government will take note of your system of humanitarian slavery and create some real change here."

Joseph was expecting more vitriol from Eliza, but when she began to talk this way, he brightened up. His eyes began to shine like a doctor who was getting credit for having saved a patient. All this talk by Eliza excited Joseph immensely, as he began to respond.

"Eliza, you mentioned that Jefferson has a slave, Ben, who has applied for a patent on an invention, and the government keeps turning him down because he is a slave. This same man traveled up north on our business and could have run away at any time but did not. Ben negotiated all our business and purchased equipment for Jefferson. He didn't run away because he has a happy life here, and he is part of our business success. He has become a big part of our life here. He is as close as any family."

Eliza nodded affirmatively.

Joseph went on, "What about our slave court for redress of grievances? What about our conditions of employment?"

"I know, Joseph, that's just what I was thinking about when those two Reverends were talking."

"Eliza, maybe the government will take a look at these things when it tries to find a way to end slavery in a humane way."

"How do we get rid of slavery without destroying our economy? That is the big question," Eliza continued. "We have quite a good life here, and it all comes from slavery."

Now that he was all fired up, Joseph paced the living room, thinking out loud.

"Some of the northern abolitionists claim that we could hire our Negroes like they do with their mill workers and pay them a workable wage after they are freed. I'm not sure this would work here. If they are freed men, they might not want to work in the fields anymore. They might want to be cooks, or work on railroads, or become sailors.

"There have been some Negroes who became successful pirates until they were hanged. They sure made wonderful sailors. Even if this could be made to work, the dislocations would destroy us.

"Our productivity of crops like cotton is keeping the whole country afloat in hard times like the recent years. It is a very delicate balance. If the northerners had their way and tried some of their free labor ideas on our slave population, it might destroy our cotton production. Our slave-labor system has been around a long time. Our slaves are used to it. You can't go from one economic system to another without severe dislocations."

Eliza shot back with a pained look on her face, "Joseph, we would be the ones who would be dislocated, along with all our slaves. Who is going to compensate us for these losses? Not the free-labor northerners. Some of them are so tightfisted that they won't part with a penny. It just wouldn't work!"

"I agree," said Joseph. "We need workers in our fields picking cotton every day. Many of the people up north don't understand the conditions here. We could have our cotton-picking crew work from sunup to sundown, and a hurricane could still destroy everything. Eliza you know there are already hurricanes, tornadoes, droughts, floods, insects, and blights that can destroy all our work. Who knows what will happen if we lose all our workers to a free-labor scheme."

Joseph suddenly stopped dead in his tracks and turned to Eliza with a searching look. "The Austrian Empire just abolished serfdom in 1848. Serfdom is a lot like slavery, except you don't legally own a serf, as you do here. I think Russia is planning to do the same thing. I don't think that, when these relationships break up, the lord of the manor is ever properly compensated for his losses.

"Eliza, how do we get rid of slavery without destroying the South that we know and love. As much as I hate the people who want us to secede from the northern states, they have a point. Maybe by standing up to them we could negotiate some kind of arrangement that would allow us to slowly unwind slavery without the dislocations that would destroy our economy and our way of life."

"I just can't imagine it, Joseph, but maybe it is possible."

"I hope so." Joseph added.

Fatigued by the encounter with the two ministers and the heavy discussion that followed, Joseph and Eliza sought refuge in music and wandered over to the grand piano. Eliza played the piano and Joseph accompanied her on the cello. They played a suite by Beethoven. The melodies resonated off the wooden floor in the parlor and appeared to change their mood to a brighter one.

CHAPTER 18

FAMILY LIFE IN MISSISSIPPI

One morning about a month later, the music of Schubert emanated from the parlor room at the Hurricane Garden Cottage and lit up the atmosphere. Nate and Jackson found some piles of sheet music near the dark ebony grand piano, and between lunch and dinner Nate took the lead, because his master had originally taught him how to read music as well as recipes.

"Let's have some music," Nate said to Jackson, and he sat down and stretched his legs out and began pounding rather heavily at the keyboard.

Jackson, who had also learned to sight-read music when he came north and who had often performed with his local church choir, then pushed him out of his seat in a good-natured way and said, "Let me take over." He stretched his long arms out gently on the keyboard and began to play the Schubert so naturally and beautifully that Joan and Wilma came into the room. They had been doing cleaning chores upstairs.

Joan said, "I know that piece, "*Gretchen am Spinnrade.*" I studied that piece in Switzerland in German. I can sing it!" she said enthusiastically.

"Go ahead," Jackson said, "you turn the pages, Nate."

Wilma, in a long beige and brown dress with wide lace sleeves, stood at the entrance, her brown face and dark eyes lighting up with admiration.

Joan's rich soprano voice resonated off the wooden floors and wood paneling to create an ethereal, magnetic sound, which quickly drew Josh and Emily from the next room. They applauded wildly when it was finished.

Josh's face then turned beet red with embarrassment as he added a warning. "I don't want to rain on your parade. You all know that you are not supposed to be people of high culture. If folks nearby hear this type of music, they may get suspicious. It's too high falutin' for slaves to be playing this type of music."

Nate and Jackson went back to the kitchen to start work on lunch, and Wilma and Joan went back upstairs to finish their cleaning.

Back in the kitchen, standing behind a row of copper pots hanging from hooks below the ceiling, the two had a follow-up discussion on Nate's advice to Jackson.

"I think Wilma likes me," Jackson said, talking to Nate as his confidant and mentor. "That stuff you told me about looking and acting romantic seems to have gotten her attention! I've been joking around with her, and she seemed very responsive to me. What do you think?"

Nate took one of the pots off the rack and started wiping, as it was dusty. "It sounds good to me. If I were you, I'd continue what you're doing, but now I'd get ready to be more aggressive." He hung up the now clean pot and decisively stated, "What I mean here, is to look her right in the eyes, and give her a real passionate kiss. That is, when the time is right!"

Jackson, breaking eye contact with Nate, stared at the ceiling thinking—yes, but maybe I should make one more romantic gesture before I start with the physical stuff, then things can take their own course from there. On the other hand, Nate's previous advice had certainly worked out well. His heart was divided between loyalty to his friend and uneasiness about disregarding his friend's advice.

Back in the living room that morning, Emily and Josh had received a letter from Josh's parents, Will and Katie, inviting them to come back north for part of the summer. If that were not practical, they also suggested the possibility of their coming down south to Davis Bend and visiting during the winter season. Josh and Emily had had little contact with them up until this time. The letter reflected their concerns about their health and the progress achieved in their original plan of action.

Deciding on how to respond proved no easy matter.

Josh said, "Emily, we have been here almost four months. Planting won't start until the beginning of April. Why don't we invite my parents to come down for a few weeks in March. It would break up the winter for them. We could show them around here and take the fast packet to New Orleans. We could all have a good time there, and the trip would give us some distraction from our work here. And I could take advantage of the visit to meet with a cotton broker there who Joseph uses to sell cotton to England.

"As far as us coming up to New England, it would have to be early in the summer after planting but before the harvest."

"What are you going to do about the harvest?"

Josh looked and saw Emily staring nervously at him. Josh then immediately saw the reason for Emily's anxiety, and began a discussion of the season of diseases, hurricanes, and tornados.

"I plan on us leaving during the mean season for the most part, but we could return at the end of September or the beginning of October, depending on how the growing season works out. Joseph is helping us get started, but I feel I need to be there at certain points to learn the growing cycle.

"In September through the beginning of October there is still a chance of weather problems as well as disease. I mean malaria, typhoid fever, yellow fever, even cholera—but these diminish as the fall comes on. We get most of these diseases up north as well, but not as often. Remember there was cholera and yellow fever up north in Philadelphia in the 1700s. There is always typhoid everywhere. That's why I feel a few extra weeks down south should not be too dangerous."

"Still, Josh—I'd feel better if we could get away for the whole summer."

"I promise, next year we'll get away for the whole summer. I've just got to learn the ropes here."

"Josh! You are not here to learn the plantation business. You're here to teach the Negroes, and raise their awareness of the world outside!"

"That's all true, Emily, but we have to appear real to the other planters, and I have to be able to talk the lingo, otherwise no one will take me seriously and people may become suspicious."

"Okay, Josh, I understand. But we all know Mississippi is not the safest place to be in the summer."

CHAPTER 19

MUST BE THAT WILMS BOY

The telegraph office in Vicksburg, Mississippi, was a small but busy three-room office on Main Street. It was composed of a back room for supplies, telegraph batteries, and wiring; an operations room for the telegraph apparatus; and a third room for the operators. There was a customer space and window up front. All day long, passersby heard clicking at high speed from the sending keys and a different-sounding electric type tone from the electromagnets in the receiving apparatus. In addition, there were registers which recorded messages when an operator was unable to listen to the message. Vicksburg also had a message repeater, which transferred messages from the Nashville section on to New Orleans by way of Vicksburg.

John Wilms was a reporter for the Vicksburg Daily Citizen, and he liked to hang out in the telegraph office to pick up stories that came through the wires. His cousin had taught him some Morse code, and he was able to understand some of the messages, provided that they were not sent too fast.

On this day, Wilms stood outside the telegraph office listening to the sending and receiving in code. Today he was able to decipher the following messages: *MISSISSIPPI HIGH*

ABOVE VICKSBURG. STOP. JAMES HENRY HAMMOND TO ARRIVE. STOP. Unfortunately, he could not make out the rest as it was sent too fast.

John Wilms was a pleasant, nice-looking young man with an aquiline nose and dimpled chin. He was of medium height, with brown hair and an easygoing manner. He was well-dressed in a light suit and black cravat. He studied medicine but then turned to journalism after writing articles on medical practice. He could be charming with women, even though he was somewhat awkward on first meetings.

John grew up in Atlanta, Georgia, where his father owned a hotel with a restaurant. He worked in the hotel when he wasn't in school. In the four years he had lived and worked in Vicksburg, John learned a lot about what was considered newsworthy and what was not, particularly from the standpoint of plantation high society.

Despite his frequent amiable contact with them, he had never regarded himself as anything but a workingman. His family had never owned any slaves. As much as he lived in the heart of cotton country, he secretly was very much against slavery.

Today, he stood outside the telegraph office till the bustle died down inside. Planters were corresponding with cotton brokers, and there was a large number of people with personal messages as well.

He walked back and forth outside until there were only two people left in the office reading telegrams. Ezra Hoyt was the chief telegraph operator. He had a stooped appearance from hunching over his sending keys for hours on end in an almost fetal position. Ezra had a bad back which gave him pain and did not always help his disposition when dealing with the public.

Ezra had a very attractive blond daughter named Cathy who often helped him with messages. John always enjoyed talking and bantering with her. Cathy was a skilled operator herself and could sometimes take over her father's work completely if he was too busy or not feeling well.

A casual observer could quickly deduce that John had a secondary motive when he went into the telegraph office to "troll for news." The first person he saw was Cathy. Dressed in a long, rich-brown dress with ruffled sleeves, her blond hair hanging down in ringlets, she presented a pleasing picture to Mr. Wilms. He noticed that her attractive face blushed as she said hello, and she quickly scurried away to take a telegraph message off a telegraph register that had stopped sounding.

As Wilms watched her graceful form move away, the thoughts went through his mind: "I wonder if she saw me walking back and forth outside. Does she think I like her? Why was her face so red? Does she really like me?"

He walked over to her awkwardly with a blunt declaration. "I came to see your father."

"He's in the other room refilling the registers. We'all had a lot of traffic on the lines from Nashville today."

"That's just why I came to see him," John said. "It sure would be good for my newspaper to have something to write about. It's been pretty darn boring around town these days."

Cathy's face lit up in an impish smile. "Well, I got some news for y'all! Remember that Senator James Henry Hammond who made that speech about cotton being king? He is coming here to Vicksburg to make a speech next Saturday. It's been out on the repeaters all day. I expect thousands of folks will come to hear him speak. It could be real fun!"

The thought flew through John's head–she does like me! Cathy was looking right at him in a preoccupied way, adjusting her hair at the same time.

All of a sudden, his face lit up as he asked the big question. "Miss Cathy, can I take you out of this sweatshop and accompany you to the speech? I've got press credentials so I can get us right up front."

"I don't see why not."

A thrill of excitement passed through John's body as he felt the success of his efforts. Now he needed to make a transition out of the office to fix his success before his ecstasy got the better of him and he committed some sort of imagined faux pas, such as tripping on the floor or drooling in front of her.

John knew from experience to take Cathy's news tips seriously because she was very well-informed from listening to the telegraph all day. In the past, Cathy and her father had been in the habit of throwing him a "bone" from time to time, which his editors appreciated.

"Miss Cathy," John said, "I've got to get right back to the press to meet the deadline today for advance notice on the speech. Tell your father I'll come see him soon. This is big news!" He then awkwardly stumbled out of the telegraph office.

John had made this abrupt transition out of the office as much to ensure he made the deadline of his paper as to get away from a sudden flood of anxiety, having asked Miss Cathy out. He left feeling a bit lightheaded over his success and didn't want anything to spoil it.

Back in the telegraph office Ezra called Cathy, and when she did not come to him fast enough, he came up front to ask her to send a telegram for him. He noticed that Cathy had a great big smile on her face, and the thought quickly raced through his mind–must be that Wilms boy.

CHAPTER 20

TERRAPIN TROUBLE

Two weeks before the date of the big dinner arrived, Nate was busy ordering food for the banquet. Running back and forth to the telegraph office in Vicksburg was a bigger job than it appeared. Some of the food had to be ordered from up north. A large amount of ice had to be shipped south by railway car.

Nate ran into the biggest difficulty with the terrapins for one of the entrées of the banquet. He located a seafood supply house in Maryland which would sell him the turtles, but they couldn't guarantee railroad delivery on time. He then asked Emily to speak with Eliza about interceding with Joseph, whose brother had big connections in the senate with the railroads. Emily had arrived early in the morning at Eliza's front door, about two weeks before the banquet.

The discussion began with some small talk about the weather and the river being high. Then they got down to specifics.

"You know, our chef Nate has been working on our big meal all this week–arranging food orders," said Emily. "He will work on it next week as well. One of the things he makes best is roast Maryland terrapin. He tried to order some turtles, but the railroads can't guarantee delivery on time."

"Let me talk to Joseph," said Eliza. "You all know his brother was the Secretary of War, and is a senator. He knows all those railroad men. I'll bet he can help you get your turtles shipped! Just give me some information on whom you're purchasing them from, and the dates you need them, and we will see what Joseph can do. Is everything else going all right dear?"

"Everything else is going on schedule," "Emily replied.

"I'll come over tomorrow or the next day to let you know if Joseph can help us," Eliza said.

Good as her word, she was back two days later with good news. "When he went to Vicksburg yesterday, Joseph communicated by telegram with a railroad man who was one of Jefferson's biggest supporters. He gave Joseph the name of his right-hand man to whom Joseph promptly sent a telegram. He told Joseph to give him the name of the supplier and the number of terrapins that you want. He said he will take care of delivery to Vicksburg. After that, y'all have to arrange with the fast packet to bring them down here to Hurricane Island."

"Oh Eliza, that must have been powerfully difficult."

"You know, Joseph likes to do things for his friends and family anyway. I know this is going to be a memorable meal. Another thing–Joseph likes to do things like this just to see if they can be done. He loves the challenge!"

After Eliza left, Emily went into the kitchen to talk with Nate to see how things were going with the meal preparation.

"This is an awful lot of work, Emily," Nate said with a pained look on his face. "I really do feel like a slave!" He wiped his hands on either side of his long white chef's apron, which he wore over his double-breasted chef's coat. His voice had a wavering note as he spoke which gave off an air of anxiety.

"First, I had to set this kitchen up for quantity cooking, and now I've got to begin preparation as the ingredients are coming in. Two tons of ice are due to arrive from up north. This should keep the prepared food cold for our banquet. I can only hope everything arrives on time so we can pull this off."

Nate's normal calm demeanor looked different today. He

appeared sweaty and anxious as he moved away from the hot brick stove. He looked odd and out of character to everyone in the kitchen, especially because he was wearing a white chef's toque, which he never wore normally.

Although he used to cook on a grand scale for his former master, it was some years since he had done that. As a chef in a restaurant, he rarely had opportunities to organize banquets. In the past he had had his own kitchen all set up for him.

Here, he had to set everything up from scratch, and some of the normal implements that he regularly used were not available, so he had to improvise. His stress level began to rise as he proceeded with the task, which unfortunately made it difficult for everyone around him.

After Emily finished talking with Nate for several minutes, she too had absorbed some of his worry–and after informing her husband of the situation, he also began to feel the pressure.

"Emily, this is a huge undertaking," Josh said with a concerned expression on his face, "suppose that the ice doesn't arrive on time. How can we keep the food from spoiling? All Nate's work may be for naught."

"Well look," she said, trying to take a more practical tack. "If some of the ingredients don't arrive on time, we can probably make substitutions. Nate has drawn up a list. But if the ice doesn't arrive early enough, we may have a disaster."

Stress over the upcoming dinner began to spread to all six of them. They saw this meal as portending a collapse of all their plans. Jackson tried to calm Nate down with a good analogy. "You know Nate, if the captain of a ship gets frightened and shows it, the whole crew will usually panic!"

Nate appeared to listen for a while and seemed to calm down, but as the afternoon wore on and he mulled over all the potential logistical pitfalls, he began to fret once again. The stakes were high, and this was not going to be an easy job, given the tools he had to work with.

CHAPTER 21

IS THE SOUTH ANOTHER COUNTRY?

On the day of James Henry Hammond's big speech, John Wilms went to pick up Cathy at her house, which was a few blocks away from the telegraph office. For this outing he had arranged to take the newspaper trap that the office used for courier work and fast transportation. It had been purchased from the Vicksburg Taxi Company several years before. Because the rear of the cab was full of old newspapers and boxes of used type, he spent a good part of the morning cleaning it up and polishing it.

He hitched up Nostradamus, the old newspaper horse, who had been one fast pacer in his time. He had a fast trot, which was almost as fast as many horses could go at a full gallop. Nostradamus was slower these days, but he could still show flashes of his former brilliance, especially if another horse tried to pass him too quickly. Even when restrained by the reins, he would leave the other horse in the dust.

John loved to take him because he enjoyed speed, and Nostradamus was one exciting horse that John was very skilled at controlling. He put his press signs on both sides of the cab and went off to pick up Cathy.

She was waiting for him wearing a beautiful dark blue dress which enhanced her curvy figure. When John saw how pretty Cathy looked, he felt a little wobbly on his feet until they got into a conversation. Then his anxiety slid away.

As they drove the two miles to the plantation where Mr. Hammond was going to make his speech, they spoke about some of the past week's events.

"Boy, have we been busy in the telegraph office this past week! There's been a huge amount of message traffic regarding Mr. Hammond's upcoming speech. Then, one of the planters with a lot of pull has been sending telegrams to the president of one of the railroads to arrange delivery of some turtles. I'm not sure what it is for, but it must be real important, for they held up a train full of people to send them through instead. This could be a good item for a newspaper, couldn't it?" Cathy ventured to ask.

John answered, "Maybe for up north, but I think I know who the planter is, and I'm not going to write it."

"Well, why not?" Cathy asked.

"I don't bite the hand that feeds me, and he's an awful nice man." Joseph Davis treats his slaves almost better than he treats himself, even though they are still slaves. His brother, Jefferson, is a senator and was Secretary of War. No ma'am, I don't want no trouble, no how! Not me."

"Well, don't say I didn't give y'all a good story, even if you won't write it."

"I really do appreciate your stories and tips, even though I don't always publish them. Y'all please keep giving them to me, as they are very important to me."

"Well, all right–I will."

The vehicle traffic heading to the speech site at the plantation was fierce and slow-moving. John was feeling almost claustrophobic, trapped in the line of carriages, and he had an urge to show off his horsemanship to Cathy. He felt a little speed and excitement would add some spice to their relationship. He knew a shortcut trail that no one appeared to be taking, except for one other buggy that was hightailing it for the shortcut.

As he came abreast of the other buggy, he shook the reins and called out *giddyap* to Nostradamus, but he did not really have to say anything. Nostradamus read his mind and showed why he was called Nostradamus. He took off at his famous trot and began to pull away from the other carriage.

Cathy enjoyed the thrill of the trot and had a big smile on her face. At just about that point, the other vehicle, not to be outdone, went into a full gallop—and when that was not fast enough, a dead run, which was about forty miles per hour. Nostradamus then broke stride, matched the other buggy's speed, passed the other buggy, and got to the shortcut first.

Cathy's smile had vanished, replaced by a look of fear. "Y'all please slow down." John rapidly complied, and now that he was out in front of the other vehicle, he lapsed back to a comfortable trot.

Cathy's mood had taken a turn for the worse, and she did not hesitate to speak her mind. "John, honestly, why do you want to frighten a poor little girl like me? What is this for?"

"I beg your pardon Cathy." John looked at Cathy and saw that she was not too impressed with his apology. Her mouth was still frozen in a pout. Crestfallen, he began to own up to his behavior. "Aw, Cathy, I was just trying to impress you with my control of Nostradamus. I just wanted this to be a memorable experience for you because I like you."

"And I like you too, John, but please talk to me before you do something like this again. The trot is fine with me—but not the gallop!"

"Okay, Cathy. I promise not to do anything like this again without telling you first."

John and Cathy were the first to arrive at the plantation speech area thanks to the speedy Nostradamus. They picked out a nice seat just below the podium where a slave had placed a pitcher of water. They were ideally situated to hear every word in the speech. The rest of the crowd began to arrive quickly. Very soon all the seats were taken, and the latecomers moved onto the large lawn area where some of them spread out blankets.

Mr. Hammond was comfortably ensconced in the middle of a group of planters who were busy shaking hands and slapping each other on the back. John noted that neither the Davis's nor any of their neighbors or friends were in attendance. He had heard slanderous stories in the past about Mr. Hammond's bad treatment of his slaves. These had included stories of sexual liaisons with slaves, both mothers and daughters, as well as his own nieces. These stories had come from other slaves as well as workers who worked at Mr. Hammond's plantation. He now wondered if some of these stories were true.

After about ten minutes of handshaking and back slapping, the tall, famous orator got up on the podium to begin his speech. His powerful, resonant voice echoed off the barn and manor house.

"It is great honor to be here in the great valley of the Mississippi, now the real and soon to be acknowledged seat of the empire of the world."

He then went on to compare the gross domestic product of the South with that of the North. He spoke about how the cotton crop had helped the North in the recent financial panic, how powerful cotton therefore was as a crop, and how necessary it was to the whole world. There was a vague reference to England's need for cotton being so great that she might back the South in any conflict with the North over slavery.

He then turned to the condition of the Negro slaves and gave his justification for the institution of slavery, comparing the treatment of the slaves with the treatment of the industrial workers up north. James Henry Hammond raised his voice further and hammered home his next point with sweeping gestures of his arms.

"The difference between us is that our slaves are hired for life, and well-compensated. There is no starvation, no begging nor want of employment among our people. The northern workers are hired by the day, not cared for, and scantily compensated. Why, you would meet more beggars in one day in New York than you would meet in a lifetime down south." He finished the speech by praising the glorious contribution of the South to human history.

Mr. Hammond, in drawing such stark contrasts between the North and the South, gave the impression that secession of the South was a possibility—at least in his mind. The audience went wild with applause. Some voices in the audience yelled for more, wanting Hammond to continue speaking. He politely declined, offering instead to answer a few questions from the audience.

John Wilms of the Daily Citizen asked one of the first questions. It was a very thought-provoking question.

"Suppose we'all had trouble with the northern states, as some folks are already talking about seceding from them. Suppose we'all did secede from them, and they blockaded all our southern ports. And we couldn't get our cotton out, or anything else in. The United States government currently controls most of the Navy. What would we do?"

Hammond answered, "Young man, that's why I'm speakin' today, to tell folks not to worry. Other countries won't stand by and watch cotton being shut down. They will help us. We have powerful friends in London who have assured us that if the North ever tried that, the British navy would intervene. Remember, Britain's textile and clothing industry is critical to their economy! The mills in the North compete with them. They would be very happy to take all our cotton, and cut the mills in the North off without any.

"Their mills and factories are critical to their industrial revolution," Hammond went on. They don't want most of their workers thrown out of work. No, Britain will not stand idly by. Not only would they break a blockade, but they might help us build a navy. Y'all got to remember, we got a lot of money right now. We can buy a lot of things we don't have, and we don't have a panic or depression like up north!

"Remember, our slave system is the heart of our cotton growing and picking enterprise. You take away our slaves, and we've got nothing. Remember Dr. Newton's famous law–*bodies in motion tend to stay in motion*. Well, we sure got the motion; we got the cotton crop–that's what is moving for us. The North has nothing quite like it. They are still bogged down in hard economic times. Let them try to mess with us!"

Another reporter, who had come all the way from New Orleans for the occasion, also asked an insightful question. "When I was up north many of the northern factory owners and industrialists were scared, now that the south is expanding slave states. They are afraid that the South is going to compete with their system of free labor and destroy it by bringing in slave labor to work in factories and mills in new slave states."

"Young man," Hammond answered, "they should be scared. You can't take workers, have them work from dawn to dusk, and pay them scanty salaries–where they can't even make enough to take care of their families. Then you cheat them out of the few dollars they make in company stores. They know that by our taking care of our workers from cradle to grave, they can't compete with us. Their treatment of workers under what they call free labor is much worse than the way we treat our workers in our slave system. Let them try to compete with us, and we will bury them in a sea of cotton!"

A new round of applause broke out, and the meeting broke up with scores of well-wishers mobbing the podium to shake his hand.

As John and Cathy walked back from the speech to their buggy, a headline kept popping into John's head. Try as he might, he could not keep it from coming back. When they got into the buggy, he said to Cathy, "What do think of this front-page headline: TWO THOUSAND MORONS CHEER SPEECH BY JAMES HENRY HAMMOND!"

Remembering their earlier discussion, Cathy came back with, "That's a great headline for up north. But honestly, not only would you lose your job and your livelihood forever down here–you might also lose your life and get the newspaper burned down as well!"

"I was just joking, Miss Cathy."

"Well don't ever joke about that again, except if you all want a heap of trouble!"

Then John added, "I can't get the words *cradle to grave* out of my head. Is that the way anyone would want to be taken care of–from cradle to grave? Did you hear all that bull? He says the slaves are treated better than northern workers. Those slaves are not free to leave the plantations. Some plantations are hellholes and slave-labor camps. Many slaves are beaten and whipped. That doesn't happen in employment up north. Worst-case scenario is you lose your job and may have to move somewhere else.

"Hammond never dealt with the industries that are connected to the South–like textiles, agriculture, and tobacco. Most of the management and workers in these factories and mills are proslavery and pro-South. It appears that he doesn't care a hoot about them. He is ready to throw the baby out with the bathwater."

"Is he right about difficult conditions for the northern worker?" asked Cathy.

"He is right there." John replied. "Since the panic and depression, things have gotten much worse for the northern workers. Still, it's a far cry from slavery. The main thing is that this man is ready to go to war with the North! You can really feel it, can't you, Miss Cathy? This man is a United States senator and he doesn't care about the United States of America. There are, after all, bigger things than just the South!

"James Henry Hammond is perfectly willing to turn the defense of our ports over to the British navy. Even Andy Jackson would turn over in his grave. What did we fight the War of 1812 for? This just illustrates how bad things are getting. These guys aren't thinking about the United States anymore. It's almost as though the South is another country."

CHAPTER 22

FAST PACKET AND THE FEAST

It was a beautiful late-fall day with pleasant river smells wafting through the air. The day of the big meal had arrived. It had been a difficult week at the Lawrence household. Everyone was scrambling to make sure that the big feast would be a success.

The first sign of apparent trouble began earlier in the week with the two-thousand-pound ice shipment. It was supposed to arrive on Tuesday to cover all the fresh ingredients that had been coming over the last few days. Jackson brought the rig down to the landing dock to meet the riverboat which was supposed to bring the ice, but there was no ice.

The fast packet was tied up at the dock, and Jackson started to make inquiries. "Da master done sent me to picks up a rail big heap of ice, anyone done seen it?"

No one had heard of an ice shipment—neither the captain, the pilot, nor any of the crew. Jackson was visibly upset over what appeared to be a major disaster and was getting ready to go home to discuss how to proceed from there with Josh and Emily. As he was walking back to the rig, feeling downcast, he ran into another tall, strong-looking Negro slave wearing blue overalls.

The slave said to Jackson, "Shoa is a nahce day."

Jackson quickly changed from the disgusted, down look that had taken over his face and put on his best slave talk. "Foa some folks it is, not foa me, doe. Da masr sent me to pick up some ahce from the riverboat, but nottin done arrive, and nobody know nottin about it! Dis is rale bad, we is goin' to cook a meal, an we needs it!"

The other slave cocked his head to the side, deep in thought. "Wayl, you know we'all had to unload a big heap of ahce yestaday, but no one come to take it. It's behind dose cotton bales. You reckon that could be youren?"

As Jackson went to look, he had to cross a small river of water flowing from the ice. He took off the blanket covering the ice, and saw that three quarters of it was still remaining. "'Spect that's enough foa us," he said out loud. "Can y'all help me load dis in da wagon?"

The dockworker nodded yep and called to another dockman, "Rasamus, y'all help us!"

When Jackson got the loaded wagon back to the kitchen entrance, he found everybody was in the kitchen, busy preparing food under Nate's direction. He went off and transferred the ice in a piecemeal fashion into the underground root cellar.

The day before the reception, everyone was pressed into service by Nate, who proved to be a tough taskmaster. Distressed because he had neither the kind of kitchen he was used to working in, nor all the ingredients and tools required for the preparation, he often had to improvise. If he didn't like the way something was prepared or the way it looked, he threw it out or gave the preparer a stern lecture. Tempers began to flare. There was a terrible din in the kitchen.

"You call that a salad? It's too wet! Never, never leave water on a salad. It's gauche; it's got to be perfectly dry. That's the mark of a fine kitchen."

As the other three people in the team brought over spoonsful of gravy and sauces, Nate began to taste everything and snap orders like a general based on what he was finding.

"Let me adjust the seasoning. Don't add anything. This is the most important part of the cooking. You can make several good dishes as part of a meal, but if these dishes aren't compatible, the overall effect is diminished or ruined. That's why seasoning is so important."

Nate appeared to be almost in a manic-like state. His speech was somewhat tight and pressured, not like his usual calm demeanor—and he kept giving everyone a lecture when he wasn't muttering under his breath, "Look what I have to work with. I have to turn out a fine gourmet meal, but I'm working with botchers who don't understand how a kitchen works."

The more Nate snapped orders, the louder the kitchen staff got. Pots began to bang, glasses rattled, dishes crashed, and knives came down harder from the chopping.

Then Nate turned his attention to the Terrapin Baltimore, now that the terrapins had arrived without incident. "Keep working on that chicken stock from the cooking chickens. Now watch how I cut the terrapin meat and watch how I cut the guts. Separate the liver this way. You guys think you can copy me? I'm watching! Bring that sherry wine over here. Now this has to cook real slowly, otherwise it'll be ruined!"

Nate then noticed Jackson, who walked into the middle of the turmoil. "You got the ice? Good! We are almost out of ice." He didn't give Jackson a chance to explain about his difficulty at the dock.

"Here is the menu for the dinner." Nate showed it to Jackson. It read as follows:

Glass Dishes of Fresh Beluga Caviar
Clear Green Turtle Soup with Amontillado Sherry
Terrapin Maryland
Dressed Roast English Pheasant with Full Plumage of Red, Black, and Orange Feathers

Wild Rice
Heart of Palm Salad
Bombe Nesselrode
Demitasse
Napoleon Brandy

"The pheasant is in the oven," Nate continued. "The terrapin should be ready when the guests arrive. The caviar is on the little ice we had here. I made the soup yesterday. It has been sitting on ice all day, which is real good for the ingredients to mix and work in."

The women are working on the heart of palm salad. "*I hope it's not watery!*" Nate yelled out sarcastically. Wilma slammed down a pot filled with lettuce with a big bang. Both Wilma and Joan frowned and began to chop the salad harder and louder with their knives.

"The wild rice is ready," Nate announced, "we'll just keep it warm in the pot."

For Jackson, Nate's aggressive behavior was an opportunity for him to show his sympathy for Joan, and most particularly for Wilma. Out of Nate's earshot, he mumbled to them, "I wouldn't get too upset over Nate's aggressive comments. He's under a lot of pressure to deliver a near-perfect meal. He doesn't have the kitchen he used to have or the same ingredients available to him."

Wilma shook her head. "He's been yelling at us all morning. We've taken enough nonsense from him, and we are both getting very angry! We've never seen him behave like this before."

Joan agreed. "The only way to describe him is *slave driver*. He'd better cool down."

Jackson answered with a shrug of resignation, "I don't think that is going to happen until the meal is delivered, which should be in a few minutes, and then we'll have the Nate we know back."

At that moment Nate yelled out. "Finish setting the table if you please. The guests should be here soon!"

CHAPTER 23

BANQUET OF CULINARY RAPPORT

About half an hour later the first guests began to arrive. Dressed in his dark swallow-tailed coat with cravat, Jackson played the role of butler. In his best servile role, he showed the guests into the gathering room.

There, he and Joan, who was dressed in a long skirt and apron, served drinks and hors d'oeuvres to the guests.

For the most part, these guests were friends of Joseph and Eliza. Politically, they had for the most part a similar view of the country and slavery, even though they were slaveholders. Many had either been given land by Joseph or had been helped by him to purchase their land with the stipulation that they treat their slaves humanely.

More carriages began to arrive, and fifteen couples filed into the gathering room. Joseph's niece Dee Ann arrived with her friend Marie and two male escorts. Everyone was well-dressed for a banquet. Dee Ann and her friend Marie were stunning in their low-cut dresses.

Jackson and Joan scurried around to make sure all the couples were well-satiated with drinks and generous portions of caviar. Joan's serving attire appeared to enhance her shapely figure, and she received lots of glances from men when their wives weren't looking. All the guests had a nice warm glow from the copious flow of alcohol.

There was much discussion of James Henry Hammond's speech, even though most of them did not attend it; rather, they had read about it in the *Daily Citizen*.

"Speeches lahk thayt miahht lead to wahr," said Sam Vreeland, one of the closest neighbors to Josh and Emily.

Will Smith answered back, "Guys like Hammond mahht help us all out, because the North can't meys with us so easily if they are looking over their shoulder waitin' for England to intervene. This maht buy us the tahme to figure out how to solve the problems with slavery."

Then Joe Foster added his input. "But you know ain't nobody's going to do anything 'bout slavery. There's no consensus or political weel to change it. Folks think if it's not broke, don't fix it. All we will get out of this is a wahr–and a big one!"

Sam came back with, "Y'all know one aspect of Hammond's thinkin' is correct. Our sale of cotton and other slave agriculture has helped America develop to where it is today. Many of the workers in textiles and tobacco up north owe their livelihood to us. Much of our relations with Britain and the rest of the world came from the development of our slave agricultural system.

"Without us, the North could not have developed the way it has, and as fast as it has. Y'all have to read *De Bow's Review* to understand this stuff. They're a hurtin' rail bad up north now. A bank in Ohio started it when it went broke a few years ago. Everything is gitten bad up north now.

"They're a startin' to look around for someone to blame. Since we don't use their free labor system here, they're afraid we're agonna take over everything with our slaves–including their business. Y'all know it's got to be us that catches the blame. Now that we'all have outlived our usefulness to them, they want to destroy us out of fear of our slave-labor system. That Dred Scott decision by the Supreme Court is makin' them even more scared of us. Now they think we are agonna to take over all their factories and wipe them out. They think we're the cause of all their troubles. When times get hard, they look for someone to blame!"

"That's it," said Joe Foster. "Them folks up north are scared of us because it looks like we're wiping out their economic system. For that reason, they're starting to persecute us. It doesn't matter how successful we are. The more successful we get, the more frightened they get of our slave-labor system."

Sam Vreeland jumped up, his brain stoked up to full capacity by his resolve and a generous supply of alcohol. "Of course, it's true!" Vreeland added as though pontificating on this subject. "They don't care a hoot for what we did for this country in the past.

"Even if we wanted to get rid of slavery, how could we do it? Are they going to pay our expenses while we all dismantle our agricultural industry? How would we then earn a living without our major source of income?

"Don't forget, people in New England are rail cheap! Can you see a town meeting in Vermont voting to reimburse us for our agricultural losses? New England's full of skinflint, tightfisted farmers—and miserable dirty mill workers and greasy mechanics. They work from sunup to sundown, and they mostly don't accumulate any money by the time they hit old age, and no one takes care of them when they get old or sick. They have a miserable life. It is far worse than that of our slaves. Will they all want to pay millions of dollars to reimburse the South for her losses? *No, suh!* And besides, they got no money anymore up north!"

Sam continued, all fired up. The redness in his face had now spread to his neck as well. He was sipping his drink when he let loose with, "When folks up north get into trouble they put up tariffs! Remember the Tariff of Abominations? That took place in hard times just like today. Our parents sure had a hard time with it.

"Many people up north, with the exception of businesses related to textiles and crops," he went on, "think we'all are getting away with murder down here. They don't understand our system, and they blame all the ills of the country on us. I don't know how we'all are going to work things out with them!"

Vreeland was so worked up that no one dared enter the conversation for fear of giving him a stroke. The conversation then gradually modulated to more gentle topics, such as agriculture and horses, when Nate rang the bell for dinner. Everyone retired to the tables for the meal.

There were three big tables set up in banquet style for all the guests. Jackson, Wilma, and Joan, well-dressed in their serving uniforms, bowed and scraped as they waited on each diner with attention and delicacy. The guests ate everything that Nate made with real pleasure, copiously complimenting the quality of the cooking.

"This is the best meal I ever ate in America."

"Why, the last time I ate like this was in Paris!" Sam Vreeland roared out, not to be outdone. The dinner conversation was more revealing as the planters made an effort to get to know and understand their northern hosts.

Normally, many of these planters used more indirect communication to ferret out information. These were northern visitors, however, and this was a chance to discover more about the North. Although they expected some level of questioning, Josh and Emily were in for a surprise. The questioning took the tone of a genteel and elegant inquisition.

Sam Vreeland finished off the questioning with, "Many folks from up north want nothing to do with us. Whah deed y'all come down south in the middle of a mess like this? Y'all know things may never be the same as they was before. There'all has been a change in the quality of our relations with the North."

The color came into Josh's face, and his jaw began to twitch. His heart began to pound as he prepared his answer. He opened his mouth, and it took a few seconds for his brain to catch up to his mouth. At first, he was worried nothing was going to come out, then the words started to flow.

"You all should know that I spent some time down south when I was young and in training for the Mexican War. I immediately noticed the relationship with folks was different then up north. There appeared to be a code of honor between people, almost like the old code of chivalry. I liked that very much.

"Up north everyone is out for himself. It's a dog-eat-dog world. Everyone is so busy making ends meet that there isn't time for relationships between people. I don't like that at all. The workers fight with each other to get someone to watch their kids. The kids get the short end of the stick. They don't get to know their parents well. At night there is terrible crime in the streets. It's not safe to go out without weapons. None of these types of behavior are evident down here."

Josh conveniently omitted any reference to the treatment of the black slave population who were people, as well, even though he knew that if he made mention of that, his whole argument to this group of people would appear patently false. He knew this argument was believable to people down south.

"I always liked farming," he continued, "and I wanted to find a good life to raise kids with good values. People down south seem happier than folks up north."

Emily echoed his previous phrase. "We came down here to start our life under different circumstances then up north. It may be a bit difficult adjusting, but we're committed to doing it."

Their presentation to the group appeared to move some of the planters and helped establish a rapport with them.

Eliza was looking across the room when she noticed Dee Ann standing in front of a mirror in the parlor arranging her dress and fixing her hair. Dee Ann, hungry for attention, then took a deep breath and walked into the gathering room where Josh was shaking hands and talking to the guests. She got behind some of the guests and patiently set up her ambush, calmly waiting for her turn to talk to Josh.

Gazing wide-eyed at him she began, "Why, Mr. Josh, that sure was an interesting speech y'all made. I wonder if your chef could teach us all how to cook. He sure enough did a great job on this meal."

Dee Ann seemed to exude a sexual chemistry which hit Josh like a cannonball. "I think we can arrange something along those lines," he added, very much thrown off balance by her forwardness. He was almost relieved and disappointed at the same time when two male neighbors broke into the discussion, also showing interest in conversing with Dee Ann.

Josh used the opportunity wisely to move on to some of the other guests, even though he missed staring at the beautiful apparition that had been in front of him.

The quality of the meal was having its intended effect. "I have never had a meal of this quality ever before," mentioned one of the guests. And, "This is the very best," Joseph Davis said, "—even in Washington, New York, or New Orleans—we never ate this well!" Every plate was picked clean.

When Eliza commented positively on the quality of the cooking, Emily said within earshot of everyone, "You know, I'm sure our cook Nate would be glad to teach your cooks how to make meals like this. If you're interested, just let me know, and we'll see what we can do."

Sam Vreeland's wife, Lorraine, piped up, "Boy, would I like that," as did several other women.

It was decided to have everyone who was interested come back to arrange expert group cooking lessons for all the cooks whose masters wished them to learn.

The meal was finished with the Bombe Nesselrode and

brandy. Josh then called the guests back into the parlor where he had arranged for Jackson to sing several Stephen Foster songs as well as the Negro spirituals, "Deep River" and "Swing Low Sweet Chariot." Joan accompanied him on the piano. His powerful resonant voice accomplished the desired emotional effect on their audience. Emily noticed tears in some of the guests' eyes.

CHAPTER 24

THE WORLD IS TOO MUCH WITH US

Not completely content with her first effort, Dee Ann made a second pass at Josh as he was shaking hands with some of the departing guests. "Thank you, Mister Josh, for a great evening. I sure am looking forward to your introducing me to your chef!"

"We'll be in touch when we work out a time," said Josh. "Goodnight." Uneasy with Emily around, he gave her his most noncommittal smile and moved on to the next guest.

Jackson walked toward the kitchen carrying a lush magnolia flower that he had picked in the garden. Wilma and Joan were cleaning the dishes, pots, and pans. As they worked, they were talking away in disconnected snatches of conversation like birds chirping in a tree.

"Boy, was that meal ever a success. Did you see the way that food was lapped up? Did you see the way Dee Ann was dressed? She is really on the prowl for men. I guess everything was worth all the torture we had to endure with Nate."

"Speaking of Nate," said Wilma, stopping to look across at Joan, "I think he likes you. I saw the way he was looking at you."

"Now that you mention it—that's funny, I saw him looking

at you too," said Joan. "I can't have a relationship with a man with a mean streak in him. Did you hear the way he treated us all? Isn't he one angry man?"

"I'm not sure about that," said Wilma. "I think he just got himself in deep water, over his head. I know him. He was cooking a gourmet meal without being in his usual kitchen. Not all the ingredients arrived on time for us. We're not professional cooks, you know. I think he saw this whole thing as a potential disaster that would all be blamed on him. It would all be his fault. My father always told me, Joan, that anger equals fear and that angry people are frightened people. I know I never saw him get angry like that before, did you?"

"Well, no." Joan shrugged. "But he sure frightened me with his behavior." All this discussion warmed Joan up to Wilma, and she started talking to her more personally.

"Did I ever tell you that I had a boyfriend who was mean and abusive? He was really something. He used to tell me to do everything. If I didn't do what he told me to do, he'd ignore me."

"That must have been real tough for you." Wilma looked at her sympathetically.

"Worse than that, he used to hit me—and I took it from him, but I kept getting madder and madder. If anger equals fear, I can tell you—I was real frightened."

"Good heavens," said Wilma, "what did you do?"

"Well, one time he punched me, and I just snapped. I swung and knocked him out." Her body mimed the violence of the blow as she spoke. "That's when we broke up. Oh Wilma, why can't Nate behave more like Jackson? Then I wouldn't have to think these terrible thoughts about my old boyfriend."

Wilma smiled sympathetically, her powerful but shapely frame almost towering over the more diminutive Joan. "But Nate is not Jackson, and Nate is not the same person as your boyfriend, Joan. Whatever meanness he showed at the meal did not come from abuse, it came from fear of messing us all up. By the way, speaking of looks, I saw Jackson looking at you as well."

This did not cheer Joan up. "Jackson doesn't want me," said Joan. "Can't you tell he wants you? I'm so sure of it. He always looks like he is trying to be near you and please you. Oh yeah, he will look at me if I'm wearing a dress, but I don't think he's really interested in me. You watch his behavior, Wilma. I think you will see what I mean."

It was almost as if Jackson had been eavesdropping on the conversation when he made his move. Joan had gone back to the dining room to get more dishes, and Jackson saw his chance to pounce. He had well-integrated Nate's talk on being romantic. Jackson quickly walked over to Wilma with a big smile and said, "This is for you." He handed her the flower and held his breath, praying that Nate's advice would hold good.

Wilma, though visibly weary and emotionally drained from the stress and strain of the day's trials, instantly broke out in a most radiant smile, showing her pure white teeth. "You are so sweet giving me this flower after the long day I've had."

A thrill went through Jackson's body when he saw the effect of his gesture. "Gee," he thought, "Nate's method actually worked."

When the meal broke up that evening, Josh and Emily both felt they had accomplished their objective of establishing a good rapport with their neighbors.

That night Josh was flush with success from the first stage of his plan down south. He should have slept well, but he did not. Maybe he was overtired and overwrought from the events of the last week leading up to the dinner.

He had trouble forcing the image of Dee Ann in her sexy dress and flirtatious manner out of his mind. He thought about the cotton crop, the dinner, and the guests—but it always ended with the image of Dee Ann. All night he tossed and turned, and awoke four different times.

Toward morning he had a dream that a dangerous snake was crawling in the grass near a river. He saw a dog nearby begin to follow the snake. When the snake turned, the dog ran over and grabbed it just below the head, and clamped onto it like a vice. The dream then shifted to a different scene. The dog, holding the snake, got inside a small, high water tower for trains that was somehow extremely high. With a violent spasm the snake shook the dog, still clamped onto it, out of the tower and onto the ground one hundred feet below–killing them both.

Josh, thinking about the dream when he woke up, tried to interpret it. He got the feeling that the dog was a hero in killing the snake but had sacrificed his own life to do it. Somehow, he saw himself as the dog in his "attack" on slavery. This dream was so real that, when he woke up, he couldn't get the image out of his head.

After breakfast he asked Emily to take a walk with him, and they went down to the banks of the Mississippi to sort out his thoughts. The mist was rising off the river, but the east bank was still partially obscured by a light mist. They heard the whistle of a fast packet heading for New Orleans and saw the riverboat silhouetted against the white mist. It must have been making fifteen knots or so running with the current.

Two feelings were overwhelming Josh as he and Emily watched the packet head downriver.

He had been focusing all his attention on the big meal and making a connection with the other planters. When they started questioning him, he realized that many of the things he spoke of about dealing with quality of life down south were true. Except they did not extend to the black slaves. He didn't like the endless work up north which interfered with the overall quality of life. He didn't like the crime up north either.

As they strolled along the riverbank hand in hand, Josh said, "Emily, in New England everything is focused around money and hard work, the ethics of the Puritans—you remember—in Wordsworth's poem, "The World Is Too Much with Us."

They paused at a large rock and Josh motioned to Emily to sit down and enjoy the river view.

"You know, when I was telling everybody at dinner why we were here, I really began to believe what I was saying. It made sense. In some ways the quality of life is better down south. In some ways even the slaves here on these particular plantations are treated more like human beings than the workers up north. It's true they're not free to come and go as they please—but if you compare the two groups—the slaves here do get medical care, they are treated like family, they get acceptable housing, and they even enjoy a social life.

"We came down here to destroy slavery, and I am committed to doing that, but these thoughts still disturb me. This area is not the same as other parts of the South. I have to keep telling myself that. Things are not quite as simple as I imagined they would be."

"Oh Josh," Emily said, tugging on his arm, "we must always remember that this place is not the whole South. How do you think James Henry Hammond treats his slaves—at least judging by his reputation? Joseph Davis and his family, followers, and friends are the best of the South. Just because we see better things happening here does not mean they are happening everywhere. We know it's impossible to humanize slavery. You can only go so far with that line of reasoning."

With nervous energy, Josh got up and paced back and forth in front of Emily as she stared up at him.

"That brings up another issue. When I was up north, I hated all slaveholders. I wanted to destroy them and destroy slavery, which I still do. But now that I know some of these people better, I found myself liking many of them and their wives at the dinner. I kind of made friends with them, and now I feel a bit peculiar, but of course not peculiar enough to change my feelings over slavery in any way. We know that if any of these slaves revolted and did not want to work, they'd face severe sanctions, including corporal punishment or even being sold to a less desirable master."

Josh brought up many of the issues that had bothered him that night, but he did not bring up Dee Ann in particular. He thought it might create needless suspicion in Emily's mind. His thinking was, "Dee Ann wasn't really doing anything too obvious, and maybe that was the way she deals with all men. I don't want any sort of misunderstandings on this level to interfere with our larger plan—and this could ruin things. We can't forget that she's Joe Davis's niece. What's more, Emily has gotten jealous before, and at times she has a bad temper."

While Josh was talking with Emily that morning, Jackson was helping Nate prepare lunch in the kitchen. After an hour's work in the hot kitchen, Jackson decided to take a walk out by the woodpile to get a breath of fresh air. There he found Wilma splitting wood at the back of the house, which was the job that he did most of the time.

She was wearing a sleeveless shirt to keep cool in the humid heat. Keeping his distance, he watched her out of the corner of his eye. She had beautiful form chopping wood. Her muscle definition in her arms and shoulders was alluring to watch. She cleaved the wood easily with one stroke and did it in a graceful motion. Her heroic proportions very much attracted him, and he felt desire for her rising inside of him. An inner voice told him it was a perfect opportunity to talk with her, and he eased his approach by complimenting her on how well she was splitting the wood.

"You're doing a beautiful job of splitting the wood. I wish I could split it that neatly," said Jackson.

"Thank you. I've been splitting wood since I was a girl. I love the exercise."

"Maybe I can get another ax, and we can work together."

"I'd surely like that," said Wilma.

Jackson went to get another ax, and they worked together side by side for about an hour and finished off the woodpile. Then Jackson suggested that they take a walk down by the river to cool off.

"I would love to go for a walk with you," said Wilma, brightening up considerably at Jackson's offer.

In the time it took to reach the bank of the great river, Jackson was pleased to notice that, little by little, it was feeling more and more natural to be with her and that he was no longer really nervous in her presence. Almost surprising himself, he took the lead in the conversation.

"Wilma, how do you really feel about this enterprise—the slave scheme that we are engaged in?"

Wilma remained silent for a moment, brushed her hair out of her face, and looked Jackson in the eye.

"It certainly gives my life some meaning," she replied.

Jackson pressed forward. "Might I ask what are your other goals in life are?"

Wilma looked down at the ground, and then up at Jackson. "Well, first, I certainly want to abolish slavery."

"And then?"

She paused a moment and stared quizzically at him. "I think I would also want to get married and raise a family, but it would have to be with the right person. I don't want to get married just to say I'm married, and I don't want to have kids with the wrong person because then I might not have control over how they are raised."

"Could you ever imagine that I could be the right person?" Jackson stopped, and asked awkwardly but boldly, with his heart pounding.

Wilma paused and looked out to the river for a moment. Then her gaze came to rest squarely on Jackson's eyes, and she said, "Maybe, but I still don't know you half well enough."

"Well, perhaps we can do something about that?"

She nodded in agreement with a little shrug of her shoulders.

Jackson, emboldened by Wilma's response, immediately put his arms around her and gave her a passionate kiss, which she fully reciprocated.

CHAPTER 25

UNDER THE COPSE OF TREES

About a month after James Henry Hammond's speech, John Wilms was visiting Miss Cathy at the telegraph office. He had been coming to visit her almost every day since Hammond's famous speech. Her father, Ezra, did not object as he had gotten used to John's manner. He had always liked the young man and did his best to pass newsworthy information his way.

Cathy and John would often go out and have lunch together and would discuss national events, as they had a similar view of the world. Local gossip and goings-on about town were all fair game for discussion. They had gotten closer to each other and had very good communication between them. John was very careful not to surprise Cathy without giving her warning of what he intended to do, as he had done the day of Hammond's speech, when he frightened her by racing with another buggy.

Today John and Cathy, in her long gingham dress, went out for a walk to the copse of trees behind the telegraph office. They stood under an oak tree in the breeze and began by discussing the past election.

"I was for Jeff Davis," John said. "I read the speech he gave in Boston, and he appears to be against secession. With what I know about him and his family, he seems like a moderate. We need more moderates like Jeff Davis to avoid a war."

Cathy flipped her hair off her face in the breeze and quickly cut him off. "John, we can talk about Senator Davis as much as you like, but with politicians you never know where they really stand till the chips are down and they have to make a decision. What has been coming in over the wires seems highly significant right now. I'm talking about the Border Ruffians coming here from Kansas. It looks like a war had already begun there. If things had gotten that far out of control, what about the rest of the country?" She stared at him intently waiting for a reply.

"You are sure right, Cathy. Why, when I went to Missouri last month I met with another reporter named John McReynolds, and he told me how bad things had gotten over there. To this day people are still killing each other and families are continuing to get murdered–all over the Kansas Nebraska Act and its expansion of slavery in that territory.

"While most of the killing is over with, there are still some bad feelings between the pro and antislavery groups. Things will never be good in those communities because people are still holding a grudge. I hope this doesn't happen here! That Dred Scott Decision is still riling folks up on both sides of the Mason-Dixon line. The planters like the decision, but it is sure angering many folks up north who are now seeing the South as wanting to extend slavery into their states. Things are getting out of control quickly. You would think the Supreme Court would calm things down, but it has done just the opposite. It's getting harder and harder to avoid a war."

Cathy broke in, "I'm so glad we'all have moderate good people like the Davises here. They'd never let things happen like that. I heard on the wires that some of the Border Ruffians who been doing the fighting in Osawatomie are headed down to New Orleans and should pass through Vicksburg tomorrow.

Some of the planters are preparing a celebration in their honor. A celebration for a bunch of murderers and child killers!"

Cathy's face had a look of both sorrow and revulsion when she added, "Oh John, honestly–what is this world coming to!"

After his outdoor lunch with Cathy, John returned to the newspaper office to write up an article that he had to finish for the press deadline. When he walked in the door he found an unusual surprise awaiting him. There was a faint whiff of Parisian perfume, and he noticed that someone was in the outer waiting room. It was Dee Ann McCross. She was wearing a stunning, low-cut, long black dress.

As he approached her, he was quickly affected by her flirtatious charm.

"Whayl hello there, Mr. Wilms. I always wanted to meet you," she said as she stared him boldly in the eye. "I've been reading your stories for a number of years, and I really do like them. I am here to see if I can get your newspaper delivered by packet to Davis Island, where I live."

"Are you related to Joseph and Jefferson Davis?"

"Why certainly, they are my uncles. Do you know them?"

"I've met them both, and they are the most impressive men in the South at this day and time."

"Then you really should come out and visit Davis Bend some time. I could try to arrange it with my uncles. If I remember the concerns you voice in your articles, I think you would find the treatment of Negro slaves there interesting and exemplary. A write-up in the paper might be good for Jefferson's political career as well, and might also prove a feather in your cap."

She batted her eyelashes and almost seemed to exude her perfume in John's direction. "I think you would most definitely enjoy a little trip downriver and some of my family's hospitality."

Dee Ann bent down to pick up a scrap of paper that had fallen to the floor, revealing an exciting view of her ample and well-formed cleavage and translucent alabaster-toned skin.

John felt a powerful and electric charge pulse through his body, much like the consequences of the shock he had experienced when he hit the wrong part of the telegraph key as he was practicing Morse code.

This time it was a very pleasant experience. He found he had completely forgotten about Cathy, which was unusual for him. Dee Ann left, promising to get back in touch when she could arrange a visit with her uncles.

John had some difficulty doing any more work that afternoon on finishing the story he had come in to write. Probably, a hit on the head with a billy club would have made a significantly lesser effect than Dee Ann's unannounced visit.

The next morning, freshly returned from her shopping trip to Vicksburg, Dee Ann was having tea in the home of her best friend, Marie, talking about two men she was currently interested in.

Marie, ten years older that Dee Ann, was in her early forties. If now somewhat less energetic and vivacious in her pursuit of male company, she was nevertheless still an extremely attractive woman. She had auburn hair and a shapely, petite hourglass figure—and was capable of charming men just the way Dee Ann did. Through aging she was wiser and more mature, and could view Dee Ann's mistakes through the backdrop of her own mistakes when she was younger. When Marie pressed for details, Dee Ann began by saying, "one is married and the other has a reputation as a ladies' man."

Marie's reaction was immediate and knocked Dee Ann off center. "Dee Ann, y'all are always picking men who are either unapproachable or hard to get. I'm thinking about the last two men you kept company with. Jeb was married and so was Martin, but that did not prevent you from making a play for them both."

Feeling obliged to defend her choices, Dee Ann shot back, "I like men who have more experience. It makes them more attractive. I've been thinking about that in the light of this new book I just read, the one my cousin brought back from England, *The Origin of the Species* by Mr. Charles Darwin. He says, if animals can't adapt to their environment, they become extinct. Well, if a woman can't hold onto her man, maybe she should lose him. Only the strongest animals survive and only the most attractive woman should get the man. This feels like many of the same laws of nature that Mr. Darwin talks about in his book."

When Dee Ann finished explaining her rationale, Marie shook her head, looked her straight in the eye, and replied in a wistful tone, "I used to think like you do, Dee Ann, but I'm older than you and I've learned from my mistakes. Once upon a time, when I wanted something badly enough, I could convince myself that I needed to start relationships with people that way. But sooner or later I understood it just wasn't a decent thing to do."

Dee Ann rolled her eyes impatiently, and it appeared that Marie was losing her quickly.

"What about the damage you cause to the person's spouse or girlfriend? You're only hurting people who haven't done anything to hurt you. It's just not worth it. Why not choose someone who doesn't have a wife or lady-friend," Marie suggested. "Live and let live."

Dee Ann shrugged her shoulders and answered glibly, "because I'm not attracted to people who are not involved in other relationships."

"But why bust up their hopes and dreams. That's mean."

Ready to administer the *coup de grâce*, Dee Ann's jaw tightened into a snarl, showing her teeth in a less attractive light. "Look, Marie—you broke up relationships in the past. Maybe now you are not as young or attractive. You're just jealous 'cause you can't do it anymore."

Marie, visibly taken aback by Dee Ann's forcible blow, still managed an even tone. "Honestly, Dee Ann. But, you know, sometimes I do think I understand why you're doing this. I know your father was a ladies' man, and he went out with scores of women while he was married to your mother. Could it be you're just trying to get back at him?"

Dee Ann then started tapping her hand on the table as her patience was wearing thin. "So, you're going to bring up my father again."

Marie went on, not reading the signs that Dee Ann was getting hot under the collar. "I know your father was gone for long stretches of time on trading voyages, and you were raised by your grandmother."

Dee Ann came back at her, yelling loudly. "That's just like you, Marie, always trying to figure me out! Well, you're not going to get a chance to do it anymore!" She ran out of the room and slammed the door so hard a picture fell off the wall.

Marie sat there dumfounded, and after a few minutes began to speculate on some of the causes of Dee Ann's behavior. She knew that she had married young to an older man who was killed in the great hurricane that struck Davis Bend. But try as she might, she was not able to come up with any real answer. The closest she could get was that Dee Ann's father was not around very much, so she craved having a male who paid attention to her. Then, when she lost her husband at an early age, she still craved male attention. What confounded her most was that Dee Ann had shown the same flirtatious behavior when her husband was still alive.

She had to let Dee Ann know that her errant behavior with men was wrong and that it could go as far as to cause a duel or other tragic consequences. What's more, that was at least the fifth time she had confronted her on the subject.

Dee Ann blew her stack in roughly the same way. She would have nothing to do with Marie for a week or two, and then something would bring then back together. Marie would refrain from bringing up the topic until the next great confrontation, which could be six months or a year later. She was therefore pretty sure this occurrence would follow the same track as all the others, so she was not too worried about the temporary loss of her friend.

Several weeks later, John Wilms received a perfumed letter from Dee Ann which read as follows:

> My dear Mr. Wilms,
>
> Since our last meeting, taking in mind your wish to see the plantation, I thought I would go ahead and arrange a visit to Hurricane Island. I have spoken to Uncle Joseph, and he would be glad to show you around the plantation. If you can come on Wednesday the fifteenth, it would be a most opportune time. Joseph will be conducting his court session to adjudicate disputes which take place among the slaves—a very interesting process!
>
> Your faithful correspondent,
> Dee Ann

On receiving the letter, John's heart skipped several beats, and he made haste to clear his calendar, even though it included several important interviews and a meeting with Miss Cathy.

CHAPTER 26

WE A LIVING HAS GOT TO MAKE

Returning to the telegraph office the same afternoon, Miss Cathy found her father eager to speak with her. In between the arrival of customers, they sat in the front room discussing John Wilms. They often had father-daughter talks, and had been even closer to each other since Josephine, Ezra's wife and Cathy's mother, had died from yellow fever several years before.

"How do you feel about John?" Ezra asked Cathy. "You all have been keeping company for quite a while. Is there a wedding on the horizon?"

"Oh Dad, I really do love him, but he's worried whether he can get enough money to raise a family. He has saved about fifteen hundred dollars so far, but he doesn't feel it is nearly enough."

"Cathy, why don't you have him come talk to me. You know I have some money saved from the sale of our old house in New Orleans when you were young. Maybe I could help you all get started."

"Well, all right Dad. It's just not the right time—but when it is, maybe we can come talk to you."

At that point Josh walked into the telegraph office. He filled out the form to send a telegram to his family in New England, which read:

EVERYTHING GOING WELLADVISE WHEN YOU CAN COME DOWN FOR A VISIT THIS WINTER FOR A GOOD TIME. JOSH

After he handed in the telegram, Ezra asked him, "Did y'all get your ice and turtles and stuff from up north on time? It's a good thing for me to know—when people order things from far away or up north—whether they arrive on time."

"Everything worked out fine, a few little problems—but, overall, it couldn't have worked out much better! By the way, I have a question to ask you about telegraph service. Is it possible to string telegraph service to Hurricane Island?"

Ezra stopped and scratched his head. He looked Josh in the eye and said, "Well, I just don't know. Twenty miles of poles and wire, I bet you it would cost an arm and a leg. And then you would need an operator who knows Morse code, and you'd need to pay his salary and keep up the maintenance of the poles and wires. There's a lot involved with that. Trees and branches fall on the wires, hurricanes destroy the poles, and varmints like polecats climb the poles and mess up the wires! It's a real wonder that we have any telegrams at all! I know the Davises have a heap of money. But do they all want to spend it like that—keepin' up a telegraph system? I don't think so."

"You're right," Josh quickly added, "our money has to go into the cotton business." The conversation ended abruptly when Ezra had to return to the telegraph to read an important message.

Josh then headed out to do some shopping in town. Emily wanted a new dress, so he headed over to the general store to pick up the fabrics she had ordered. Seth Feinberg, the Jewish proprietor, and his wife Sarah waited on him.

Seth, a diminutive man, and Sarah, of equal stature, had moved here from New York five years ago to leave his dying business in dry goods. It had gone on the rocks in the troubled economy.

Since then, he had prospered immensely in Vicksburg. He had no real competition, as the other stores did not have either his zeal or his drive to please his customers. Both he and his wife had easy, pleasant manners, which made a big hit with the local population.

Seth had grown up in Hamburg, Germany and had left after the 1848 revolution had made him persona non grata in post-revolutionary Germany. He still had a heavy German-Jewish accent, which made his speech remarkable for Vicksburg.

When Josh left the store, Feinberg groaned to his wife, "If my revolutionary friends could see me now, selling merchandise to slave owners. Boy, to a new low level I have slipped. What a capitalist won't do to a living make."

As she listened to her husband, Sarah's face took on an irritated expression, then she shot back, "What's not to like about this place, Seth. It's warm in the winter–the quality of living is good here. Even the quality is good for many of the black slaves in our area around Vicksburg!"

"Sarah, what are you saying? These slaves are not free to speak their mind. I'm not free to speak my mind either. Look what happened to Cohen, the druggist. He made a few of the wrong comments and got beat up and tied to a tree!"

"Seth, we both know you have got a living to make. You lost everything in the revolution in Germany. We, while the sun shines, must make hay."

All this remembrance about the revolution made Seth feel weak in the knees. He felt unsteady on his feet, and a wave of nausea came over him. "I don't want to talk about this anymore, but you're right, Sarah–we a living has got to make."

"And Seth, this is the best place to do it," Sarah replied.

CHAPTER 27

VISIT TO HURRICANE ISLAND

Wednesday the fifteenth arrived, and John Wilms came to the dock early to catch the fast packet boat to Hurricane Island. Since the river was running very swiftly, the trip downriver took only about an hour and fifteen minutes. The speed of the boat combined with the speed of the river current was quite fast.

During the entire trip down, John felt an excited anticipation, as though he was on his way to a romantic tryst with a beautiful woman. He had to constantly remind himself that his real objective was to collect information for a very important story on Hurricane Island. He knew that, rationally, he should not let himself be distracted by Dee Ann's attractiveness.

After the boat docked at Hurricane Island, it seemed that no one had come to meet him. Then the steamboat let out its big whistle to summon its passengers to get aboard, and he noticed a horse and rider approaching at a canter. The rider was riding astride and at first Wims thought it might be a man but then Wilms realized it was a woman.

It was Dee Ann. When she got close enough, he could see that she was dressed in a striking riding habit with dark breeches and gleaming black boots that set off her blond hair tied up in a bun. The horse came right up to the boat landing.

"Mr. Wilms, I'm truly sorry I'm a few minutes late. I brought my mare. We can ride back to the barn and get another horse for you, or you can ride the mare. She is fast and spirited–and exciting to ride. You do ride, Mr. Wilms?"

"Of course, I can ride. I need to be able to ride to do my job. Why are you riding astride?"

"All the women ride astride in the plantations in this area. We had two accidents with sidesaddles on the plantation. One of them involved my cousin whose skirt got caught in the stirrups, and she was dragged. It was lucky that she wasn't killed. After that Uncle Joseph sold all the sidesaddles, and forbid us to use them. It wasn't the sidesaddles fault, I think it was poor training but stylish or not, his orders are the last word around here. Many famous woman such as Catherine the Great and Marie Antoinette rode astride, so I guess we can too."

"Well you look lovely in that riding habit, it fits you like a glove, maybe you will start a new fashion."

"Well then hop on, and we'll get another horse, and take the trail which runs along the river. It's most beautiful."

Dee Ann dismounted and let Wilms mount up, and got on behind him. Having Dee Ann hugging his waist and the Parisian perfume wafting into his nose was almost more then he could take. They quickly got to the barns and saddled up a fast Arabian for him, and headed out.

As they rode, he found himself agreeing about the beauty of the river ride. Blue herons and snowy egrets flew by, and he heard birds singing throughout the whole trail ride. To these pleasant sounds was added pastoral scenes of the river flowing by. The departing riverboat blew its steam whistle and headed downriver, silhouetted against the far shore.

Dee Ann led them to a clearing, where she suggested they dismount for a few minutes and walk around.

"This is a place where we'all come for cookouts. We can watch the boat traffic on the river while we dine." As they walked toward a wooden bench, John was struck by how attractive Dee Ann appeared in the sun. Her figure was beautifully curvy, and her gleaming black riding boots seemed to add a grace-note to her almost perfect figure. He found himself staring at them for a moment, and Dee Ann caught his stare. "You like my boots?" She lifted her leg to show them off.

"They are very beautiful."

"Yes, but they're getting a bit dusty." She uncrossed her right leg and gently rubbed her boot against his right leg. "See? It's much more shiny now."

A shock coursed through his body and an overwhelming urge to kiss her came over him. Taken by surprise, he barely fought it off by saying to himself, "You are here on business, and you can't afford to mess up what you are here for. Dee Ann is a very important person, the niece of Joseph and Jefferson Davis. You don't want any trouble."

Nevertheless, he felt he should say something, so he added, "Miss Dee Ann, you're a very attractive woman, but I'm here on business. There is a time and place for everything."

She fixed her hair, which was blowing, in her eyes, and stared boldly at him and answered, "Oh, I know you're here on business, because I set this whole thing up and invited you down. It looks like you and I have a different view on how to conduct that business–but as you just said, there's a time and place for everything. So I hope you have in mind a time and a place for the other aspects of our relationship."

He answered quickly, "Miss Dee Ann, I most certainly have it in mind." As soon as these words came out of his mouth, he wished he could take them back. In fact, at that moment his mind was close to overheating in trying to deal with a number of rapid-fire questions: Have I really encouraged her? What have I done? I just wanted to flirt with her a bit, but she looks like she's taking this very seriously! Will I be able to extricate myself from this relationship? Do I really want to extricate myself from this relationship? Look at her hair—look at her figure—look at her boots. I don't feel the same way with her as with Miss Cathy. She makes my blood boil, but Cathy doesn't do it like that. What will I do now?

Dee Ann walked toward her horse and remounted, motioning him to follow, and they both headed for a garden cottage on the plantation, which was in fact a giant Greek Revival building with enormous space for meetings.

When they first arrived, Joseph was meeting with a handsome-looking slave couple. They were both tall, with attractive features and well-cared-for white teeth, which was unusual for slaves.

When John walked in with Dee Ann, Joseph introduced him to the couple. "This is John Wilms," he said to the slaves, "and he is interested in how we settle our disputes and problems. Is it all right if he sits in? He is a newspaper reporter, and he wants to write about what goes on here so that other plantations can learn to do similar things."

"It's fine wid me boss, I doesn't mind at all."

"What about you, Hattie May?"

"Ifn he wants to see how a no 'count man acts, its okay with me."

"You sound mighty angry, Hattie," Joseph said.

"Ah sure is."

"We will talk about it in a few minutes."

While the couple was getting settled, Dee Ann explained to John that Tibor and Hattie May, for all intents and purposes appeared as a married slave couple. Joseph had bought them both fifteen years ago. They had already been living together for ten years before having had two young boys, ages two and four.

Since then, their relationship had begun to deteriorate markedly. They didn't show each other much affection and would often snap at each other. This was affecting the atmosphere in the house and affecting all the other slaves, and it was also upsetting the Davis family.

Hattie had recently become very friendly with another slave, Jonas, the gardener, who was treating her in a very affectionate way. The two men vying for Hattie May's affection had provoked a fistfight between them. After meeting with all the parties together, Joseph determined that the cause of these problems lay in the relationship between Tibor and Hattie May.

"Let's get started," Joseph began. "Hattie, you called Tibor a 'no 'count man.' Why did you say that, Hattie?"

"Causin' he don't do nothin'! He don't help wid da children. He don't seem to care about me anymore. He expect me to do everything. He don't want the children sleepin' in the bed with us. We bin fighten over dis for da last year."

Joseph broke in, "Tibor, what have you got to say about this?"

"She'all says ah doesn't do nothin'. Does she ask why I doesn't do nothin'? Ah tells you why I doesn't, boss. She doesn't listen to a ting that ah says. She used to, but den she stopped. Boss, ah gots no say in what goes on in da family. So why should I help her. She don't help me!"

"So, if she listened to you the way she used to, you would be more willing to help her, Tibor—is that right?" Joseph asked.

"Dats right boss, you has got it! You knows how ah feel boss when y'all cut off da balls of a chicken so it done grows bigger? Dats how ah feel, 'ceptin instead of growen bigger, ahs agettin meaner, and smaller."

"Are you saying that you feel Hattie is castrating you?"

"Ah shoa does boss!"

"Hattie May, what do you have to say about this. Are you castrating Tibor?"

"Ah done never heard a such a thing. Ah'd never cut his balls off, but iffen I caught him messin' wid dat pretty maid he was talking to, ahd take mah big knife and tear his guts out!"

"But seriously, Hattie."

"Oh, ah is serious boss, an he knows dat!"

"Hattie! I don't want anything to happen to either of you, and that's why you're here—to work out this problem so it doesn't turn violent."

"We knows dat boss, dats why we is here."

"Let's talk about your feeling of being castrated. First of all, Tibor, when did this start?"

"After da kids waz born. When Grover, he's de oldest, would done cry, and I tells her—let him cry hisself to sleep—its good for him so he can learn to sleep by hisself—so Hattie and me has time for lovin' at night. But no, as soon he starts a cryin loud, she say no, Tibor, you is wrong. An den she done put Grover in da bed so we can't have no lovin'. And she done do da same thing wid Paris. He da youngest. Dats when things comencin' to go rail bad."

"All right, I got the picture. Now you both have to listen to me carefully" said Joseph. "I want you to act out a fight you had recently over putting Paris in the bed. Hattie May, I want you to be Tibor, and I want Tibor to be you."

"Ah can't be Tibor, and he can't be me! We is two different people boss," said Hattie with a perplexed look on her face. What iz you doin', boss?"

"You done lost me too, boss. What is dis all about boss?" asked Tibor. "Dis don't make no sense to me."

"I want you to act like Hattie would act as close as you can, and I want Hattie to act like you as close as she can. Don't stop till I tell you to. I'll explain after we do it what it is all about."

"I think I got it, boss," said Tibor.

"What about you, Hattie May?"

"I has got it too, boss." The perplexed look had vanished from both their faces.

"Let's begin now," said Joseph, directing his remarks to Tibor, who was to play the role of Hattie May. Joseph spoke to Tibor, but now called him Hattie May. "Hattie, you bring Paris into the bed here," and then speaking to Hattie May, who was now Tibor, "Remember, you are now Tibor and you are going to object and begin the fight."

The hostilities commenced quickly after Joseph's directions.

"Honey, Paris is afraid of something and is commencing to cry. I'm a bringin' him into the bed," said Tibor, playing the role of Hattie May.

"What you do dat foa? Let him cry hisself to sleep. It will be good for him," said Hattie May, playing Tibor.

"Why you no 'count man—doesn't you care about your son ,he needs us," said Tibor as Hattie May.

"I have seen this before in my family. Crying works." said Hattie playing Tibor.

"The only reason you is doin this is 'causen you wants lovin'. You doesn't care about Paris. You is a no good, no 'count man who only cares about hisself!" said Tibor, playing Hattie May.

"And you iz trying to cut off my balls like a chicken," said Hattie May, playing Tibor.

"Okay, let's stop at this point." said Joseph. "Go back to being yourselves. Did you learn anything from this?"

"Yes, boss," was the reply from Hattie. "I learned what it felt like to be Tibor," she said, looking thoughtful.

"What about you, Tibor—did you learn anything here?"

"Boss," Tibor said sheepishly, "I think I understands Hattie May better."

"Dat goes for me too. I understands Tibor better," said Hattie May.

Joseph was turning to Hattie May to get more on her response, when the building shook from a loud explosion outside. Everyone ran outside and found that the boiler on the steam engine which was turning the fans to cool down the cottage, had blown up from overheating. No one was hurt, but the explosion had damaged the far end of the cottage. Several workmen came over to clean up the mess.

Joseph then added, “It’s almost lunch time. The workmen will straighten this out. We have a new steam engine in the warehouse, and we were going to replace the old one soon, so this will all work out. Dee Ann, why don’t you take Mr. Wilms over to the plantation dining room for lunch. You have most often participated in on our sessions here, have even run them yourself, and can explain more about what goes on and how we solve problems to make this a happy place to live and work. I’ll finish up with Tibor and Hattie May. If you’re still eating when I get there, I’ll fill you in.”

CHAPTER 28

DAVIS PLANTATION TOUR

"That was a most fascinating experience," said Wilms enthusiastically. "I never saw anyone try to work out slaves' problems before. I learned a lot by watching." Dee Ann tucked her arm around his elbow, and marched him over to the Davis Bend plantation dining room, where the cooks had set out a luncheon for the three of them. They sat at a huge dark mahogany table. Dee Ann and John Wilms occupied a small corner of the table.

"Wayl, boss and Miss Dee Ann, what can we'all get you?" said Toby the cook and waiter. "You know'd we'all got some fresh-baked Virginia ham. Prissy, my helper, just brought it over from da boat. Or does you want somtin else?"

They both nodded their heads.

"That'll be fine, Toby."

As the waitstaff served them a leisurely lunch of the baked ham, Dee Ann asked, "Well, what do you think, Mr. Wilms?"

"I never realized how difficult it can be to run a plantation with thousands of workers and keep them all getting along with each other."

"Most plantations don't do anything like this," Dee Ann

added. "The only ones who are doing this that we know of are the plantations in this area where Uncle Joseph either sold or gave land to the owners."

"This makes good sense from both a humanitarian and business point of view," said John Wilms, crossing his leg and munching on his sandwich.

"If there is no way to redress grievances, the slaves can turn mean and revolt," Dee Ann said, looking him in the eye, "but in some plantations I wish they *would* revolt. It would teach the plantation owners to do more of what we do here. Uncle Joe feels it is important from both a business and humanitarian sense."

John looked over at her with interest.

"Just imagine Hattie stabbing and killing Tibor. What would happen? She would wind up in prison. Uncle Joe would lose the labor of two valuable slaves, a multi-thousand-dollar loss. What about their kids? Who would take care of them? Or Tibor kills the gardener while vying for Hattie's affections–what a terrible loss! Imagine the effect on the other slaves."

"It must be a huge job for your uncle to keep all these workers content and producing. Doesn't that take a toll on him?"

"Uncle Joe has adjudicated all kinds of disputes involving property, objects of inheritance, domestic disputes, fights, and lunatic-type behavior. Unfortunately, he takes all the stress and worry on himself."

"It sounds like he's not only running a business, but also acting the role of lawyer, judge, and doctor in a lunatic asylum," John said.

Dee Ann lowered her voice and began to speak in a whisper. "I will tell you a little secret about Uncle Joe, because I believe you are sympathetic to his way of thinking. But you've got to promise not to tell anyone. Uncle Joe believes the black servants are as capable as the white folks. He believes that they can do anything white folks can do, and just as well. They just need a little confidence, though. He has thirty-five years of hard work and experience in the field from running plantations, and he believes this, as do I."

"Do you think the other planters who use his methods have the same beliefs as he does?" asked Wilms with interest.

"I'm not even sure what my uncle Jefferson Davis believes because he is a politician, and it is hard to tell exactly what he believes in. As far as the others, I'm not sure whether they believe everything that Uncle Joseph does, but using his methods to the letter of the law has made many of them rich men. Everybody knows these methods have made Uncle Joe wealthy, and nobody in this area sneers at them."

"So, the brothers don't think completely alike on the subject of the slaves' abilities?" Wilms asked.

"I have heard my uncles Jefferson and Joseph discuss this very issue. Jefferson has said that these Negro servants come from an inferior race and will never be able to do things on the level of the white man without very strong direction. I'm not sure he actually believes this, because he thinks his slave Ben Montgomery is the equal of any white man. He has said that many times. Uncle Joe is the boss here, and his system works very well."

"So," Wilms added, "Jefferson Davis, the famous politician and former Secretary of War gives in to Uncle Joe's thinking and methods, even though he may not believe in them fully?"

"They work better than any other methods," Dee Ann said. "Most of his friends around here use a lot of his methods, even though they don't all believe the way he does."

"Could that be because they want to get rich, like him?" Wilms queried.

"Everyone around here respects him as a man who really knows how to run a plantation and get the last drop of work out of his slaves. His servants and workers put in a hard day's work for Uncle Joseph—not because they are slaves, but because he treats them well and rewards their work. When a bountiful harvest comes in, he makes sure they all get a piece of the rewards."

"But isn't it backbreaking work?" Wilms asked, playing the devil's advocate.

"For you or me—yes, but we are not used to working in the fields. The workers sing in an antiphonal way while they work. It's very inspiring to watch. At times you feel like you are in Africa watching a tribal ceremony."

"Maybe," said Wilms, "we'll get a chance to see and hear this on the way back to the boat."

"I'm not saying it's the kind of work any one of us would want to do," continued Dee Ann, "but if you go out in the fields with them, you can feel the power of their labor. What a difference between watching a bunch of mill workers up north in a mill and Uncle Joe's workers in the fields. You get a feeling of elevation—like watching a good musical performance or hearing an inspiring sermon in church."

They continued talking for about an hour in the dining room. As the servants leisurely brought them desserts and beverages, Dee Ann said, smiling, "Uncle Joe always says he will be right along but often takes much more time resolving disputes."

Since Joseph never returned from the meeting, Dee Ann took John on a tour of the plantation. First, they visited the slave quarters. Although, by and large, the housing was neat and tidy, the first house Wilms visited proved to be an exception. While it was larger than the usual plantation housing, it was not as neat and clean as he would have imagined, and the bed was not even made.

"It looks like this slave left in a big hurry."

"I think we had some problem in the fields this morning, so he had to leave in a big hurry," said Dee Ann, cognizant of the house's less-than-perfect appearance.

"I will show you some other houses."

They went to a small bungalow-style house which was bigger than the first house and appeared to have a small barn attached. This house was indeed very neat and clean for someone working in the fields. There appeared to be some animals in the barn, which were being tended to by another slave. There was also a blacksmith's forge there.

"When people work hard for him, Uncle Joe makes sure he does something special for them. He even makes it possible for them to earn money and buy their freedom. The slaves know that, and it makes them work harder for him because they feel he is fair to them."

As Wilms inspected the rest of the housing, it appeared that most, albeit not all, of these particular houses were as good as the workers' housing he had seen in the New England area.

"Remember, Uncle Joe has created a system which rewards hard work but does little for those who don't work, other than providing for their needs and medical care. For that reason, you will see big differences in the size of the quarters. The best workers get the best housing. In fact, they get the best of everything.

"Don't be fooled into thinking that all the plantations are like this," said Dee Ann. "They are not. Some are awful. But those plantations don't get the work quality and production that ours does. We believe that only by treating our workers right will they go all out for us."

For the preparation of Wilms's forthcoming article in the newspaper, Dee Ann proceeded to lay out the benefits that the slaves get, and they were quite formidable without any real freedom. It was almost like a benevolent jail where the inmates were very well treated, but it was still a jail. The slaves benefited from good working hours, time off for religious worship, health care, good food, incentive rewards for good work, and help for their families when running into difficulty. This included Joseph presiding over adjudication of disputes.

"We all know they are not free to pursue their dreams as they see them," conceded Dee Ann. "Still—neither are workers up north, working from sunup to sundown."

"In theory," said Wilms, "wouldn't you be better off free, even if you worked from sunup to sundown? You could always pull up stakes and move somewhere else where your life would be easier and better. These slaves can't pull up stakes, even if they're well treated. I grant you it's the most exemplary treatment of slaves I've ever seen. But ultimately, they are not free to pursue their own destiny."

"Off the record, I find slavery repugnant, Mr. Wilms. But considering that our economic system is dependent on it, we are forced to continue it at this time—as Uncle Joe often says—until someone comes up with a good way to dismantle it without any severe dislocations to our economy. We could have our whole economic system dissolved and all of us end up in the poor house if we replaced slavery too quickly in today's world. Who would take care of the slaves then? This is a very complex problem, and no one has been able to solve it yet."

The planters would wind up in the poorhouse, Wilms thought to himself, and could no longer reap fortunes off the slaves—but the slaves would be free. While it might be difficult for them for a while, eventually they would find their way. He did not say anything more, however, and let Dee Ann's quotation of Uncle Joe's stand be the last word on the subject.

Having made a tour of the plantation, Dee Ann and John mounted their horses and started back to the dock to pick up the next steamboat heading upriver to Vicksburg. The next boat was not due for about two hours, so they made their way back slowly.

She took John by the fields where the slaves were working, and they were indeed singing as they worked. John felt the surge of an emotional high as he listened to what appeared to be an African chant. As he looked back on this experience at a later time, he was not sure if this was caused by the beauty of the natural voices, the environment with the earthy smell of the soil, or Dee Ann's having predisposed him toward witnessing a religious experience during their prior conversation.

They stopped to talk to one of the slaves, a powerful looking man stripped to the waist who appeared to have a position like that of a foreman for a group of slaves.

Wilms took the opportunity to ask this slave how he liked his work. "Well, masa, there ain't a body here who likes dis work, but it's got to be done. The plantation ain't gonna be here if we stops, and who knows where we gonna end up."

"How does master Joseph treat you," asked Wilms.

"We all likes masa Joseph. We works for him. He treats us good. We likes working for him. Dats why we works here. He comes 'round to watch our work and he done tells us when we done do a good job. We likes dat! When hesa younger he done work right wid us sometimes. His brother, da senator, he still work wid his mens in da field 'causen he's younger. We'all likes folks like dat. Deys not too good to get deys hands dirty!"

As they walked along, a cool breeze blew off the river carrying the smells of all the alluvial deposits it had picked up and carried from Cairo to Saint Louis, Minneapolis, and beyond. It was a breath of air that carried the smell of the heartland of America in its grasp. This smell of the river-borne soil, coupled with the herons and egrets feeding on the riverbank, etched a powerful image in both their minds as they walked along.

They went by the big warehouse where the cotton gins were separating the seed from the cotton. The workers there were busy at their jobs. In response to Wilms's questions about Massa Joseph, everyone had good things to say about him.

"He helped my family when I got da typhoid! He done helped us work out de big trouble."

Wilms found himself trying to figure if he was getting honest answers since everyone was so positive about Massa Joseph. Then he remembered having done a piece on a plantation where the slaves were not so well treated, and their responses were much more guarded. They did not give information as fluidly and talked as though they really did not like the Massa. The slaves in this other plantation were sullen and angry. Some even seemed surly when questioned. Wilms got the feeling that something good was going on here. He left the warehouse in a pleasant mood, buoyed by the warm response of the slaves and his attraction to Dee Ann, which seemed to grow stronger as the day went on. Normally, a plantation tour was a trying experience for him because he did not like slavery and he had decided to do something about it as soon as he was able.

As they made their way back to the dock, Dee Ann suddenly stopped and dismounted. "Wait a minute Mr. John, I think my horse threw a shoe." She walked over to pick up his front foot. John quickly dismounted and came over to help.

"Let me help you." He lifted the horse's front foot. "Nope, not a shoe, but a rock is wedged there." He quickly took out a penknife and pried the rock out. Then he picked up a nearby rock, and banged in the shoe nail to make it tight.

"When you get back, show this to the farrier. I didn't have a hammer, so it might not be tight enough."

Dee Ann was standing incredibly close to him, looking into his eyes intently. With her hair blowing in the wind she was a beautiful picture, juxtaposed against the backdrop of the river. When their bodies touched, some of her hair blew into his nostrils. It had a pleasant smell of the earth and fields as well as aromatic soap.

He inhaled this aphrodisiac odor, and a powerful urge came over him. He turned Dee Ann around and gave her a lover's kiss. She seemed quite responsive, but he felt he had violated her boundaries.

He quickly added, "Ah am most sorry, Miss Dee Ann, I just don't know what came over me! I couldn't help it."

"Now, Mr. John, come look me in the eyes."

When he did, she put her arms around his back and a thrill coursed through his veins. She pulled him down to the ground where they fondled each other, and she wrapped her legs around him, but they dared to go no further because they could hear the voices of workers in the nearby field.

After a few minutes they got back on their horses and headed to the steamboat dock. By the time they reached it, the packet was just rounding the bend and battling the current. A big wave was coming off the bow. The boat labored hard in the turns as the river fought back, trying to turn the riverboat broadside. It blew its whistle to announce its arrival. As it approached the dock, Dee Ann said goodbye to Mr. John with a polite handshake, and they parted ways.

"Miss Dee Ann, I surely had a most memorable time here."

"So did I," she answered. "I do hope we will see each other soon, and you will write about your experience here. Well not about everything, that is."

"Don't you worry Miss Dee Ann. I will do you and your uncle proud!"

CHAPTER 29

DESCENT INTO THE BELLY OF THE BEAST

Josh and Emily were headed to New Orleans for business and a brief vacation from the cares of the plantation. Josh had received a response to his telegram that said that his father was suffering from gout and couldn't walk. Will would have to stay in New England for the time being. This meant the family wouldn't be able to visit Josh and Emily for some time.

Josh was upset about it, but he was not in a position to leave his affairs and go north for the near future. So, he put his family plans on hold and decided to take a short trip to New Orleans with Emily, instead. They took Nate and Joan, officially as servants, and left Jackson and Wilma to look after the plantation. They gave them instructions to go to Mr. Joseph or Miss Eliza if there were any problems they could not solve while Josh and Emily were gone.

Josh and Emily had been working hard adjusting to plantation life, and they were now ready for a little change. Josh wanted to get to meet with the cotton broker who had been helping sell all the cotton harvested by the Davises and their friends and relatives. The price for cotton had been running low, and he wanted to see if anything could be done to raise it up.

He felt a little distraction would be good for Emily, as well, as she was used to more of a city life. As long as he was ensconced in the role of a plantation owner, he wanted to act the part, so he felt it was incumbent on him to meet with cotton brokers.

Josh also had an ulterior motive. He wanted to check out the slave market, if he could find it, and talk to other planters. Unfortunately, he did not realize how all this would affect his emotional state, as well as that of everyone who came along with him.

They caught the fast packet and made it downriver in record time. The river was flowing quickly with melting snow from faraway Minnesota, and the boat put on extra steam. It felt like they were making at least fifteen knots due to the combined steam and river current. The only problem was the boat was visibly harder to control in the river bends. The captain, nevertheless, was a real veteran and handled it expertly.

As they headed downriver, Josh brought Emily up front so they could both watch the changing spectacle of the Mississippi. He scanned the surface for meandering eddy currents, as the pilots in previous trips had shown him how to do. He was scanning these currents to reveal the possibility of underwater obstacles which could turn the boat broadside to the current and cause disaster.

Emily quickly noticed Josh's withdrawal of attention from her and his intense focus on the river. "Josh, what's going on? Why are you staring at the river so intently? This is supposed to be a little vacation for us. What are you looking for?"

"Emily, I've learned to love this river. You see those ripples over there? They are probably caused by a tree that fell in the river and washed down here, or something else which is stuck on the bottom." Josh wisely omitted any reference to the danger that could come from underwater objects.

"Well, I'm glad you are enjoying yourself staring at the river, but I was hoping you would pay a little attention to me."

"Oh Emily, don't worry, I am sure planning to. Our trip has only just begun." At that point he stopped looking at the river and put his arm around Emily and gave her a whimsical smile. He thought, "These riverboat pilots know their stuff, and they certainly don't need me to do their job for them. I'm going to have a nice romantic weekend with my wife—that's all."

Then they walked back to the cabin to join Nate and Joan inside the recreation and gambling room. On the way there, they heard the couple in front of them talking about New Orleans.

"Honestly Lulu, it's the biggest slave market in the world. There are slave auctions on almost every corner."

Josh was suddenly sorry he had not been able to discuss his upcoming trip with Joe Davis and his wife before they left on a trip to Washington, DC. Joe and Eliza would not be back until the day after the foursome left for New Orleans. Had he known the city was rife with slave auctions on every corner, Josh would probably not have brought Joan and Nate along.

As Emily and Josh walked back to the recreation and gambling room, they ran into Joan and Nate. "I thought you all were never coming back. It seemed like hours," Nate said uneasily.

"You left us all alone here," Joan added. They were visibly ill at ease standing out all by themselves without the protective cover of a master to take care of. Then they retired to the cabin suite Josh had rented for the four of them to discuss plans for the next day.

"Now, Joan and Nate—Don't be shocked by what you see tomorrow! I'm hearing New Orleans is the biggest slave market in the whole country. There could be slave auctions going on all over the city, depending on what the slavers have brought in. There are also masters who have fallen on hard times and have to sell their slaves. Keep your emotions under control and just keep catering to the two of us. Remember, of course, that you're supposed to be our slaves."

Nate and Joan both appeared very anxious in reaction to

Josh's revelation. It was obvious that Josh's forged ownership title for Nate was the only thing keeping him from a lifetime of slavery.

Nate wrung his hands nervously before blurting out to the group, "Everyone knows that under the Fugitive Slave Law even free blacks are kidnapped and taken away in disputes over ownership. The magistrates get more money for cases when Negroes are taken away, and laws don't allow the Negroes to present evidence to defend themselves. These laws are full of abuses that work against freed slaves, runaway slaves, and free men who are black."

With a taut look on her face, Joan added, "If they determine you are a runaway, you are guilty of being a runaway. It's like a rubber stamp."

To which Nate added grimly, "There is no due process of law for a black man."

"I share your concerns," said Josh thoughtfully. "We all know that you are guilty of being a runaway unless you can prove otherwise—but at the same time, your testimony as a freed man or free slave is not allowed in court. You are considered property—and not a human being who could bear witness to testify.

"If one of you got caught in the wrong way, you could wind up in the meat grinder. I know that, and you know that. But that's not going to happen here. We are in the Deep South, as far south as you can go, except for Florida. The issues you are talking about are mostly happening in northern cities, where slaves are running away.

"These laws were designed for northern cities, and while they are in force here, they are not paid as much attention to. Slaves rarely run away to New Orleans. I would not worry about this happening down here. You are both here with Emily and me, and you are both officially our slaves. Look, we have got to go through with this. Just imagine we are all soldiers with an unpleasant job to do."

Josh's perspective on these issues went a long way to calming down Joan and Nate. "I don't think we have anything to worry about here with the fugitive slave laws," he continued. "Now let's plan to do a little relaxing here, if it can be done."

Later, in a somewhat calmer atmosphere–Nate, well-groomed and dressed in his best tan traveling suit, began to make overtures toward Joan, resplendent in her Sunday best, a long blue dress. Since they were in public on the boat–standing in front of a bench outside their cabin, Nate had no choice but to communicate in slave talk, even though he was seriously trying to woo her.

"Wayl, honey chile– wha don't you all sit down next to Uncle Nate."

He was immediately rebuffed in slave talk.

"Ah doesn't want to sit next to a no 'count man like you."

"Wayl, why not? What you got against Uncle Nate?"

Joan faced him squarely and let fly, showing off her pretty white teeth, her curly hair blowing in the wind. "'Causen you is mean, you done has a mean, angry streak. Now you is nahce 'causen you wants me now. But before, when we done cooked together, you done yelled at me! Joan don't forget that. Why can't you be nahce like Jackson is."

"Aw honey chile, dat meal was da biggest thing ah done did in years. Ah didn't have my kitchen set up right. Ah didn't have ma ingredients. Ah was scared it would be a disaster. Ah is not like dat. Has you ever seen me like dat before?"

"Well no, but ah can't take a man who behaves like dat. Ifn you promises me not to be like dat, I'll be nahce to you."

"I promises." Nate put his arm around Joan and she cuddled up next to him. They both enjoyed the close contact as she snuggled in his arms.

Despite the plan for some sort of vacation, the four of them spent a restless night on the boat, worrying about what tomorrow might bring as they descended into the belly of the beast.

During the night Nate thought about what Josh had said, and it all made sense except for one fear. If his last master was visiting New Orleans at the same time, and if he saw Nate, which was highly unlikely because he never went anywhere, he could report Nate to the authorities. Nate and everybody else might have to deal with the Fugitive Slave Law after all.

The next morning, they docked at Wharf Street. Coming into the port of New Orleans, they noticed two large churches towering over the river. One of them had three large steeples. The other had one large steeple and four smaller corner steeples. There, a great array of four- and five-story buildings spread out from the Mississippi in all directions. Every street was crowded with pedestrians. It seemed like ages since they had been in such a large city. The city took on the form of a veritable metropolis. As they descended from the boat, a man walked over to Josh with a printed handbill that he was giving to everyone. It read, *Slave Auction, Jackson Square. Best Quality Agricultural Slaves at 11:00 a.m. Don't miss it.*

Josh thought it wise to skip Jackson Square due to the probable emotional impact on Nate and Joan. They walked up to Saint Louis Street to the Saint Louis Hotel, where they were staying, after circumventing Jackson Square by taking St. Peters Street and Chartres Street.

Josh's attempt, however, to evade the slave auction came to naught as they ran right into a higher quality auction with more sophisticated slaves. This auction contained butlers and cooks. When they got to the hotel, they found it had a slave auction in the rotunda of the hotel that they could not escape. It took place alongside another auction of high-quality art.

The auctioneer's voice echoed loudly through the hotel lobby "What am ah bid for this gorgeous negress. She has perfect teeth, a perfect figure–y'all know she is quite strong, and her former owner said she'all was a wonderful cook and great with the children." The poor young lady looked down in embarrassment as the auctioneer praised her attributes.

"She is being sold because her former master died, and his family is asellin' her to pay off his estate."

This woman was indeed quite a looker and the four of them heard these comments from prospective buyers as they passed through the room: "I wonder what Joe's agoin' to do with her? He's getting his money together to bid on her. Why, there's only one thing to do with her, an ah bet she does it rael well! Hey Joe, ahl beyt sheel make a great maid for your whaf!"

Josh tried to lead his party quickly through the rotunda to the main desk of the hotel to register, but not before the auction had a terrible effect on them. When they were alone in their suite, both Josh and Emily noticed that Nate and Joan were quite shaken by what they saw.

They both had turned silent. Josh pushed them to find out what they were feeling.

Finally, Nate said, "Its worse than I can ever imagine. What must that young lady be feeling—being presented almost like a prostitute, being pawed over by men, and not knowing where she is going or where the rest of her family is going to wind up?"

Josh replied, "I thought something like this might happen, but we have got to remember why we are here. Our purpose here is to destroy slavery so that these types of things don't happen to people any longer."

Although Josh put on a brave face for the benefit of the other three, he too was quite upset by what he saw at the auction. In fact, it came back to haunt him with a vengeance in the middle of the night. At 2:00 a.m. the recurrent thought kept going through his head—I could have bought that poor woman! I had the funds to outbid anyone else. Why did I not act? What is wrong with me?

In fact, he was so upset that he woke up Emily to discuss

his actions. She could always be counted on to help him work through his feelings.

She reminded him, "Josh, you have a job to do, we all have a job to do. Wouldn't this have jeopardized our whole mission here, as we would have been acting impulsively by buying this woman? This whole act of buying any new slaves has to be carefully thought out. We don't know anything about this woman. She could turn out to be a blabbermouth and give all our plans away."

By the time Josh got up the next morning, he was sure Emily's appraisal of the situation was correct, and he was able to put the matter to rest. But occasionally it came back to haunt his thoughts. He could not meet with the cotton broker till the next day, so he took Emily and his "slaves" for a tour of the city as far away as he could find from any slave auctions.

CHAPTER 30

LOST AND FOUND IN NEW ORLEANS

The group of four traveled back to the wharf in two hansom cabs, as was appropriate for masters and slaves, to see if they could find a suitcase of Emily's clothes that failed to be delivered from the boat.

There were a large number of powerfully built dockworkers, stripped to the waist, holding onto various musical instruments. It was hot in the sun, and the dock smelled of pitch. The workers all moved into a shady alcove where the air smelled pleasant from nearby plants.

Just outside a dockside restaurant, there were a few flashily dressed black women—slaves with low-cut red dresses and enormous black sash belts. They worked in the restaurant, and they joined the group of musicians because it was between meals and they had free time.

After arranging and tuning the instruments, the group began playing, singing, and dancing in rhythm. Josh seemed surprised, not only by the liberty of the music, but the freedom the musicians had to play it between loading and unloading the Mississippi riverboats.

Josh went up to one of the musicians to ask him how long

the music would go on. His answer was, "Wayl, boss, dis music go on till da next boat comes through. It's been slow today. Nona da boats dats due today show up, so we plays music while we waits. Da big boss says okay, so we plays music and dance. We tink he done like our music. We used to go Congo Square every Sunday to sing and dance and play da drums. I doesn't know why dey stop dis, but dey did, so we plays here when we isn't too busy."

The dockworkers began and played melodic variations of rhythms using banjos, fiddles, a marimba, pan flutes, and African drums–as well as brass instruments. They improvised on songs, played double-syncopated passages, and even worked in antiphonal choruses. The four of them had never heard music quite like this.

Almost as soon as the music started, Emily began swaying her hips–and soon all four of them were moving in time with the insistent rhythms.

The music had such a powerful effect on the group that they found it impossible to leave the dock for half an hour. The spell was finally broken when the dockworkers took a break from their music. When the four left the dock, they all felt rejuvenated, as though they had been through a kind of religious experience. The elevated spirit stayed with them, even though they had no luck trying to find the lost suitcase.

Invigorated by their impromptu musical experience, the group went shopping in town. They found a store that specialized in cooking equipment. Nate was able to point out some good values on copper pots, knives, and bowls for the upcoming cooking classes he was planning to conduct with other slaves from nearby plantations.

Then they left to go to a women's dress store to look at the latest Paris fashions. Josh bought Emily a new, white low-cut gown. They all agreed it suited her particularly well.

As they were leaving the store, Emily noticed that Joan was

looking at a similar gown with interest. Emily whispered to Josh when she saw Joan turn away, "Can slaves wear something like that?"

"Of course," he whispered back. "She's supposed to be my slave. She can wear anything we want her to wear, or rather what she wants to wear. How about some of the planters who dress up their maids like Parisian harlots! I wonder what that slave woman who was for sale in the hotel will be wearing," he remarked bitterly.

Emily marched over confidently to where Joan was standing and informed the sales clerk of her decision to have Joan try the dress on. When she came out of the fitting room with it on, Nate couldn't keep from sneaking an admiring peek at her, which she in turn pretended not to have noticed. As the dress was a perfect fit, no alterations were needed. They purchased it for Joan and left the shop.

Since they were loaded up with pots, bowls, cooking knives, and women's dresses, they arranged for cabs to take them back to the hotel to unload their packages.

The driver was very talkative since he was used to showing off the city to tourists. "This evening I'm a gonna be reel busy bringin' folks to the Cotton is King Ball raht heah in the hotel. You folks gonna 'tend?"

Emily looked longingly at Josh. "Oh Josh, could we?"

Josh replied, "Well, I don't know, I'll try to get us invited if I can. Joan and Nate will probably have to fend for themselves for the evening." Then Emily, Joan, and Nate went back to their suite, while Josh inquired at the desk about the ball.

The manager at the desk said, "It's only for select guests who are planning to attend the cotton broker convention later this week, but if y'all know a cotton broker, maybe he could get y'all invited to the ball."

Then he suddenly looked down at his feet and said, "By the way, are you the Lawrence family?"

"We are," Josh replied.

"I believe this belongs to you," the manager said, and he handed Josh the lost suitcase. "A cab just brought it over from the dock."

"Can you hold onto it for a little while longer," Josh asked, "I've got to see a man about some tickets to the ball. I'll be back in a little while."

The clerk nodded yes, and Josh then quickly left in a cab to visit his cotton broker's office. He was able to snag an invitation from the cotton broker's secretary, an attractive brunette with a vivacious personality. "Now y'all have a rail good tahm there. Hey, and y'all know you can bring your servants there too?"

At that comment Josh paused and looked at her inquisitively, "Is that really so?"

"Ah understand," she nodded, "they has got a special ballroom raht next door where the black servants can have theymselves a good tahm too! Wayl, I guess wheel see you back here tomorrow, and you can tell us about the fun y'all had. Be sure and bring this invitation with you. It bears the ball director's signature, and it will get y'all into the ball."

Josh scampered up the hotel steps to tell everyone the good news about the ball. When he got to the suite everyone was seated in the gathering room.

"We are all going to the ball," he said excitedly. "And here is the missing suitcase, just delivered to the front desk." He set it down on the floor.

"The only issue is that we can't all attend the ball together. The servants have to dance in a separate room, although they can see the same orchestra and hear the same music. The ballroom is set up that way."

"And the servants have to be available to wait on their masters if necessary," Joan said. "Well, at least I'll get to wear my new dress."

To which Nate reacted joyfully at the prospect of seeing Joan in the dress. "We'll just have to make the best of it!"

"This should be fun and maybe useful too," Josh replied, "as a chance to mingle with other slaves."

Nate added, "Maybe we can learn something from this event that we can use when we start our cooking classes."

Josh said to himself that this was really an immoral experience. But in his thoughts he was able to quickly rationalize the situation: "The whole country is going through an immoral experience with slavery. Our purpose here is to undermine slavery. So why can't the ladies and all of us have a little fun."

He kept his thoughts to himself, however, so as not to spoil the others' fun, even though he wondered if they were possibly thinking the same thing.

The women took the whole afternoon to get ready for the ball, which was an evening affair. "You women are really lucky," Josh said. "This is a frontier ball, a bit more casual, and you can wear the dresses you bought. If this was a formal ball, European style, you would have to spend upwards of a hundred dollars to get ready for that type of occasion."

"You're right," Emily answered. "Those hoop skirts with all the accoutrements are not only spectacular to look at but endless work to prepare for. It could take a whole day's work to get ready."

"In addition, we would have to memorize *The Ladies Guide to Gentility* by Emily Thornwell. I found a copy in the library at Hurricane Island, and I brought it along. It has the latest on dressmaking, deportment, conversation, hygiene, care of teeth, and bad breath."

Emily opened the book and said, "Let me read you some from a chapter: 'A lady ought to adopt a modest and measured gait. Too great a hurry injures the grace which ought to characterize her. She should not turn her head to one side and on the other, especially in large towns or cities, where this bad habit seems an invitation to the impertinent. A lady should not present herself alone, or in a library or a museum, unless she goes there to study or work as an artist.'"

Nate added, "Boy, it must be tough to be a woman. You got to do all that just to do the right thing. Men don't have to worry about any of that!"

Josh added, "I think this refers to women's behavior in high society, either in England, Washington, or among the very rich. We Americans on the frontier can't afford the time or effort for this type of luxury."

Any observer could see that both Emily and Joan were very excited about the immanent ball. They both chattered away to each other intently, trying on their dresses and accessories. "How does this shawl look, Emily?" Joan said, quickly flipping one side of it over her shoulder.

"I like the other one, Joan, it's a better color for you. Do you think I should wear this purse, Joan, or carry the smaller one?" Emily turned towards her, her face flushed with excitement.

"Let's ask Nate," Joan responded. "Nate, does this necklace go with my silver earrings?" Before he could answer, Emily took an appraising look at her, shook her head and said, "I'll lend you my gold earrings if you'll look after them very carefully."

They were in a mood to have some fun, and it was an easy rationalization after a few months of deprivation on the plantation. After several hours of hard work for the women and mild torture for the men, Emily and Joan were ready to attend the ball.

In the thick of these preparations, qualms about the morality of going to a ball in a city where slave auctions were being held everywhere seemed to slip away for the moment, replaced by a feeling of respite from the tensions of their double life on the plantation.

Josh was attired in his Sunday best, a slim-cut, tan cotton suit, and Nate wore his best slave suit, made of dyed-blue cotton with a jacket cut in back with big swallowtails. They both looked quite handsome, but the real attractions were the stunning women who were sure to turn heads at the event.

Emily and Joan did their hair in the new Grecian curly style that was very much in vogue. After a light dinner at the recommendation of Miss Thornwell's book, they made their way to the ballroom at a slow pace, the women being very careful not to disturb their carefully arranged coiffure and makeup.

As they approached the ballroom there was a big crowd gathered around the entrance door, which had a receiving line where the guests lined up to show their invitations. All eyes were on the two beautiful women, which seemed to allay some of their anxiety in attending a strange ball in a strange place.

As the line slowly moved toward the door, other guests began to make small talk with Emily, Josh, and Joan—not realizing Joan was black. The entrance went well, and Josh and Emily were introduced to the floor as planters from Davis Bend in Mississippi, which was a well-known area to everyone.

Joan and Nate went to the side of the ball meant for the servants. Other guests came over to introduce themselves. Some of them were stunned by Josh and Emily's northern accent. "Why, we never expected to see a northerner running a plantation with slaves. Do y'all lahk livin' here down south?"

"We love it," Josh replied. "Our plantation is just starting to run very well. If the weather keeps cooperating, we should deliver a mighty fine crop!"

Two distinguished, handsome men walked in. One was Josh's cotton factor, Brett Hume. The other was his associate, William Armistead. Brett was dressed in a blue suit with a maroon cravat, loosely tied in an easygoing style. He had well-shined shoes and curly blond hair. This, combined with his bright blue eyes, gave him a very striking, formidable appearance. Armistead's appearance was also striking. He was a tall man with dark brown hair and a dimple when he smiled. He was wearing a gray suit with a shiny pastel-colored cravat and well-shined shoes. Both men had tanned complexions from working outdoors.

Having been apprised of Hume's appearance beforehand, Josh made his way to him. "Are you Brett Hume? I'm Josh Lowell." They both shook hands and went through introductions, since they had never met before. Joe Davis knew Hume very well and had already arranged for him to sell Josh's cotton

CHAPTER 31

COTTON IS KING BALL

Hume's face was flush with confidence as he prepared to welcome some foreigners to his domain. "Ah can hear you're a northerner from your accent. We'all have had a few northerners who came down here to make their fortune. Most of them have done rail well down here. We think it's because folks up north work rail hard for a living. We think they have to work real hard, cause life is harder there. Bah the way, how is it going up north?" Before Josh could answer, he went on, "We heard that jobs are scarce since that panic started a few years ago."

Josh, who was a little bit uncomfortable with what he thought might be the beginning of another gentle inquisition replied, "I think you're probably right, things are bad in the economy up north right now. Hopefully they should improve soon."

At that point Armstead asked Josh if he could dance with Emily as the orchestra had just started up.

"Fine with me," Josh replied, glancing at Emily, who appeared to give him the okay, "if it's okay with Emily." Emily nodded affirmatively, and they went off to the dance floor. The grand march was just beginning. Emily and Armistead took their place at the back of the line as the couples circled the dance floor, progressed to march and file, and proceeded to quadrille as they broke into groups of four.

Brett and Josh continued their conversation. Hume was in an expansive mood for the benefit of his guest and his oversized ego. "Thank providence that we'all can help the north get back on its feet," Brett continued, "'cause things is boomin' here, and cotton prices are going to get better, which y'all will soon see."

He spoke with great animation, waving his arms emphatically as though he was conducting a symphony. "We'all are sellin' to England as well as to up north. Just yesterday we got a huge order to fill for the mills that make the uniforms for the French army. And other mills in France have been buyin' too. This just caused a big spike in prices."

Josh smiled, "That is really good news." From time to time, Josh kept an eye on Emily on the dance floor.

"Don't worry, we'all are gonna get real good prices for you. The last few days have been very good for cotton prices. Let's hope we don't get any hurricanes or weather problems."

At that point Emily and Armistead came back. Emily looked very pale and wanted to sit down. Armistead explained, "We were whirling around, and she got dizzy and came close to passing out."

Josh asked one of the waiters to run and get Joan to come sit with Emily for a few minutes so she could get back her balance. In the meantime, Armistead ran off to get some punch for her to drink.

Joan came hurrying into the room to keep Emily company, holding up the hem of her long dress as she did so. Almost immediately, several of the men began staring at Joan. As she arrived, Joan whispered with her back to the dance floor, "Well, you got me here to help you, Emily, at least we are on the same dance floor if for only a few moments."

At that point Armistead came back with the punch and appeared very much taken with Joan's appearance and striking figure. After receiving Emily's reassurance that she was very much improved, Armistead asked her if her friend would like to dance with him.

"Joan is not my friend," Emily replied to him curtly, "but my servant. She is supposed to dance over there in that hall."

"Well," Armistead replied, pointing his finger, "we can dance over there." He escorted Joan over to the entrance where the two halls met, and they began to sway into a waltz. He seemed almost mesmerized, and continued dancing number after number with her, punctuated only by his considerable intake of alcoholic beverages.

His compulsion to dance with her continued unabated until another gentleman presented himself and tried to cut in. Disconcerted by the interruption of his pleasure, Armistead hardly noticed that at that same moment a Negro in a swallow-tailed coat was standing in the connecting ballroom, glowering at him in anger.

Seizing the opportunity to make her escape, Joan excused herself to her aspiring dance partners with a worried frown, "I've got to get back to the dance floor over in the black ballroom," and left hurriedly. Her abrupt exit threw a bucket of ice water on Armistead's mood. He quickly gravitated to where Josh and Emily were standing and looked for an opportunity to break into their conversation.

"Your servant Joan is quite an excellent dancer," he said to Josh and Emily. "Is there any possibility that she is for sale? I would pay a good price for her!"

"I'm gratified that you hold her in such high esteem," Josh replied, "that you would want to purchase her. It shows us that we have done a good job of training her. But we've had her now for a number of years, and it would feel like losing part of our family. No, we could never sell her."

"Well, how about renting her to me for a few weeks," Armistead said.

"Maybe some time in the future," Josh replied, trying to mask that his face was reddening with anger. "But for the next few months we are going to be very busy developing our plantation, and we sure are going to need her."

Hume and Armistead then bid their farewells for the moment, and left to head over to a corner where some other attractive women were standing.

Hume, noticing Armistead's glum look, said, "Sir, you look downhearted. You cannot enjoy a ball looking like that."

As the evening progressed, Emily and Josh had several more glasses of alcohol-laced punch, which had almost no effect on Josh, but great consequences for Emily's behavior. She got into the spirit of the night and danced with increasing gusto as the evening progressed with no return of dizziness that had bothered her early in the evening.

Many men began to notice her by her natural grace on the dance floor, and several took their turns asking Josh's permission to dance with her. "Do you mind if I dance with your partner?"

This happened two or three times in succession during the course of the evening. Emily danced with beautiful movements, especially in the waltzes, which created a magnetic force that kept drawing men in her direction.

Before the evening elapsed, at least half a dozen men had asked Josh's permission to dance with her. As the alcohol began to affect her, she became somewhat flirtatious with several of the men to the point that Josh began to worry about her losing control, but fortunately that never happened. He was only interested in making sure she had a memorable time at the ball, so he did nothing to reproach her for her behavior or to discourage the seemingly endless flow of men.

Late in the evening, Josh noticed that both Armistead and Hume were thoroughly enjoying themselves, dancing with some single young women. He was considerably relieved to think that Armistead must have gotten over his infatuation with Joan.

The ball came to an end at about 4:00 a.m., when Josh and his party returned to their rooms. They got to bed just before sunrise, and slept in past noon.

When Josh finally arose, he quickly realized that he had a 3:00 p.m. appointment with Hume to discuss cotton prices, even if they had already done so the night before at the ball. He felt he should go anyway in order to broaden his contacts in the South. It would make further inroads into laying the groundwork for the delicate mission of raising the awareness and education of the slaves.

CHAPTER 32

IN SPITE OF THE PERILS

Mr. Hume was in his office when Josh got there, and the same secretary who got him admitted to the ball ushered him in. Hume looked a bit under the weather from the wild evening before, but he quickly got his second wind and began to engage Josh in the same type of conversation as the night before.

"Mah associate was verah much taken by your servant Joan. Boy, she is a real looker—that one—and smart too! But he knows she is not for sale. You know, Mr. Lawrence, can ah call ya Josh?"

"You may," Josh replied.

"Our cotton crop is in such demand worldwide that other countries would do almost anything for us to keep the cotton flowing. If things get rail difficult with the North, Great Britain and France would support us if we had to go it alone without the rest of the United States."

"Do you think the rest of the United States would let the South separate from them without a murmur?" Josh asked him.

"Of course not," Hume said, "but we'all can negotiate for more favorable arrangements with the North if we also have the strength of Europe backin' us if necessary. Since the economy up north has gotten so bad, y'all woulda thought they'd be happy the southland is pullin' them along, but no such thing. They want to control us and destroy our economy by takin' away our slaves. They want to bring in a free labor system to replace slavery, but it jess won't work down here. What are they tryen to do, bite the hand that feeds them? It don't make no sense!"

Josh tapped his fingers on the desk. He was rapidly getting bored with the conversation but was trying hard not to show it. So Hume went on, "It's like taking a roundhouse swing at yourself. Don't they all realize they're punchin' themselves in the face?"

Josh answered carefully but diplomatically so as not to tip his hand as to what he believed in. "Many of the folks up north feel they can't live with slavery. They would rather risk damaging the country so as to get rid of slavery, especially since the Dred Scott Decision by the Supreme Court. Some northern folks are also scared that the South will bring slavery up north and wipe out their free-labor system."

"We all could do that if we all chose to, but I don't think we want to do that. It also shows you that mill owners can't cheat workers in company stores, work them from sunup to sundown, pay them next to nothing, and not take care of them in old age. Their poor treatment of workers is one of the reasons they are so afraid of us. For the most part our slaves are better off then these northern workers."

Annoyed more by Hume's bellicose, self-satisfied tone than by the comparison itself, which he himself had sometimes made, Josh fought to master his feelings of resentment in order to keep his real opinions carefully hidden.

"People here see the North as cutting off its nose to spite its face. The northerners don't see it the same way, and it is leading to a serious conflict. I don't know how we are going to get out of it," Hume continued, "the Democrats, they seem to understand us. But those new Republicans, they are some of the stupidest folk ah ever saw. Those are the ones who all want to cut off their noses to spite their faces! Don't they realize that much of their manufacturing depends on our supply of raw material?"

Josh bit his tongue and agreed with Hume in the interest of not arousing suspicion. When the meeting was over, Josh took a cab back to the hotel. After packing up and checking out, the four headed down to the wharf to pick up the fast packet heading up the river.

Their business and vacation had come to an end. In spite of the perils, they all agreed that the days away from the plantation had been a breath of fresh air. Emily and Joan seemed much buoyed up by the festive animation of the ball and the dancing, as well as the thrill of having been the center of attention.

The trip had also brought Nate and Joan much closer to each other, perhaps fueled by his newfound feelings of possessiveness on seeing her dancing with Armistead. Nate now seemed to pay much more obvious attention to Joan.

They decided to continue their voyage on the fast packet up to Vicksburg before returning home to the plantation in order to pick up some supplies and clothing that had been ordered at the general store and haberdashery.

The trip upstream was naturally much slower because the steamboat now had to fight the current in the river going upstream. Josh and his party took little notice of time, as they were all thoroughly exhausted from the night before.

They lounged on deck sleepily, although a pianist was playing rather strident music in one of the staterooms, which carried up onto the deck. Several attractive-looking couples strolled by, going to and coming from the stateroom from which the music was emanating.

Only half-awake, Josh thought he recognized one of them before exhaustion got the better of him and he dozed off again.

The steady repetition of the steam engine's piston and the chunking of the paddle wheel lulled the party irresistibly into dreamland. When they finally arrived in Vicksburg, they were all well rested.

CHAPTER 33

FEINBERG'S GENERAL STORE

The group got off the boat and headed into town. Nate and Joan stayed in the town square, while Josh and Emily made the rounds of the stores. They came to pick up food and supplies, and planned to bring them down to the dock for loading on the next boat downriver.

Seth Feinberg's General Store in Vicksburg occupied the corner lot in a row of two-story buildings uphill from the port. A sign above a covered porch advertised *Staple Goods and Groceries.* Inside—sauerkraut, molasses, and vinegar were stored in large barrels on the floor near the entrance. Several aprons hung from a shelf. Large bags of flour were stacked up next to them. The smell of sauerkraut and pickles permeated the air in this part of the store. The fanciest clothing and fabrics were located on the upper floor of the emporium. That area was usually tended by Mrs. Feinberg.

Open wooden shelves that went up to the ceiling displayed an array of salt, sugar, canned goods, cigarettes, tobacco, soap, and a display of candies in glass jars. A lower shelf was filled with stacks of fabrics, shoes, and boots.

As there was no one in the store, Josh and Emily strolled past a cutting table with knives and a large cash box, and headed towards the back of the store where they heard voices. They had come here on the recommendation of Eliza Davis, having sent their order in the previous week. On the way across the room, they both sniffed the pleasant aromatic smells of soaps and nearby spice bins.

In a back room of the store John Wilms was sitting with Seth Feinberg at a small wooden farm table in avid discussion. One would have thought that Wilms might have come for a story for the newspaper, but after listening to them, they sounded more like conspirators for the Underground Railway. Feinberg, they saw, was an older German man—short and slightly stooped over, almost bald, with thinning grayish hair, wearing wire-rimmed glasses.

The first strains of conversation they heard interested Josh and Emily greatly. They pretended to look at items near the back room and continued to stay in place to eavesdrop. They were able to witness virtually the entire conversation between the two men.

"What do you think about this bad situation between the North and the South? What do you think is going on here?" asked Wilms.

"Two economic systems are what we have here, competing against each other, they are doing. Capitalism it is, or free labor, for the North—versus slavery, or a kind of feudalism, for the South."

Feinberg spoke with a heavy German accent, but he appeared to be confident in what he was saying.

"How did we get to the terrible situation we have now?" asked Wilms.

"Before the Mexican War," Feinberg continued, "to northern people it seemed slavery was dying out. Slavery, most people thought, would eventually be replaced by capitalism and free labor. Other ideas the South had entirely on this subject."

"What about all the territory President Polk captured?" asked Wilms.

Both Josh and Emily cupped their ears to hear the conversation going on between the two men. At one point, Emily made a noise, and Josh put his fingers to his lips in a sign for her to keep quiet as Feinberg continued.

"Huge territories we did capture in the Mexican War. The size of the United States was doubled. To make much of its slave states, the slavocracy decided. They were in control of the White House at that time. For the first time, direct competition between free labor of the North and slave labor of the South."

"What about the recent panic in 1857? It seems things have gotten worse since then," Wilms added.

"People up north have become for the first time scared. In an economic sense, it looks like the South is besting the North for the first time and calling attention to their independent success."

"You mean the workers thrown out of work by hard times up north?" Wilms asked him.

"Right," said Feinberg. "Workers thrown out of work at the same time the South's slave labor economy is sailing along with bumper crops of cotton and a huge flow of money into the coffers of the South. This to the northerners is very frightening. We revolutionaries have always been taught to look at the economic causes that underlie all conflicts. Then, as part of the Dred Scott Decision it appears the compromise of 1820 is unconstitutional, so slavery can go anywhere up north now. This terrifies the factory owners and workers up there."

"But how do the black slaves fit into this picture?" said Wilms. "Many people, not just abolitionists, are ready to fight just over the slavery issue and see no connection to the big picture of warring economic systems."

"These two issues are inseparable. Up north, some people are fighting for their economic system—and some for abolition are fighting—and thirdly, some are fighting for both. Right now, the three groups are fighting together against the South and slavery. But that may change at some point in the future."

"Could these groups turn on each other at some point in the future?" Wilms queried.

"Of course, they could. Those are the dialectics of history and its revolutions."

"That brings up another question," Wilms said. "How do we instill in the slaves a revolutionary consciousness when many can't even read.?"

"You know, John—I, a revolutionary was;" said Feinberg in his thick German accent, "the most oppressed people have the highest revolutionary consciousness. All revolutionaries knew that in Europe."

"Shouldn't the blacks, according to that theory, have the highest revolutionary consciousness?"

"Yes," Seth added, "when you are talking about revolutionary consciousness. Education and schooling, you don't talk about. You don't to the university need to go. To make a revolution you need to have several requirements met. One is a revolutionary consciousness on the part of the oppressed masses. Number two is a will to power on the part of these masses—and number three, the collapse of the old order. This is how a revolution you start."

John then added, "This is very interesting. I can see how this could work. It makes good common sense. But why didn't the revolution succeed in Germany and France in 1848, with these principles?"

Emily nodded to Josh and he motioned back to her to keep listening in silence.

"Because enough revolutionary consciousness we did not have. There was not enough will to power on the part of the masses, and finally, the old order did not collapse completely. It confounded us by changing its character.

"But this I tell you with complete confidence—succeed, these revolutions will! Nothing is more certain. It is the dialectic movement of history. It has to happen. History says that oppression is doomed and slavery is doomed. It may take fifty years or more, but the slaves may be running this country.

"People who try to hold on to slavery are on the wrong side of history. History moves from misery and oppression, to resolution of grievances. We in the dialectics of history, must believe."

Josh thought he saw a puzzled look on Wilms's face when the reporter asked Seth, "Does that mean that things are always going to get better in life?"

"Well yes, over the long term if you measure things in hundred-year increments," Seth replied. "Things improve, but in the short run they may worse get. But history is always moving to a redress of the bad conditions. The interplay of two ideas or forces creates a third idea or force, which is a combination of the original two. It is an improvement, also, on the original two. It is just like a husband and wife fighting, which gets resolved for the better most of the time."

"You really have an optimistic world view. It is a real pleasure to hear this, Seth, compared to the misery you hear from people in the street."

After about fifteen minutes of listening, Josh and Emily thought they had heard enough, and not wanting to be caught eavesdropping, they returned to the front of the store. They opened and closed the front door so that it made a loud bang, and Wilms and Feinberg promptly returned to the front of the store. "We the storeroom were just checking," Feinberg said to his customers.

The couple checked the order that was ready and waiting for them, paid the bill, and had everything sent to the steamboat dock. Then they met up with Nate and Joan, who had stayed closer to the port in search of foodstuffs and fresh produce.

They arranged for the transport of the rest of the provisions and left on the next boat going downriver.

Nat and Joan went off to the top deck of the boat to get some sun. Josh and Emily had quite a bit of discussion over what they heard in the store. "That Mr. Feinberg sure has a funny accent, and most of his sentences are backwards," Emily said.

"That's the way Germans and Jews talk," Josh added. "We had an instructor at West Point. He had been in the Prussian Army. He was a very good teacher, but he talked like that. By the way, I understood everything we heard in the backroom, did you?"

"About half of it," Emily replied. "I didn't understand all of what he was saying about revolution."

"He is still a revolutionary–he thinks and talks like one. I think he feels that the black slaves can be molded into a revolutionary class. I read some of these European revolutionary writings from 1848. I also regularly read the *New York Daily Tribune* because Charles Dana, the editor, was one of my heroes. Did you know that many revolutionaries used to write for the *New York Daily Tribune*? Some of them presented brilliant views on abolition. I was also interested in Robert Owen's work with the underclasses, so these revolutionaries interested me as well.

"Emily, didn't you find that discussion with Feinberg quite an eye-opener. I didn't think we had people like that around here. Maybe we can find a way to include him in our plans, since he has almost the same goals we have. We don't want to tell anyone what we want to do here, but this man knows how to make a revolution!"

"That reporter from the newspaper in Vicksburg also seems to have an awareness of the situation, doesn't he?" Emily added. "You know, a lot of people down here think the same way we do, but they just don't have any power to change things. Do you think we could involve him in our plans as well?"

"We will have to discuss this with the others, but it looks like he could be useful."

CHAPTER 34

INNOVATIVE IDEAS

During the whole ride downriver Josh's brain was running in overdrive, processing ideas on how to start a great revolution among the black slaves to cast off their oppressors. He was more eager to get started right away on Nate's cooking school for other slaves so he could start getting their consciousness raised to the point where they would be able to shut down Mississippi's economic system and end slavery there.

Normally, on riverboat runs Josh would sit on the upper deck and pay careful attention to the bends in the river as well as the currents and crosscurrents, as the pilots had shown him. This time his brain would not shut down. Strongly influenced by what he had heard from Feinberg, all he could think about was how to make the blacks into a revolutionary class.

That night he dreamed strange dreams, and at dawn he had a nightmare where he was leading thousands of blacks in a revolution against the cotton growers. At one point in the dream he was making a speech in which he said something wrong, and thousands of blacks with sticks and knives beat and hacked him to death. He woke up Emily, crying out, "Whoever makes a revolution, has it turn on them. What about Danton and Robespierre? They were guillotined."

Talking to Emily calmed him down. "What about George

Washington or Simon de Bolivar?" she asked him. "They never died from attacks from their own revolutionaries."

After breakfast the next morning, Josh asked Nate, "When will your cooking school begin?"

"We are all set for next Saturday."

"What is the plan, Nate?" Josh asked.

"I'm going to bring out a book on cookery and teach the slaves to read the recipes. In the process I will teach them to read," Nate said. "We will have to tell the masters that, in order to make great cooks out of their servants, we are going to have to teach them to read some simple recipes."

"This is Mississippi, not Virginia," said Josh. "Remember that Nat Turner was taught to read before he led a revolt that killed scores of whites. Thanks to the revolt, it became illegal to teach black slaves to read in many states like Virginia, where the revolt happened, but not in Mississippi."

"Do you think we have to worry about this," Nate asked?

"This law is not strictly enforced even in other states because slaves have to manage some of their masters' affairs. They are the only ones to do it in some places. In these cases, they need to understand writing. Hopefully, no one will make too big an issue out of it."

Nate continued to spell out the plan. "First, we teach them to read—then make available revolutionary material for them."

"I would love for many of these slaves to be able to read the *New York Daily Tribune*," Josh added. "We could even start by reading it to them. If we plan on starting real slow, nobody will realize what's going to happen. Eventually, we will create a revolutionary class of slaves who will be ready to take power from the slave owners. If we use a very gentle approach, appearing to support slavery and its institutions, nobody will be able to tell what is happening until it's too late."

Nate added, "That sounds like a good solid plan."

While Emily and Josh and Joan and Nate were in New

Orleans, Wilma and Jackson stayed nestled in the comfort of the Hurricane Garden Cottage at the plantation, doing their chores.

They were close and intimate friends now, and while the rest of the group was away, they spent their days and evenings together as a couple.

Early one sunny morning, a sweaty Jackson entered the kitchen at breakfast time after doing some blacksmithing work and found Wilma bent over the black iron stove stirring some hot porridge for them. Wilma was in the kitchen cooking them breakfast because Nate was away.

Jackson came in and looked at Wilma, his dark eyes intent. "I've been outside doing some thinking," he said. "Nate's cooking school is a great way to get started. I feel a bit envious though. I wish I could do something like that, or something else to help."

"Oh, but you can," said Wilma earnestly, putting both hands on his shoulders and looking him directly in the eye. "Jackson Greene, you know the Bible better than most preachers. You could do bible studies and teach the slaves to read scripture."

"You're right. I could explain to them how awful my second master was," Jackson said, wrinkling his nose, "and encourage them to read the scriptures in order to move ahead with their freedom."

"And you could teach them blacksmithing too—and other things," said Wilma, rubbing her hands on her apron.

"You're right. That's just what I need to do." Jackson said determinedly. "The Bible is a revolutionary document if you interpret it properly. I can use the strike by the Jews when they were slaves in Egypt, and Exodus as a model for the revolution."

"Maybe you can convince the ministers that you want to teach the slaves to read the Bible. It will surely make better Christians out of them," Wilma added, encouraging him on.

"I'm feeling fired up now. That's a great idea. I'll bring it up when the others get back."

The next morning after the four returned from New Orleans, Jackson, looking flush with energy, began a discussion at breakfast. "I would like to work on another project of raising the awareness of the slaves in the area as a supplement to the work that Nate is doing with the cooking. I am well-versed in the Bible, and I believe that I can present it to the slaves in our area as a revolutionary document to help with the other work we are doing. I am also thinking that we could enlist the Anglican ministers in setting up a program to teach the slaves to read in order to better understand the Bible. Little will they realize that we are going to use reading to teach revolution."

"Hold it a moment!" said Nate raising his hand in a stop sign. "This is a lot of stuff to do in a short period of time. I'm just getting going with my cooking classes. If we do too many things too quickly, we could squander our resources and energy. I think we should succeed at one thing before we move on to the next. We don't want to stick out too much in the community too quickly. However, I like the idea, it is a very good one."

"So do I," said Josh.

This was seconded by Joan and Wilma.

"Maybe Josh could explore the idea with the ministers, or discuss the idea with Joe Davis," said Emily. "If we can get him to support the idea. I'm sure it will work."

"I think this should be our second line of attack," said Josh.

* * *

Dee Ann and Marie, in keeping with their previous history of friendship, began to warm up to each other again. They both missed each other terribly since they were best friends and neither of them had very many other friends. This was partially due to plantation life, which did not put them in a very active social milieu much of the time.

They both had a few friends and some extended family in the Vicksburg region, but neither could get away that often to see them or talk over problems. Both women were widows. Marie's husband had died from consumption a few months before Dee Ann lost her husband in the great hurricane which had hit the area five years before.

The similarity of their joint losses had provided the glue that cemented their friendship ever since. Marie had been much closer to her husband and had been married a longer time. Dee Ann dropped by Marie's house to return a plant of Marie's that she had taken care of while Marie was gone.

"I'm planning to go to Atlanta for a couple of weeks to visit my cousin," Dee Ann said, "so I thought I would bring this back." The conversation quickly modulated into other subjects, and they were soon talking about both eligible men and men who were taken.

"I really like that newspaperman John Wilms, but I heard he was keeping company with the telegraph operator's daughter. I think he likes me a lot too. You know, he kissed me–and what a kiss! Another beau I like a lot is that new planter Josh from up north."

"Y'all be careful, Dee Ann. He's happily married!"

"He can't be too happily married. I caught him sneaking a peek at me."

Rather than criticize Dee Ann for her improper or somewhat distorted thinking, Marie chose to continue the conversation, considering she had just gone through a major fallout with Dee Ann, by criticizing her moral code.

So, she bit her tongue and asked her a question. "What are y'all planning on doing to meet these two men?"

Dee Ann gave a gentle sigh with a big dimpled smile that showed her beautiful white teeth. "Well, I'll tell you. For John, I plan to visit the newspaper office the next time I go to Vicksburg, which should be very soon. And for Mr. Josh, I understand he is having his servant-chef give cooking lessons to some of the cooks in the area."

Again, she smiled that dimpled smile. "Well, I haven't worked it all out, but if he is going to be there, I'm going to find a way to show up there as well. I understand it's to be this coming Saturday."

"Well, good luck and happy hunting. I'd tell y'all to be careful with these men, but you're not going to listen to me anyway about this sorta thing. So maybe next time we meet, y'all will have caught a man. I do hope this works out for you. I don't agree with everything you are doing, but ah can't change you, so good luck with your plans."

CHAPTER 35

A CULINARY REVOLUTION

Saturday had finally come, and Josh and Emily were home as some of the cooks from nearby plantations began arriving. There were a few masters along to check on what their servants were going to be learning. Dee Ann came with her friends, Tom and Nellie Selby, who brought their cook. Almost all of the cooks were women, but two men came in the first of what was to be successive groups of prospective chefs.

The first group was therefore comprised of ten women and two men. Nate began the lessons by introducing himself. He tried speaking the language the black slaves used to get his point across, but occasionally his vocabulary was not understood.

Nate told the group that his former master was a well-known chef who taught him everything he knew about cooking. His master, Nate said, always preferred to work in the kitchen, even though he had servants to do this work for him, as he loved cooking. When his master could no longer stand in the kitchen due to health problems, he had Nate do all the cooking for the household. He always critiqued Nate's meals so that Nate was constantly improving.

Nate did not tell them the rest of the story, the part that

dealt with his owner eventually dying, and how he was sold to a new master who did not appreciate his skills. He did not share the anger and misery at his new position which led him to escape.

Nate advised the group that they would start very simply to get them to cook better basic meals, before giving them the "crown jewels" of his knowledge.

He began by giving them a short lecture, trying to use the simple slave talk that most slaves understood.

"Don't worry if y'all don't understand everything the first time. One of da principles of cooking is simplicity. Y'all should done try to make your meals simple. What I means here is don't fix them too fancy—adding too many ingredients, gussying them up too much, or adding spices until y'all get a good feelin' of how to use da spices. If y'all are makin' fresh fish, don't add sauces to it dat hide the fresh flavor of the fish, because dis messes wid da taste of fresh fish.

"Fresh fish don need nottin'. Nottin' you can add to it will improve its taste over its natural one. Undercooking a meal makes it unappetizing and makes some folks sick so that many cooks *overcook* da meal. Dis is no good either, as it dries out da meal and does not give the experience of a well-cooked meal.

"Fish is better cooked on da rarer side to a cooler temperature den steak, chicken, or pork. Most fish is not made properly—so dat many people hate fish, and never develop a good taste for fresh fish."

At this point Nate scanned the audience to see if they were paying attention to his lecture. They all seemed very attentive to this strange black slave who did not talk like them. He noticed that several of the cooks were stretching their necks to listen carefully to him since his manner of speech was different.

After taking a quick peek at his audience, the thought crossed Nate's mind that becoming a good cook could have great value to these slaves, as it could curry favor with the master's house. It had worked well for Nate with his first master.

Nate continued with his lecture. "No one wants to make da master or his family sick. Y'all should pay attention to what you put together in da meal. Da ingredients dat don't fit together can create bad aftertastes in da person's mouth, or indigestion afterwards.

"Y'all try to arrange your plates in an artistic way—da way a painter arranges his painting. A plate that is well-arranged in an art-like way actually tastes better, according to most chefs.

"Next time I will show you how it's done. Salads should be put on ahce before serving. You gotta wash da salad ingredients well, but make sure dare is no water or grit left in the salad when you all are finished. All da salads you make must be carefully drained of water and thoroughly dried. A wet salad is the sign of a poor chef.

"To enjoy food y'all need three senses—smell, sight, and taste." Nate motioned to his nose, his eyes, and his mouth. "But to cook good food you need a fourth sense, which is a good developed sense of touch." He the pointed to his fingers. "You need to feel your way among fruits, meats, doughs, and batters. To make a good pie crust you has got to handle the dough real gentle like.

"A good chef can tell whether a steak or chop is gonna be medium, rare, or well done by feeling the meat. If it springs back quickly, its rare. If it don't spring back, it's medium, or well done. Y'all can tell ifn a young chicken is tender by feeling da breastbone."

"Wayl brother, dats not all you can tell by feeling the breastbone!" said Will, one of the cooks, causing an outburst of laughter.

Nate continued, "Ifn it's soft and you can pull it, y'all has got a young tender broiler. After the broiler has been cooked, y'all can tell if its ready to eat by pullin' on the drumstick. Ifn it comes off easily from da second joint, da bird can be served.

"Hey, I'm not expectin' you to remember all dis da first time. We all are goin' over and over dis many times till y'all get it in your heads. I'm gonna teach you how to cut and chop with knives and how to keep knives sharp. I'm gonna cook along wid you to show you some tings. Some of you will learn some tings faster than others, but others who are slower on some tings will learn different tings faster. It doesn't matter, 'cause y'all are gonna learn a lot. When I gets done with you, your gonna cook meals as good as da finest restaurant.

"Today we is going to learn the rahte way to chop with a knife. But first—does any of y'all have any questions?"

"I'm Jake from Maser Seeley's plantation. Hey boss, you doesn't talks like we talks. I knows you was raised like a servant like us'n, but is you still a servant, 'causen you don't talk like no servant!"

"Well, Jake," Nate went on, trying to sound as illiterate as possible, "I done was raised by a master who grew up in New York. He had a different way of talkin', and he taught that to me along with cookin'. I'm still a servant, but I talks different like 'causen I was raised different."

"Whale, boss," Jake said, "I understands most of what you said but not every word 'causen you talk different."

"To this Nate added to the group, "Did y'all understand me?"

To which one of the women in the group said, "Boss, we done got most of what you says but not maybe all." The rest nodded their heads in agreement.

"Y'all stop me if y'all don't understand someting! It's very important. I'll go over anything you want many times. You may hear dis many times, but dona you worry. Y'all gonna get it."

One of the planters, Joe Jakes, walked into the room and asked Nate, "How did you learn all that cooking knowledge? How do you know just what to do in all these situations?"

"Ma master done taught me everyting he know about cooking before he done died. I doesn't know why I can do dis. I jest can!" Nate answered.

Thinking this was a good time to separate the servants from the few masters who had come with them, Josh and Emily invited the masters who came to have refreshments with them and discuss the cooking enterprise. This left Nate alone with the servants.

As they drank coffee, the masters gave Josh and Emily feedback at what they had seen. "Ah gotta say, your man Nate sure knows his cooking. He'all sounds like a walking cookery book," Joe Jakes said.

Dee Ann, hanging out of one of her most provocative red dresses, added, "I sure learned a lot about cooking from your servant Nate." Then she sighed and leaned over, making sure Josh got a good view of her more than ample cleavage. "It made me want to be a cook myself, even though I never did it much before."

Josh fought his urge to stare at the breasts hanging out in front of him. By then, Emily was registering a look of disapproval at Dee Ann's forward behavior.

The planters who came made future plans with Josh and Emily to return twice a week for two hours at a time. Emily and Josh planned to socialize with them as the cooks worked with Nate.

After Nate worked with the cooks for the two hours to complete the first lesson, the planters left with their entourage. After all the guests had left, Josh and Nate were in a very upbeat mood.

"Well, we have finally started the first phase of the plan."

Everyone in the house was in a mood to celebrate, except for Emily. "What's wrong, Emily?" Josh asked, "You don't look very happy."

"It's that woman Dee Ann. I don't like her. I don't trust her. She doesn't act like you are married!"

"Remember, she is the niece of Joe and Jefferson, we don't want any problems with that family," Josh said. "We have to think about our plan. We can't afford any conflict with her. We will just have to eat crow for the time being."

Emily, however, would be the one who was really going to eat crow. Josh, although he wouldn't admit it, enjoyed having a beautiful, sexy woman pay him a lot of attention, even though it injected a feeling of tension into their plans. Emily appeared willing to accept this reality, although she did not appear that happy with it.

So, Josh sought to change the subject, called Nate over, and said "I noticed that you gave Joe Jakes a very superficial explanation in illiterate dialogue of how you learned to be such a great chef. It is something we wondered about."

Nate perked up and went on "I'm not going to cast my pearls before swine, but since you are asking, I'll tell you. Please bear in mind that I was just giving a lecture to these cooks from the plantations. I feel I've got an awful lot to say on this subject. The way I can present it best is almost in the form of a lecture, so forgive me for my pontification. As you are learning to cook with spices and other ingredients, you use them over and over again. You are also constantly tasting meat and fish as well as all dishes that you make. After a while these ingredients and spices become ingrained in your mind, and you can picture how they are going to taste before you even make the meal. I can actually taste the way it's going to taste and smell before I even make it. And if it doesn't come out quite the way I want, I can figure out ways to adjust it so it will come close to what I want."

Josh shook his head to indicate that he could never do anything like that, since he hadn't the skill or experience to differentiate between spices.

Nate continued, "These skills were learned over my whole

young life, and they are firmly ingrained in my head. I don't need a book to tell me what to do. I can improvise most recipes."

Josh then asked, "Why are some chefs so much better than others, and often with less experience?"

Nate explained further, "I can best illustrate this by using the analogy with music and musicians. People learn scales and intervals until they get these notes into their heads, and they can reproduce them with instruments when called upon to do so. All works are made up of these different scales. For the purpose of my explanation, these scales are equivalent to spices and ingredients in cooking. Some musicians are more skilled than others. For instance, you have a rare number of musicians with perfect pitch where a C is always a C in their head."

"I am very familiar with perfect pitch because my sister had it, and she was a wonderful musician," Josh replied, "who was always correcting us as being slightly off key."

"Certain chefs have this facility," Nate went on, "that is either learned or a gift, and they can hold all these ingredients and spices in their head—and when new ones are introduced, they are quickly added to the repertoire. This seems to me to be close to perfect pitch. When they are planning a meal they can taste, visualize, and smell the ingredients in their head."

"These skills are not unique to cooking. The men who make perfume in Paris also memorize different smells and can combine them to create powerful effects. Some of these men have noses as developed as a dog. Anyway, that's the best explanation for what I have learned."

"That's fine for you," Josh said, "but I can't even imagine holding these things in my head. Emily and I are happy if we follow a cookery book and it comes out close to what it is supposed to."

Josh, realizing that there was more to learn from Nate, quickly sat down on a chair and motioned Nate to do the same.

"Nate, your explanation makes my eyes spin 'round in my

head! I had no idea cooking had such depth. It is really an art form of the highest level. When I looked at the hash houses and little restaurants in Lowell, Massachusetts, I thought of a crude toothless cook wearing an undershirt in a hot kitchen and slaving away, dripping with sweat. His clothes were covered with food and grease, and every word coming out of his mouth was an epithet or an angry oath.

"When the food was finally delivered to you, it was sometimes not even edible! The cooks are always fighting with each other and with the waiters and waitresses. Sometimes, in extreme fits of anger they stab each other as well."

Josh wrinkled his brow with a look of distaste and continued, "You know, I can feel a wave of nausea when I think about one particular restaurant in which one meal was enough! Your explanation of cookery puts it in the realm of the sublime. What a contrast."

Nate then added, "You know, that stuff about restaurants is true in many cases. Many people who are unhappy with their jobs working in a factory from sunup to sundown crave opening their own restaurant or tavern. But it can be a terrible trap!

"Meals have to be delivered at breakfast, lunch, and dinner, when everyone comes in to eat. Most people come in at the same time, so the cooks are under timely pressure to deliver all their meals at this same point. The chef has to manage his inventory of food so that he has enough for a menu. If he doesn't keep track of the inventory, the food can spoil and make the customers sick. Sick customers are the kiss of death for a restaurant. When the food is made, it has to be delivered hot to the customers."

"Yeah," Josh mumbled in agreement, "I hate cold food."

"Cold food," Nate went on, "is unappetizing to customers, and it will often be returned to the kitchen, making more work for the cooks. If the cook sees that the waiter did not pick up the food quickly, he has an ax to grind with him because he destroyed his creation and made him do double the work. Meats and fish have to be kept on ice continually, or they will certainly spoil. Waiters talking to each other and not paying attention to the timeliness of the food are targets for angry cooks. Irritable customers returning perfectly good food to the kitchen are another source of stress for the kitchen."

Josh added, "I sure saw that type of thing in the restaurant I was just talking about."

Nate continued, "If the chef or cook thinks the waiter did not handle the situation well, he may vent anger at the waiter. In this high-pressure atmosphere, if the cook thinks the customer is unreasonable in returning the food, he may take it out on the customer's hide by spitting in his soup or gravy, or rubbing the steak in his crotch or ass. The customer is totally unaware of this process, but most cooks and chefs have watched this happen in the heat and pressure of delivering a meal. If you eat in a restaurant, *never* return food to a kitchen. If it is not to your liking, just take it on the chin and eat it, or don't eat it."

Josh appeared to be strongly affected by the discussion.

Nate went on, "Waitstaff can also have a bone to pick with chefs and cooks that they perceive to be hostile and abusive. They will gossip behind their back and try to get them into trouble with the owner or manager. If the stove does not work right and does not heat properly, the whole kitchen can go into a panic—and this can happen with kitchen fires as well.

"The butchers, fishmongers, and produce suppliers who supply the restaurant with food are mostly crooked. They will try to cheat you if they think you don't know what you are buying or not too skilled at cooking. If the chef is not the owner of the tavern, they will try to pay you off with graft and then sell you lower cuts of meat and cheaper fish or produce that is not fresh. Once you accept graft, the restaurant is finished as a quality place to eat! All and all, cooking and managing a restaurant or tavern can be the most stressful profession that anyone could want go into."

"I've certainly learned a lot about cooking," Josh said, then he sat up in his chair and ended the discussion with, "I'm not going to send food back in a restaurant ever again!"

CHAPTER 36

DAT SLAVE CATCHER!

As Nate's reputation as a fine chef spread around the region, many people were talking about his magnificent banquet meal at the dinner party. They mentioned it in church and other places. Unfortunately, all this publicity had some negative consequences for the group.

One rainy fall day while Josh was out working in the fields with his overseer and Emily was away for the day in Vicksburg shopping at Feinberg's store, Jackson and Wilma were loaned out for the day to Eliza to help her with some chores around her house.

There was a knock at the front door. Nate opened the door, and a large, powerful, rough-looking, white man stood there with water dripping off his hat. He was carrying what looked like a medical bag in his left hand.

"I'm alookin' for Nate the chef," he said.

"I is Nate de chef, boss, what does you want me for?"

"I hear tell, you is the best cook around these parts. Why, everyone is talking about your cookin'."

"I sure lahks to hear talk like dat boss," Nate replied. "Does you want me to make you something?"

"Not jest yet. Ah wants to talk to you first. Can I come in?"

"Why sure, boss—but da masser, he out in the fields workin' on da planting."

Joan was in the next room folding linen, but she decided to eavesdrop on the conversation because this white man was new to the area, and she had never seen him before.

"Where did you learn to cook like that?" he asked Nate.

"Ma old master done taught me to cook before he done died. He done waz a famous chef."

"The reason ahm askin' you these questions, is thayt a nigger named Cassius, who was also a great chef, escaped from his master in Virginia. Everybody thought he skedaddled for up north—the trail led north, but no one ever found him. He had the same kind of reputation as you, and there's a powerful big price on his head. See that scar on your arm? Cassius had the same scar. Based on the description, height, and weight—I have to assume you're the same person." He drew a pistol and pointed it at Nate.

"I is not, boss, you done got the wrong man," Nate said, looking very tense.

"Well, we'll see about thayt. Is anyone else home?"

Deres another servant in dat room, boss, and another servant doin' carpenter work on a table. I tink he went outside to get some nails."

At that point Joan walked into the room, carrying some folded wash.

"You sure are a pretty one, I'd like to get with you. Come over here, ah wants you to put these handcuffs on Cassius. Ahl show you how to do it. Ah wants them rail tight." He took a pair of handcuffs out of his black bag, and held them for Joan to use.

As Joan walked into the room, Nate noticed a strange look on her face, a look he had never seen before as she walked past. Nate heard a distinct metallic click from the pile of wash she was carrying. As the slave hunter held up the handcuffs to demonstrate how to put them on Nate, Joan walked over to him, still carrying the wash.

The huge white man put his arm carrying the handcuffs around her waist and pulled her toward him hard. As she was pulled into him, he stared at her with greedy eyes, like a tiger looking over his prey. Then Joan let the wash drop, revealing a large Italian stiletto, fully open. Before the slave hunter could realize what had happened, Joan used the momentum of being pulled into him, combined with the power of upward thrusts, to stab him through the heart two times.

Before he realized what had happened, he went into a dying mode. He staggered around for about a half a minute, dropped his gun and handcuffs, and collapsed on the floor, never to rise again. There was not much blood outside the victim, since Joan had used a stiletto, which made narrow self-sealing entrance wounds, remarkably clear of external blood As Nate rushed to her and profusely thanked her, she cleaned up her knife, folded it, and put it away.

"Boy, I thought I was a goner. Those slave catchers take away black slaves and send them back to masters whether they are free or not. I saw this whole thing happening to me."

At that point Joan began to show a reaction to what she had just done. Her whole body began to shake, and she appeared in a daze.

Nate put his arm around her and tried to console her. "You saved my life. That was an evil man. If the Lord was watching, which he always is, he would have approved of what you did. He would have ended my life for me, and Josh and Emily might have been charged and gone to prison under the Fugitive Slave Law. It would also be the end of our plan. Let's drag his body into that closet until Josh gets back. Then we'll figure out what to do."

Josh returned later from a hard day's work alongside his slaves. He was exhausted by the hard work of plowing a new field, but he was in for a big surprise that he did not enjoy at all. The first inkling he got that something had gone wrong was when the carpenter, Elijah, came running to him.

"Boss, you all shoulda seen what done happen this afternoon while you was gone. "I was in de side room workin' on da table when Nate let dis man in who turn out to be a slave catcher. He try to put de handcuffs on Nate—says he is an escaped slave. Nate say no, you is got da wrong man, but he wants to take him nohow! Boss, I is in da next room, and I listens carefully. Den he wants Joan to help him put da cuffs on Nate. Den, when he grabs her she done knifes him a few times wid a long pointy knife, boss!

"Dat slave catcher was up to no good, but he is done dead, boss, last ah sees, he was lying on da floor dead as a chicken. What we gonna do, boss? Dat man was no good. Ah wants to help Nate too, but ahs too scared—dat man done had a gun. Dose slave catchers are powerful mean men. One done took my brother away, and he never did come back. Dat happened when I was young and worked for a different master."

Josh responded, "Don't you worry about this, Elijah. I'll figure out what happened and take care of it."

He accompanied Elijah back to where he was working and told him to continue working there, and then he quickly walked to the gathering room, where Nate and Joan found him. They began to tell him the story of what had transpired. When he walked over to the closet where they had put the body, he felt a lump in his throat, and his knees felt as though they were going to give way.

He opened the door quickly and gazed on the body of what appeared to be a large, powerful man lying on the floor. He wondered how this woman Joan could possibly kill this giant of a man with a knife—a man who had a gun in his hand. Josh then closed the door and listened carefully to their description of the murder versus Elijah's and found that they both added up to pretty much the same event.

Then he put his finger in front of his mouth, signaling the need to whisper, and added, "We have a few problems, though. First, we've got to get rid of the body. These slave catchers often work in groups of two, so we may get another visitor at any time. I've got some ideas about that, but I'll tell you about it a little later."

Josh noted that Joan was still in a state of shock over what she had done and did not participate in the discussion, so he went over to her, put his arm around her shoulder and said, "You did a great job in saving us from certain disaster. We all owe our lives to you. All our plans would have been destroyed. You know we could have all been charged with many different crimes!"

Nate hugged her also and said, "I can't thank you enough for saving my life. We are so grateful you were there. I saw myself returning to being a slave again, but then you saved me."

Joan repeated in a monotone voice, "Yes, I saved you," and then became quiet again.

Josh said, "Let's have a meeting tonight with the six of us to discuss what to do." Joan and Nate both agreed.

CHAPTER 37

GETTING RID OF THE CARGO

That evening, the group of six met in the kitchen to process the day's events and come up with a solution. Emily came over and gave Joan a big hug. "I'm glad we had such teamwork," she told her. "This was the bravest thing we've ever seen." All of this discussion seemed to soothe Joan, and she began to function more normally. All six members of the group participated actively, including Joan, who—on realizing that they all stood together on the crime—began to get over her shock.

Wilma added, "Thank heaven you were there, and not me. I don't know how I would have handled that situation." Jackson also gave her a hug and thanked her. All this support and affection went a long way in ameliorating Joan's trauma over what had happened.

Jackson then whispered, "If Elijah was in the next room and heard everything that happened, what are we going to do about him?"

"You can trust him," Nate said, "I've gotten to know him very well in the last few weeks. He is very much against slavery. You should hear the story he tells about his life before Joseph Davis bought him. He is not as confident as a man living up north who did not grow up in slavery. But I think that is normal for anyone growing up in slavery. You can't really get too confident, because everything is done for you, like a man in prison—except here, you grow up in prison instead of going to prison after you grow up."

Jackson nodded to Nate and shared his memory. "I also felt these same issues during different points of my life."

"Luckily," Nate continued, "I had a master who treated me like his son. He nurtured and taught me everything he knew. It was obvious to him that blacks and whites were equal. He did warn me about the world outside in the South, and that it would be unforgiving if I acted in a way that appeared too confident. If I had grown up with my second master who I escaped from, I would not have been very confident. I still have bad memories and nightmares of my life with him."

"I think, with a little help from us, Elijah could grow and become more confident," Jackson said.

"That may be all well and good, but will he crack under pressure?" Josh added. "All our plans depend on no one talking!"

Nate answered right back. "Do you think all the black slaves here tell their masters everything they are thinking or doing? As a former slave, I can tell you—they do not! There are whole parts of their lives their masters have never been told and will never be told. That Fugitive Slave Law that President Fillmore supported has affected everyone, not just people living in the North!"

"I will tell Elijah not to mention what he has seen to anyone. I don't need to mention this to him, as he knows this already. I think Elijah feels that our family is closer than master and slave," Nate continued.

"I still think he should be told not to mention this to anyone," Josh said to Nate.

Elijah returned to his slave quarters with an admonition from Nate not to mention to anyone what he had seen. This was quickly followed by an animated discussion about what to do about the situation regarding the murder.

"The first order of business is to get rid of the body," Josh began. "We all have been working to clear a new field for planting, so we have a big pile of brush which we have been getting ready to burn in a ditch. We were going to start burning tomorrow morning. I think we should head out tonight and bring the body over there in the wagon. There shouldn't be any one around, so we can place the body in the middle of brush, and that way no one will be able to recognize it or find it easily. When the fire is out, we will cover the ditch with dirt. That should help to hide any remnants of the body that are left."

Everyone thought this was a good idea. Josh then asked a question. "Can any of you think of any way this plan of disposal could go wrong or backfire? Think carefully, this is important!"

Jackson added, "Only if somebody sees us put the body there."

"That's not going to happen," Josh replied. "This is my land to use, and no one should be anywhere near there tonight."

With an anxious sigh, Joan added, "I think I'll feel better when the body is burned, buried, and out of sight."

It was agreed that Nate, Jackson, and Josh would take the body out after dark and put it in the middle of the dried brush for burning.

"I'll get up real early, pour some kerosene on the pile, and start it up," Josh said.

"Now, coming back to the big issue with the group, what do we do about Elijah? He knows too much. In the old spy days, they would say he's got to disappear!"

"You mean kill him?" Jackson added. "None of us could do that. We did not come down here to kill black slaves. None of us could live with ourselves if we did that! So, what do we do?"

There was a long silence, and Emily blurted out, "We could buy him and then set him free."

"That's a great idea," Nate said, and Joan and Wilma liked it as well.

Wilma added, "Could that really be done?"

"I hope I can do it," Josh said determinedly. "When Joseph rented Elijah out to me, he told me he was renting me several real good servants. He said if I like them, we could talk about purchasing them for our plantation. I'll talk to Joseph right away to see if this can be done. Are we all resolved on this?"

Everyone was unanimous in agreement, so they moved to the last problem. What if the slave catcher was not operating alone? What do we do if another slave catcher comes along looking for Nate?

"We have to be more vigilant," said Jackson.

"This is why I trained you with firearms," said Josh. "But remember how Joan killed the slave catcher. We have to practice stealthy, devious ways to protect ourselves. I think for the time being we will have to carry well-hidden weapons all the time, at least while we are on the plantation. I'm thinking of a small derringer and a stiletto like the one Joan used. Remember, if a slave is caught carrying a gun in public, it could be a capital offense unless he can prove his master gave it to him to hold. A stiletto is a better weapon to be carried concealed as many people don't think about it the way they do a gun."

With their business completed, the meeting broke up, and Jackson, Nate, and Josh carried the body out to the wagon and drove to the ditch filled with brush. It was a clear moonlit night, and it was easy to follow the ruts in the road out to the ditch, about a half a mile away.

Half the sky was clear, and most of the brighter stars were visible despite the bright moonlight. When they turned in the direction of the river, they noticed a fine mist covering most of it. They also noticed what appeared to be a lantern light on the bank of the river, but they could not tell whether it was on the riverbank or out in the water.

Josh spoke up, "Let's check out that light after we get rid of our cargo."

They carried the body on a waterproof sheet to the fire ditch, and with the help of a lantern, buried the body under a pile of dead brush so that it was completely invisible.

Nate said, "Make sure it's real deep because, when the fire starts, some of this brush will burn off the top, revealing things underneath!"

When their task was complete, they headed over to where they had seen the light earlier but could find no evidence of anyone on the land near the river.

"That light must have been out in the river—maybe on a raft, maybe someone fishing for night catfish," said Jackson.

"It might have been a reflection of the moon off a shiny object in the distance," Josh responded. "Anyway, it's too dark to find anyone out here."

Every member of the group had a difficult night, waking up several times to process the prior day's events. Joan had night terrors and woke up screaming at several times during the night. Emily also slept fitfully. The screaming added to the macabre atmosphere, and no one slept very well.

The weather that morning had changed dramatically from the night before. A warm front had come through during the night, and now the air was thick with fog. The air was dense and oppressive. All the low areas and hollows were under a blanket of fog, but the high ground and the much of the river was visible. The speed of the river created some air currents near the surface of the water which helped carry away the fog over the river.

Josh, Nate, and Jackson got up at dawn, brought a couple of gallons of kerosene to start the fire, and headed off to the pit. When they got there, they found the pit pretty much the way they left it, but at one end they found some big brush separated from the rest.

"Nate, do you remember seeing that brush over there?" Josh said.

"I don't," Nate said, "but it could have been there. It was pretty dark."

Due to the change of atmosphere, it was hard to make comparisons from the night before. They then poured the kerosene on and got the fire going. The fire burned for two hours, and when it was just a pile of glowing coals they began to fill in the pit.

The area where they put the body was covered by a huge amount of coals, and then they added a layer of rocks and boulders. The fire had covered the whole area, and they could not see any evidence of a body.

Nate added a final comment. "I don't think anyone could find this body easily—and if they could, they could never identify it."

CHAPTER 38

PURCHASING ELIJAH

After they completed their work, Josh went over to see Joseph Davis about purchasing Elijah. Joseph was at the plantation but was planning a trip to Washington, DC to discuss his feelings about the Kansas-Nebraska Act. Josh knocked on the front door and Eliza, who was about to go out, answered it.

"Why hello Mr. Josh, we haven't seen you all week."

"Hello, Eliza. I was trying to see if I could talk to Joseph about something important to me and the plantation."

"He is just finishing breakfast. Why don't you follow me in. This could be a good time to talk to him, you know. He's leaving for Washington next week."

Eliza led Josh in to see Joseph, who was busy reading the newspaper.

His spectacles were low on his nose, and he squinted over them to meet Josh's gaze. "Oh, hi Josh, good to see you! It's amazing how up-to-date our newspaper is. It's all due to the telegraph. We get news from all over the country instantly. For someone like me, who grew up with news coming by horseback, this is a giant change."

Joseph inquired about how Emily was doing and how the plantation was running.

"Everything is going real well. In fact, as it's going so well, I wanted to ask about purchasing Elijah." Joseph turned silent and appeared deep in thought, and Josh continued, "Remember when we discussed our plan for the business. You said that you would lend us some workers, and if it worked out, we could discuss purchasing them. Elijah is a great worker, and he gets on really well with my other servants. They like him a lot, he fits in like part of our family."

"I actually never thought about selling Elijah because I, too, am very fond of him. What you are saying is that it might be good for him to have other opportunities to develop his skills. I'll tell you what–we'll meet with Elijah, explain that you want to buy him, and see how he feels about it. If he likes the idea, we will go ahead with it.

"I know many plantation owners don't do things this way, but to me, my servants are like family, while they are also part of a team of workers. You also have to think of the consequences of selling someone off to another plantation, and how it affects your workforce. I don't take these issues lightly."

Since Joseph was free that morning, they walked over to where Elijah was working in the guesthouse where Josh was living. On the walk over, Josh felt weak on his feet as he strolled along the path with Joseph and went up the steps. He also felt a lump in his throat. The thought kept racing through his mind that, considering Elijah had just seen the murder–how was he going to act? Would he spill the beans? Suppose he doesn't want me to buy him. Will our plans go down the drain?

Joseph was in a good mood getting ready for his trip to Washington and did not notice Josh's tension over the prospective purchase. They both walked over to Elijah, and Joseph began. He looked Elijah straight in the eye and said, "Elijah, you have been working for me for many years as a servant. You know we like your work, but Mr. Josh here, who y'all have been working for, has asked to purchase you for his plantation. For most folks I would say you are not for sale. But Mr. Josh likes you, and likes your work, so I wanted to ask you what you think of working for him from now on and belonging to him?"

The way Joseph dealt with the sale of Elijah disturbed Josh. He began to see the possibility of all his carefully crafted plans unraveling.

"Boss, I is real happy workin' for you. I doesn't really want to leave, though I does lahk workin' for Mr. Josh. Mr. Josh is a good boss too–but I worries, if something done happens to Mr. Josh, what done happen to Elijah."

"If that's what's worrying you, we will write the contract to say that if you are not happy with how things are going with working with Mr. Josh, I will agree to buy you back. But remember, I am much older than Mr. Josh, and he is likely to live longer than me, so long-term you might be better working for him."

"Can you do dis, boss?"

"I can do anything I want in a contract," said Joseph.

"How can you tell ifn ah wants to come back to you?"

"After about a month, I'll come over and talk to you and ask you if you are happy. If you are still happy with Mr. Josh, I'll come back after six months and ask you again if you're happy. I will have the right of first refusal on the contract."

"What dat done mean boss?"

"It means if he wants to sell you, he has got to offer you to me first. You all know you can trust me to do right by you."

"Ah knows dat, boss, you hads always done good by Elijah. Boss–dis is okay by me. Ifn you do dis way, Elijah is willin'."

Josh went through the mill with these negotiations but was satisfied when all the smoke cleared. Joseph drew up a contract, and they both signed it in front of a witness, a Mr. O'Shaunessy, who was visiting the plantation at that time. Josh paid a nominal fee of one hundred dollars, which was considered a bargain for a first-class worker.

After Elijah went back to work, Joseph ended the negotiation by adding, "I could have asked a lot more for one of our top servants, but I'd like to help you and your wife succeed here with your plantation. We are getting older, and we want some fine people from the younger generation to live and work here. We want people whom we can trust for the future. Having a good home for Elijah is very important to both my wife and me."

After another sleepless night, Josh told his wife, "Well, Emily, I'm a slaveholder now. If my friends back in Massachusetts could see me now, what would they say? Events are happening faster than we can keep up with. I don't know what is going to happen next. Everything is not going so badly, except for our worry over the slave catchers coming after Nate. Maybe this guy worked alone so he would not have to share the reward with anyone else. I sure hope he worked alone, but we have to be careful. If this guy found Nate, others could also. We need to remain vigilant and remain armed in case of another visit."

A week later Josh received a visit from the local constable from Vicksburg. "Sorry to bother y'all, but I'm a lookin' for a man named Brett Toothaker, a real big fellow who waz huntin runaway slaves. Hiz wife sez he was headin' downriver and he paid a fare to the downriver wharfs, of which there be seven.

"The boat was having engine trouble the whole way down, so the crew did not look over the passengers the way they usually do. They was not sure where some of them got off. We'all are not sure if he was going to pick up another boat going downriver or not, but he sure is missing, and his wife sure is worried about him. The last place someone saw him was in Vicksburg. Have you seen a real big strong fellow hangin' out around here in the last week?"

"Sorry, constable, but I can't recall seeing anybody who looks like that. We don't get many visitors here, so we remember everyone who stops by. Do you know if he was traveling alone or with anyone else?"

"We'all believe he was traveling alone. We know he was alone in Vicksburg. Joe Davis said he didn't see him either. Mehbe he headed further downriver. You know, huntin' slaves is a dirty business. My cousin used to do it. It is real dangerous too. A slave who is runnin' is desperate. They'll do anything to escape, even kill you!"

"We've got to have slaves to keep our plantations running," said Josh, playing the role of a plantation owner.

The constable then drew close and looked Josh right in the eye and said, "I don't know what it's all for. You say the plantation needs slaves to keep running—yes suh, but think about this—a slave who's been up north for several years ain't no good for the plantation anymore. Maybe he can read now, but he knows how to escape 'cause he done did escape before. He knows where to go, how to go—and he knows who to see, who can help him. Ifn he helps the other slaves by telling them all this, then he helps more escape and wrecks the plantation."

Josh cut in at that point and said; "I heard that from other plantation owners too."

"It's a crazy business to take a runaway whose been up north back here," said the constable. "You might just kiss your plantation goodbye. The thing that makes catching slaves profitable is that you can get a lot of money in many different ways."

"Like how?" asked Josh

The constable looked up and rubbed his head while he collected his thoughts, and said, "Here's how—straight from the mouth of my cousin. The slave owner pays you for your time to watch, catch, or maybe kidnap the slaves. The slave could pay you even more to let them go and say you never saw them. Or you could take the slave's money and turn him over to his owner anyway and get paid double."

"But slaves don't have much money," said Josh.

"That's where you're wrong, young man. The slave who has been up north has lots of friends who want to help him—church groups, abolitionists, real rich men like the Tappans, benefactors, rich newspapermen. They all will pay thousands of dollars to free the slave, and some of that money goes to the slave catcher. My cousin made one hundred times more money than me until he got shot in the leg by a slave and had to give up the work. You know, he's still got a lot of money, even though he can't work anymore."

"What about that new Fugitive Slave Law? Does that help or hurt this business," asked Josh.

"Don't make no difference," said the constable. He looked down and spat on the ground and said, "My cousin said to stay away from the courts or legal stuff."

"But the slave can't testify on his own behalf. Most of the time he is going back to the plantation," Josh stated.

"That's true, but it takes time and money. Crowds of blacks mob the courts and try to abduct the escaped slave, and jailers who don't like slavery let them escape. No sir, you're better off kidnapping them. No one knows, and few will try to help them."

"I never realized what the profession of slave catcher was all about," said Josh.

"Well, I got to leave and go downriver to look for any sign of Mr. Toothacker," said the constable.

"Well, I sure hope you find Mr. Toothacker," Josh said.

When the constable left, Josh called everyone together to discuss the developments. "We may be okay for the time being. The slave hunter's name was Brett Toothacker, and his wife is looking for him. He bought a ticket from Vicksburg downriver, which means he could have gotten off here or at any of the docks the boat stopped at in this vicinity. It seems no one saw him get off here, and he may have been a solo hunter. So far, only his wife is looking for him, and he was only seen alone in Vicksburg. This situation looks better than I thought it would, but we still have to be vigilant."

At that point Nate said that he wished they could take Elijah into their confidence and plan. "I'm sure he would support us," he said.

"Not yet," Josh replied. "Why should we upset him with knowing about our plans? He was close to Joseph. This stuff would only upset him. This is not the right time, but maybe it will come in the not too distant future.

"Another thing I wanted to tell you all about is that Joe Davis's brother Jefferson, our senator from Mississippi, has come here for a visit. Joseph is due back tomorrow because a family visit is planned. Emily and I have been invited for dinner. I fought with Jefferson during the Mexican War. Jefferson is a very powerful man in the senate, and recently, he was the Secretary of War in the Pierce administration.

"I'm not sure he still remembers me from the war, but I remember him very well. It was by salvaging his mail that I learned a lot about his plantation system, and it gave me the idea to come down here to help destroy slavery."

CHAPTER 39

OUR COUNTRY DIVIDED

Two nights later, Josh and Emily came over to dinner with Joseph and Eliza, as well as Jefferson and Varina, his wife. Joseph introduced Josh and Emily to them both.

"I don't know if you remember me from Buena Vista," Josh said to Jefferson after the introduction.

"Of course, I remember." Jefferson's eyes lit up. "You saved my mail! That was the day before Santa Anna attacked us," Jefferson recalled. "You led a company of the Third Indiana, right?"

"Yes, you're right there. That was when I got hit in the shoulder—That ended my military service. It's just recently that I have been able to use my left arm well again. Working on the plantation has been good for healing up my injury," Josh told him.

"Well, you should know, I got shot in the foot at almost the same time. That's why I walk with a limp sometimes. It's much better now, but it still bothers me occasionally."

"I still remember that great chicken meal you cooked with Major Bragg the night before the big battle," Josh recalled "That was the best meal we had in Mexico! Major Bragg was one great artillery officer. His howitzers helped stop those Mexican charges."

"Are you men going to talk only about the war," Varina broke in. "What about us? We don't want to talk about the war!"

"I'll second that," Eliza added.

"I'll third that," Emily added. She added her voice only after the other woman had come in first as she was anxious to see Josh make a connection with Jefferson.

Jefferson then asked Josh how he liked life here, compared to New England.

"It's taken some time, but I've come to love this place. The work in the fields, the traffic on the river—you never know who you are going to meet. We live in a rural place, but the river is a great big highway that brings people together from both the North and the South. The smell of the river gets in your blood, and you can't forget about it."

Jefferson said, "We've lived part of our time in Washington, DC, and when we come down here we've always noticed some of the same things that you're noticing."

"When I first came down here," Josh continued, "I went back up north to get my affairs in order. I kept dreaming about the river. You know it has a powerful force that pulls you in—the smell of the river and the smell of the freshly plowed fields."

"That's just the way I feel about it," Jefferson sighed. Then he added, "You already know the downside of this place—and every place has its downside. The summer weather brings disease. You've got to get out of here July and August, and maybe the end of June. Don't make the same mistake I made. I lost my first wife to malaria in August. I still get recurrences from time to time. Quinine helps, but I've gotten used to the fact that I will occasionally get sick with it."

"Joseph and Eliza warned us about it a long time ago," Josh said. "I don't want to be here during the summer."

"Joseph told me you bought Elijah from him," Jefferson said. "You sure got a top-notch worker. He has got real ability. I think that if he was properly trained, he could run a plantation like my man, Sam Pemberton, who is my overseer."

"Not many planters would let a black slave run their plantation. I also have a black secretary who runs my business affairs. His name is Ben Montgomery. He does anything I ask of him. I taught him to read and write, and he has paid me back a thousand times for all I have taught him."

"That's an unusual arrangement," Josh added.

"We are unusual people here," Jefferson said.

"Joseph studied Robert Owen's industrial system in England and made it work here—and it has made him wealthy. I am trying to do the same thing, but I'm also interested in politics. It always helps to have a thriving business that can supply money if you need it. Senators and cabinet officials don't make very much money—unless they are crooked."

As the three men talked, Emily began to chat with Eliza and Varina. "Jefferson stands up for the South," Eliza began." He keeps the legislature honest in Washington. Thank God we have him, otherwise the North would overrun us. Do you know that he was named after Thomas Jefferson?"

At that point Varina stepped into the conversation and added, "He has brought out a point that most people don't realize—and that is, our slaves on our property are better treated than workers in factories and mills up north."

In the interest of forming a relationship, Josh agreed with Varina. "My family used Robert Owen's methods, the same as Joseph, and our workers were also treated well. I agree that most of the mills and factories up north do not treat their workers well."

"We have an exceptionally close relationship with our slaves," Varina continued. "I would say that, for us, it's similar to a dog owner who takes special care of his pet. He takes great pains to make sure nothing happens to him. If the dog gets sick, the owner gets very upset, just like it was his own family."

"Usually he develops feelings of love for the dog. If it runs away or dies, the owner is inconsolable. Do mill owners treat their employees with that kind of care?"

"On our plantation," Josh said, "we have found an even more powerful bond can develop between master and servant. I've seen this happen many times with our servants."

"On other plantations," Varina went on, "when a servant runs away, the master begins to wonder where he went wrong, and this can set off a bout of melancholia."

At that point Jefferson, seeing his wife starting to explain his philosophical rationale for slavery, broke into the conversation and continued the discussion. "I think we have all discovered that slaves are much closer to their masters in a plantation such as ours, than are typical workers to the owner in a northern mill. The big boss usually has no connection with his workers and may not even know their names. This is rare in our type of plantation, although it does happen when there are hundreds of slaves and where the master has groups of people between him and the slaves.

"Overall though, the slave-master connection is much closer than boss-worker relations in the North. Look at some of the problems that develop in industrial societies up north or in Europe. Problems such as poor worker treatment, strikes, and labor unrest rarely happen here."

Jefferson turned and saw a look of impatience in Varina's eyes at his intrusion into the conversation. "Well, enough talking on my part, I'll let you alone to do your talking."

Josh asked Jefferson about General Quitman, who had land close to the Davis's land. "What do you think about his ideas on secession from the Union?"

"I think he is way overboard in his thinking," Jefferson replied. "Why, I traveled up to Maine and Boston not too long ago, and I found a lot of support for the South from northern democrats. The talk from people like Quitman could alienate the people up north and push them into the arms of the Republicans.

"The Republicans are the party most dangerous to the South. They believe, first and foremost, that slavery must be destroyed and replaced by a free labor system. They don't seem to care about the effect on our economic system of losing our slave laborers. I've always stood for the Union. I was willing to give my life for it in the Mexican War. I still stand for it just as strongly as I did in 1847. We are a wonderful reciprocal country. We in the South grow cotton, and the mills in the North buy the cotton at a good price. They make clothing and products that they sell back to us at a good price. This is a winning situation for all involved. Why would I want to destroy such a good situation?"

"How does Quitman fit into this equation?" Josh asked.

"Even though Quitman is a close friend of ours, I think his thinking is faulty," Jefferson added. "Look at the support we have in the White House. We have had two presidents who have been mighty supportive of the South. Pierce was terrific, and Buchanan is turning out to be almost as good. Having this kind of support from the North warms our hearts. With this kind of support, why would I want to destroy the Union?"

"Suppose the Republicans win the election coming up. The Democratic Party is split in half, and there are other parties involved. Everything is split in two except the Republicans, who are solidly for abolition. What happens if they win?" Josh asked.

"What you are talking about would be the worst calamity for the country," Jefferson answered. "That would be the saddest day of all our lives. If the Union were to abandon the South, we would have to abandon the Union.

"It's what Thomas Jefferson spoke about. If the government no longer reflects the will of the people, the people have an inalienable right to overthrow it. We probably wouldn't want to overthrow it because the northern people might be happy with it, even though it doesn't reflect our needs. We would just want to go our own way without intrusion from the Republicans.

"Please, let's not discuss this anymore, not this evening. We can only hope and pray that this scenario does not come to pass because it would destroy our beautifully run economies and set us back to the Bronze Age. There is still some time before the election. We can only hope that cooler heads will prevail and things will work out the way they have gone in the last ten years."

Book Two

Admiral Porter's fleet running the rebel blockade of the Mississippi at Vicksburg, April 16th 1863

CHAPTER 40

SECRET AGENT

The beginning of the second year of the Civil War took place approximately two years after Josh's meeting with Jefferson Davis at Joseph Davis's plantation. Jefferson was now the president of the Confederacy. Through Nate's cooking school, Josh's plantation had made significant inroads into raising the consciousness of slaves in the surrounding properties. Josh, his family, and their house slaves had been accepted into Mississippi society in the area.

Over this time frame, Wilma and Jackson became closer to each other and now were lovers. No other slave catchers came looking for Nate. Emily had become more and more comfortable in her role as mistress of the plantation. Various masters and mistresses in the surrounding plantations accepted her as one of their own.

Elijah continued to remain a slave in Emily's and Josh's household. He always knew that something was different about this plantation, compared to the others he had known. His new owners never took him further into their confidence in order to avoid subjecting him to more stress. Once the war began, all communications with Josh's family were quickly cut off as a protection for Josh as well as his parents.

At the very start of the Civil War, Josh communicated to his family up north the idea of offering his services to the North. He contemplated fleeing with the group to return to Massachusetts. He was all set to go when word came from his parents that he was to meet with another man in Vicksburg. This rendezvous was set up through the northern War Department, but Josh knew nothing about it at the time.

The man Josh met with turned out to be none other than John Wilms, the reporter who Josh had eavesdropped on in Seth Feinberg's store two years earlier. Wilms had been recruited as an agent by the War Department in Washington due to his political connections and his allegiance to the North.

The meeting took place in the newspaper office where John Wilms worked, and on that day, John was the only person in the office of the *Vicksburg Sentinel.*

The War Department had gotten all the information from Josh's parents about his abolition mission down south and how it was proceeding, and they were in the process of facilitating a commission for Josh.

Officials at the War Department decided that Josh, his wife Emily, and their four slaves were worth much more to the Union ensconced at the Davis Bend plantation. They were close to Jefferson Davis's property, and they already had a good relationship with Jefferson and his family. There was an excellent chance they could come by intelligence as to what Jefferson Davis was planning. It was definitely possible that, in communications with his brother Joseph and his family, there might be secrets they could learn—especially through Dee Ann, who was very talkative.

In view of his training at West Point, Josh wanted a battlefield role. John Wilms quickly talked him out of that idea by telling him that this was his chance to do something bigger for the Union.

Josh could obtain intelligence on Jefferson Davis and pass it on to John Wilms. He was also free to continue his work on raising the consciousness of the slaves, with the goal of engineering a slave revolt that could help to destroy the South's economic base.

"The Secretary of War told us," Wilms said, "that what you are doing now for the Union is a hundred times more important to us than even becoming a major general and winning a big battle. This whole situation must remain hidden, but when the war is over we plan on presenting this to Congress for a possible military title regarding your role.

"The Mississippi River is the lifeline highway for both the North and the South, and what we do here will have a gigantic impact on the whole war! We will provide you with funds in gold, dollars, or Confederate currency, because the rebels are now printing their own currency."

"I have a question," Josh said. "All the planters are volunteering to join the Confederate army. I've told some of them that, as soon as I get my affairs in order, I would be joining them. That's why I wanted to flee and head up north with my family and slaves. If I remain here, I will have to join the Confederate army in some role."

"According to our records," Wilms said, "you were trained as an army engineer but you went into the infantry in the Mexican War instead. Why was that?"

"Because the Governor of Indiana raised an infantry unit, and that was the only chance I had to go at the time."

"We have already thought about that," said Wilms. "Your engineering background will be very helpful because the rebels are starting to build fortifications on the Mississippi River. We have some important contacts on the staff of several of the major generals, including Albert Sidney Johnston and General Pemburton. We are going to try to get you transferred to an engineering battalion."

Josh turned toward Wilms with a sarcastic look on his face. "So instead of giving me a commission in the Union army, you are going to wangle a commission in the Confederate army for me?"

"If it works," said Wilms.

"Also, if I'm building fortifications on the Mississippi, how will I be able to collect intelligence for you from Davis Bend?"

"There will be six of you involved. We plan on using all of you to collect information. When we'all have to capture any enemy territory on the Mississippi River, you sure could be very valuable to the Union. And it might save thousands of lives knowing where fortifications, gun emplacements, and river defenses are located."

"Do you really think you can get me a commission in an engineering battalion?"

"We are going to try."

"Another thing, suppose I'm caught by the Union troops in a rebel uniform. Wouldn't this be bad for my reputation–not to mention, for my life?"

"We all thought about that as well. The Secretary of War and his office know about you, and every precaution will be taken, but we can't guarantee anything with capturing troops. If this plan works, we will tell you what to say if you're ever captured in a rebel uniform."

There was one more issue Josh raised with Wilms. "We have made quite a few inroads in teaching some of the slaves to read. We also have been passing them a lot of information about what is going on outside the South. Many slaves are beginning to develop a feeling for potential revolt."

"I'm going to bring someone to our next meeting," Wilms told Josh, "who knows how to conduct a revolution. He should be very helpful in creating a revolutionary consciousness."

An arrangement was made between the two of them to meet at Davis Bend and the newspaper office on a weekly basis to develop plans.

Back on the plantation, Josh called for a meeting of his

group to inform them of the new plans with the federal government. Josh called this meeting of the group to discuss the possible change in roles for everyone.

He began the meeting by saying, "I have been in touch with the federal government through a third party, and they want us to provide them with any information we can pick up regarding goings-on in Davis Bend. They are looking for any rebel generals visiting here, or any important information on Jefferson Davis.

"This information could be very valuable to the government in Washington. They also want us to continue with our work waking up the black slave population. We must prepare the slaves for revolution. The government is willing to provide us with both money and assistance to continue our original endeavor and also obtain intelligence on goings-on at Davis Bend.

"Since this is a change in our original plan, if any of you want to bow out and go north, now is the time to let us know. Emily and I will stay here no matter what."

Jackson stood up, looked out the window, and walked back and forth for a few moments. "We came here for a purpose, nothing has changed," he blurted out.

"That goes for me too," said Nate. "Why should we quit now that we are beginning to get somewhere."

"That goes for me too," said Wilma.

"Me too," said Joan.

Then Nate added, "Things have been going quite well. Many of Quitman's slaves have learned to read, as well as slaves in many of the other plantations. The whole river for about fifty miles south from Vicksburg is saturated with plantations that we have worked with. At most of these plantations we have a few slaves who know how to read, and we can give them written instructions if we have to."

"Our whole plan is going into a new phase now," Josh said.

"I'm going to meet with a man who has some experience conducting revolutions. He is going to help us move the slaves toward revolt and destruction of the rebel's economy."

"These plantation owners and their wives don't suspect a thing," Wilma added. "They are so busy looking out for invading Yankees that they don't want to look over their shoulder in their own backyards."

"We have been very lucky so far," Joan said. "We can only pray that our luck holds out."

"Things may get a bit more active during this next period for all of us," Josh added. "The rebels are fortifying the Mississippi with the intent to cut the northern states off from using the river. They want to prevent the North from sending goods downriver and out to other destinations and markets."

"The federal government will never stand for that," Jackson exclaimed.

"You are most assuredly correct," Josh agreed. "Removing our products from their markets will not be tolerated. We can expect the full power of the federal government down here within the next few months. We can try to increase our social activities with Joseph Davis and his family and slaves, with the intention of getting as much information as possible. Remember that Joseph Davis shares some of his slaves with his brother, Jefferson, so that will give us some insight into what goes on at Briarfield, Jefferson's plantation, as well.

"Can we invite Joseph and family over for a dinner and entertainment soon?" Josh asked everyone.

"Sure," Nate said. "We'll cook him a great meal, even though we won't have all the ingredients we used to have due to the war. We've still got some great chicken and some squab from downriver. We can build a great meal around them."

"Remember your promise not to turn mean if you do any more cooking," Joan broke in.

"Dona you worry, honey chile—my word is my bond!" said Nate in his best slave talk.

"Let's invite all of Joe's family that we can," Josh added. "I hope a commission in the rebel army comes through by then for me because it may be embarrassing for me not to be involved in the fighting. I'd like to get this going quickly. Still—perhaps I'll wait to see what can be done about a commission in the rebel army before we invite the Davis family over for dinner."

CHAPTER 41

WHO DO VOODOO

Over the past two years, Elijah had become very well integrated into the Lawrence plantation and had attained a higher status in the Lawrence household. The original six considered including him in their inner circle but finally never did. This was more to protect him than for any other reason.

Things went well until Elijah was stricken with a mysterious illness after eating some cooked crawdads that he caught and cooked, himself. He was losing weight rapidly, so Josh took him to Joseph's doctor, who gave him a diagnosis of colon cancer and believed he could not live more than six months.

In a desperate attempt to get well, he went to see his cousin Marie Laver, who was the local voodoo queen. Since he was very weak from not eating well and had no appetite, Josh brought him over to Marie, himself. At the back of Josh's mind was the memory of what the curandero did with the sick soldiers during the Mexican War many years before. Marie's home was unusually attractive from the outside. It was built of nicely finished wood, in two stories much like a New England Cape Cod style house.

This was similar to the housing many freed blacks lived in.

They were quickly ushered into Marie's office, a most unsettling place for Josh. Jars filled with strange powders and medicaments were on shelves and lined the walls. On one shelf there was a skull which seemed to be smiling at everyone. As Josh moved into a corner, he recoiled from a huge snake hanging on the wall near him, which almost appeared alive.

There were several types of chairs arranged around her office. Marie led Elijah to one and pulled up another one right in front of him. She was a mulatto woman wearing a black dress with a large bright-colored scarf draped over her shoulders. Another scarf was wrapped around her head in turban style. Marie began to take a thorough history of Elijah's symptoms, what happened to him, and how he felt about the whole thing.

"Did you go to the doctor, and what did he say?" she asked.

After a half an hour of abrupt questioning, she came up with a diagnosis. "Elijah, y'all have been cursed by an evil spirit!"

"How dat happen to me, Marie? I always been a hard worker—isn't I, boss. I does my work rail hard—doesn't I, boss. Why dis done happen to me?" Elijah began to sob softly.

"You must have seen an evil deed. I need to talk to you alone." She motioned to Josh to wait outside and spent another half hour talking to Elijah. Then, when she was finished, she began to talk to Josh.

"I am ready to begin the treatment now. I may need your help for part of it."

"I am willing to do anything to help Elijah," Josh replied.

"George," she called out the window to her assistant, "bring two chickens in for Mr. Josh to hold, and bring in the dead moccasin snake." She began to shake a rattle.

While George went to get the items, she brought one of the jars, which had a red powder, down from the shelf. She poured some in a glass with water and stirred it with a spoon. Then she took off Elijah's shirt and had him lie down on a couch. She dipped her index finger in the powder and began to draw a cross on Elijah's stomach. Next, she made a circle at the apex of the cross and began to chant African words.

George arrived with the live chickens and handed them upside down, feet first, to Josh, who was a bit startled by their flapping wings. Marie told him to wave them back and forth over Elijah while she continued to chant in some African language. Then she motioned to George to bring the dead moccasin over. Next, she got on top of Elijah, straddling him.

She opened the moccasin's mouth, exposing its fangs, and lightly pricked Elijah on the arm with the fangs of the dead snake. She had Elijah drink the red liquid, completing the ceremony. His face contorted and he quickly threw up. She mixed up a weaker batch, which he was able to keep down. She gave Josh a glassful of the liquid, and told him to give it to Elijah over the next day, claiming it would eventually restore his appetite.

After the healing ceremony was completed, Josh brought Elijah back to the plantation house to help take care of him. After putting him in one of the bedrooms to rest, he walked into the kitchen where Jackson and Wilma were preparing some food.

"You can't believe the ceremony I've just been through involving dead snakes and live chickens," said Josh. "I don't see how this is going to help him, but I saw some strange things during the war in Mexico that worked, even though I did not believe they could possibly work."

"If Elijah believes it will work, maybe it will," said Wilma helpfully.

For two days Elijah showed no improvement and even seemed to get worse with repeated vomiting. On the third day after the treatment he began to rally and even began to eat again. Within a week he was eating normally to the puzzlement of Joseph's doctor, who had pronounced him in mortal danger. Elijah's success was attributed by everyone to the intervention of his cousin Marie. He rapidly got his energy back, and he returned to productive employment within two weeks.

CHAPTER 42

SARTORIAL SPLENDOR

To Josh's surprise, Wilms was able to facilitate a commission for him in the Confederate army. He found out about it two weeks later at their weekly meeting in Vicksburg.

Wilms began by announcing the following news: "Albert Sidney Johnston has agreed to bring you onto his staff, and he is the most able general the rebels have, except for Robert E. Lee. This is quite a feather in your cap!"

Josh gave him a dirty look. "That's just ducky!" Josh shot back. "I want to make a big splash so everyone back home gets to know what a traitor I've become!"

Wilms then added, "Don't worry. It will only be for a little while until we get enough information and get this part of the country under control. Then we'll pull you out of here and fix things up for you."

"You are going to get a telegram from the rebel war department confirming your position and attachment to General Johnston. They will probably give you about two weeks to wind up your affairs on the plantation before you report for duty at General Johnston's headquarters."

"There is also someone I want you to talk to. I know you know him, but I don't think you know how important he is to our war effort. Let's go over to Feinberg's General Store and speak with Feinberg. He is the revolutionary who can give us some ideas on how the slaves can help us win the war."

Arriving at Feinberg's store, they found Mrs. Feinberg waiting on two customers near the entrance. Seth Feinberg ushered them into the back room and closed the door.

"I would like you to share some of the ideas of how the slaves could destroy the economy of the South and bring the rebels to their knees." said Wilms.

"Well, all right, if that's what you want, I will tell you how. To start a revolution there are some basic prerequisites. First of all, one must have a revolutionary class that wants to take power, with a revolutionary consciousness. This class must have an awareness of the class struggle between the rich and poor.

"Next, this class must have a means to seize power. Finally, it must have the will to take power for that revolutionary class. And lastly, there must be a collapse of the old order, to be replaced by the new revolutionary order.

"Mr. Wilms has told me of the work you have been doing with the slaves in the area—teaching some of them to read and making them more aware of some of the conditions outside their area.

"He told me they are reading some northern newspapers and abolition pamphlets. This is a memorable achievement, and it sets the stage for the underpinnings of a revolution, but they are still not there yet.

"Remember, I follow the theory that says that the most revolutionary person is the person who is the most oppressed. As I study this situation with an eye to creating the type of revolutionary situation we are looking for, I think the quickest way to make it happen is to strike where the South is most vulnerable. It is in this area that the revolutionary consciousness of the blacks could destroy the southern economy.

"Think about this. Suppose the black slaves began to run away on a mass scale, refusing to work in the fields picking cotton or any other crop. The southern economy would be brought to its knees. The South has been scraping the bottom of the barrel, trying to get men to fight for the cause. Most able-bodied men are at the front. At this point the South doesn't have the manpower to watch over and catch masses of runaway slaves, or force them to work. They are having terrible trouble even catching their runaway soldiers.

"The South depends completely on everyone doing their job to support the war economy, and that includes the slaves working in the fields to produce food and cotton as well as slaves helping with manufacturing. They might be able to control them with armed forces, but if a huge number of slaves refused to work, what could they do?"

At that point Wilms jumped in. "Seth, your English is much easier to understand than it used to be. You no longer make all your sentences backward like you used to."

"The wife and I had a big talk about this because we live here and not in Germany. We decided we have to make a better effort to talk like everyone else. Sometimes, when I am tired I forget and go back to the old way, but it feels a lot better being more fluent."

"We want Josh and his team" said Wilms, "to continue their work with the slaves in this area, and that may mean mostly the rest of his team—as Josh is going to be at General Albert Sydney Johnston's headquarters for an indefinite period of time.

"Since the rebels are fortifying the river, there is a great likelihood that Union troops will get here before the other parts of the South. For that reason, we want your team to prepare the slaves to be ready to abandon the fields when the fighting begins. We would like to work toward creating a general strike in the territory not yet captured by the Union army. This could bring the rebellion to its knees.

"From Tennessee to Northern Mississippi, the Union Army has encountered thousands of displaced slaves from captured territories and plantations. They have been employing them to cut wood, build roads, and other tasks."

"I also heard," said Josh "that many of these slaves have been refusing to leave their plantations and desert their masters because they don't know what's coming next.

I don't think this will happen in our area because there is a higher level of consciousness and desire to be free among greater numbers of slaves."

"We are also" Wilms resumed, "trying to figure out a plan with the Union generals, as not all of them are going to be sympathetic to large numbers of slaves leaving the plantations, choking up the roads, and hanging out with the Union army. It could be one of the biggest moves of the whole war if we can get the slaves to go on strike and leave their jobs!"

"I think this is a good, solid plan," Josh added, "which will utilize all of the work we have put in and move it in a great direction, but the people who are going to do the heavy lifting here are the black slaves.

"If this works, it is *their* effort that will destroy the South, even more effectively than the battlefield. These slaves are going to be the real heroes of the war, although I doubt that they will get the credit they deserve."

Feinberg added one more grace-note to the plan. "Remember one of our basic revolutionary principles. It is the most oppressed peoples or workers who have the highest revolutionary consciousness. Therefore, it is most fitting that they should have the hardest job."

As Josh left Feinberg's store to head for the next downriver steamboat, he found Emily getting off. She had just arrived.

"I'm glad I was able to meet you," said Emily "This letter just came in from the rebel war department. It gives you a commission of Lieutenant Colonel, and authorizes you to pick up your uniform at headquarters in Vicksburg. It says you can meet General Johnston while you're there, even though you don't have to report for duty for two more weeks."

"Let's go right over there," Josh replied. "I'm not sure they will let you in, Emily, but if not, you can wait for me—unless you would rather go shopping in town."

"Actually, military posts bore me. I would rather do some shopping. I haven't been in town for a long time, and there are a few food items and supplies we can use. I think we should buy extra now because we'll never know what to expect as the war gets going here. I want to buy as much as we can get now and buy additional seeds for our crops in case we can't buy food easily."

"That's a great idea, Emily. Buy as much as you can and have it brought down to the landing. We'll put it on the boat and we'll have everyone help offload it at Davis Bend."

They then went their separate ways. Josh met the sentry outside the post and told him, "Colonel Lawrence reporting to pick up my uniform. I'm here for a meeting with General Johnston."

"Wayl suh, you can get most of yow uniform heah, we have a tailor here today who can take all yow measurements. It wayl take a half an hour or so, but unfortunately, suh, General Johnston has gone back north. He was only heah for a few hours. The Major can fill you in on what's happenin'."

Josh went in to meet the Major, who told him that the army had been falling back from Kentucky and Tennessee. It was now ready to strike back. General Johnston had left to lead the battle after meeting briefly with President Davis.

Josh asked if he knew where the battle would take place.

"Ah think one of the landings on the Mississippi, but ah could not hear where. Ah think he'll stop them Yankees from comin' down heah. He said heel meet you when he gets back heah, but it maht be quite a spell."

"As far as the uniform is concerned, our tailor has quite a bit of material to work with, and ifn you can hang around here for a few hours, I spek he might be able to finish the job today. I'll go in the other room and see if he'all can do it."

After a few minutes the tailor came back and said, "I have two partially completed uniforms for tall men similar to your height. If I can modify one, I can make this work out well. You're going to have quite a bit of material to carry. That uniform will be your size, but you can have your own tailor make any further modifications if you feel it is uncomfortable in any way. Some officers here do that, and some have others make their uniform from scratch. It all depends on your taste and fit."

After the job was done Josh looked in a big mirror on the wall. "I think this is a perfect fit, but I'll have to show it to my wife to get her opinion."

"We'all can send a man to help you carry it back to the landing. We'll also need you to contribute some money to the cause to pay the seamstress who made it originally. One hundred dollars should cover everything."

After paying the tailor, Josh tried on his Colonel's dress uniform, and decided to wear it for the boat ride back to shock Emily when he met her at the landing. He was carrying a package of his field uniform and his regular clothes, and one of the orderlies from headquarters helped him by carrying all the accoutrements. When he found Emily standing by the landing with many packages of her own, she was indeed quite shocked to see him wearing a dress Confederate Colonel's uniform, although he did look quite handsome in it. She quickly approved of the fit.

Before they could settle down and begin to discuss the day's events, Josh realized he had to talk to John Wilms as soon as possible. He needed to inform him of the information he had just received from the military headquarters post, so he went back to the newspaper office. There he found Wilms just about to leave in his horse and buggy. He asked Wilms to drop him back at the dock, and on the way he quickly filled him in on what he had heard about an upcoming attack.

"It looks like the rebels are getting ready to attack at one of the landings just over the border in Tennessee," Josh said, "but I don't know where."

Wilms shook his head and said, "Boy, if we'd got that information yesterday, it would have saved a lot of lives. The attacks started today," he told Josh, "and it has developed into quite a big battle. I don't have too much information about it at this time."

"The attack started at a place called Pittsburg Landing. We should find out in a few days what happened. If the Union wins the battle, troops will keep coming downriver until they reach Vicksburg. This might still take quite a while. On the other hand, if the rebels win, they will only buy some more time for themselves. Eventually, the Union armies will reach Vicksburg and wind up here."

They arrived back at the landing dock, and Josh got off to meet with Emily and head home downriver. "That is quite a handsome uniform, even though you are now a lousy rebel," Emily exclaimed when Josh came back to meet her.

"All the better to make love to you," was Josh's answer to her.

"We'll deal with that when we get home," said Emily.

The fast packet boat, *Lacy*, was now loading, and a deckhand helped them stow their packages for the trip downriver. As they headed downriver at a rapid pace, they passed quite a bit of river traffic, mostly steamboats carrying troops upriver to reinforce the defenses against the invading Yankees.

As the boats drew near them, a band came out from the upper deck of the *Lacy* and broke into "Dixie." There was wild cheering on the other boats, and everyone blew their steam whistles. Josh noticed the crowd was deferential to him on the boat, as his uniform stood out to everyone.

Josh mentioned to Emily "This feels very strange. To play the role of a hero to a group of people fighting for a cause I don't believe in."

"You're doing a great job, keep up the good work," Emily added. "We'll discuss this when we get home!"

At the landing they carried their packages over to a wagon. The wagon had just transported Joseph Davis and his niece Dee Ann to the dock to head downriver on the same boat that brought Josh and Emily back to Davis Bend.

"Well how do you do!" said Joseph staring at Josh in his uniform. This created an awkward moment for Josh, since Joseph was well aware of Josh's connection to his parents in New England. He felt pain for both Josh and his parents, since he was now on the opposite side in an increasingly bitter war.

What Joseph felt was hard to make out as he made no reference to this problem and only said, "Doesn't he look handsome in his uniform?"

Dee Ann quickly seconded that with, "You better believe it!"

After a few pleasantries, Joseph and Dee Ann got on the boat and headed downriver, while Josh and Emily rode home with Joseph's driver in his wagon.

This meeting with Joseph, seeing him in his rebel uniform, created a feeling of doom for Josh. The war, his northern family origins, and his dress in a rebel uniform all made his position appear all the more tragic. Yet, once having thought this, he quickly began to rationalize the situation. Remembering that Joseph himself had several relatives in New England, his intuition told him, "Maybe Joseph has some of these same kinds of problems in his own family. That's what makes this war a civil war."

CHAPTER 43

TROUBLE UPRIVER

When Josh showed up at the plantation, his four "slaves" got quite a fright due to his uniform. They quickly adjusted to his changed status, and started calling him "Colonel" in jest.

"Colonel, sir," said Jackson with a sloppy salute, "there is a Yankee battalion on our left flank, what shall we do?"

"Colonel, sir," said Nate with a god-awful salute, our thirty-two-pounder just laid an egg."

"Colonel, can we'all join the rebel army," asked Wilma and Joan?

"You can all go to hell," said Josh in a joking way.

Emily broke in, scolding them good-humoredly with, "Leave Josh alone, he's had a very busy day."

They then went back to their planning. They all agreed it was time to invite Joseph and Eliza over for dinner to see if they could get any intelligence on Jefferson, or to figure out any new moves by the rebels.

Food was getting scarcer, so it was decided that Nate would bake a pie, and Emily would bring it over and invite the Davis family for a meal. Nate made a delicious apple pie in which he used some of the last Calvados they had in their cellar to give it a truly exotic taste.

Jackson then drove her over in the buggy. Emily knocked on the door, carrying the pie. Their butler Toby answered the door and brought Emily into the kitchen where Eliza was making some fresh peach jam from a nearby orchard.

"We've got to prepare for a rough time," Eliza said, "with food shortages and all, as the Yankee blockade is making it harder to get some foods we were used to before. Is that a pie you're carrying?"

"Oh yes, we brought this for you! And speaking of food we wanted to invite you all to a dinner over at our place. We don't have as many fancy ingredients as we used to, but we can promise you a good, solid, tasty meal. If you and Joseph and anyone else in your family are available, that would be a great pleasure for us. We are planning on next Saturday night at six. Would this be convenient for you?"

"I'll have to discuss it with Joseph to be sure he doesn't have anything planned, so we will be in touch with you soon. Joseph is away today, so I won't see him until tonight, but I will discuss it with him tonight."

They chatted for a while, catching up on recent events, although Emily was not able to glean any new information. As she was getting ready to leave, Eliza said, "Why don't you take some of this jam I made, and we'll call it an even trade on the pie."

Emily left with an ample supply of peach jam to await Eliza's response. She did not have to wait too long as one of Joseph's slaves brought over a note from Eliza the next day after lunch. The note said that Eliza, Joseph, and Dee Ann would be glad to come for dinner. Jefferson, she mentioned, might come by if he was in the area, but he was very busy, and his attendance was not likely. Varina was not with him because she was back in Richmond.

The next day, however, Eliza dropped by to let the Emily know that this week would not be a good time for dinner because the Davis family was in turmoil. Events were happening upriver in regards to a huge battle, which might have a big effect on the war in the western part of the Confederacy.

"Jefferson might be around," she told Emily, "but he will have to concentrate on what is going on in Tennessee, just over the border. If things go badly there, the Yankees may be down in this area sooner than we thought. If things blow over, maybe we can get together in a month or so."

The next morning Nate was in the kitchen at the Hurricane Cottage stirring a large bowl of oats with a wooden spoon when Joan came down to see him. She had been busy making beds upstairs and doing some light dusting.

Nate really enjoyed Joan's company, and they had become more than close friends. Joan appeared in the kitchen in a long blue dress with a white lace apron, her hair in a bun.

As he placed the bowl of oats on the fire to warm up, he glanced over at her with a quick smile. "Let's go for a walk down by the river honey child, and why don't you wear that dress you bought in New Orleans."

Nate was dazzled by Joan's appearance and would often try to get her to dress up in one of her low-cut dresses, especially since there were fewer and fewer opportunities to do so. The war had begun to restrict all chances for leisure and enjoyment.

He turned to her, dusting some oats off his brown suede pantaloons. "I'll wear my special blue suit so that we can both dress up together."

"We never do anything exciting anymore," Joan said. "If I dress up, I'd like to do something special, like go to a ball or a dinner party."

"There are no more balls and few dinner parties, or anything like it anymore. We will have to wait till the war is over," said Nate. "We will have to make do with this bad situation. But I really do enjoy looking at you when you are all dressed up."

"If you put it that way, let's do it. At least it's a positive change in our lives. But let's set the date for a Saturday within the next month so that we can both look forward to it."

With their social engagement set, they both anticipated a little spark of excitement.

CHAPTER 44

A THORNY PROBLEM

Josh was on his way to the cotton warehouse one morning to check on his supplies when Marie Laver came walking along from the opposite direction. Josh greeted her warmly.

"How is my patient doing?" she asked.

"Very well," Josh responded. "He is back to work and working very hard to make up for lost time."

"I was sure I could help him, especially after he told me about the bad experiences he had been through."

"What experiences?" asked Josh.

"I can't tell them to you as they are confidential, but I can tell you that I got a pretty good picture from Elijah of some of the things going on in this plantation. He thought he was dying, so he told me a lot of things that went on here."

"Like what?" Josh inquired.

"It's confidential between me and Elijah. All I can tell you is that this is not like any plantation I have ever seen before. Something fishy is going on here. I'm not going to tell anyone, but I have my suspicions about this place."

Josh's face turned red, and he felt his throat get tight as he answered her. "I don't know what you are talking about. There is nothing fishy about this place," he said.

"You don't know what I know! Do you see that field over there? I would like to run a ceremony over by the cotton gin."

"Is that what you would like?"

"Yes," answered Marie.

"All right, but I need to discuss this with my wife and others. If you come back in a few days I will see what we can do. I'm not promising anything, but we will see what can be arranged."

They said goodbye. Josh was so agitated that he returned immediately to the house to discuss these developments with the others.

The group was just finishing breakfast as Josh burst into the kitchen in an agitated state. "We've got trouble. I think Marie Laver is onto our scheme."

"What are you talking about?" asked Nate.

"I think Elijah may have spilled the beans about the murder of the slave catcher to Marie when he thought he was dying and getting treatment from her."

"Those voodoo queens operate that way with everyone," said Emily. "They talk to someone and get some information. Since no one is perfect, everyone has some type of skeleton in their closet. They use that information to get an advantage over others. In this case it is us. Sometimes they are bluffing–they don't really know anything, but they assume that you have done something wrong, and they use it to manipulate others."

"I am so angry!" said Josh. "I feel like we are being blackmailed. She wants to run a voodoo ceremony here on the premises. We can't afford to take a chance as to whether she has information on the murder or not."

"Wait a minute," said Wilma. "Wasn't the slave revolt in Haiti set off by a voodoo priest called a houngan? Maybe we can find a way to join forces with her. She has a lot of followers among the slaves."

"I don't like that religion," said Jackson. "It warps and twists the Bible for its own purposes. Look at what Marie is trying to do to us. Blackmail is immoral."

"Jackson Greene!" said Wilma. "In Exodus 23-22 doesn't it say, 'I will be an enemy to your enemies and will oppose those who oppose you.'"

"That's true, but I still can't stomach voodoo ceremonies," said Jackson. "They may have a different way of dealing with what they consider enemies than we do. I think we should spend some time with them before we even think of throwing our lot in with them."

"I agree with Jackson completely," said Nate. "They could prove to be great allies, or they could prove to be a real stumbling block in reaching our objective. We don't know what they would do if they took power. We need to know more about them. I think we should let them run their ceremony if we can find out what they want to do with it. It will let us study them in a better way."

"It's okay with me," said Josh, "as long as it doesn't get out of hand."

CHAPTER 45

WAR CORRESPONDENT

Back at the telegraph office, John Wilms found that his usual source of information had almost dried up because things had changed dramatically since the war began. First Ezra and Cathy had been impressed into service as employees of the Confederate State of Mississippi. They had to sign an oath of secrecy regarding confidentiality of transmitted information.

There was now an armed guard at the telegraph office, and an extra locked door was added to prevent anyone from eavesdropping or looking at military transmissions of important messages. Many of these messages were in cipher code and could not be easily read.

But the Confederate States of America was now dealing with John Wilms, who was a formidable operative for the Union cause. Wilms had originally tried to enlist in the Confederate Army but was rebuffed. The Confederate leaders felt he was more useful as a propagandist and war reporter who could raise funds for the South and possibly bring in thousands of dollars in needed currency.

From his days of courting Cathy before the war, John knew about the copse of trees behind the telegraph office, which was very secluded. It was the place where he often ate lunch while waiting for Cathy to get off work. He discovered very early on that, on certain days when the wind was favorable and there was not too much noise in town, he could hear the distinct clicking of the telegraph keys both sending and receiving. Curiously, it was only when he sat in one part of the copse of trees. Still, it was a marvel of acoustics that the sound traveled to this one little area. If his deciphering of Morse code was still less than perfect, the regular practice he was now getting greatly improved his deciphering ability.

Mornings, just before lunch, and early evening were good times to listen for material for newspaper stories. Now he was on a mission to glean what he could from the telegraph lines. It was impossible to get military information directly because it was sent in code cipher and very rarely sent out in the open. Just the same, private messages often revealed sensitive information about ongoing events.

On this day, April 8, 1862, John Wilms was sitting in the copse of trees when a message came through that he was able to readily understand. It came from Corinth, Mississippi, requesting that doctors in his region travel to Pittsburg Landing, on the Mississippi. There were huge numbers of wounded soldiers from both sides being brought in to Corinth, which was overwhelming all medical services in the area. They spoke about thousands of casualties in a very small area. Obviously, a huge battle had taken place on a larger scale than anything that had come before. According to the message, the casualties were pouring in from just over the border in Tennessee.

In the space of two minutes, John's nervous system went on high alert. He realized the Union army was now coming quickly down the Mississippi. This battle was close by, just over the state line in Tennessee.

Still, he wondered who won the battle and what was the outcome. He realized Vicksburg was a formidable obstacle for the Union army to get around.

John waited till lunchtime and walked over to the front

door of the telegraph office, just outside the area where the soldier stood guard, until Cathy came out. He then walked along with her. They were both carrying some food, so they strolled over to the park to eat together as they had often done.

John had been feeling more and more pressure from his family and friends to marry Cathy because they had been keeping company for several years, but they both had resisted this move for some inexplicable reason.

Perhaps it was the war, perhaps it was Cathy's attachment to her father and her work at the telegraph office with him, or it may have been the fact that John was a Union spy who did not wish to implicate Cathy in any of his clandestine activities if he should be caught. He felt no need at the present time to move toward matrimony.

As they ate lunch together, John said, looking at Cathy intently, "I know we should be talking about getting married, but things are so uncertain right now. I don't know where I'm going, and I don't know where the country is going. I have such a feeling of uncertainty right now."

"I do too," said Cathy. "Maybe it would be wrong to start out a marriage in the kind of world we are living in."

"You are right, Cathy. The Union army is trying to strangle the South, and we are living in that part of the South that corresponds to the neck of a person being strangled. But what are we going to do?

"This situation casts a pall over everything. My intuition tells me that the Union army will be down here before long because they have to be here to keep the Mississippi open. Maybe we should wait."

"Oh John, I see what you are saying." Cathy looked at him thoughtfully. "But things are never going to be perfect. When all our relatives were married, there were wars, cholera epidemics, and all sorts of calamities–but that didn't stop them."

"You're right Cathy, but we are right on the cusp of a major battle and giant dislocations. Shouldn't we wait for these events to play out? I feel something big is going to happen before very long!"

"Oh, I guess you're right, John," Cathy sighed, "we've waited these last two years, maybe we should wait a bit longer."

"Cathy, speaking about war and battles, I know you can't discuss much of the telegraph traffic coming through, but my sources tell me a huge battle just took place at Pittsburgh Landing just over the border in Tennessee."

Cathy nodded her head affirmatively and then added, "By tomorrow everybody is going to know about it. I think the battle was lost because the Union army is still there. Don't talk or print anything just yet, John, unless you can confirm it from somewhere else."

"We all heard Albert Sydney Johnston was killed in the battle as well," Cathy said. "This battle at Shiloh was maybe the biggest battle of the whole war."

Thoughts began to enter John's mind about Josh and what he would do now that General Johnston was not going to be there, if the news turned out to be true.

At that point John decided to take the next boat upriver to verify what happened.

"Cathy, I'm going over to the editor to get an okay to go upriver and check out this story."

"Y'all be careful, John. You may wind up in the middle of a battle up there," Cathy replied with great concern.

"Don't worry, Cathy, I'll be very careful. I'll drop by and see you when I get back."

He went off to see the editor. It took less than five minutes to convince the editor of the need to cover the aftermath of the battle.

John quickly found himself heading upriver. In about an hour he began to pass river traffic headed downriver carrying some wounded soldiers, which passed their boat very closely.

The soldiers all had a hangdog expression that made them appear to be depressed.

John's boat stopped at a landing near Milliken's Bend, and he took the opportunity to interview troops returning from the battle. He found one sandy-haired young man with bandages on his arm and chest who was very willing to talk about his experiences.

"We started out real well. We surprised the hell out of the Yankees, and we almost drove them into the river. They was hanging on by a shoestring by nightfall. I thought we all had won, but the next day more and more of them kept comin', and on the second day we all got driven off.

"Boy, that was one huge battle. I ain't never seen nothing like thayt before. My ears is still ringin' from the noise. We lost a lot of folks." At that his eyes began to tear up, and he had difficulty finding the words. As his voice was cracking, he made the transition to, "But them Yankees did also."

Then he was able to go on.

"Most of the army pulled out, but I couldn't go with them cause a shell exploded above our heads, and I got hit with shrapnel. Ifn you were to come over in our boat, I'd give you a piece of it. Them doctors were pullin' pieces out of my arms an chest yesterday afternoon. I got seven different pieces here."

John thanked him for the offer, but politely declined it. He thought, "Poor boy, he doesn't even look twenty. He has such a good-natured pure character, he should be happy working at a job, or working on a farm—but instead, two days ago he was running across the field with a gun trying to kill Yankees. He was one of the lucky ones." John could envision the battlefield at Shiloh covered with lots of dead bodies of young men just like him.

"My brigade commander also got wounded," the sandy-haired soldier went on, "and he is in the same boat here also. He knows a lot more'n I do about what happened on the battlefield."

John walked over to the boat where Brigadier General Wilcox was standing, with his left arm covered in bandages. He introduced himself.

"I can't give you too much information because I haven't been given clearance to talk about our troop dispositions. I can tell you, we took a good whipping from the Yankees, but they lost a lot of men too. We almost drove them into the river, but we couldn't finish the job. The next day they got reinforcements and drove us back. If you want information, I'll try to answer your questions if I can, as long as you don't ask about troop dispositions."

"General Wilcox," John asked, "we had information that General Johnston was killed in the battle. Is this true?"

General Wilcox had trouble talking for a few seconds as his voice cracked. He fought to get control of his emotions and began. "I'm afraid it's true, but he did not have to die. That's what makes this so difficult.

"I was right near when he got wounded in the boot by a Minnie ball. The doctor was right next to him, and asked him if he wanted him to look at his leg, but General Johnston waived him off yelling, 'Its just a scratch.' Then he said, 'Doctor, you've got men who need your services a lot more than me.'

"Well, it wasn't just a scratch. It wasn't five minutes after the doctor left that the General turned all white and collapsed in the saddle. By the time they got his boot off to treat his leg, he was unconscious, and he quickly bled to death. It's the saddest day for the Confederacy–he was one of our very best generals."

"Well, I hope y'all recover fast," said Wilms, "so you can return to your brigade, because the South needs men like you real bad. I sure am sorry about General Johnston, and he will be sorely missed."

"By the way, is your boat going back to Vicksburg?"

"I believe it is, that's where we're supposed to go to get transferred to a hospital," Wilcox answered.

"Well, I'm going to see about changing boats because I realize I need to get back to Vicksburg."

Wilms spoke to the pilot who helped arrange his fare back. He parted company with the soldiers and went inside the boat to a quiet corner in the lounge. He began to ponder his front-page story of the battle, since he had interviewed one of the generals, albeit a wounded one.

He couldn't publish, YANKEES WIN BATTLE OF SHILOH ARMY RETREATS, GENERAL JOHNSTON KILLED, HEAVY CASUALTIES. This would be the last headline he would probably ever produce because he would be suspected of treason. Not a good position for a Union spy to take. He needed to keep a low profile and still appear patriotic, so he worked and reworked the headline till it came out like this: DIFFICULT MAJOR BATTLE AT SHILOH. HEAVY LOSES ON BOTH SIDES. MANY MORE YANKEES KILLED. YANKEES RETREAT TO HIGHER GROUND AND IMPREGNABLE POSITION. It gave the impression that the Yankees were on the defensive and the rebels were only waiting for them to abandon their temporary position prior to resuming the attack. He then added: GENERAL JOHNSTON MORTALLY WOUNDED. DIES ON BATTLEFIELD. This appeared to be a good mix of truth and exaggeration, which would accomplish his purpose without calling too much attention to himself.

As they headed downriver back to Vicksburg, the riverboat overtook another towing a barge behind it. Wilms noticed that there were no passengers on it, which appeared strange considering all the comings and goings in the aftermath of this great battle on the river. As the boats drew abreast the captain spoke with the hailer megaphone:

"*Where are your passengers?*"

"*Look carefully, and you will see!*" came the reply by loud hailer. Wilms climbed some stairs to get a better view of the deck on the other boat and instantly spied a huge number of coffins lining the deck and the barge as well. There must have been at least a hundred coffins between the barge and the riverboat.

"Boy, we must have lost a lot of men in that battle," said the captain.

"Y'all think *this* is a lot," the other captain replied, "y'all should see what is waiting for us back at the landing on the river. Thems ten times as many bodies there, and these are only the whole bodies. Them other bodies can't be returned to their relatives in parts, so they probably will be buried in Tennessee. We got a lot of trips ahead of us. The General said we can't take no passengers as it would be bad for morale. But what about our morale"

At that point, Wilms asked the pilot if the other boat was headed for the main dock in Vicksburg.

"I believe that it be headed there," said the pilot. "I suspect them dead boys's relatives will be there to pick up the coffins. This be only the first batch. That boat may take an hour more to get in to Vicksburg towing that barge."

The two boats having separated, Wilms fought to rid his mind of the grisly image of all the coffins lined up side by side, an image which left him in a trance-like state all the way to Vicksburg.

CHAPTER 46

PROBLEMS WITH THE MEDICAL PROFESSION

At Vicksburg, Wilms got off the boat and said goodbye to the soldiers onboard. He noticed a line of relatives nearby waiting for the boat to arrive with the coffins. They were all wearing black, and the women had on funeral veils. They all had the same look of loss and trauma on their faces. Two local constables kept them away from the other passengers.

While waiting on the dock for the bag he brought along with his writing and clothing, Wilms ran into Doctor Evans, the local doctor who was called out to go upriver and help tend to casualties.

Wilms had known Dr. Evans since he was a child. They had a very friendly relationship and often discussed the medical profession, as it was a topic that had always interested Wilms. He had started medical school training in his younger days and had completed the program. But he had quit the profession when he could not make a living at it because too many people owed him money for his medical services, and they couldn't afford to pay him.

Wilms turned instead to newspaper work but kept his interest in the medical field and still craved helping patients with their problems. Dr. Evans was well-respected in the community as a man who was almost always there when you needed him. He was very competent and was credited with saving many lives. An outspoken man who saw no reason to maneuver around the truth, he was nevertheless capable of doing it in a sensitive way when dealing with patients.

Today, Dr. Evans was a bit agitated at having to leave his practice suddenly; there were many sick patients and a pregnant woman who would soon be due. He was expected to go to a field hospital near Shiloh. Wilms found him in a chatty mood, perhaps from the fear of the unknown as he went to a scene of immense casualties that was sure to be a trauma for him.

He had nothing good to say about some other members of the medical profession that day. "Some of those fancy doctors from New Orleans are nowhere to be found, and the aftermath of this battle is falling on a bunch of country doctors like me. We are glad to do this for our country, but what about those fancy doctors in New Orleans? They came to the big city down south to take advantage of the rich folks who live there. All they see are dollar signs when they look at their patients."

"I remember those doctors well," said Wilms. "It certainly was maddening.

Those specialists were making hundreds of dollars in fees, and many of their patients died from the operation or the complications of the operation."

"I found their overall diagnostic skills to be poor," said Evans. "All they want to do is find enough evidence to do a big operation and perfect their skill in that particular type of surgery."

"I also found," said Wilms, "that they were not necessarily interested in what was really wrong with the patient, or even if it corresponded to the surgery being done."

"These bloodsuckers are nowhere to be found," said Evans, getting more agitated by the discussion. "In a situation such as this big battle there are too many patients, and there is no time to perfect their operations. They can't make any money doing it, so they are not interested. I take my fees in chickens, cows, and pigs—but not *these* doctors. They want gold—and fast! It's a terrible thing to see our profession warped by these polecats. I'm sorry to mouth off to you like this, but I needed someone to talk to."

Wilms then added that it was good that they had Dr. Evans in Vicksburg because those other doctors would decimate the local population.

Dr. Evans shot back, "You don't have to ever worry about them coming here. They only follow the money trail, and they would never settle in an area where fees are paid in chickens and pigs. As far as decimating a population, each of us in the medical profession has our own private graveyard, patients who succumb after a treatment or operations. Luckily for me, my graveyard has always been much smaller than that of other doctors. The type of doctor I am talking about has a huge graveyard because he does not care as much about what happens long term with the patient, as long as he can perfect his surgery. This type of doctor expects a fifty percent mortality rate on his operations, and still looks for reasons to operate on a patient."

At that point Wilms began to surmise what was really bothering Dr. Evans. After arriving at the battle at Shiloh, he was going to have to greatly expand his own graveyard as disease and infections were rampant in dressing stations and field hospitals. This terrified him. He was afraid his whole life might change, given what he was about to undergo.

This very issue of death haunted Wilms. He had given up his own involvement in the medical profession after a beautiful young woman who was his patient died in childbirth. This experience had soured him from continuing in the medical field, especially when he heard from his colleagues that it would be the first of many deaths he would have to encounter close at hand.

Wilms considered mentioning the expansion of the graveyard but thought better of opening this can of worms and instead bit his tongue and said nothing.

After a few minutes, the boat blew its deep whistle to depart. Dr. Evans said goodbye, and Wilms wished him good luck, even though he knew Evans was going to a ghastly scene.

As he headed in the direction of the telegraph office he ran into Bill Jones, a reporter for the *Augusta Chronicle*. Bill was known to everyone as a muckraker who was always criticizing the Confederate regime and finding fault with it. Recently his newspaper was attacked by angry mobs for publishing material that was antagonistic to the government in Richmond, Virginia.

After talking with Jones for several minutes he was able to tell that Mr. Jones had no idea the coffin boat was about to arrive. Wilms did not want to be the one to publish the story behind the coffins and compromise his favored position with the Confederate government. He knew, however, that it was an important story to tell to the public.

"So, Jones, I guess you're here to interview the mothers and fathers of the dead heroes in that line over there. I hear they've been waiting for a couple of hours for the coffin boat to arrive."

"You better believe that I am," said Jones, pretending that he knew all about the arrival.

"That will be quite a story—telling the country about the parents whose sons gave their lives for the Confederacy. Many people will be most interested in what the parents have to say. It could be a chance to whip up some patriotic fervor," said Wilms, knowing that probably wouldn't happen at all among the grieving parents.

As Jones said goodbye and rushed over to the line of grieving parents, Wilms felt a grim feeling of accomplishment, knowing that many of these grieving relatives might not have nice things to say about the Confederacy and that Jones would probably amplify them.

His business with Jones concluded, Wilms walked over to the telegraph office and waited outside the office for Cathy, as it was the end of her work shift. When Cathy came out, she was so surprised to see him that she blushed deep red.

"I'm sure glad to see you back here, I was worried all day you all were going into a war zone. How come you're back so quickly? Did you go at all?"

"I only made it to Milliken's Bend when I ran into some troops who fought in the battle and were wounded. I got a first-hand account of the battle from a wounded general, including the part where General Johnston was killed. I could not have gotten a much better account even if I had been right at Shiloh. I'm going over to the press now. We have a few hours to set the type, which is plenty of time. I've had to water the story down and change a few things so I won't be suspected of being unpatriotic. I think the war is going to go just as I expected, and the Union troops should wind up here within the next six months or so, but I won't dare print anything like that!"

Cathy wore a look of concern when she said, "John, these events are sure moving fast. I wish we had time to relax and do things together like we used to before the war."

"Well Cathy, now that this battle is over and both armies are licking their wounds for a while, maybe we can take a carriage ride down the river to Warrenton and have a picnic if you're not working on Saturday."

"I'd like that John, and I am free."

A few days later Josh picked up the newspaper and read Wilms's account of the battle, including the eyewitness account of General Johnston's heroic death. This death of General Johnston, whom he was supposed to report to, left him with a rootless disconnected feeling, and he decided that he needed to meet with Wilms right away to determine his course of action.

The deadline for the next day's stories would be that evening, so he gambled that he could catch Wilms in town.

Josh decided to catch the next boat leaving that morning for Vicksburg. He just made it to the dock on time as the boat was getting ready to shove off. It was a slow, difficult trip fighting the current upriver, and he spent the time formulating questions for Wilms.

Now that he had enlisted in the engineer battalion of General Johnston, he wondered what was he going to do now that there was no more General Johnston. Since he was a colonel with battlefield experience, could he be given a battlefield command of troops instead? Would he now be forced to fight on the battlefield with the wrong side?

This thought was revolting to him. Would Wilms and his ring of spies have any influence to get him posted to work on the defenses at Vicksburg as originally planned, and who would he report to?

His brain was teeming with worries when the boat docked at Vicksburg. He felt unsteady on his feet as he walked down the gangplank to the dock, and at one point he almost fell in the water.

He quickly walked over to the newspaper office and found Wilms talking with the typesetter about the next day's headline. When Wilms saw Josh he promptly excused himself, and the two men walked down to the copse of trees to talk.

Josh began, "General Johnston is dead, what am I going to do?"

"Well," Wilms responded, "I have been giving this a lot of thought already. Because you graduated with honors at West Point you were destined to work in engineering, and that is how you have been presented to the general staff. We don't know who will take over the defenses in Mississippi. It could be generals Price, Van Dorn, or even General Pemberton. If it is any one of these three, your job will be essentially the same.

"Make no mistake, these generals are not of the same caliber as General Johnston, but they are all competent, committed commanders. I would not worry about this. It is highly unlikely that you will be offered a direct battlefield command. The general staff is most concerned about fortifications on the river to prevent the Union capturing Vicksburg.

"That is the job you have been selected for by the Confederacy. It also gives us our best opportunity to find a way around the defenses when the time comes."

Wilms's answer went a long way to calming Josh's worried mind, and he began to finally relax a bit.

"How is the education program with the slaves going?" Wilms asked.

"Reasonably well, and we have about a score of slaves who are reading well enough to understand simple books," Josh told him. "We're getting better every day."

"Liberation is coming for them," Wilms said. "Within three to six months they will be putting that reading into practice."

CHAPTER 47

MILITARY CONFERENCE AND AFTERMATH

In the aftermath of the battle at Shiloh, Dee Ann was getting ready to attend an impromptu dinner that had been hastily arranged at the Davis mansion, as General Van Dorn, General Price, and General Pemberton were visiting for a meeting with Jefferson Davis. He had come to meet with the generals to decide who would take the place of General Johnston.

Today was their lucky day, because when Dee Ann was out riding she saw the generals arrive much earlier than anticipated. She galloped up to the house to greet them before Jefferson got to the door. She cut a striking figure in her attractive riding habit with gleaming black boots on her flashy Arabian horse, and she skillfully dismounted.

"Well gentlemen, this is a pleasant surprise. It's not often that we get a visit from such handsome and distinguished guests."

General Van Dorn quickly answered back, "And it's not that often that we get a chance to sample such beauty." Dee Ann's face blushed quite red at that comment, and from that point on, Van Dorn was well-hooked—but so was Dee Ann.

Jefferson asked to speak with the generals alone in the parlor, and Dee Ann left to dress and make herself up to prepare for an early dinner. Just as she was looking over some low-cut evening dresses to decide on what to wear, the butler announced her friend Marie to her. Marie had come to pay her a visit, knowing she would be at the Davis mansion but not knowing about the generals' visit with Jefferson.

"You've come at just the right time, Marie. I can use some help deciding which dress to wear tonight. Some generals are here for a meeting with Uncle Jefferson, and I want to look my very best. By the way, that General Van Dorn is quite a hunk of manhood. You should get a look at him. And I think he likes me. He called me beautiful!"

"Watch out. He is a charmer of women. Haven't you heard about him before? He is famous all over the state both as a hero and a womanizer. He has broken women's hearts before. You should be very wary of him."

"He just hasn't run into the kind of woman who can handle him," Dee Ann shot back. "Men like him intrigue me. It's quite a challenge not to have them get the upper hand with me. I've narrowed it down to these two dresses, the red one or this blue one. Which do you think is most suitable for the dinner tonight?"

"They're both nice colors for you. Let me see you try them on."

As Dee Ann tried them on, Marie ran commentary on the dresses. "The red one fits you like a glove–it really looks great. But do you want to show off that much cleavage? You've got a lot to show off up there, but it will drive those generals wild. It may be hard for them to concentrate on their work."

"That's just what I want them to do," Dee Ann responded. "I want them to pay attention to *me*." She then tried on her blue dress.

Marie walked around Dee Ann, cast her face down, hesitated a moment, then blurted out, "That blue one is too obscene to wear. I wouldn't want to wear something like that. It could be construed in bad taste. It's just too sexy for the occasion."

Dee Ann raised an eyebrow.

"The red dress is not far behind, but at least it could fit an occasion where women want to look their best–if not, sexy. It shows off all the attributes of your figure quite well."

"You are right Marie. I'll go with the red dress and wear it with these French high heels."

That afternoon the generals were having cocktails with Jefferson in the smoking room after a long strategy session of going over maps and plans. Jefferson had just handed out his last best Cuban cigars to the group, and they each had a cigar in their mouth when Dee Ann made her grand entrance into the room.

The cigars of the two generals Price and Van Dorn almost fell out of their mouths as they stared at the beautiful, enticing creature who walked in the door. All three of them were equally stunned, and everyone rushed to pay attention to Dee Ann in their best chivalrous manners.

Most notable though, was General Van Dorn, who followed the apparition of beauty in the red dress the way a trout follows a fly that has just landed in the water. The room was overflowing with compliments as even Jefferson was shocked at the impression his niece made on the group. At first, he seemed mildly annoyed that an interloper had broken up his serious planning, and he gave her one of those intense stares that he was known for.

Then realizing that his serious discussion was over for the moment, he decided to flow with the events and let the generals enjoy themselves. Everyone quickly got into the spirit of the occasion.

Not to be outdone by anyone there, Van Dorn stated loudly, "Mr. President, you certainly have the most beautiful niece I have ever seen." The others, who rushed to pay their compliments to her, quickly seconded this.

One of Jefferson's slaves had been sent over to the Lawrence household earlier to invite Josh and Emily to the hastily arranged dinner and reception, which took place after the strategy planning session. They arrived just as the generals finished paying their second round of compliments to Dee Ann.

Josh arrived wearing his new dress uniform and saluted the generals, who were also in uniform. He shook hands with all of them. Then they got involved in a discussion of the how to reinforce Vicksburg to make it even more formidable as a defense against the Yankees, who were surely planning to take it.

Dee Ann had tried to lead Emily into an adjoining room, not realizing how much hostility Emily had toward her for her overt flirting with Josh. She was very fortunate this time because Emily was not going to make a scene, since this was Jefferson's meeting. Emily had her eye on the bigger task at hand, the destruction of the Confederacy. It was very difficult, but she fought to get control, and even complimented Dee Ann on her dress, which she said was stunning.

Later on, during some mixed-group discussions Emily still nervously eyed Dee Ann, well aware that the generals were stealing glances at her from time to time. Emily was also well-dressed in an off-the-shoulder green taffeta dress but had not dared to dress in Dee Ann's sexy style. Consequently, she did not attract the same level of attention, even though she herself was quite attractive.

After the women left the room to have tea, the group began talking in general terms about Vicksburg. The specifics had already been discussed in the private planning meeting.

"Have any of you inspected the Rock of Gibraltar?" Jefferson asked. No one had, but they all were familiar with its impregnable fortifications. Jefferson then addressed his remarks to the team, but most specifically to Van Dorn, who was then the commander of the Vicksburg region.

"I heard General Sherman had procured a map of its fortifications when he was the superintendent of the military academy at Alexandria, Louisiana, and I also heard he did not take it with him when he left to join the Union Army. I would like to get that map so we can use it for a basis of planning our defensive structure."

"Gibraltar did not have a Mississippi River flowing through it," said General Pemberton, "which carries produce from the Midwest to the South and New Orleans."

"Well, Gibraltar had the Mediterranean Sea running through it, which was the major sea lane for commerce between Europe and Africa," said Jefferson. "As far as the river is concerned, one of our telegraph operators was telling me about a way that torpedoes anchored in the river have been exploded using electricity from a battery—and conducted through an underwater cable. This was the way messages were sent in the transatlantic cable during the fifties, when Buchanan was President. We have already sunk some Yankee shipping using that method. I think it should be included in Colonel Lawrence's plans when his combat engineers work on strengthening the fortifications at Vicksburg."

Josh quickly agreed to study the idea, saying there would have to be a safe channel for Confederate shipping to use and thinking that, later on, this might afford an effective way to sabotage the very river fortifications themselves.

At this point Josh decided to play it safe and not take too active a part in the conversation unless he was asked specific questions, of which there were no further ones posed.

Walking back into the room with Emily and noting that the conversation had taken a more technical turn, Dee Ann deftly steered it back in her own direction.

"Gentlemen! All this talk is too complicated for us women.

Can't we talk about some other things, such as a military ball or a picnic where everyone bids on a lunch basket? Why can't we do that to support the war effort, of course?"

This quickly transitioned the conversation to a lighter note and set the stage for the small talk that brought the military conference to a close. Jefferson had long since met his goals of deciding the big picture of Confederate plans for the next six months.

As the sun was beginning to set, and the last rays of sunlight moved across the drawing room, Dee Ann spent a few minutes charming each of the generals, paying the most special attention to General Van Dorn.

"General, I would love to show you around my Uncle Joseph's plantation, you must come visit us sometime."

"I would love to, but you know the demands this war makes on me," Van Dorn replied, "I don't know when I'll get back this way." Suddenly his face lit up with a flicker of recognition. "Wait a minute! I don't have to go back till tomorrow evening. Is it too soon to go to see the plantation tomorrow morning?"

"Why of course not, General, I had no plans other than baking a cake, and I'd much rather have your company than do that. My horse is here as are my riding clothes. He'll stay in the corral for the night."

"Why don't you stay over in the guesthouse, and we'll go out first thing in the morning, bright and early."

After breakfast the next morning, they hit the trail.

"We can take my horse over to Uncle Joseph's stable and borrow one of his horses. He owns another fast Arabian like my horse Beelzebub, named High Hat, but High Hat is very spirited and needs a very skilled rider."

"Why Miss Dee Ann, didn't you know I was a cavalry officer? We need to be good riders. Our life depends on our skills."

Dee Ann quickly dressed in her most appealing riding habit, put on her riding boots, bobbed her hair up, and was ready to impress the General. They went to the barn together to Beelzebub, put the bridle and saddle back on him, and mounted him. Van Dorn took the reins with Dee Ann putting her arms around his slim waist.

When they got to Joseph's stable, she introduced Van Dorn to High Hat, Joseph's fast Arabian, which appeared to be a match made in heaven. Van Dorn quickly took charge in a no-nonsense way, and before long Van Dorn and Dee Ann were galloping across the fields and jumping fences.

After they got the sudden, almost-compulsive craving for speed out of their systems, they took a more leisurely pace, and Dee Ann gave Van Dorn a tour of the plantation. They dismounted at the cotton gin warehouse, tied up their horses, and went inside.

Horace, the black warehouse manager, was just leaving for the Davis plantation to get some instruction on the excess cotton inventory. Cotton was piling up in the warehouse because most of it could not get through the Union blockade of all the southern ports.

"Sorry, Miss Dee Ann, ah gots to go and meet with mars Joseph. Sorry ah cants show you around today. Ders a lot of cotton piling up, and we doesn't know whats to do wid it. Sure is a shame."

"It's all right, Horace, I know my way in here. I'm just showing the General around." The warehouse was empty at that time, and there were big cotton bales waiting to be taken down to the dock. These bales would be sent down to New Orleans for shipment up north to a few mills in Virginia if the ships could run the blockade. They could also be sent out through the blockade to English ships waiting to take them to Britain.

Dee Ann used a ladder to climb up on one of the bales, and Van Dorn quickly followed and sat down beside her. Starting to describe the workings of the warehouse but hearing no response to her commentary, she turned back towards him, whereupon in a flash they seemed to lose themselves in each other's eyes. Van Dorn gave her a passionate kiss and was about to tell her that he was going to go off to battle and might be killed, so they might never have a moment like this again.

Before he could say anything, it seemed Dee Ann had read his mind. She looked him boldly in the eyes and said, "I know you are going off to war tomorrow, and we may never have a moment like this again."

Her sensitivity to his feelings stunned him, and he blurted out "Now I have something to want to come back to." They engaged in a long passionate kiss, and decided to head back to the stables because Van Dorn had to depart for his command. The chemistry between them was fantastic for the moment. Still, an unbiased observer might have questioned whether there was any deeper connection between these two other than love of horses and the sexual energy they both exuded.

The next morning, Dee Ann hurried over to Marie to give her an impassioned account of the day's events. She found Marie making breakfast, so sat down to have a cup of coffee.

Marie began, "So how did that meeting with the generals go?"

"Just wonderful," Dee Ann told her. "I think I've found the love of my life! He is very handsome, he's a superb rider, and he thinks I'm beautiful."

"Are you referring to General Van Dorn?"

"Oh yes–you know, my heart pounded when you mentioned his name."

"Really, tell me more."

"We went for a ride together," Dee Ann said glowingly. He handles a horse masterfully. I took him by the cotton gin warehouse, and he kissed me–and what a kiss! I dreamed about it all last night. If we got married, it would be a match made in heaven."

"Don't you think you're rushing things? You just met him yesterday!"

"Marie, I can tell he's the man for me. I know we were meant to be together."

Marie was a long way from sharing Dee Ann's exuberance. However, rather than throwing a bucket of ice water in Dee Ann's face and risking yet another blow-up, Marie backed off, hoping to be able to bring Dee Ann to her senses at a later date.

"Well, Dee Ann, when is the wedding date? Is he going to give you a ring?"

"It's too early for that, but it's coming—nothing is surer!"

"When is he coming back here?"

"I just don't know due to the war. He's a General you know, anything can happen. But he wants to come back soon."

At that point Marie decided to leave Dee Ann's fantasy intact without raining on her parade, as it seemed harmless to let her have her dream of her handsome General, even though she knew Dee Ann's modus operandi. This always involved exaggerating the future potential of her romantic conquests. Beside all of this, maybe he was a good match for Dee Ann. She was a female version of what he had a great reputation for being—a womanizer. Life was getting harder for everyone as the war continued. Her last thoughts to herself were—who knows, anything could happen for better or worse. They might live happily ever after, or he might just as easily be killed in battle like General Johnston.

CHAPTER 48

LAYING FINAL PLANS

Just before Josh began his new job as combat engineer of Vicksburg, he met with his group at the plantation. They discussed strategies of how to deal with issues while Josh was away at Vicksburg. One issue was what to do about Marie Laver and her wish to run a voodoo ceremony on the plantation.

"Based on our last discussion," Josh began, "I decided to let Marie Laver run the voodoo ceremony on the plantation. I thought I'd ask Joseph Davis about this matter, but I remembered that freedom to practice religion was one of his basic rules for running a plantation."

"What if the ceremony gets out of hand?" asked Jackson.

"I don't think it will," said Josh.

"There have been some strange occurrences that have taken place at Quitman's plantation next door," said Nate, "right after Quitman made fun of the voodoo ceremonies."

"Weren't there a lot of poisonous snakes found in his warehouse?" asked Wilma. "And didn't one of those snakes bite and injure one of his overseers?"

"And what about his cotton gin building burning down mysteriously?" asked Joan. "All that set his production of cotton way back. I heard they found strange dolls all around the plantation," Joan continued. "When I saw Marie Laver the other day, I said 'Marie, I hope nothing will happen here like some of the strange things that have been happening on the Quitman plantation.'

"She told me not to worry and that they protect their friends. Then I asked Marie that if I weren't her friend, would bad things happen to me? She had a tight look on her face and she told me not to discuss this anymore."

Jackson rolled his eyes.

"But those were some evil deeds that happened to Quitman."

Joan finished. "Marie Laver told me that an evil deed in the pursuit of freedom is not an evil deed. Then she added, 'I think you know what I mean, Joan.'"

"I still think we ought to let her run this ceremony," said Josh, "and see where it takes us. The rest of the group hesitated and then nodded assent. "I'll see if we can do the ceremony before I leave for Vicksburg," he concluded.

"Now, on to more important things," Josh continued. "We just got word that New Orleans has fallen. There is going to be greatly increased Union traffic on the river. The Davises are leaving to go inland and start a plantation in a safer area. Dee Ann is going to stay here in the mansion for the time being to keep an eye on the area for her Uncle Joe.

"I have arranged through my contacts in Vicksburg to first tell the Davises that we are also leaving, then stall until after they leave and remain here as a base of operation until Vicksburg falls."

Nate sighed at the news of New Orleans falling and asked, "Do you think Vicksburg will fall soon?"

"It's a tough nut to crack," Josh answered. "It may take quite a while, but it has to fall eventually.

"Be sure you keep me informed," he continued, "on what is going on here, even if one of you has to come to the city occasionally."

At that point Jackson showed a look of concern asking,

"suppose we are picked up by rebel forces on the way in and impressed into fortification work? Won't it be better for Emily to go with one of us?"

"Good thinking, that might well happen," Josh answered. "We could give you a letter to deliver in Vicksburg, but the uncertainties of war could strike at a black slave traveling alone with an important message. He might indeed be carried away by the rebels to work on their fortifications.

"I've got a lot of important stuff to cover with you, so try not to interrupt me until I get all these details out," Josh said, facing the group who all shared the same anxious looks.

"Remember, I'll only be a few hours away. Also, be ready to leave the plantation at a moment's notice. That means keep a suitcase packed and ready to go if necessary. The Mississippi River and the tributaries are going to be the biggest battleground of the whole war, except for Virginia, because the Mississippi is a main artery for commerce for the middle of the country.

"All rebel obstructions to the river will have to be routed out and destroyed. We anticipate the fighting will be in this area or close by. General Sherman has been made aware of our situation, according to my contact in Vicksburg. If you need to make it to the Union lines, you should ask for General Sherman or General McPherson. He is also aware of our situation.

"If our troops come close, all of you can make a run for it, with Emily providing ownership of you to satisfy the rebels, if necessary. When you get to the Union lines, report to them. We will meet later after the battles of Mississippi are decided. Remember, all slaves are free if they are under Union control.

"I'm doling out almost all of the money I have left from running the plantation. I'm giving each of you one hundred dollars in Confederate currency, and the same in Union currency, as well as twenty dollars in gold. Use the Confederate currency first. Remember, people will be suspicious of anyone with northern currency or gold. If you have to use it, have a good story ready as to why you have it. I want each of you to hide it or sew it into your clothing. You will probably need it at some time in the future.

"Don't worry about leaving without telling anyone, it's better if you don't. If you need to go, just go! Emily can be making a trip with her slaves if you have to pass through rebel hands. This is what we think is going to happen in the future, so this is only a contingency plan. If things turn out differently, this may not need to happen as I have described.

"Since I will be away in Vicksburg, you may be on your own, so I want you all to be ready to act independently if necessary."

Jackson then added in a lighter tone, "Don't worry, boss, we is ready to skedaddle if need be. It might be a relief to get back up north where we don't have to play the part of dumb field hands anymore."

Josh then added, "I'm not your boss. We are all in this together. This is like a giant chess game. We have to think a few moves ahead to try to figure what is going to take place very soon. Things may happen that we could never foresee, knowing that our best guess may not be good enough. These are only my best guesses as to what may occur.

"You all might be called up to construct fortifications or trenches to protect the South. If that happens, you will have to go. If it looks like you will be called up, try to escape with Emily traveling and going as her slaves.

"Okay," Josh went on, "that's the plan for escape if we have to go, but now let's discuss a plan for a strike among all slaves in this region. Slaves have been running away from plantations when battles have been won and territory captured, but not yet on the large scale that can happen if we make a huge general strike in this state.

"Nate," Josh said, "when you meet with the cooks for their class do you think you could tell them that the Yankees are close by? Can you help them set up a plan where they can all leave their plantations around the same time? This would be when we get word that the Yankees are right nearby, so at that moment can you have everybody head for the Yankee lines?"

"We have cooks in training," said Nate, "from just north of Baton Rouge—all the way north to Milliken's Bend. If each of these slaves tells the other slaves on the plantation to spread the word and tell other slaves on neighboring plantations, this could spread everywhere in western Mississippi like wildfire."

"This could be one of the biggest labor movements in history," Josh responded. "If we can get someone from each plantation to go to other plantations and advise them of the situation, we could shut down all agricultural work in Mississippi."

"From information I've gotten from other slaves," Nate said, "things are getting pretty ratty on all the plantations with shortages of food. Due to the blockade, little production of cotton is getting out to the external world market. Many of the plantation owners are away in the army, and skeleton crews of overseers—many who are too old to fight—are trying to keep up production. Much of their production is piling up in warehouses and on wharfs. No one has any money to buy anything or pay anyone. The only labor left is slave labor, and the slaves are not treated as well as in the past—even here, because there is just not enough money to keep up the infrastructure of the plantations."

"No one is being treated as well as before." Josh continued, "This is war. Well, this is our revolutionary situation. The question is, can we do this from the point we are at now?"

Nate replied, "We can make this work in western Mississippi, but I don't know if this will spread to the whole state. We can give it our best try. Maybe we can set up a system where we have riders like Paul Revere running from one plantation to the others to warn all the inhabitants that the Yankees are coming.

This would be the cue for the slaves to skedaddle and run to the Union lines.

"Hopefully many of the movements and battles will be north or east of here because this is not the best ground for a battlefield, so then we will get a chance to work this strike out. I can feel that the moment to strike is getting very near."

After spending an hour discussing future plans, Josh made ready to leave for his job as a combat engineer in Vicksburg, which he would begin several days later.

CHAPTER 49

WHO DO VOODOO WE DO

The day of the ceremony had arrived just before Josh was to leave for his new job in Vicksburg. Marie Laver brought many of her followers from the nearby plantations. Some of them were carrying boxes containing powders. Others were carrying live chickens, and yet another follower held a large snake. All told, there were about a hundred people at the ceremony.

Before the ceremony itself started, Josh's group decided to volunteer and participate if Marie would have them.

"Can we take part?" Joan asked Marie at the start of the ceremony.

"Of course, you can, all are welcome," said Marie shaking her rattle. "You newcomers don't know everything about the ceremony, so watch others, and participate in the dancing. Just do what everyone else is doing. We will try to explain things to you as we go along."

Joan, Emily, Nate and Wilma all went along with the big crowd. Neither Josh, who had business elsewhere that day and could not attend–nor Jackson, who would have had trouble hiding his distaste for the ceremony, were in the assembled crowd.

The first thing Marie and ten of her assistants did was to cleanse everyone in preparation for dealing with the spirit world. Marie and her helpers rubbed a white powder all over their faces. Everyone began to dance around a cross that the followers had brought. The cross had a circular wire around it, about six inches from the apex. Some of the helpers carried black and red dolls, which they spread around on the ground. Next, the chickens were killed and the blood was poured into cups that were passed around, and everyone either drank a small amount of blood or rubbed it on their faces.

The four outsiders, looking doubtfully at one another, decided to rub the blood on their faces, rather than drink it. The dancing got more and more violent. People began to aggressively shake hands with others, pumping their arms up and down in a powerful manner. They formed a bond with those whom they shook hands with, and the new couples stayed together for the rest of the ceremony. Everyone danced around the cross with great gusto.

Joan and Wilma took pains to make sure Marie saw their bloody faces and were satisfied when she nodded approvingly to them. The woman carrying the large snake danced around with a bloody face and the snake draped over her shoulders.

Marie began to chant in French "*Le jour de la liberation arrive bientôt.*" The followers took up the chant in an antiphonal response. The use of French was an attempt to disguise the true intent of the meeting from outsiders, but it did not fool Joan, who spoke fluent French–or Nate, who studied cooking in France and had to know how to read French recipes for cooking. Emily and Wilma were not fooled either because they both knew quite a bit of French. Many of these slaves had great familiarity with the Creole language and easily understood Marie's intent.

Marie completed the ceremony with the statement "*Nous attendons le moment juste! Çà arrive! Çà arrive!*"

When the four new "converts" returned to the Lawrence

plantation after the ceremony, they expressed wonderment at what they had seen as well as relief that it was over.

"Did you see the size of that snake? It could have been poisonous! Did you see the way she was holding it? It could have bitten anyone in the group!" said Wilma.

"It was an Indigo snake," said Nate. "Nonpoisonous snakes are not aggressive as long as they are well fed and not injured. Some of their rituals involve poisonous snakes as well."

"Are you going to tell us about that ceremony?" Jackson blurted out impatiently. "I don't want to hear about snakes. They make my skin crawl!"

"Yes," said Josh. "I want to hear about the ceremony. Tell us what happened!"

"I'm not sure any of us fully understood the significance of what happened, since we don't understand the religion," said Wilma, looking puzzled, "but the dancing was fun. What we picked up was that Marie is trying to set off a revolution."

"*Le jour de la liberation arrive bientôt. Nous attendons le moment juste*: The day of liberation is coming soon. We are waiting for the right moment," said Nate, translating the French.

"There is no doubt that we agree about what needs to happen, but do we agree about the means to get there?" asked Jackson. "Can this shocking religion, which uses all these bloody props, go along with more nonviolent methods to accomplish our goals?"

"Did anyone hear any dialogue pushing violent revolt?" asked Josh with an intense look on his face

"What does it matter now, we are in the middle of a Civil War," said Wilma.

"That's all true," Josh replied thoughtfully. "We have put in a lot of work here and we need to do things in an orderly way. To start chopping off heads is not the way to go for us. We have a double role to play in order to ensure our access to the Davis's plans. We don't want to blow our cover prematurely. Marie and her followers could be very useful to us down the road but just not yet. As Marie said, the day of liberation is coming soon, and we, too, are waiting for the right moment."

CHAPTER 50

ROMANCE BLOOMS

Dee Ann had been receiving letters regularly from Van Dorn, which excited her and with the passage of time worked her into a positive frenzy of longing to see him. In the midst of the intensity of the war, their letters spoke of their hopes and plans for a tryst.

General Earl Van Dorn had had some serious battle losses at both Pea Ridge and Corinth, and was at a low point in his career as a leader of troops. He had just been reassigned to the cavalry, which had always been his forte. Moving into the Vicksburg area, he saw an opportunity to meet with Dee Ann and rekindle his ongoing love affair.

Van Dorn had just gone through a court of inquiry for the way he had lost these battles. The Confederate general staff felt he had made some bad judgment calls and failed to plan in advance for contingencies that had arisen.

In one of the battles, as rarely happens in the Confederate army, he actually had more troops than the Yankees did—yet he lost the confrontation. Although the court of inquiry exonerated him, these losses left a big question mark next to his name, as one fit to receive a battlefield command.

Van Dorn did receive command of a troop of cavalry, and quickly distinguished himself by destroying much of the supplies for General Grant's expedition to Vicksburg. This was estimated to have set Grant back three to six months.

It was while basking in the glow of his latest success that he planned a surprise visit to Dee Ann. He arrived at a most unusual time. Dee Ann had ridden down to the dock to pick up a package that was brought for her from Vicksburg by her friend Marie, when she ran into General Van Dorn, who had just arrived on the same boat Marie took downriver.

Almost struck dumb with the shock of seeing him, Dee Ann quickly recovered and introduced Marie to Van Dorn, who began in his usual gallant manner, "The company of two beautiful women is the best treat I have had for some time."

Dee Ann was more used to his flattery, but the sudden shock of running into him in such an unexpected way caused her to blush deeply. The General's comments had an effect on Marie as well, and they both walked off the dock glancing at each other and smiling.

After a short conversation, Marie went on her way and Van Dorn focused all his attention on Dee Ann. He began by handing her one of the packages he was carrying.

"Oh, by the way, this is a present for you. It came from the raid on General Grant's supplies. I guess it was intended for some officer's wife, maybe even Julia Grant. Since I liberated it from Yankee hands, I am bestowing it on you. Open it."

When Dee Ann opened the package, she gasped and ran her fingers through the beautiful folds of fabric. It contained some lush blue velvet dress material, which was stunning.

"I believe this merchandise is straight from Paris," Van Dorn said. "Notice the French writing and the French mark. I am told that this is the mark of the foremost couturier in Paris. I'm sure one of our dressmakers in Vicksburg could do you proud."

Dee Ann looked up at him with shining eyes. "I'm not sure I want anyone else to make it, as I'm pretty handy at making dresses myself. I haven't seen any material of this quality in two years, with the blockade and all. Only a few ships slip through, and much of the goods is mostly spoken for. Thank you so very much!"

They mounted Dee Ann's horse together, put the packages in the saddlebags, and headed to the guest cottage where Dee Ann was planning on having Van Dorn stay.

"Uncle Joe is away in Vicksburg buying some land for a new plantation–inland, away from the river and the Union gunboats. We don't expect him back for quite a while. Are you hungry? You know, we have a few eggs and some bacon if you are hungry."

"Well, I brought some cans of cooked turkey in that package, some other goods we liberated from General Grant's supplies, but I guess we can have all that later. It's really decent to eat, although it's no home-cooked meal."

Looking at him out of the corner of her eye, Dee Ann added, "Things have changed a lot in the last two years. We rarely ate anything out of a can two years ago. Everything was fresh cooked–but now, if we can even get canned food to fill our stomachs, we are happy. I did save a bottle of excellent Bordeaux wine. I was saving it for a special occasion, but now that occasion has come."

Van Dorn appeared distracted and deep in thought for a few moments, then turned to her and blurted out, "You know, Dee Ann, there doesn't appear to be anyone around the plantation today. All the white folks are gone, and the slaves are all working in the field. If we are seen alone in this house, won't this compromise your reputation?"

Dee Ann's pleasant smile, which had been set on her face since Van Dorn had arrived, began to fade slightly as she thought about his statement. "Earl, the white folks won't be back till tomorrow afternoon, and we can act as though you just arrived. No one is expected here till tomorrow. Some servant might come across our land, but I'm not worried about my reputation at all."

"You know, Earl," she went on wistfully, "about two years ago, before the war began, every woman was terrified about her reputation and the need to maintain it, but this war has changed all that.

"After Shiloh, when the casualty lists came out so many women had lost their husbands and beaus. Things changed after that. What good is a reputation if you don't have a husband or a beau? There are a lot of woman hurting terribly who just want a little warmth and love. There are a lot fewer men to go around these days. Many men are dead and wounded, and most of the rest are in the army."

"The way I see it," agreed Van Dorn, "who is going to deny us a little pleasure? This old way of looking at things doesn't really apply anymore—at least not to us. We may be separated, forever, at any time, so why not seek pleasure when it comes our way."

Dee Ann turned to Van Dorn with shining eyes. "Whatever moment we are living in, life should be as good as possible. The books I read on Japanese Buddhism teach that way of thinking on morality."

Van Dorn began to smile as he listened to Dee Ann with growing interest. He nodded in agreement and said, "A little love and affection is a good thing for me, after the things I have been through in the last few battles. Before the last two battles, war seemed simpler. It was you against the enemy. You fought a battle—either you won or lost, and that's all there was to it.

"Now the situation has changed completely," he went on. "I never saw such a sea of Yankees trying to engulf us. If you cover one area, the Yankees turn up somewhere else. Dee Ann, it's like a colony of angry fire ants that get all over you. You have to anticipate what is going to happen before it happens, and even if you do, it's not good enough.

"You must carry all your supplies with you all the time

because the Yankees may prevent you from coming back. There are Yankees everywhere, even in the swampy countryside of Mississippi.

"I am sorry to unload this all on you, Dee Ann, but it's hard to live in a happy moment with this sea of Yankees invading our country."

Dee Ann nodded in empathy for Van Dorn's powerful emotions. "A little distraction may help move you to more happy moments." She walked over to the seated Van Dorn and gave him a hug and a kiss. He responded by seating her on his lap where they kissed passionately for several minutes. Then he took her by the hand and led her into the bedroom.

CHAPTER 51

YANKEE SHIPS RUN GAUNTLET BEFORE VICKSBURG

Josh began working in Vicksburg as a combat engineer. He met with some of the generals in a planning meeting. They were assigned the task of developing the defenses of Vicksburg against an imminent attack. These generals were John Bowen, Martin Luther Smith, and Carter Stevenson.

Josh was the only officer below the rank of general, but was readily welcomed by the other three. He looked resplendent in his new dress uniform with gold braid on the sleeves, and was unmistakably the handsomest man of the generals' staff present.

Josh had a familiarity working with black powder from a job he held briefly at the E. I. du Pont de Nemours gunpowder factory on Brandywine Creek in Delaware. He also had experience with electricity from a job repairing telegraph lines he had held before he worked in the family mill. His firm grasp of engineering led him to be chosen to construct the river obstacles and torpedo mines, which were installed to prevent use of the river by the Yankees.

This was a very tricky job because the Confederate troops

and navy also had to be able to use the river to ferry troops to different dispositions and to use their own ships to attack and ram any river traffic. Cutting off the river to all traffic was simply out of the question. While the Mississippi River was the most important artery of the North, it was also a critical artery of the South.

After much discussion with the generals, it was decided to set up a huge in-depth defense, using three or four different modalities of defense. The first was to move all available cannons to the bluffs above the river. This involved all sizes of cannons. There would also be a series of forts or redoubts all along the river all the way to Warrenton, several miles away. Any unfriendly river traffic would have to run the gauntlet of these forts and gun emplacements, which would pour a withering fire down on them.

The second modality was to mine the river with electrically-exploded torpedoes, which would sink any ship not destroyed by the guns. These torpedoes would be placed in channels used by most shipping, and could be set off by crews standing on the shore or up on the bluff.

The third aspect of the defense was the use of ships called rams to sink Union attempts to run the river and get past the fortifications.

The fourth and final modality was a plan to fortify the eastern, western, and southern approaches from inland by use of a series of forts or redoubts as well as a continuous perimeter of earthworks.

The DeSoto peninsula, across the river from Vicksburg, would be fortified if possible, but this ground might not be able to be held because it was too far away from the city. There was concern about sinking any Yankee shipping in the middle of the river channel because it might tie up the Confederate use of the river as well.

Particular care had to be devoted to the placement of

torpedoes. This was to be Josh's main job. As the day's business drew to a close, Josh went for a walk through the fortifications on one of the bluffs over the river, where he enjoyed the cool river air. As he walked along briskly, trying to get some exercise, he noticed there were at least three tiers of gun emplacements that ran in long lines along the river. He heard the bugler blow *attention*, which puzzled him. This was a warning in preparation for battle, yet there were no Union troops nearby.

He walked up to the nearest fort, which held some twenty-four and thirty-two-pounders in the process of being wheeled into position. Running over to one of the cannons, he found the battery commander and asked, "What is going on here?"

"Colonel sir, we just spotted two Yankee ships just off the point. It's getting dark, and they may try to run the river just like they did last week. Last week they hung tight just under the point until dusk, when the glare made it hard to guess their intentions. Then they slipped downriver. They made it half way down before we caught on to them. An ironclad stood between the transport and us. By elevating the howitzer to maximum height, we were able to drop a few shells on the transport, but it made it through. Ifn they try that again tonight, we will be ready for them. We'all brought up more howitzers, and we even got a ten-inch mortar that we stole from them Yankees."

Josh asked to borrow the battery binoculars, and quickly trained them on the ships hanging out at the point, out of artillery range. He saw the ironclad very clearly and made out three guns right up front, but the transport was partially obscured by the bigger vessel. He could clearly see the Stars and Stripes flying from the mast. It was quickly getting dark, and there was still a glare from the setting sun, but there was no movement from either ship.

Josh thought they must be adjusting their compass to line up with the proper channels to get by the fortifications. He kept his eyes glued to the ships for the most part, and when it was fully dark the order came to start a bonfire on shore and send up a flare. An orange light illuminated the river, clearly showing the two ships headed downriver, with the ironclad taking the inside passage closest to the forts and guns. This shielded the smaller ship from the batteries on shore and on the bluffs.

At that point more flares and bonfires were lit along the river, and the whole river began to glow with an eerie orange light. The bluffs and the partial cloud cover were illuminated with this orange light too. As the boat drew nearer, the bugle sounded *commence firing!*

Josh covered his ears as the big thirty-two and twenty-four pounders began to fire at the ships. The solid-shot cannonballs had almost no effect on the ironclad except for leaving large dents in the superstructure at point of impact. The howitzers were also elevated very steeply, and their shells rose high in a steep arc. Their trajectory was well illuminated by their burning fuses. The shells from the howitzers just cleared the ironclad, and began to fall near the transport, hitting it several times. The closer it got to the forts, the more difficult it became to control their accuracy because the guns had to be elevated higher and higher, so the shells began to drop on the ironclad with little effect.

Josh heard the battery commander call out twenty-second fuses, which surprised him, and he went over to the battery commander to ask him why.

"Colonel sir, these shells are hard to control due to the high trajectory. We are having great difficulty hitting that transport due to the ironclad standing in the way. Explosions underwater are powerful and could do great damage to ships. Our fuses will burn underwater, and if these shells bounce off and roll into the water or miss and fall into the water nearby, the blast might rupture the hull and cause a leak. This could sink the ship. The extra ten seconds gives us enough time for that to happen, but we may need to go up to thirty seconds."

Both ships held their position well and made good speed down the river, running fast with the current. The scene on the river looked like an illustration out of Dante's *Inferno* as the piercing orange light illuminated everything on both shores. This orange glow also lit up all the gun batteries on the bluffs above the river.

It must have been fully apparent to the gunners on the ironclad how heavily fortified the bluff was with guns of all different calibers only a few feet apart for long stretches of the rock formations.

Josh knew these emplacements ran irregularly for about ten miles. The ironclad took advantage of the illumination to get a fix on the rebel gun emplacements and began to return fire. The ship's nine- and eleven-inch shells thundered overhead with a low shriek. It was a very impressive reply but had little effect on the fortifications.

The big eleven-inch explosive shells sent showers of shrapnel and rocks flying in all directions. As the ships headed downriver and turned slightly, Josh could barely make out smoke rising from several hits on the superstructure of the transport.

Although well-illuminated by the flares on shore and overhead, he could not tell how severe the damage was from these hits. It seemed that the whole riverbank, as far as he could see, was alive with a continuous artillery barrage directed only at the two ships.

There were occasional columns of water sent up as shells exploded underwater near the two ships. It was impossible to tell how seriously the transport was damaged as it kept pace with the Ironclad, but it did appear to be running lower in the water than previously.

The forts and gun emplacements kept a steady fire directed at both ships. After about fifteen minutes of a continuous barrage, the transport turned away from the ironclad and made a dash for shore on the opposite bank. As it broke away from the protection of the ironclad, Josh could see what appeared to be quite a bit of damage to the ship illuminated by the flares.

Josh thought that the underwater explosions must have damaged its hull, and the crew was trying to beach her and attempt to escape onto the DeSoto peninsula. The ironclad drew too much water to get close to shore, so they were powerless to help the crew and passengers of the transport, who appeared to jump off the ship near the shore and run away.

A party of troops was sent after them in rowboats to capture them while gunners at all the batteries cheered as they saw the effect of their cannonade. The ironclad proceeded down river without the transport, but this was to be a valuable lesson for the Union navy.

Inwardly upset over seeing the destruction of the transport vessel flying the Stars and Stripes, Josh went out for the evening to meet with Wilms, his contact in Vicksburg. He found him giving directions to the typesetters for the next day's edition on the destruction of the Yankee transport.

"This is going to appear like a great victory, and I'm going to make the city appear invincible, but I want to discuss this with you further. Let's walk over to the copse of trees, and we can talk about this," said Wilms.

As they walked, Wilms noticed that Josh appeared a bit down in the dumps and began, "Something eating you?"

"I'm just heartsick over the loss of that transport flying the Stars and Stripes," Josh began, "and me in a rebel uniform helping make these things happen."

Wilms shot back, "Think about this, Colonel—this may be the beginning of one of our greatest victories."

"You mean that transit was planned?"

"Of course, it was. That transport had a skeleton crew, and an artist was on the ironclad who made a rendering of the gun emplacement locations as closely as he could. That boat was expendable! We did have every rebel cannon on the river firing on us. The big twenty-four and thirty-two pounders each fired twenty or thirty shots at the two ships. Each shot used quite a bit a lot of gunpowder, and just to sink one old scow of a ship! They couldn't tell at night, but that ship was in bad shape. Its timbers were eaten through with worms, and part of the crew was keeping it afloat with pumps. Without constant pumping the ship would have sunk anyway!"

"Boy, did the gunners have a hard time hitting it obscured behind the ironclad," said Josh. "This was a brilliant move to test the defenses. They must have used a huge quantity of gunpowder sinking that ship."

"On the subject of gunpowder," Josh continued, "the rebels main gunpowder factory is in Augusta, Georgia, which manufactures the highest quality powder. Some of their powder came from Mexico and is inferior quality. I can tell because I worked at Brandywine Mill, and I know good gunpowder. They appeared to be using a great deal more powder to get the same range out of the guns near me."

Wilms gave him a quizzical look and said, "How can you tell the difference between good-quality gunpowder and poor-quality gunpowder?"

Josh gave him a look and then quickly said, proud to show off his knowledge of the gunpowder industry, "You have to watch the explosions of the bursting shells. Good gunpowder gives a bright, distinct flash followed by a sharp, clear report. Inferior gunpowder gives a muffled report with an indistinct flash, which is buried in smoke and less visible because it is hidden by the impurities in the gunpowder. In addition, shells and cannonballs filled with inferior-grade powder have many duds that don't go off at all.

"I worked in quality control in Brandywine Mill, and part of my job was to test the powder. I developed a real eye for discerning good powder, and some of the powder the rebels are using is not that high quality, although to an untrained eye it appears to work."

Wilms was somewhat awed by Josh's knowledge on this subject and asked,

"Why do you think the rebels are using inferior grade powder?"

"Because they only have one major powder factory in Georgia, and most of the other powder comes from what they stole from our armories back in 1861 when they seceded from the Union. This powder is getting old, especially in the humid air down here. It has picked up impurities in the last two years since it was made. Let me tell you one more thing about gunpowder. It's like baking powder. If you want a cake to rise you use fresh baking powder. If you want a shell to explode with maximum force, you use fresh gunpowder!

"This is good," Josh added. "Based on what we are discussing, I can formulate a strategy which might work to get the rebels out of Vicksburg. First, if the railroad and boat traffic on the rivers is cut off, the rebels won't have enough powder to keep all these guns supplied because they won't be able to send it in bulk.

"Next, instead of just one transport, we bring up fifteen or twenty of them, all protected by ironclads standing between them and the fortifications. In the same way that we saw today, many of them would probably get through, as the gunners would have real difficulty shooting over the top of the ironclads. All the guns would have to concentrate on twenty or thirty ships instead of just two.

"In addition, we now know the placements of many of the guns, so we should be able to silence some of them. If we can ferry our troops down the river, we could decide at what point to attack. We could fan out across the country and cut off all the roads and railroads, and then try to capture the city, which would be cut off without supplies.

"I know General Grant tried digging a canal to bypass the city and the fortifications, but that didn't work, and I heard the canal collapsed and filled in."

The next day a big headline appeared in Wilms's newspaper: TWO YANKEE SHIPS ATTEMPT TO RUN THE RIVER IN FRONT OF THE GUNS AT VICKSBURG–ONE SUNK AND ONE DAMAGED–ALL BATTERIES FROM VICKSBURG TO WARRENTON HEAVILY ENGAGED–A VICTORY FOR THE CONFEDERACY!

CHAPTER 52

VICTORY FOR THE CONFEDERACY

In the days when things were heating up in Vicksburg and the southern end of the Mississippi River, Wilms spent a substantial amount of his time around the telegraph office, often going to the copse of trees behind it. He would go to get more information on the war situation but also to meet with Cathy to develop their future plans—a pleasant way to put the war out of their minds for the time they were together.

The day after the headline appeared concerning the attack on the Yankee ships, Wilms was eating lunch with Cathy in the copse of trees. "We can't make any plans for ourselves until this war gets resolved," said Wilms. "But if I were you, I would store up as much food as you can because the war is coming to Vicksburg. Buy and trade everything for food as we are sure going to need it. Every day, more and more troops appear to be coming in from the countryside. Both sides are spoiling for a fight here. I'm afraid that Vicksburg is the key to the whole Mississippi River, and both sides know it. This is going to be the heart of the battle, and we are going to be right in the middle of it.

"Let's talk about some other things now as this scenario

may not play out for a couple of more months, and we have to think about the here and now," Wilms said to Cathy. "We'all certainly have a right to pursue some more enjoyable pursuits."

As they talked, his hand moved around Cathy's waist, and he pulled her to him, and they kissed. With the sword of impending doom hanging over their heads, their interests turned to more pleasurable pastimes.

"You know, Miss Cathy," Wilms brightened suggestively, "I could take you for a ride on Saturday and I would really like it if you were to wear the red dress that I like so much."

"I sure would like that very much," Cathy smiled. "All I've been hearing for days are dots and dashes coming over the wires, and it feels good just to speak ordinary English. Getting out of the telegraph office will be refreshing for me. Maybe we could ride down the river. Could we go as far as Warrenton?"

"There is a tavern near Warrenton," Wilms said. "We could stop off and have a drink if they still have anything to drink with this war and all."

"Oh John, if we all want anything to drink, we had better bring it ourselves. You never know nowadays what is going to happen, or if anyone has anything to eat or drink." Having made plans with Cathy, John headed over to meet with Seth Feinberg in his store, which he found surprisingly empty both of goods and customers. Feinberg was taking inventory of the scanty amounts of clothing and supplies.

His face turned down, he frowned and murmured to himself, "Most of my goods the army has been taking, and they pay me in these dollars–dollars that are almost worthless. It's getting harder and harder to make a living. The only bright spot is that I pay my bills in this same worthless currency, and everyone has to accept it. No one pays with gold anymore."

Continuing his despondent tirade, "A few northern dollars that were captured I've gotten paid with, but the army wants this very badly. If they find I have it, they will pay twice the value in Confederate money."

"Can I ask you an important question?" Wilms said gently. "Did you put away goods, supplies, and foodstuff as I told you to do?"

"That I have been doing since before you even told me, Mr. Smarty. You won't believe how much I've put away, but this does not a business make—this is war. You can't expect to make any money during a war unless you're living up north and selling to the Union army—shoddy supplies, like the articles you read about in the northern papers."

"The Union Army will be down here in a few months, and you may be able to sell them some goods anyways," Wilms said, trying to appease him.

"By the way, I thought you revolutionaries don't like capitalism and think it is evil," Wilms remarked, trying to change the subject and get Feinberg onto a more comfortable topic.

"Well, we felt it was evil in Europe, but in America life is much simpler. Life in the South is closer to feudalism then capitalism, although capitalism is present here as it was during the Middle Ages. Whatever the case," Feinberg went on, "a living I have to make. I have no slaves to take care of me, and I don't have any plantation, unlike other people around here. We are also in wartime; food and clothing are getting scarce. It's become a dog-eat-dog world, and I have to think of survival, for my wife and I."

"I hope you have all these supplies and food well-hidden because if anyone finds out about them, especially the rebel army, they will disappear fast!'

"Don't worry about these things, I have them well-cached. I have drawn you a map of all the places where they are hidden. I hope the Union army will respect my property, as I haven't been able to pay my suppliers for all of these items and don't have receipts. I don't want to have to go bankrupt when the war is over," Feinberg said, shaking his head with a look of despair.

As he was ready to leave Wilms asked, thinking of Cathy, "Oh, by the way, I don't suppose you have a good bottle of wine, or if not, maybe a bottle of *Oh Be Joyful*? That would do fine. It's very hard to come by these things these days."

"Both these things I do indeed have." Feinberg told him, "and on your account I will put them. I trust you will make good use of them."

Wilms did intend on making good use of the wine and spirits, and brought them along on the jaunt with Cathy the next Saturday down to Warrenton in the company carriage. They did find the tavern almost dry as all the spirits had mysteriously disappeared, except for some weak hard cider which most of the patrons had to put up with. A few eggs were available for a considerable charge, which most patrons could not afford, but Wilms had considerable funds from his two careers. He was easily able to treat Cathy to a good meal of eggs and potatoes. They ate on the outdoor tables right alongside the river.

"Honestly John, I don't know where you get all this money. Being a newspaperman sure must pay well. You always have enough money, even if no one else does!"

Wilms quickly changed the subject. "Cathy, do you realize that the water flowing past us comes all the way from the north in Minnesota–from a lake called Itasca? This is one long river. Of course, it's mixed with thousands of streams all along the way. This river represents what this country is all about, a mixing of waters from everywhere.

"It's like the mixing of all the different types of people who make up this country. The sum of these different types of people makes a bond stronger than just the individual people alone. It's unfortunate that this river represents the lifeblood of this country, and that's why some of the biggest battles are going to take place right on our doorstep."

"So, you think the major battles are going to take place right here around Vicksburg?" asked Cathy.

"Think about this," said Wilms. "Neither the Confederates nor the Union can afford to lose it. If the Confederates lose it, it cuts their territory right down the middle and separates them into two parts. If the North loses it, it means they can't bring their goods up and down the river to market. It also makes it hard to trade certain goods and crops with foreign countries. This issue has to be decided fast. You know what–the Union can't lose; it will have to win eventually."

As they were talking, a stylish-looking couple sat down at the table next to them. John immediately spotted Dee Ann, who did not recognize him right away as he had grown a beard since the last time they met. With his tall stature, his full beard, and dark eyes he looked very distinguished as Cathy's escort. He glanced at Dee Ann intently, giving her a long look, but she did not notice him due to his excess of facial hair.

As the couple walked by, Dee Ann appeared to be much taller than the man she was with. He was wearing a cavalry general's uniform. Wilms quickly recognized him as General Earl Van Dorn.

Since there were so few patrons at the outdoor tables, Wilms had nowhere to hide and proceeded to introduce Cathy to the couple. The introduction went surprisingly well, and both Dee Ann and Wilms gave no hint of their earlier relationship, as it would have caused trouble for both of them.

Wilms took careful note of Van Dorn's presence in the proximity to Vicksburg, and wondered whether it was a harbinger of a large rebel cavalry contingent in preparation for a Yankee assault on Vicksburg.

He pulled his bottle of good French wine from out of the basket, and asked the waiter for some glasses. The four began a rare moment of relaxation. The waiter brought the cooked eggs and potatoes, and when Van Dorn saw this he quickly wanted the same thing. Wilms cautioned him on the expense, but he persisted.

"I just collected my last month's pay, and I've got nothing to do with it, so I might as well spend it here. Dee Ann do you want the same thing?"

"I'd love it," she quickly added, and the waiter left with two more orders for eggs and potatoes.

Wilms began a general discussion of the Vicksburg situation, hoping to glean some information from Van Dorn. "The Yankees have been sending a lot of boats past the guns of Vicksburg, trying to run the river. Ever since New Orleans fell, things are getting hotter and hotter down here. The only good thing is that they don't tend to come through on the river during the day. It's too dangerous for them."

"You know what I think," said Van Dorn. "I think they're just testing us to check out our defenses in preparation for the big assault. They won't tolerate the river cut off from their traffic without trying to free it up, and we can't tolerate our country being cut in half by the Yankees."

"Do you think you can help the city with your cavalry?" Wilms asked.

"It depends on where. Cavalry is not much good in swampy, muddy areas, and it doesn't give us the freedom to wheel across the country in any direction we wish, as in Georgia or in Virginia. We may be able to help out some if needed."

With a grimace of impatience Dee Ann burst out, "Can't you men talk about something other than the war? I declare! It's getting harder to get by these days. Can't we take our minds off it at least for a day or two?"

This put the kibosh on Wilms's attempt to glean more military information from Van Dorn. At that point the conversation moved into a discussion of much lighter topics, and Wilms dared not discuss heavy topics of war any further. He felt he would appear too interested in military goings-on, which might seem suspicious to other people.

Dee Ann and Van Dorn received their food and ate it with great relish. After about a half hour of talking and finishing the bottle of wine, Van Dorn said, "I've only got a short period of time before I have to get back to my unit, and I promised to spend some time with Dee Ann before I left. So, we'd best be on our way. Nice to have made your acquaintance."

On their carriage ride back to Vicksburg, Cathy talked to Wilms about her perceptions of their newfound friends. "What a handsome couple those two are," Cathy observed.

"Yes," said Wilms, "they are truly very impressive looking."

CHAPTER 53

FROG LEGS PROVENÇALE

Nate ran Joseph's plantation buggy at a fast trot on the road from Vicksburg to Warrenton. At one point the horse broke stride and went into a gallop, sending a shower of dust and small clumps of mud back toward Nate and Joan. "Slow down, slow down!" yelled Joan and grabbed Nate's arm with a vice-like grip. Nate quickly complied but not before a few bits of mud hit both of them.

Nate and Joan headed down to the river as they had planned to do. Emily gave him a note, which gave them permission to use the buggy and be on the road.

As had been planned, Joan was wearing her New Orleans dress and Nate was well-attired in the same suit he had worn to the ball in New Orleans several years before. Both of them were wearing a duster over their fine clothes.

Going to the tavern, as the four white people had just done, was out of the question for them. They tied up the buggy and walked down to the river.

Standing on the riverbank was not as free and easy as it had been in the days before New Orleans was captured. Both

Confederate and Union boats now used the river, and if they ran into each other, a battle ensued.

Nate carefully scanned the river to make sure there was no hostile traffic there. When he was satisfied, they walked down to the river and found an abandoned boathouse filled with water and rowboats tied up in a cove. This cove was cut off from the river, so it resembled a small lake.

They sat down to eat some morsels of food they had brought with them. "It's really nice here," said Nate. "I would love to bail out that boat and take you out here in the cove. The water appears to be very shallow, and there is no one around for miles."

Joan turned towards him, put her hand on his arm, and said with a concerned look, "Aren't you forgetting we are still both slaves officially? Slaves don't go out boating. They don't have the luxury of that kind of behavior. If we got caught, what would you say? It's going to appear suspicious. Slaves out having a good time may not be acceptable behavior in Warrenton."

"Aw, come on honey, let's just go for a little boat ride. You said that we never do anything exciting anymore."

"I'm sorry Nate, I think it's too much of a risk."

Nate looked crestfallen for a few moments and suddenly said, "I've got an idea. There are frogs out there along the shore. If we take off our Sunday best and strip down to our underclothes, we can catch some frogs for food. I know how to prepare delicious frog legs. We can say we are searching for food for Miss Emily. Since I have a reputation as a chef in the area, I believe everyone would buy our alibi."

"You're right," said Joan. "This will work, let's do it."

They started off by bailing out a rowboat with a jug that had been left in it. They pulled the boat down to the water and put it in. It leaked slightly, but not enough to cause them any trouble.

Nate and Joan took off their suit and dress, and stripped

down to their underwear. They set up their plan of attack to catch some frogs. Next, they went up to the boathouse, where they found a large box with a secure cover that held anchors for the boats. They took the anchors out and brought the box to hold the frogs. After that, they took the boat out in shallow water and scanned the shore for frogs, which were very noisy at that time. After a few minutes of searching, a huge bullfrog was spotted with his head sticking up near the bank of the cove.

"Let's land the boat up a way, past the frog," said Nate, "and walk back and try to catch him. I'll sneak up on him from the shore and jump in the water to catch him."

"You take the first one, and I'll try the next one," said Joan.

They rowed slowly past where the frog was, and pulled the boat up on the shore about fifty feet past the frog. Nate slowly snuck up on it, with Joan following behind him. Unfortunately, when they got to the spot where they had seen the frog, it was no longer there.

Nate blew a sharp breath of exasperation when he saw nothing there. "This isn't going to be an easy job," he told Joan and was about to get back in the boat when Joan called out. "There he is—right near the shore!"

Nate resumed his stealthy shadowing of the frog and slowly got within five feet of the monster bullfrog. When he felt the time was right, he jumped in the water, grabbing the frog, and made for the shore. Just as he got back on land, the frog—in a desperate attempt to get free—pushed Nate's hand apart with his powerful hind legs and sprang free on the shore. He took two enormous bounds of seven feet at a time and jumped into a shallow pool of water near the bank.

Joan jumped in after him and quickly caught him—but again, the frog was too strong and burst out of Joan's hand, only to be caught a second time by Nate, who wisely held onto it by its abdomen, avoiding its strong legs. They took the frog to the box, closed it up, and went back to look for more frogs.

"Let's see if we can catch a few more like him. Then we can make a real good meal out of the legs," said Nate.

"I hope they are easier than this one," Joan responded. "He sure was a lot of work!"

They found another big bullfrog, but not quite as big as the first one. This time it was Joan's turn, and she snuck up, copying Nate. She jumped in the water and caught the frog, but when she got it back on the bank the frog broke free, just as the other one had done. Nate had to assist her in capturing it.

They caught five more big ones a bit more easily by working together. They went on to the eighth frog, which was comfortably ensconced in some lily pads nearby. Nate jumped in, but the frog got loose and started to swim away.

Joan followed suit by jumping in also, landing awkwardly on her side right next to him, but it was too late. Laughing at her determined but clumsy dive, Nate brushed away several strands of her wet hair from around her mouth. They kissed passionately among the lily pads before retiring to the boathouse where they proceeded to make love on the floor.

Before leaving, they put everything back where they found it and put their frogs in a sack they found in the boathouse. They got dressed, joyous to be working together as a team, and carried home their haul of frogs.

When they arrived at the plantation carrying the sack, Nate said to Wilma. "Guess what we are having for dinner? Frog Legs Provençale!"

CHAPTER 54

THE BEGINNING OF THE END

On a mild February day in 1863 on the riverside of the plantation, Wilma was outdoors walking toward the river close to where two Confederate rams were anchored in the river, building up steam. She saw the Union gunboat *Indianola* run slowly past, towing two barges. A few minutes later she heard the booms of cannon fire and ran to get Jackson, Nate, and Joan to watch the battle.

They all came running out at the same time and ran down to the river together. The two Confederate rams got on each side of the *Indianola* and rammed it several times.

Heavily encumbered by the two barges it was towing, the *Indianola* could not move very fast. The boats kept maneuvering and turning in the water to avoid being rammed, but the *Indianola* was getting the worst of the ramming because it was so sluggish in maneuvering. After a struggle that lasted about twenty minutes, it nosed into the riverbank, struck her colors, and surrendered.

Some of the crew climbed onto the bank and ran away. The four watching the river battle were downcast.

"I hate to see a rebel victory," Jackson said. "I don't think there have been very many rebel victories in this area."

"Hey! Wasn't *that* rebel boat once named the *Queen of the West*? But now she's flying a rebel flag," said Nate. "She must have been captured. Look, those are two ironclad rams captured by the Confederacy."

"Is the Union really winning this war?" said Jackson sarcastically.

"We are looking at the winners in a losing cause," Nate answered as they continued to gaze at the aftermath of the battle.

Everyone had a dejected look on their face, as these results would obviously impede any Union victory for a while.

After a period of tense jockeying around, the Union army began to make some headway in the area around Joseph's and Jefferson's plantations. Having made raids all along the river, they finally reached these Davis plantations as well. They destroyed the Davis's property and furnishings and set fire to the main house. Confederate raiders had come, trying to recapture the slaves but did not succeed.

Through all of this chaos the team continued to live in the guesthouse unmolested due to the good graces of the marauding Union troops, who knew they were Union spies. Josh and his group had even helped the slaves on the Davis plantation to organize a defense and repel the marauding Confederate raiders, who planned to steal the slaves for themselves.

In the middle of April 1863, the Union fleet had been running the guns in front of Vicksburg several times a week with mixed results. There were many hits on the Union ships, with sailors killed and wounded, but overall light casualties, considering the scope of the operation.

Grant had been trying to capture the city, with poor results to date. He tried everything—from digging canals to bypass the city, to a direct assault on the fortifications on the north side of the city. His soldiers were repulsed everywhere. At this point, after a council of war with his generals, he made a major change in his plans.

One particular evening, a large force of ironclad gunboats came down the river bearing many transports. At around the same time, Grant's army marched down the western side of the river across from Vicksburg. It appeared to be a repetition of the events Josh had witnessed several times before. It began with the bugle blowing *attention* as the fleet hung near the point at dusk. Instead of the fleet taking the path out in the middle though, which was mined with torpedoes, they took a path closer to Vicksburg to evade Josh's submerged explosives.

Josh had conveniently passed on the location of the torpedoes to Wilms, who forwarded it to Grant's headquarters. The first ship to start the transit was a rickety transport covered with sheets of iron, with two tall masts bearing glowing lanterns.

It headed right for the channel filled with torpedoes, and the Confederate soldiers on shore let out a loud cheer as a large column of water erupted alongside it. Within a couple of minutes its deck was awash, and it sank in shallow water. Much of its superstructure was still above the river, but its bottom squarely rested on the river bottom.

Its lanterns were still glowing brightly to warn other ships not to use the main channel. Grant had been waiting for the river to be at full height with the melting snow from the Midwest, and he now made use of channels that had been heretofore impassable.

Josh knew full well that the torpedoes had only been planted in the main channel. Two weeks before, when the work was done planting them, the water level in the side channels was not even deep enough to cover them. Without the pressure of an underwater explosion, they would have little effect on an ironclad hull.

All this information was available to Grant and Flag Officer

Porter, thanks to the information Josh had passed on to Wilms, who promptly sent it on. As the rest of the river fleet was almost abreast of the sunken transport, orange flares went up all along the river. Flares and bonfires were also lit along the riverbank. The eerie orange glow made the ships stand out clearly in the moonlit night.

The cannonade that followed was deafening. Eight, sixteen, twenty-four, and thirty-two pounders and several large caliber mortars let fly with everything they had.

Josh was on a ledge about two hundred yards back from the river and about one hundred feet above it, where his team was waiting with his telegraph apparatus and wires to set off the torpedo when the fleet passed over them. The fleet, however, was not going to pass over them due to his timely intelligence. The fleet began to draw abreast of the sunken transport, and it was clearly being slammed by the massive batteries of guns on shore.

The boats blocking the transports were taking multiple hits on their superstructure, and their smokestacks were even perforated. In some, the smokestacks were carried away.

One battery commander next to Josh's position ran a running commentary of the events. "One transport down, let's see how many we can get. How many more torpedoes do you have out there?"

"About ten," Josh replied, "but the rest of the boats are not going near them. They are using the river crest to take a short cut across an area they could not get across before the river got high."

"See those stacks that are carried away?" said the battery commander, "That means the ship is filling up with coal smoke and heat from the boilers. It must be a living hell for the crews on those ships. As long as they keep up their speed, they can get some ventilation from the smoke and fumes being pulled out by the air rushing over the top, but God help them ifn they slow down."

He called out to all the guns in his battery, "Have all the eight- and sixteen-pounders take five-second fuses and go for air bursts above the ships. Ifn we knock off enough of those stacks, maybe we can asphyxiate the crews, or force them out of the engine rooms. The solid shot is rarely penetrating the armor belts. It looks like you have to hit the same spot three or four times to make any penetration. If we can force the engine room crew above decks, they may become disorganized and stop screening the transports, and then we can get to them with our guns."

By now all the ships were returning fire. Shells from the ships came shrieking overhead, often showering his position with shrapnel and rocks. While it was difficult for the gunners on shore to damage the ironclads and get at the transports behind them, it was also quite difficult for the ships' gunners to knock out any of the gun emplacements. Many of these emplacements were well-installed and protected on the rocky bluffs.

As the battle wore on, Josh took note of some of the gun crews injured by shrapnel, but he could not find one major battery who had lost any of their big guns due to enemy fire. He did see several small eight-pounder fieldpieces put out of action by the ships' cannonading, but that loss was insignificant to the defense of Vicksburg.

Eventually, the fleet fought its way past Vicksburg with only two transports sunk. Many more were damaged but still usable for ferrying troops across the river. About one-third of the smokestacks were gone or severely riddled with holes from the shrapnel of the exploding shells.

All the ships held their position in the convoy, and Josh did not notice any ship that had left its station due to smoke or fumes. With the hellish din in his immediate vicinity gradually subsiding, he heard more ongoing commentary from the battery commander nearby.

"Well, they'all made it past us, but they're not out of the woods yet. We still got big guns all the way down the river. Send a telegraph message to Warrenton to be ready for them."

Josh then felt a pang of worry coursing through his body. He had set up three more torpedoes at Warrenton, but they were in the main channel. The plans were given to Wilms for this channel to be bypassed. The river was narrower at Warrenton, so the fleet would have to approach closer to the torpedoes than at Vicksburg.

There was a possibility of the ships being damaged or sunk, depending on their proximity to the torpedo placement. Josh also knew that the rebel army had two rams with reinforced prows to attack and ram any river traffic breaking through the guns at Vicksburg.

The order came from the battery commander asking to telegraph on to Warrenton to make sure the boilers were stoked on the rams to raise steam in order to be ready when the fleet made it to Warrenton, about twenty miles away. As the fleet pulled away, the guns around Vicksburg gradually fell silent as their targets moved steadily downriver toward Warrenton and Hurricane Island.

Josh began to ponder the reason that the flotilla ran the guns at Vicksburg, protecting the troop and equipment transports, and quickly figured out what the Union army intended to do. This transit of ships was taking place at the same time Grant was marching his army down the west side of the Mississippi opposite Vicksburg.

Josh realized he needed those transports to get his army across to the east bank of the Mississippi. He quickly realized Grant could cross at any point in the river down below Hurricane Island. This meant that he had better get word to his plantation to put their plan into operation because the Yankees were coming fast.

As soon as he could stand down from the aftermath of the river battle, he decided to meet with Wilms to discuss his interpretations of the events that were now unfolding.

He walked over to the newspaper office, and had to walk around a large shell crater made by a forty-two-pound shell that had exploded about one hundred feet in front of the newspaper office. It left the front of the building defaced by shrapnel from the blast.

Inside he found Wilms working on one of the presses. Some of the type was in a box. The rest was scattered all over the room. "Boy, were we lucky this time. The building sure got riddled with shrapnel, but the only damage to our printing presses was to that box of type that we are cleaning up now."

Josh quickly added, "We need to talk as soon as possible." They decided to go to their usual spot in the copse of trees. Josh quickly spelled out what he surmised regarding the purpose of the transit by the river fleet as well as the movement by Grant's army down the west bank of the river at the same time.

"It is quite obvious to me that Grant is going to use those transports to put his troops on the east bank of the Mississippi, strike at the soft underbelly of the Confederacy, cut across Mississippi, and lay siege to Vicksburg. Is the time right to put our plan in place, to warn all the slaves on the other plantations to give up their work and flee to the Union lines?"

"We are real close, but no cigar yet," Wilms added. "It's been four hours since the fleet blew through here. We might have some news from the telegraph station the rebels set up down the river–certainly by morning. It's getting late," Wilms said. "Why don't you get some sleep and come by in the morning."

CHAPTER 55

CREATIVE PLANS

When Josh came by the next morning, Wilms had the news he was waiting for. Grant had indeed marched his army to way down south on the Louisiana side of the river and crossed at Bruinsburg using the transports. No additional transports or ironclads had been sunk at Warrenton by either the guns or the torpedoes.

A small rebel army was moving to Port Gibson, however, to stop him. This meant the Union army would eventually have to move north to capture Vicksburg, which was the intention of their campaign. The time for the "strike" by the slaves was near at hand.

Josh's heart jumped in his chest when he realized what he would have to do—and very quickly. "I'm going to meet with General Pemberton," he told Wilms, "to discuss plans to move the torpedoes into the shallower flats, under the pretext that if the Union troops decide to use the river again, we will get them for sure."

"But Grant may not need to use the river much anymore, now that he has landed his troops," Wilms countered.

"Anyway," Josh continued, "I'm just going to use this as a pretext to go out on the river in a canoe at night. What I really want to do is use the canoe to escape Vicksburg and paddle down to Hurricane Island. I think I can do this at night. Then we can put our plan in motion to warn all the slaves on the other plantations and have them warn still other plantations. This can spread like ripples in a pond."

Wilms agreed with the plan but added, "Remember, this is a dangerous undertaking. You are going to have rebels on the east bank of the river, and Union troops on the west bank of the river. Both armies are going to have pickets stationed on the banks to prepare for an imminent attack. And there may be sharpshooters looking for targets on the river."

"Well, I'm going to go at dusk, and if I travel all night I can reach Hurricane Island well before dawn. The river is flowing swiftly—it is very high, and if I paddle fast, I can go as fast as a steamboat. I won't have to worry about underwater obstacles because I draw only about six inches of water under the canoe. I'll cover my uniform with a black poncho and get some black paint to cover the canoe. I should only be visible in daylight, or maybe if they send up enough flares to light up the river—but again, maybe not. I'm going to try it."

"You know, it's not a bad plan," Wilms broke in. "Maybe I can go along with you. With two people paddling fast we could make really good time, and I get the feeling that my usefulness in Vicksburg is drawing to a close. But I will miss Cathy terribly if I leave. With Grant on both sides of the river, however, Vicksburg is going to be doomed. It should be only a few months till it collapses."

"We could do this, John, but how do I explain your presence? I can get out in the boat to the torpedo area, but what reason do I have to take you?"

"Well, I used to do a lot of fishing in that area for catfish, and I know the holes where the fish hang out. You can tell the generals they would be real good placements for torpedoes. You'd be taking a guide who knows the river very well in these spots.

It's a mighty changeable river, and you have to know what you are doing."

"John, that's a great idea. I think I can convince them to try it. I'll also have to convince them to requisition some black paint for the canoe to protect us from sharpshooters on the west bank of the river."

Josh left Wilms to go over to headquarters to talk with General Pemberton. He asked one of his staff if he could meet with the general. The staff member announced him, but General Pemberton was deep in thought perusing a map of the Mississippi below Vicksburg.

The general raised himself from his chair, sighing, and gave orders to his adjutant. "Tell General Bowen to hold the high ground at Grand Gulf as long as possible, but I'm afraid I can't help him. It looks like a simultaneous attack is shaping up at Haines Bluff, which the enemy wants real bad."

Pemberton then became quiet and returned to the map. Josh saw his chance to break into the conversation. "General, the torpedoes have not been as effective as we had hoped for. Many of them are just in the wrong places right now. We had placed them just before the river got real high, and the Yankees are making use of other channels to bring their boats through. Their present placement is now ineffective against Yankee shipping.

"I want to move the torpedoes to better placements. If the Yankees try to run the river again, they will get a nasty surprise. I have a man who used to do a lot of fishing in the river, and he knows all the catfish holes in the area. I would like to bring him out in a canoe and have him mark the holes for repositioning the torpedoes. We will need a canoe and black paint because there are still sharpshooters reported on the DeSoto peninsula on the west bank of the river."

Since there was trouble brewing at Haines Bluff, north of the city, it looked like an attack was imminent at the same time that Grant was embarking his army at Grand Gulf. Pemberton was unsure of where Grant would strike next, and whether the fleet would make another attempt to run by the city, so he quickly acquiesced to Josh's plan.

While Josh was meeting with General Pemberton, Wilms went over to the telegraph office to tell Cathy that he might have to leave the city for an extended period. He walked over to the telegraph office and found two sentries outside who stopped him.

As he was talking, he raised his voice above the clatter, as both telegraph keys and repeaters were all sending and receiving messages at the same time.

"Sir, we have a lot of high priority military messages going through at the moment. Your message may be held up, as they have priority over civilian messages."

"I don't want to send a message," Wilms said, "I just want to talk to one of the operators for a moment."

"Okay, go ahead," said one of the sentries.

Wilms found Cathy at the key sending a message. Ezra was nearby, writing out a message he had just received. As soon as Cathy finished, Ezra said "Cathy, you take a break–you have been on that key for hours. I'll cover you. Why don't you get some air outside?"

As they walked outside, Cathy looked fatigued. Her usually pretty face looked tense. She had circles under her eyes as though she had not been sleeping well. "Oh John, things have been so out of whack, so confusing. We're taking so much telegraph traffic through the lines. Dad and I are working twelve-hour days. Our wrists are aching from all that work on the keys. Sometimes you start to send out a regular message, and an adjutant comes in with an urgent dispatch. Then you have to wait for answers–sometimes three or four answers–and then more dispatches come in. It makes things totally disorganized here. At the moment it's pretty quiet, but it can start up at any time.

"Another thing. Due to all the fighting nearby, the lines

are being cut all the time. We'all are having difficulty getting through to Jackson lately. We also got an army telegrapher to help us during the night, but his handwriting is almost illegible. I don't want to whine too much, but that bombardment by the gunboats is terrifying everyone."

John added, "I think things may go bad for a while, but eventually it will get better. If the Union forces keep coming, the war may eventually pass us by.

"This brings me to an important thing I want to tell you." Wilms swallowed hard and got to the kernel of what he wanted to tell Cathy. "It looks like I'm probably going to have to leave town for a while. And don't be surprised if I'm not able to get back for a few months due to the fighting in the area. You and Ezra should really leave the city. It may be cut off soon, and food and supplies are going to be very tight."

Cathy stared straight in John's eyes and said, "John, you know I can't leave town. The whole city garrison depends on my father and I for communications. If either of us left, they would see us as deserting our post. We are trapped here until the battle is over or the city is captured."

Wilms grabbed her hands tightly and looked her in the eye and said, "Well, when I get back maybe we can make plans to get married."

Cathy's eyes filled with tears, and her chin began to quiver with emotion. "I'm afraid of us being separated, even for a little while."

"That's another thing I wanted to tell you about," Wilms said solemnly. "If the Union fleet comes back and starts shooting, go for the caves. As long as you all stay in the caves, you will all be safe. Now this is between you and me–and don't tell anyone you know, but Feinberg has some extra food stored away. I told him about you, and if you get hungry, go to him. He will see that you get some."

Cathy turned her head away for a second, then faced John

squarely and looked deeply into his eyes. "Thank you very much for thinking about me, John, but I did hide away quite a bit of food when you told me to be prepared. I may not need it, but thank you anyhow. John, can you tell me where you are going?"

"I don't want to sound mysterious, but you've got to trust me. It is better not to know. If I can get a letter into Vicksburg, I will advise you by mail when I can. I know there are things that you can't tell me and things I cannot tell you, but after the war, and when we are married, we'll tell each other everything."

"All right, John, we'll have to leave it that way. I'll wait to hear from you then."

They embraced and he gave her a kiss goodbye that was deliberately not too passionate–so as to not engender longing for either of them. Wilms headed back to the newspaper office to wait for Josh to finalize the rest of the plan.

An hour later, Josh came back carrying a bag and a can of black paint with some brushes.

"General Pemberton said to go ahead with the plan, so we begin tomorrow morning. We'll paint the canoe tomorrow morning and leave it to dry all day in the hot sun. We'll head out tomorrow evening at twilight. We'll bring little floats, as though we were planning to tie them to some rocks to anchor them in the new spots for the torpedoes. But as soon as we get out there, we'll dump everything in the river and paddle down-river like hell!"

"I just hope the Union gunboats don't try to run the river tonight," Wilms added.

"We should be okay in that area because all the boats are busy embarking troops across the river down in Bruinsberg. The rest are going upriver to Haines Bluff. This should be a good time to leave," Josh said, "but there could be some problems across the way at the DeSoto peninsula. It's a long shot for the sharpshooters that have been reported over there, but we still have to be careful. That's why we are going to work at dusk."

CHAPTER 56

ESCAPE AN EVASION

The next morning, Josh and Wilms met at the Vicksburg landing and found a canoe nearby, which Josh had spotted the day before and hidden under a tarpaulin. It appeared to have no damage despite the shelling by the Union fleet. They pulled it back past some bushes and set to work painting it black. They also painted the three paddles for it as well. There were two fishing poles in the canoe, and Wilms wanted to take them along.

Josh's face crinkled, an obvious sign of displeasure, and he objected. "We're not going on a fishing trip. This is deadly serious business. Why would we want to take them along?"

"Well, you never can tell, we could get stranded out there and we might need food, and they're pretty light weight–besides, they belong with the canoe." As they worked, a few flies, gnats, and mosquitoes landed and stuck on the paint, but they did not care. They were only doing a quick job to camouflage the boat for night work. When they were done, they left it to dry and went off to talk with Seth Feinberg in his store, which fortunately was undamaged.

They found him comfortably ensconced behind the counter with his feet propped up on a chair. "Not much business these days," he said. "Even if there was, I wouldn't have any merchandise to sell. The river is cut off, and pretty soon the railroad will also be, so the only things to sell are in the inventory that I have had for a long time, and even that is dwindling.

"A store I might not have if not for that oak tree out front. When you leave, I want you to inspect it where those branches are missing. A big shell it stopped from a thirty-two-pounder headed right for us. I always hated that tree, you know, because it blocked my view of the river. Last year I was going to cut it down. Well I'm glad I didn't. It saved our lives."

"That's quite a story. We're glad you're all right," Josh said. "We are heading south to put our strike plan into place."

"Good luck! To help you I wish I could do, but I am now too old for that. All I can do is give you advice on how to conduct a revolution. We have learned a lot from the mistakes we made in 1848. Godspeed to you."

"You may be having some great difficulty in the next few weeks. I can't tell you and your wife what to do, but if I were you, I would leave the city if you can," said Josh.

"I wish Cathy could leave as well," Wilms added, "but she can't, and if she runs out of food, I told her to come looking for you."

"I will do my best to help her," answered Feinberg.

Since they were going to be paddling all night and Josh was off-duty till that evening, they went over to the newspaper office to take a nap in the storage room where they had a bed and a couch. They managed to get an hour's sleep before they woke up a bit groggy.

Wilms figured he would leave the office just the way it was so that no one would be suspicious of his motives or plans. After a quick dinner they went down to the boat dock carrying floats and markers for the torpedoes, two rifles and ammunition, two canteens, a pair of binoculars, two bowie knives, and some food for the trip. They also brought two small flags—a captured Union flag and a Confederate flag.

The canoe's paint was mostly dry, and they pulled it down to the water to launch it. The night was deathly quiet, but you could hear an occasional owl hooting, which created a ghostly atmosphere. The sun had set and the last traces of light were disappearing fast. The full moon had risen and was one quarter up in the sky. It would give them enough light for the trip downriver.

As they prepared to launch, they noticed an eerie moon shadow cast on the ground from a nearby oak tree that had fallen in the battle. All the branches were sharply delineated and seemed to point the way to the river with what appeared to be a gnarled, ghostly hand.

Before departing, they loaded their rifles and stowed them in the canoe. Then they put on black ponchos and rubbed mud from the river on their faces for camouflage. They paddled silently out to the middle where the sunken transport was resting on the bottom, its two masts still well above the water.

The current was reasonably swift out there. During much of the year it was at least three miles per hour, but now it appeared to be more like five due to the melting snow from up north.

The sunken transport seemed securely wedged on the bottom despite the current, so they took a chance and tied up to the mast above the water to get their bearings. As they were now stationary, lashed sideways to the wreck, they got a feel of the river's power. Branches and pieces of flotsam from all over the country came rushing past the gunwales of the canoe.

They realized that they should not stay there very long because the larger and more dangerous pieces of flotsam were partially submerged and difficult to make out in the failing light. If one of them hit the canoe the wrong way, it could turn them over, swamp the canoe, or even smash it into splinters.

At this realization, they picked up their rifles and fired two shots in the air, to make it seem like sharpshooters shot them so that their presence wouldn't be missed because they would both be presumed dead. They threw their float markers in the river and cut loose, trying to stay in the mid-channel where the torpedoes were resting.

The canoe quickly built up to a rapid speed, and they were going at least five miles per hour without even paddling. Then they paddled as fast as they could to maintain their speed for the long trip downriver.

They silently passed campfires on each shore, but no one saw them. As they came to the first bend in the river, they followed the moonlight's path on the water to keep dead center in the deepest part of the channel.

"This river keeps changing. I thought I knew it pretty well, but every year there are more twists and turns in it," said Wilms as they came to the outskirts of Warrenton and noticed another river flowing into the Mississippi. "That river is Big Bayou," Wilms added. "It means we're are coming into Warrenton," Wilms whispered. "We've got to be very quiet here as sound carries very well on the water."

"And there are a lot of rebel troops around Warrenton and many big gun emplacements," Josh whispered back.

As they began to pass the bluffs over the river, an orange light lit up on shore, illuminating the whole river.

"Oh shit!" Josh whispered. Then another orange flare went up from the bluffs, even further illuminating the river. But at that point they must have been sheltered under the overhanging bluffs, so no cannon shots followed.

Some small boats were launched from the Warrenton shore about a thousand yards ahead, and they headed out in the middle, which would have intersected their path downriver.

Josh and Wilms headed to the shore on the Louisiana side of the river and pulled the canoe under some branches. They got out onto the shore to await developments. Two of the boats stayed out in the river, while a third boat with two dogs and two men landed about a hundred feet from where Josh and Wilms hid their canoe.

They circled around the area while the dogs tried to pick up a scent, but the ground was swampy and not conducive to tracking. The dogs seemed to hesitate, not really going anywhere, as they had no frame of reference. Irrespective of the dog's ability to find them, they kneeled in ankle deep water behind two swamp oaks covered with Spanish moss. The air was so filled with humidity that the sweat built up in their bodies and all over their faces.

Terrified, both their hearts were pounding as they awaited their fate.

As the two Confederate soldiers came closer, Josh and Wilms drew their bowie knives, and as the men and dogs moved past them, they crept up from behind, covered their mouths, and stabbed them both in the back, killing them quickly.

The dogs then turned on them and after a frenzied tussle, they stabbed the dogs to death as well, but not before they were bitten several times. The men died quietly, but the dogs made yelping noises that must have been heard on the river.

Wilms and Josh pulled the bodies into the bushes, and went down to the river to clean the blood off themselves and off their knives as well. Josh had brought along a bar of soap to clean the wet paint off if it got on them. Instead they used it to clean the dog bites before cutting bandages out of their undershirts. Wilms, with his previous medical training, supervised the bandaging.

The two other boats were pulling for shore about one hundred yards upriver. Wilms and Josh could see them through the mist but did not think they themselves could be seen. They decided to make a run for it because their canoe was much faster than a rowboat. They pulled the canoe back in the river and took to paddling at breakneck speed. For some reason the rowboats either did not see them or chose not to follow them.

Before long they were well past Warrenton, but this episode had cost them a couple of hours.

Very soon they were going to be in the river at dawn—very soon, where they could not help being seen. As they paddled, they talked about what they had been through.

"We had to kill those guys, it was them or us," Wilms said. "All our plans could have been unraveled. We could have been shot or hanged as Union spies, or at best you could have been shot in a rebel uniform for deserting your post. We have a revolution and strike to participate in now, and it might not happen without us."

Then Josh whispered, "Where did you get the idea to wash the dog bites with soap?"

Paddling and breathing hard, Wilms answered, "I've written a lot of articles about the latest medical developments. In the last ten years there have been articles coming out that there are tiny living things that cause disease and infection, and it's important to kill them. There is a doctor in Scotland named Doctor Lister who has been writing books and lecturing on these theories."

"I read something about that just before the war broke out," Josh said. "It was about a doctor named Pasteur who was showing that wine ferments from these microscopic organisms."

"I'm not sure if it's true or not," Wilms continued, "but I'm not taking any chances. If these theories are true, all medical practices will be using them before long."

"I feel bad about killing those guys, but this is war. We have to get over this."

"Maybe if we had shot them," Josh replied, "it wouldn't have felt so bad. When you shoot someone with a gun, you don't feel like you are ripping their body apart with your own hands, even though the gun is just as deadly," Josh added breathlessly.

"We just have to get over it. We are not out of the woods yet."

CHAPTER 57

A VOYAGE FROM HELL

The eastern sky was beginning to look rosy as the sun was just beginning to illuminate some high, thin, cirrus clouds overhead, but the river was still dark.

As they came to a bend in the river, the sun was just beginning to come up. They noticed a line of eight-pounder cannons lined up on the riverbank with ammunition caissons right next to them. They were sharply delineated by the rising sun.

As they drew abreast of the cannons about two thousand yards away, one of them opened fire on them. The shell exploded in the water about seventy-five feet away, but a piece of shrapnel put a hole the size of a thumb in the hull above the waterline.

While Josh continued paddling, Wilms attached the Confederate flag with fish hooks to the fishing pole, and began to wave the flag. The men manning the cannon stopped reloading, and as they passed them, waved to them.

At that moment a fresh breeze blew up from the north, which they felt over their shoulders as they were paddling. Things appeared to smooth out on the river, except that both their hands began to ache from the dog bites, and when Josh looked at his bandaged left hand, it had swollen up around the indentations made by the hound's jaws. Wilms also complained of pain, but neither of his hands was as swollen as Josh's left hand.

Wearily looking back towards John, Josh exclaimed, "I wish we didn't have to paddle so much. It is aggravating my left hand terribly. The bite is right in the palm of my left hand. Every time I steer or paddle, it's becoming unbearable."

As a former doctor, Wilms was always one to improvise solutions for difficult situations. He said, "Let's try this, it could rest our hands." He took out his bowie knife and cut four small holes in each corner of the Rebel flag, and then unrolled some fishing line off the fishing reel. He had Josh hold up two oars, and he tied the flag to the oars, making a crude sail.

Josh sat between the oars on the canoe seat, holding the oars under his armpits, while Wilms steered with his one good hand and the third paddle. The breeze kept up and after a bit of experimenting with the new configuration, the bow was cutting through the water just like a sailboat. They navigated a long straight stretch with the wind either at their back or over the rear quarter.

After a half hour or so of sailing in this fashion, another bend in the river was coming up, which would require a radical departure from their sail configuration with the wind at their back. At the same time, they had been hearing occasional cannon shots reverberating along the river. These echoes kept repeating as though there were many cannons involved. They were both thinking that some fighting must be going on nearby.

Josh began to scan both riverbanks and came upon a very unpleasant sight.

Partway down the bend, he saw a Confederate battery of eight-pounders on the Mississippi side of the river, and two Union howitzers on the Louisiana side. The gunners were trading shots with each other from time to time.

Josh and Wilms froze in place when they realized they were going to have to run the gauntlet between these two warring parties. Josh reacted first, saying, "maybe we should get off the river and wait for night before crossing between them."

Then Wilms came up with what appeared to be a brilliant idea. "First we take down the sail," he said and cut the line holding it.

"Now give me the American flag." He then tied the two flags back to back as best he could, with fishing line and fish hooks. One was slightly bigger than the other, but he improvised well putting them together. He then tied them to the fishing pole and had Josh hold a line coming from the top hole to the front of the canoe.

"Now Josh, you must hold that line tight so that the rebels see a rebel flag and the Union troops see a Union flag. Troops are very reluctant to fire on their own flag, but if you ever let go of that line and the flags turn around in the wind, the Union troops will see a rebel flag and the rebel troops will see a Union flag and they'll all shoot at us."

They went back to paddling and drew abreast of the gun emplacements on each side of the river as a cheer went up from both sides. Almost immediately both sides stopped shooting at each other, and pulled their cannons back from the embankment.

Josh said to Wilms, "I think our gesture created a kind of peace overture, because each side here thinks that the other side let the canoe by unmolested while bearing the flag they support. More than that," continued Josh, "they cheered the transit by the canoe. Each side thinks the other cheered their enemy's flag, or was impressed by our bravery, which they thought did honor to their side."

They both agreed that this move had a definite effect of ameliorating the previous murderous intent by both sides. "You know," said Wilms, "if the North and the South could have discussed their issues in a calmer atmosphere, maybe they could have averted a war.

Just watching what played out here shows how murderous impulses can be stopped dead in their tracks by a series of events," said Wilms. "But these events were a sham—they were not real. They were created by us."

"That's true," said Josh, "but both sides were stopped in their tracks. Maybe if people had really listened to each other in discussions and had taken the time to understand each other's positions, all this killing could have been averted. That is what democracy is supposed to do, but it didn't do it here.

"People weren't able to see beyond their own preconceived ideas. Look at our side. We could not accept slavery under any condition. It violated our concept of inalienable rights. They, on the other hand, couldn't accept their economic system being destroyed. It's what they grew up with, and they knew full well that many founders and heroes of their country like Washington, Jefferson, and Jackson owned slaves."

At that point Wilms added a sharp rebuke. "Look, we have no time to speculate about this stuff. We are still not out of the woods, although we're getting closer to Hurricane Island."

They had another straight stretch, and as their hands were still aching. They decided to put up the sail even though it was now doubled in weight with both flags sewn together. As they were re-rigging it up they took their eyes off the river for a few moments, and the canoe hit a root sticking out of the water and was stopped momentarily. Before they could free themselves up, they were rammed broadside by a floating telegraph pole. It had so much mass and momentum that it stove in the side of the canoe, which immediately began to fill with water.

Josh managed to push the end of the pole out of the canoe, but held on to it, because he knew the wound to the canoe was mortal, and no amount of bailing by Wilms could save it.

They had just enough time to abandon the canoe and hold onto the pole, but unfortunately, they lost all the equipment and food they had brought with them as the canoe sank. The only thing they still had were the binoculars around Josh's neck, and their knives around their waists.

They hung on helplessly to either end of the pole as it floated down the river, reckoning that there were only a few miles left to Hurricane Island. The island was right in the middle of the river, so they knew they were eventually going to make it—that is, if their aching hands were able to keep hanging on.

Although steering the log seemed out of the question at first, Josh and John discovered that, if they kicked in opposite directions, they could make it turn slowly in a circle. This maneuver was useful when it seemed about to drift out of the main shipping channel.

They were practicing moving the log in this manner when they heard a steam whistle and saw great clouds of black smoke rising over the bend. They also heard the chunking noise of a steam paddle in the distance.

"Come to the center of the pole," screamed Josh. They moved to the center of the pole to talk, and quickly decided that they had better get out of the main channel because a riverboat was coming through and could very easily run them over.

The big question on their minds was—whose steamboat was this? Is this Confederate or Union? If it was Union, they could try to hitch a ride downriver, but they could just as easily be captured for a while, upsetting their urgent plans. On the other hand, if it was Confederate, they needed to avoid it altogether. Actually, they decided they needed to avoid capture as best as they could either way.

Maneuvering out of the shipping channel was easier said than done. They moved to opposite ends of the pole and kicked in opposite directions endeavoring to turn it perpendicular to the river channel so that they could move it forward.

Wilms screamed, "Kick as hard as you can," as they tried to move it away from the central channel.

They were just beginning to make a bit of headway as two

enormous smokestacks belching clouds of black smoke towered over the riverbank. A huge riverboat came around the bend covered in iron plate and resplendent in appearance. It quickly loomed up in the center of the river and rapidly began to bear down on them–though still some distance away.

The boat was moving at flank battle speed. Its huge paddles were chunking, giving off a very frightening sound. Black smoke continued to belch out of the smokestacks and a shower of sparks landed in the river behind it. It was an apparition from hell, and unfortunately it was flying a Confederate flag.

"Oh no, it's the *Queen of the West*," Josh hollered. "It was captured a couple of months ago. It can't stay in this part of the river long because the Union fleet will capture it. It must be headed to a tributary of the Mississippi, maybe the Atchafalaya River down below." The riverboat had four cannons on board.

As the boat drew nearer, Josh motioned to Wilms to stay on the lee side of the pole and as low in the water as possible to avoid detection. The pole was in the far end of the channel, which should have given it enough room to pass, but Josh spied an eddy current across on the other end of the channel. This meant that there probably was an underwater obstacle. To avoid it the boat would have to come closer to them than they would have liked.

All of a sudden, the boat appeared to turn sharply and at the last moment headed right at them. There was no way they could get out of its way as they both gripped the pole in a bear hug.

Josh and Wilms looked up and saw an enormous hull coming right down on them from above. They got quite a jolt as the bow of the boat hit the end of the pole about twenty feet away from where they were both hanging on. It pushed the pole away from the boat, and a part of it stayed underwater for a while, but when the pole came up to the surface, the boat had gone by and they were off the stern. Unhurt, even though they swallowed some water in the collision, Josh and John continued to keep a low profile.

The crew in the boat did not have a chance to investigate the collision closely because there was considerable glare coming off the water, which helped to hide the two men holding onto the big pole.

The *Queen of the West* was in a terribly big hurry, lest the Union Fleet discover it—another reason not to stop. As the boat receded down river, Wilms and Josh began to speculate on what had just happened. Their voices were hoarse from coughing up water.

"Whew, that was real close. We're lucky to be alive after that collision. Good thing she hit the front of the pole 'cause it pushed us away from the boat fast. That was some acceleration!"

Wilms, shivering from fear and cold, agreed. "We were so close to getting run over and getting ground up in the paddle wheels. How come they didn't even seem to notice us?"

"She must have been at least five hundred tons displacement," Josh yelled, "and maybe a thousand tons—with the cannons and supplies. Thank heavens she's a ram, which means her prow is reinforced for ramming other boats." He breathed heavily. "No way that pole could have done any damage."

"They probably did not feel anything at all," Wilms said between shivers, "and if they did, they couldn't afford to stop. If the Union fleet were to catch them, they would be dead meat."

"They would have stopped," Josh yelled, "if the pole hit the paddle wheel and damaged it along with two crushed bodies!"

"It's poetic justice," said Wilms. "First that pole rams us and destroys our canoe with us in it. Then it seems a higher power comes along and makes a big boat ram the pole, paying it back for its transgression—but again, with us holding on."

Through chattering teeth Josh declared, "All's well that ends well."

"But it hasn't ended yet," Wilms said. "This has been a voyage from hell!"

At that point Josh began to think of Emily and his team of friends, and how they were doing. He was certainly a bit shaken up by this experience, but perhaps they too were in a perilous situation. His mind was teeming with questions such as—how far away was the Union army and—what exactly was happening at Davis Bend.

About a half hour after the collision with the *Queen*, they began to make out the promontory in the river, which signaled Hurricane Island and home. They maneuvered the pole toward shore awkwardly, and when it resisted their attempts, they abandoned it in shallow water and walked to shore.

Just as they were coming out of the river, Josh yelled to Wilms, "Look out, water moccasin!" The snake was uncomfortably close to Wilms. Josh grabbed a piece of driftwood and clubbed the snake to death with repeated mechanical blows. He was in no state of mind to give the river a final opportunity to frustrate their plans.

It was only as they set foot on dry land that they finally realized how trying and tiring their journey had been. Without a word spoken between them, both collapsed on the ground to catch their breath and gain enough strength for the walk up to the house.

CHAPTER 58

ON STRIKE

Josh and Wilms began walking with great difficulty toward the guesthouse, which was home to them. As they walked across the fields, they noticed that some of them had been plowed and prepared for planting, but no planting had yet started. The aromatic smells from the soil were a pleasant change to their nostrils as they staggered across the fields very much affected by their prolonged immersion in the river.

They ran into Nate, who in spite of his modest size, did the job of a towering lumberjack breaking up big pieces of wood and heaving them onto a pile twenty-five feet away.

"You guys are all wet. Come into the house and get some dry clothes. What are you doing here anyways?"

"We just escaped from Vicksburg," Wilms said.

"It's time to put our plan into action for the slave revolt," Josh said intently. "The Union army is getting very close."

"We already started yesterday," said Nate, "when we got word from Joseph that the Union troops had landed at Bruinsburg. Joseph and Eliza are rarely here anymore, but we have use of the stables and all the equipment we need. We have been sending out our riders to all the plantations to tell them '*the Yankees are coming*,' which is the signal to head for the Union lines where they will be free under the Emancipation Proclamation. We even notified Marie Laver to advise her voodoo followers. There isn't going to be much work done around these parts now. We are all going on strike.

"Joseph and Eliza took off and left the place in care of Ben Montgomery and the slaves he had running the place. We are using their horses to warn the other plantations that the Yankees are coming. This was the arranged signal for the workers to throw down their tools, and leave the plantation, even if the masters or overseers are still there. They can't stop hundreds or thousands of slaves with just a few men.

"Look," Nate continued, putting his hand on Josh's shoulder. "You two look like you've been through hell. Why don't you rest up a while, and then we'll fill you in on all the goings-on around here."

At the same time that Josh and Wilms arrived at Hurricane Island, Jackson galloped up to the Turner plantation, a few miles further down the road, for the second time. When he had ridden up earlier to warn the slaves, there was a lot of activity going on. He noticed the town sheriff there so he decided to wait before making a grand entrance to warn the plantation.

Jackson took one look and decided the time was right for the strike to begin. There were a few slaves out front, with one old white overseer left in charge carrying some bags of grain to the stables.

Jackson came galloping up at full speed. "The Yankees are acomin'—the Yankees are acomin'!" he yelled.

Mr. Waller, the overseer said, "Where are they?"

Jackson looked down at the ground then looked down the road and said, "About ten miles down the road." Masr Davis done left, and ma masr done told me to rush over here and warn you. Da masr said warn Mrs. Vreeland too, so ah is headed over dare. Mah mistress, Miss Emily, don told me to ask you if you could warn the Wood plantation and any others you kin reach.

"Masr Joseph said to tell anyone that the Yankees done broke through the lines in many places, and they is headin' north. He dona know where they is headen, but the army can't protect this area. Everyone is warned to prepare for da Yankees comin' for a long time. Miss Emily said ifn you could tell da Wood people to warn all the plantations, dey can, and have each one warn one or two more, den everyone will be protected from da Yankees."

"You tell Miss Emily," Waller said, "that I got her message, and I'm agoin' to warn the Wood plantation raht away, and I'll tell them to warn others."

"Okay boss, I gots my orders from Miss Emily, sose I gots to head over to Mrs. Vreeland right away."

"Okay. Thank Miss Emily for warning me."

Jackson galloped off toward the Vreeland plantation with a big smile on his face. Waller had swallowed the whole story. By tomorrow all his slaves would be leaving en masse, and maybe the Wood's as well.

Jackson had a similar encounter at Mrs. Vreeland's, and gave them instructions to warn other plantations. By using Joseph Davis as the source of information, his advice was considered beyond reproach.

He was heading back to Josh and Emily's plantation when he was waylaid by two enforcement officers of the Confederacy. They stopped him at gunpoint to ask him what his business was riding a horse on the road. "Niggers on horseback on the road are not allowed unless they have permission of their master," they told him.

"Boss, I has permission. Miss Emily gave me this note to warn all the plantations in the area." He showed the note to the enforcement officers.

"I guess those Yankees are getting awful close," said one of the enforcement men. "Okay. You go about your business."

Jackson got back on his horse and galloped back to the plantation with the information on the two plantations he had notified. When he arrived, he found Joan, Wilma, Nate, and

Emily working on a grid map and chart of all the plantations in the area. There were check marks next to the ones that had been hit, and question marks next to those that hadn't.

Josh and Wilms were taking a nap after their ordeal. Those plantations that were visited by Jackson or Elijah, the two horsemen who went out to get the strike going, were listed with check marks. Those with check plus were the ones that agreed to send emissaries to other plantations to warn them.

Jackson and Elijah had warned ten plantations each so far, and each plantation had a check-plus, which meant each had agreed to warn other plantations that the Yankees were coming. Jackson explained about his being stopped at gunpoint by the enforcement officers.

Still excited and a bit frightened by what he had just been through, he spoke with clipped speech. "They swallowed the story hook, line, and sinker. Miss Emily's note did the trick. They also turned a shade of green when they heard about the Yankees breaking through. I had the feeling that they would be headed out of town real fast. I bet we don't run into *them* anymore.

"Tomorrow Nate will be on the road," Jackson continued. "Maybe Josh and John should also go out to warn any that are left. If she is still here, we could ask Dee Ann to do that as well. She is a formidable horsewoman and well-known in the area, even if she isn't in on our plan. If we can sell her on the idea of warning everyone, the message will appear more and more credible. The more people panic and run, the better for our plan to really get rolling."

Josh and Wilms were so exhausted that they didn't wake up till the next day. It was decided by everyone to take the warning all the way to the next counties and get to every plantation they could reach, using everyone who could ride.

CHAPTER 59

STRATEGIES FOR REVOLT

The next morning, when Josh came downstairs he found Emily busy writing a note to cover Nate, in case he was waylaid by any enforcement officials. Now that he was well rested, Josh was eager to speak to the group over their substantial breakfast of hominy grits, sausage, corn muffins, and johnnycakes. Provisions were now scarce, and they had been economizing for some time on what little they had in preparation for this day.

"The slaves of the South have it in their power to end this civil war. They can do more than any army can do, just by laying down their tools and refusing to work for a criminally inhuman state. I will show you why what you have started and what we are going to complete will be responsible for winning this war."

"Isn't that a bit far-fetched to say what we are doing is going to win this war?" asked Jackson.

"I'm going to show you how," said Josh.

"When any army marches in and conquers territory," he continued, "it moves in a narrow band of territory maybe ten miles across, or at best twenty miles, with a huge army. Most of the rest of the land is untouched by the invader. That land continues to operate as it did before unless it decides to change its ways or allegiance, which is not likely in a conflict like ours."

"But this is an enormous conflict," continued Jackson. "How are we going to win it?"

"Please let me finish," said Josh, holding up his hand.

"Once the invader marches through an area and leaves it, that invader rapidly loses its ability to control the population if the population does not want to be controlled. Old allegiances still stand, and the people keep up economic support of their former cause.

"Take the situation in Virginia during General McClellan's Peninsula Campaign, when he marched his whole army down to the Richmond area but failed to take the capital, and then marched his army back. All of the territory reverted back to the Confederacy war effort on his exit.

"What we are going to do here is destroy the plantation system, so that even if the Confederates recaptured this territory, it would do them no good without slaves to run the plantation. Their economic system will be in ruins! It will be obvious to everyone that their system is morally bankrupt because it was built on the backs of slaves and is no longer working. We can cover hundreds of miles of plantation territory with our method, unlike an army, which can only control a narrow corridor of territory."

After breakfast and the distribution of food packed for the trip, the team saddled four horses for Nate, Jackson, Josh, and Elijah. It was also arranged that Wilms would visit Dee Ann, using if he could, their prior relationship as leverage to convince her on the effort of spreading the word.

Little could they have imagined the shock they received when the main road came into view. From the hill they were standing on, the road appeared to have a black ribbon running down the middle, which stretched for miles. Upon looking carefully, it became apparent to them that this was a sea of black humanity using the road, which was choked up with thousands of slaves who had abandoned their plantations and were headed south.

These slaves were walking toward freedom at a rapid pace. Some groups were singing spirituals. They heard the words, "No more auction block for me—no more, no more."

The four horsemen were so choked with emotion that they dared not to speak for a while, lest they burst into tears. From a distance the slaves appeared like an enormous host heading into battle, but they had no weapons. The only thing they carried was water and food in burlap sacks strapped to their backs.

In fact, the road was so encumbered that the riders had to take trails through the woods to get to where they were going. "I'd doubt that those enforcement officers could deal with this situation," Nate said. "Their guns would be next to useless against thousands of people as inspired as this crowd is. And it's going to get bigger and bigger."

Josh, Nate, Jackson, and Elijah, seeing the results of their work, now redoubled their effort to reach faraway plantations. They had to follow more circuitous routes due to the crush of humanity on the roads. After a while the four split up according to the prearranged plan and headed to their target plantations.

While they were making their way on the road, Wilms headed over to Dee Ann's to see if he could enlist her in warning some of the plantations nearby which still had not been contacted. This, he felt, would lend more credibility to the common effort.

He found her at the stable saddling her horse. "Well hello, Mr. John. What brings you to this neck of the woods at such a trying time?"

Before he could answer, she bent over close to him and took the bowie knife he had been wearing out of its sheath. "That's quite a beautiful knife. I always wanted to have one, but I worried that it would not make me appear ladylike."

"You will always appear ladylike, no matter what you wear,"

Wilms responded, "you don't have to worry! You know what? I'm going to give it to you as a present. That's not what I came over for, actually, it is bad news.

"As you know, the Yankees have broken our lines in many places and are coming here. It's just a matter of a few days, but we don't know exactly where they're going. We are warning all the other plantations in the area. If you could warn a couple of the nearby plantations, and tell each one to warn a couple of others, it would help everyone in the area. We are asking you because you are an expert horsewoman, and you could cover this ground quickly."

"Well, Mr. John, if you're going to put it in such a nice way, I'll be glad to help my neighbors. Uncle Joe said before he left that he might not be back for a while because of developments in the area. He told me to take care of the plantation with the servants who work for him. You know he gives them a lot of responsibility. It's almost like he sees them as owning a part of the plantation."

"Be careful," said Wilms, "there may be some deserters on the road who are lawless."

He then took his belt off and Dee Ann said, "Why Mr. John, what are y'all doing?"

"I'm giving you my knife like I said I would. If there are deserters on the road, it's better that you protect yourself."

Not to be upstaged in disrobing, and remembering their past history of sexual attraction, she added "Don't you worry about me, Mr. John, see what I have."

She lifted up her jacket revealing a small but powerful-looking revolver with an ivory grip in a holster. Williams quickly recognized it as a variant of a seven-shot Smith and Wesson twenty-two-caliber, which had been very popular just before the war broke out. Well-connected people could sometimes get the Smith and Wesson factory to make it in several different calibers, and this one was an experimental model in thirty-eight caliber. It had to use special ammunition that was only made up north and not available since the war. Fortunately, Dee Ann had plenty of it available.

"Uncle Joe gave this to me a long time ago, when the war began," she continued, "and I am very good with it. It is more powerful than most of the standard twenty-twos. I can hit targets as well as anyone around here. Jefferson taught me everything about how to use it."

Wilms said, "Can I see it?"

She took it out of her holster and handed it to him. He inspected the barrel, held it so that the sunlight illuminated the inside of the barrel, slid open the cylinder, and looked it over carefully. He unloaded it, held the bullets in his hand, then cocked the hammer and dry fired it to test it out. It was in perfect condition.

"Miss Dee Ann, this gun is in perfect condition and very well cleaned."

"I told you that Jefferson taught me everything about it."

He reloaded the gun and gave it back to Dee Ann. "One other thing, though," he added, "you might want to take some of the shortcuts through the woods that you are familiar with as there may be a fair amount of traffic on the roads. I mean armies coming and going, stragglers, deserters, and plantations moving their slaves to avoid the Yankees."

Dee Ann approached Wilms with her head turned to the side and a sarcastic look on her face. "Between you and me, and don't tell anyone else, Mr. John, I don't see why the slaves don't just escape. The Confederacy doesn't have enough men to watch them anymore. If I were them, I would run away now that the Yankees are so close. What do they have to look forward to if they stay here—a lifetime of slavery?"

"Some of them are very attached to their masters," he told her, "and won't leave easily like the servants who work for Uncle

Joe. Giving someone their freedom after a whole life of work for masters is one hell of an adjustment for some people."

As the conversation grew more serious, Dee Ann sat down on a stool nearby, and John sat on a hitching post right next to her.

"I know that, John. I am torn between the good work my Uncle Joe did to try to better the quality of life of his slaves, and their general condition throughout the South, where in many places it is awful. I feel that slavery is a terrible thing, and that Mr. Lincoln did this country a service with the Emancipation Proclamation. My problem is that the closest people to me and the ones I love the most, are deeply enmeshed in slavery."

"You mean Uncle Joe and Eliza, Uncle Jefferson and Varina?"

"Exactly, and General Van Dorn as well. My heart believes in abolition, but I feel I'm stabbing my two uncles in the back! Everything I own came from slavery—my horses, all my beautiful clothes, and my good life. I feel that I'm biting the hand that feeds me, but I have to do it."

"To judge by what is happening around here, the Yankees will win this war eventually," Wilms added. "Maybe if that happens and there is no more slavery, you and your family can all be reconciled in your hearts and minds. All across America, families have been torn apart in similar ways. Don't imagine that you are the only one going through this." Wilms's sensitivity to her situation had a strong effect on Dee Ann, and she nestled closer to him. He felt she was giving him all the signals for romance, but he chose not to follow that route. There was too much serious business at hand, and they both needed to get on the road.

An additional intrusive thought forced its way into his mind, and that was of Cathy who was probably going to be trapped in the city of Vicksburg under fire from Federal guns. For him to be gallivanting around romancing Dee Ann while Cathy was suffering under shellfire dampened any urge he might have felt to rekindle his past relationship with Dee Ann.

"Well, we should get on the road if we are going to make it to these plantations to warn them." Dee Ann was still holding the bowie knife in its sheath that he had handed her and she started to hand it back to him, but he shook his head and said, "No, you keep it. You may need it. Anyhow, it's my present to you."

"Okay," she said, "if that's the way you want it." With that, she playfully tucked the knife in her boot so that the handle was sticking out. She put her boot up on the stairs to pose, as for a painting or a photograph, pulled up her jacket revealing her revolver, and said, "How do I look, Mr. John?"

"Simply ravishing," was the reply. They gave each other a hug of friendship and headed off in different directions.

CHAPTER 60

MURDER IN SELF-DEFENSE

At the same time that Dee Ann and the group were out warning plantations, the Federal fleet made one of its night sorties through Vicksburg. They were towing a barge of mortars shielded by ironclads that began to drop a large amount of shells on the town. Many buildings were demolished, and residents hid in the caves nearby, which were impregnable to the shelling. This particular shelling destroyed the town bank, damaged the hotel, destroyed the telegraph office, and did significant damage to Wilms's newspaper office.

After crossing the Mississippi at Bruinsburg, Grant's army won several battles, but instead of coming directly up the river on the east bank of the Mississippi and heading directly for Vicksburg, Grant chose a more circuitous route inland. This route involved cutting off the railroad to Vicksburg that had previously brought supplies to the city. The operation was designed to pull Confederate troops out of the city to defend the railroad.

He then marched on the state capital at Jackson, which drew even more troops away from Vicksburg to the east of the city. It was easier to defeat them there than by attacking the elaborate fortifications of the city itself.

This turmoil in the countryside went on for several weeks with Grant slowly but inexorably moving west towards Vicksburg. During the month of May, General Sherman made several attempts to capture the city. All these attempts had been beaten back, with severe losses versus minor losses for the Confederacy.

Now that supplies by railroad and river were cut off, Grant and his staff decided the time had come to lay siege to the city. He now needed more intelligence on the location of forts and defensive structures within the city. He became aware of Josh's and Wilms's whereabouts and felt they would be valuable sources of information on the fortifications in Vicksburg. He sent a detachment of troops to escort them back to his headquarters outside Vicksburg.

Thousands of slaves in western Mississippi were steadily moving southeast from the river, trying to keep away from Confederate troops, who were coming down the roads to stop the Yankees. As the Confederate troop wagons and guns came down the road, the escaped slaves would hide in the woods until they went by and then return to the road.

One slave, who had ventured too long on a trail in the woods, was captured by two Confederate deserters, who tied him to a tree and were getting ready to kill him. They kept asking him where the plantation he had come from was—because they planned to loot it, take what valuables they could, and kill anyone who tried to stop them.

The interrogation went like this: "Where is your plantation, and how do we get there?"

"Ah don know where it is, boss," replied the slave, "ahs lost in da woods. Ifn ah wasn't, ah woda find ma way home. Ah doesn't know which way to go, boss!"

After about ten minutes of questioning, they gave up. "Let's jest kill him and find someone else." One of them drew a knife and was about to cut his throat when a rider came galloping down the path with gun drawn. The rider fired two shots at the ground in front of the men, and they ran off into the woods.

It was Dee Ann, who was coming back from warning one of the plantations nearby. As she was walking her horse, she heard the slave's cries and went to help. After the deserters ran off, she dismounted and was walking over to untie the Negro man when one of the deserters who had not run very far off turned around and came back.

As she walked with her back to where the slave was tied to the tree, the deserter snuck up behind her and put his arms around her, holding her in a bear hug. Her face contorted with fear as she began to lose control of the situation.

She violently stomped down on his shoe with the heel of her boot, injuring his foot, and broke free. Then, as he came after her again, she jerked the big bowie knife that Williams had given her out of its sheath and in a panic stabbed him in the stomach. The knife buried itself all the way up to the hilt. She tried to pull the knife out for a second thrust, but it would not come, so she grabbed it with both hands and was able to pull it out with an almost superhuman effort. But when she pulled it through the gaping hole in his stomach, she also pulled out half of his intestines and part of his stomach, which slid out of the huge wound and fell to the ground.

When her assailant saw what she had done to him, he collapsed in shock, moaning, and was no longer a threat. Dee Ann's face was bright red from all the blood rushing to it. Her heart was beating at breakneck speed, and she was covered in sweat.

She went over to the tied-up slave and cut him loose—to his profound thanks. "You done saved my life!"

Taking her canteen and some rags in the saddlebags, she cleaned herself up, then cleaned off her knife and put it back in her boot. The man on the ground was still moaning, so she took out her revolver and finished him off with a bullet through his head. Then she led the Negro slave out of the woods.

After this event she lost track of time and couldn't recall getting back to the plantation. She was just going through the motions of living as she was still in a state of shock.

On returning home she looked at her eyes in the mirror of the living room, and the person staring back at her did not really seem to be her. The feeling came over her that maybe she was losing her mind. She had just committed an extremely brutal murder, the kind of murder an insane person might commit. Was she insane?

There was no recollection of how she got home. The thought went through her mind that maybe the horse had brought her back with his memory of the trails, or possibly she may have just kept enough of her wits about her to find her way home.

Still, a part of the episode was blacked out in her mind, so maybe it was a little of both that got her back. Whatever the case, Dee Ann was a wreck, and she wandered around aimlessly for several minutes until her own voice urged her to go to the Lawrence plantation. There she found Wilms just getting back from assisting the group and warning the local plantations.

"We need to talk right away," she said.

"What's wrong? Y'all don't look right," Wilms said.

"I think I just killed a man with the bowie knife you gave me as a present. No." She frowned, trembling slightly. "I think I remember finishing him off with my revolver after gutting him with my bowie knife."

"What happened?"

"I was riding back on the trail from warning a plantation when I saw these two deserters torturing a slave who had left his plantation and must have gotten lost in the woods. They had tied him to a tree and were just about to kill him. So, I came galloping in with my revolver out and shot at their feet. They both ran off. But one of them hid in the woods and jumped me.

I crushed the heel of my boot onto his foot, which made him let go, and then I pulled my knife from my boot and gutted him. I just knifed him in the stomach—but when I pulled the knife out, all his guts and part of his stomach came sliding out and fell on the ground. He was moaning on the ground and would have died eventually. So I took out my revolver and killed him to put him out of his misery—as well as my own. Since this happened the whole world looks strange, and I don't feel right. Am I a mad woman to have killed someone in such a brutal way?"

Wilms abruptly turned toward her. "Look, that guy was a murderer, he would probably have killed the slave, raped you, and killed you as well. Some of these deserters are breaking into plantations in the area stealing what they can and killing anyone who gets in their way. I think you did the world a favor by killing him. When someone is killed by a bowie knife, it is often a very brutal event. Still, I'm glad I did give you that knife. It looks like it saved your life. I'm proud of the way you handled things, even though you are pretty shaken up. You're not mad at all. You were just defending yourself. It was him or you. On the trip down from Vicksburg I had to kill someone who was trying to murder me. I know what it feels like to kill someone for the first time."

The empathy and warmth that Wilms showed Dee Ann seemed to go a long way to helping her restore her mental health, and she snuggled up against Wilms, feeling the beginning of some relief.

CHAPTER 61

TRAGEDY STRIKES

The next morning, while Josh was out in the barn checking on extra hay for the horses, his group (which now included Wilms and Elijah) was busy at the kitchen table looking over a chart of the plantations they had visited in the area. Elijah had made a successful run to some big estates southeast of Hurricane Island and started an exodus in an area that had heretofore been untouched.

"You did a real good job Elijah," said Jackson. "I didn't think we'd be able to get to those plantations. Did you run into any enforcement men on the road?"

"No sir, I sure didn't. I sure is glad, even though I had Miss Emily's note. Dem guys is real scary, but I guess dey is more scared of the Yankees now, so they done skedaddled."

While they were talking to Elijah they received a strange surprise. Two more soldiers from Vicksburg who had floated downriver showed up at their front door. They had been trying to cross to the Louisiana side in a little ferryboat, which then was destroyed by a Yankee shell. The soldiers were thrown into the river unhurt, and they found a piece of the ferry that had an air pocket in it, which kept it afloat. They floated all night down to Hurricane Island and were now hungry and exhausted.

Emily quickly removed the chart of all the plantations in

the area. Since these were Confederate soldiers, the family went back to their roles of master and slave, probably for the very last time. The group fed the soldiers breakfast, and asked them questions about the shelling in Vicksburg.

"Them Yankees have brought up a barge with mortars, they are rainin' explosive shells and huge balls of solid shot. They are destroyin' all our buildings in town. We are agoin' to have to live in the caves full time. A mortar destroyed the bank and killed the bank president, and another shell completely blew apart the telegraph office. All the bodies were blown apart. No one was left alive."

At that point Wilms jumped up from the table. "Are you telling me the truth? My fiancé worked there. Are you telling me the truth?!"

They both nodded their heads.

Wilms became highly agitated and grabbed one of them by the collar. "You better tell me the truth!"

The other man quickly said, "We are telling you the truth—we both saw it with our own eyes."

Jackson stood up. "Please boss, you has gots to calm down. Dese men didn't hurt you," hoping his soothing words would bring Wilms back to reality.

They did. Wilms let go of the man, sat down, and put his head in his hands and started to cry. "We were going to get married. Now I have nothing to look forward to anymore!" After a moment's silence, he stood up but looked unstable on his feet.

Emily advised the two men to head north quickly if they wanted to return to the Confederate lines, otherwise they were likely to be captured by the Yankees if they stayed around this area.

"Y'all know that we has had enough fightin'. Our families never owned slaves anyhow. We came in the fight because everyone said our country was bein' attacked. All our leaders are slaveholders. We don't want to get killed defending slavery. The more we got involved in the fighting, the less we want to fight for something we don't believe in. Tell us which way the Union lines are. We would rather surrender to them then go back into the fight. We had a lot of time to talk about this as we were headed downriver. We have had it with this war."

"Well, if you head due east," Emily said nodding affirmatively, "the Yankee Army should be coming along soon, if they are not there already. You all will have to be careful to avoid the retreating Confederate Army. You may have to hide in the woods, lest they pick you up as deserters. Here is some food for lunch and dinner. Good luck."

The two men headed out.

Wilms was not himself for the rest of the day, and the team tried to give him chores to do to take his mind off his loss. He chopped wood, fed the horses, and cleaned out their stalls—but his face was drawn, and he had periods of tearfulness from time to time. He kept thinking, "I shouldn't have left her there without me to protect her."

This state of mind lasted for a couple of days, and then his grief modulated into a different phase where he no longer appeared outwardly on the verge of collapse but had long periods of brooding contemplation over the loss.

Over the next few days news came in about more and more victories by the Yankees as they cut off the railroad that connected Vicksburg to the other southern states on the east side of the Mississippi River. The Yankees began to lay siege to Vicksburg.

During this period Dee Ann rode over to see Wilms. She appeared markedly different from her usual appearance, which was always carefully coiffed after an hour of makeup and preening. Outwardly, she looked far more natural in appearance but also troubled and downcast.

Wilms wondered immediately if this were the after effects of her confrontation with the rebel deserters and asked immediately, "Is everything all right?"

"I was going to ask you the same question because you surely don't look all right. But first, I have had some terrible news. Jefferson sent me a message that General Van Dorn was killed by a jealous husband in Tennessee. Now I'm completely lost. I'm very upset over this because he told me he was coming back for me. I just can't get over this."

Wilms, too, wanted to talk to Dee Ann, so he suggested that they saddle up his horse and go for a ride together. He ran inside to get the quart bottle of bourbon Josh had been saving for medicinal purposes in case any of them got wounded. They rode over to a copse of trees, tied up the horses, and sat down on a log next to each other.

John passed the bottle to Dee Ann and they both took good long gulps. She grimaced, reaching for the canteen, and took a swallow of water.

"I've had some bad news too. Cathy is dead. Soldiers coming down the river told me that the telegraph office in Vicksburg was hit by a shell, and everyone inside was killed. They were right there on the spot and saw the whole thing."

"Oh John, I am so sorry for you!" She put her hand on his arm to give him consolation.

"All my plans are gone. We were going to get married and raise a family when the war was over, but now there is nothing for me. I shouldn't have left her in Vicksburg." His voice wavered. "She was one of the telegraph operators for the Confederacy in Vicksburg."

Wilms took another swallow of bourbon and handed the bottle to Dee Ann. She took the bottle absentmindedly and then said, "Oh no, John." She frowned and shook her head. "You have everything in front of you. Uncle Jefferson lost his wife right here. You know, she was President Taylor's daughter. But Uncle Jefferson eventually remarried, and he went on to a good life, at least until now. Why don't you come over to my place? I'll show you a picture of her and tell you the story of them. You know as well as I do that Cathy really couldn't have left her post at that point. There was nothing you could have done, and it wouldn't have changed anything. She might have been hit by the shell even if you had been there with her in Vicksburg."

Dee Ann took another swallow of the bourbon, and was really starting to loosen up, as was Wilms. They walked their horses over to her house and talked.

"Talking to you makes me feel better, but what about you and your loss?"

"Mine is a bit different," answered Dee Ann. "Hearing your story makes that clear to me. I loved the general and he promised to come back for me. Still, the note I received from Jefferson gave me the idea that he was involved with another woman, because her husband shot him out of jealousy. I'm not sure he was going to come back to me, though I loved him—and he promised to. But I do miss him terribly, even if he was with another woman."

As the conversation progressed, Wilms was feeling warmer and warmer towards Dee Ann, and he held up his arms to indicate that he wanted to give her a hug over her loss. When they hugged, he felt her large breasts press against his pectoral muscles, which kicked up desire in both of them.

Dee Ann began to kiss him passionately. As they were right near her house at that moment, they quickly tied up the horses and went into the bedroom. When they woke up later in the afternoon in her large mahogany four-poster bed, they cuddled together in bed.

The losses they had both suffered seemed to be a big part of the glue that cemented them together. They were also tied together by their connection to the murder that Dee Ann had just committed, which was still very fresh in her mind. So much so that after the morning's sexual pleasures, the horrific events that Dee Ann had just been through, began to return with a vengeance. As she felt the pain again of reliving their circumstances, she talked non-stop to Wilms in a feverish tone.

Looking up at the ceiling she said, "What I can't get entirely out of my mind is the fact that you gave me the bowie knife to protect myself and you laid out the route that I was to follow. You warned me of what to expect. It's almost as though a force in the universe foresaw all these events were going to happen and endeavored to protect me. Without the knife I probably would have been dead because I had not enough time to pull out my revolver. He would have been right back on top of me. I really believe that the only reason I'm still alive is that you gave me that knife, which I really wanted. Why did you give me that knife?"

"I don't know," said Wilms. "I wanted to give you something to protect yourself as you were going on the road in a wartime situation, which had some level of danger. I felt guilty asking you to help out reaching the neighboring plantations, and I had already offered the knife, so I followed through with my offer."

"Whatever the reason," Dee Ann replied, "I felt that the whole series of events leading to what I did was almost like a sign, a religious experience, and I feel markedly changed by what I just went through."

"Religious experience?" Wilms asked quizzically.

"What I am talking about, John, is a gigantic change in my life."

"What do you mean by that?"

Dee Ann got up and paced back and forth on the hardwood floor, talking continuously.

"Well, my whole life was pretty well protected by my uncles, even though I had lost my father and husband in bad circumstances. Still, I grew up with wealth and privilege and slaves to cater to my every whim. If the way I was living led to this war, I want no part of it. It's not right for people to be living high on the hog when other people are miserable. I never saw the misery of slavery up close because my uncles were so good to their slaves. My uncle wouldn't accept anyone unless they treated slaves the same way he did."

"We all knew how well both your uncles treated their slaves."

"My Uncle Joe believed that blacks were as capable as white people, and even though other people did not have the same beliefs, they accepted his methods if they wanted to work with him.

"Folks nearby treated their slaves well, and if they didn't, they experienced my uncle's wrath. I can see clearly now that each part of this slavocracy wrote its own rules, and they were not compatible with the real meaning of the Constitution. That there are people roaming around the woods trying to kill and rob others says to me there are haves and have nots. I can see more clearly now. Even my uncle's slaves, who got the best treatment any slaves could get, were not free to follow their own pursuits. I feel like a naive fool for accepting all this wealth as uncritically as I did."

"But you weren't completely uncritical, and Uncle Joseph told Josh that you were 'the family abolitionist,'" said Wilms.

"That may be true, but when all your whims are met by slaves, it's really easy to settle in and do nothing about it. When I see those former slaves crowding the roads singing out of joy to be free, I see how completely I have missed the boat up to now.

"Another problem is I've always craved men's attention, and maybe I still do. I think I have lost my urge to chase men the way I have been doing. Maybe my best thinking in that area, as well, is not up to scratch. I felt that if I could steal a man from another woman, he must not have loved that woman, so it was okay to do it. This whole experience has been quite a shock for me. I'm just not the same as I was before. I'm questioning a lot of things I have always done.

"The biggest problem I have now is that the murder keeps coming back into my mind, and I can't get rid of it. When I pulled the bowie knife out of him and all his guts came out, a strong noxious smell of gas and feces got into my nose. Now every time I go to the bathroom and smell the air, the image of the killing comes back. It even comes when I do my own defecation. Sometimes I can still smell that smell when nothing is happening."

She looked at him wide-eyed and distressed. "I've got to find a way to get that image and smell out of my mind. Another thing I feel terrible about is a feeling of guilt for General Van Dorn's murder. I got notification of his death two days after I murdered that deserter. It feels almost like God is punishing me for violating the commandment *thou shalt not kill.* I just can't live with the person I have become, a vicious murderess. This just doesn't go with the person that I was before the murder."

Wilms came back with support and reasoning. "Look, Dee Ann, you may have gotten word two days after you killed that man, but with our communication in a shamble and the telegraph system all but destroyed, it could have happened two or three weeks before you killed him. This act would have had nothing to do with your killing him unless you think there was something else God was punishing you for.

"As far as that image of the smell and its connection to the killing, I recently published a story about a young doctor in Paris named Dr. Charcot. I took a summer off from the newspaper just before the war started, when I inherited some money from my father. I had always wanted to go to Paris because I was interested in medical research, and Paris was the place where most new developments in the field were happening.

"I sent Dr. Charcot a letter requesting an interview, and he promptly replied, granting it. Since it was a quiet time during the summer and I had told the newspaper I was going to get a personal interview and could arrange for a replacement editor, they allowed me to go.

"This doctor was relatively new to his field and wanted to get the word out to others about what he had been doing. He is a neurologist who has been using hypnosis to deal with traumatic events in people's lives. These events render people incapable of resuming their normal existence. So that I might better understand the process, during the interview he taught me how to hypnotize both myself and other persons as well."

"You know how to hypnotize people?"

"Of course, I do. We got along very well, and he showed me how to induce a trance. When I got back, I talked some of my friends into letting me hypnotize them, and I had some good practice in trance inductions, and I found some interesting results in helping people achieve things that they thought impossible"

Dee Ann looked intrigued. "Tell me more."

"It is hard, perhaps impossible, to convince people to do things they don't want to do. But it is very easy to help people if they really want to do something. According to what I learned from Charcot, if you really want to erase this memory, I can hypnotize you. We can discuss the murder while you follow with your eyes my pocket watch swinging back and forth on a chain—and then we will work out a way to erase this event from your mind."

"You really think you can do this? You know I'm willing to do anything that will get rid of this awful image; I really can't live with it. When can you do this for me?"

"I can do this for you immediately. This is similar to the trauma of what all soldiers go through in combat."

"Okay, let's do it!"

Wilms used a trance induction image representing a whale swimming on the surface of the ocean and then diving deeper and deeper into the cold depths of that ocean. He brought in the subject of sleep, relaxation, and tied it to reaching deeper and deeper levels in the cold, dark water.

When Dee Ann was sufficiently under, he tested her for response. Then he decided to relive the event and raised the subject of erasing the event from her mind while she was staring at the watch.

He finished by saying, "No one can make you do something you don't want to do, and erasing it from your mind is very important to you. It is something that will allow you to move forward with your life. You will now be able to eliminate all traces of it because it is something of the most critical nature to your future." That completed, he brought the image of the whale gradually back up to the surface and woke Dee Ann up. She was a bit groggy for the rest of the day but seemed in a far less agitated and more serene frame of mind.

CHAPTER 62

A TROJAN HORSE

A day later, a detachment of Union soldiers arrived to escort Josh and Wilms to General Grant's headquarters. Because Vicksburg was now under siege, Grant wanted to discuss the disposition of the fortifications and redoubts around the city as well as the situation with torpedoes out in the boat channel. As they rode along the road toward Grant's headquarters, they observed that the roads were choked with thousands of smiling happy slaves, singing and chanting. These were the new freedmen.

Wilms felt a deep rush of excitement and pride at what they had just contributed to. Each felt that if they did nothing else with their life, they had worked for a mighty cause.

They arrived at a church that Grant was using as a temporary headquarters during the siege. The soldiers escorted the two men to the door of the room in which the general was standing over a large map on the table that laid out the entire city of Vicksburg before him.

Grant was less than impressive looking in appearance on that particular day. He was wearing his dark-blue field uniform, which was partially unbuttoned. He had an unlit cigar stub in his mouth, and cigar ashes were all over his jacket and in his full beard. One had the impression that all his attention was on the task at hand of defeating the Confederacy, and he had no time to bother with the niceties of appearance. Probably, if his wife Julia had been with him, she would not have stood for this slovenly presentation. Here, he was the boss, and he set the tone for the whole campaign.

As they entered the room, he introduced himself, made small talk for a few moments, and wasted no time in getting down to business.

"We understand you both have been in the city recently, and we were wondering if you could give us any ideas on attacking the defensive structure of the forts and redoubts. We have the city pretty tightly encircled now. No river traffic can reach it from Tennessee or Louisiana. And the railroad has been cut off, so no new supplies can reach Vicksburg. The problem is that we have tied up a large army and river navy here, and we could be vulnerable to attack from General Joseph Johnston, who is like a rattlesnake at our rear. So we need to capture this city as soon as possible, and if we can destroy the fortifications, we can greatly speed up the process."

Josh walked over to the map and saw what appeared to be a series of forts with names of generals such as Bowen, Smith, Stevenson, and Lee. "Well, General Grant, some of these structures have been set up since we left the city. It appears that part of the army left the city to defend the railroad, and they seem to have set up new defenses since then. I have studied the soil and rock in the area, and it is conducive to undermining the forts if we can bring our lines as close as possible.

"I heard Martin Luther Smith, our engineer in chief, talking with generals Bowen and Stevenson about planting big mines around their position in case the Yankees attack. I think at least ten of these forts could be dug under if you have sappers. If this is done properly, it could disrupt the whole front."

Wilms added, "For my part, I don't think they have enough supplies stored for a long siege, and the mean season is coming soon, when diseases like malaria, yellow fever, and typhoid come out in these parts. With all supplies cut off, I don't think they're going to want to go through a mean summer trapped in this city."

Since Grant seemed unpretentious and open to ideas, Josh took a chance with him. "General, I have an idea on how to break the siege if the rebels don't surrender. Can I explain it to you?"

"I am all ears," answered Grant.

"A lot of the soil around Vicksburg is a yellow soft clay, which would be very conducive to tunneling through in order to undermine forts and set off mines under them—but my idea is a bit different. I am thinking about the end of the Trojan War."

"You're not thinking about us using a Trojan Horse, are you?" asked Grant wryly.

"Not exactly," said Josh. "I think, however, the effect would be similar. I know a place behind the telegraph office building where there is a copse of trees. What I'm proposing is that, now that the telegraph office has been destroyed by the gunboat shelling, we dig a tunnel toward the copse of trees. I could take a compass bearing from these two positions on the map during a bombardment of the line around it. We can use this compass bearing to form a line to dig our tunnel."

Josh indicated two places on the map where the copse was readily visible from the Union lines. "We could take a bearing off this map as well, but it could be markedly off target. Next, we begin to tunnel toward it in the soft clay. We can take the compass underground to compare it with above-ground readings in order to correct for any possible variations produced by iron deposits or torpedoes in the soil nearby.

"At the same time, we tunnel under several redoubts and fortifications on the Confederate line and then set off explosives under some of them. While this is going on we mount a coordinated attack at many points along the same line. The rebels will rush out of their forts and dugouts to defend the line.

"At that time, we begin to move a few hundred troops through the tunnel and into the copse of trees. We'll have them hide out there. Then we attack them from both sides at the same time. We could start the action with a big mine under a nearby fort. I think we should be able to break through the lines this way."

The cigar had fallen out of Grant's mouth as he listened to the plan being laid out to him. He picked up his cigar, brushed some ashes that had fallen on his jacket, and gave Josh a withering stare.

"This plan makes my eyes spin in my head, but it could work. If we can finish off Vicksburg before the worst part of the summer, it would avoid the season of diseases. That could save many deaths from happening–not from the battle but from all the sickness. If you want to try the plan, I could move you both up to the line to take some bearings at the point you indicated on the map. We have a company of New York sappers and miners that we could bring up as well. I'm going to bring in General McPherson to comment on the plan because he has a good feel for engineering projects. Even if it sounds a bit fantastic, it might save lives."

Grant had Josh and Wilms wait outside his office while he had an aide round up McPherson, who was in the area and arrived within a half hour. Compared to Grant's appearance that day, he was the very image of an imposing-looking general, with a full beard, moustache, and a wide forehead above far-reaching, determined eyes.

Grant asked him to come directly into his office and talked to him alone. Next, he called in the two men and asked Josh to explain his plan. McPherson asked a few questions such as, "How are you going to dig a straight line once you are underground?"

"By taking compass bearings and correcting them with above ground readings," Josh replied.

"Is this earth conducive to digging underground?"

"Sir, its yellow clay all the way to the city. What you have been digging in stays like that until you get to the rock formations over the river. The rebels have been constructing underground caves to cope with the bombardment. It is very amenable to digging."

When Josh finished his explanation, McPherson nodded approval. "I think it's worth trying. It can save lives. The undermining idea is a good one. We might also try some other variations on this idea."

Grant quickly arranged for the two men to be moved up to the trench line opposite the Confederate line. "This could be a good day for observations because there is no wind, and we can lay an artillery barrage down so that the enemy cannot see you easily through the smoke. We now have a couple of these new periscopes that can be used for observation and for taking a compass bearing on the trees without subjecting you to sharpshooters trying to kill you.

"Well, gentlemen," said Grant, "We're going to get a chance to see if ancient Greek methods work in resolving the siege at Vicksburg."

CHAPTER 63

TRENCH WARFARE BEFORE VICKSBURG

Grant arranged for a wagon to bring Josh and Wilms up to the trench line surrounding Vicksburg. Two lines of trenches, one Confederate and one Union, extended all around the city for many miles from north to south.

As the two men moved up to the line in a communications trench, the tension increased markedly. The background noises grew in intensity. Josh and Wilms heard cracks and growls as shells whizzed by overhead, exploding in front of and in back of the trench line. Occasional rifle shots rang out as sharpshooters on both sides were busy acquiring targets.

Josh explained to Wilms, "You don't have experience differentiating a shell coming close to you from another one going over your head, so watch me carefully. If I drop to the ground, you drop also and hug the earth. You've got to get used to the sound of a shell to tell where it is going. What starts out as a whistle turns into a kind of roar if it's coming close. It takes a while to learn this, so watch me and copy me."

As they moved into the main trench facing the rebel trench line, they found a bizarre underground world of men living and working where they were exposed to periodic attacks by the enemy. The trench had a periscope for viewing, and Josh and Wilms trained it on the top of the copse of trees. They both took compass bearings on that spot in the distance.

Just as Wilms was getting his bearings set as a check on Josh's, a Minnie ball hit the periscope and destroyed the top. One of the soldiers who operated the periscope said, "This is the third one we have lost to sharpshooters in the last three weeks."

Josh said, "This is not good. We are going to have to take a bearing from up on the parapet of the trench. We have to have exact bearings; otherwise we are digging a tunnel for nothing."

Josh sent Wilms back through the communications trench to ask for a bombardment of the rebel trench line facing them. In that manner he could go up on the high point of the parapet to take his bearing, without being molested or shot by the sharpshooters in the rebel trench.

After about fifteen minutes, Wilms came back with the word, "General McPherson has authorized a short bombardment of the rebel lines, which will commence in fifteen minutes. While it is at its full height we should be able to get our compass readings. Let's flip a coin to see which one goes up on the parapet. They are going to arrange a series of air bursts above the rebel line. This should keep their heads down for a few minutes."

Wilms lost the toss, so he crawled into a position where he could get up on the parapet as soon as the shelling started. After a few minutes, the artillery fired a couple of test shots to bracket the area in question. Then simultaneously, the whole rebel line was engulfed in a series of explosions—and as the bombardment continued, a series of air bursts above the Confederate position.

Wilms scrambled up and took his bearing without any return fire from the rebels. The brief exposure to trench warfare left an indelible impression on the two men.

"You should have seen the front of the trench. It was flanked by sharpened stakes waiting to impale any attacker," said

Wilms. "The rebel trench about three hundred yards away had just about the same configuration of stakes in the front of it. Those are to keep all the rebel soldiers in our field of fire so we can easily kill them off if they attack us."

While they were talking, not to be outdone, the rebels opened up a bombardment of their own. At first the shells fell long, well over the trench, but very quickly they adjusted their range. Before long, shells were exploding on the parapet, and some of the high trajectory howitzer shells were actually exploding in the trenches, causing some of the trench walls to collapse and even collapsing some of the underground dugouts where men were resting from the battle above ground. Rats and mice were scurrying around—running through the trenches as their homes were destroyed by the shelling. Josh and Wilms helped dig out a few men who were buried alive by the bombardment. But many more were interred forever in the yellow clay earth.

Wilms said to Josh, "Did we cause all this trouble by taking our bearings?"

Josh answered, "This is what a war is all about, and this may not be the end of it."

Josh was right. After a return bombardment that lasted about a half hour, the rebel guns were suddenly silent.

Josh said, "We are in for it now."

At the silencing of the guns, everyone came piling out of the dugouts and back into the trenches and the bugle blew *attention* in preparation for an attack.

All the men were ordered to fix bayonets, and they lined up along the trench wall. At that point Wilms felt his heart pounding out of his chest, for he knew he was going to be involved in hand-to-hand combat, and he didn't even have a rifle.

Some men came running with another periscope, and the captain took a look across the wasteland of no man's land, and saw a gray line of men advancing rapidly just clear of their trenches, holding a Stars and Bars flag.

At that point the rebel artillery opened fire again, and now the air bursts were timed to explode directly over the trench line. Some of the soldiers began to take serious shrapnel wounds and fell off the embrasure that they were standing in and into the bottom of the trench. They were quickly taken away to dressing stations by medical orderlies who carried stretchers.

As the gray line of running rebels got closer, it was easy to hear shrieks and yells from the ongoing wave of men. This had a terrible effect on some of the men. Josh could see some of them with their teeth chattering in spite of the hot weather. Other men were developing tremors in parts of their bodies, and yet others were urinating in their pants.

The observers at the periscope watched the line advance at breakneck speed. All at once, the Union artillery opened up, and explosive shells landed in the gray line, tearing great gaps in it. The line of men began to converge on a point not very far from where Josh and Wilms were standing. As the rebels got closer and closer, the Union artillery switched to canister shot, which brought down even more troops.

At that point the men on the parapet opened fire, killing scores of the attackers. As the enemy melted away under the withering fire, the captain blew his whistle for a counterattack. The men then rushed over the top of the trench with fixed bayonets and engaged the enemy in hand-to-hand combat. The Union troops chased the remnants of the rebel army back to their trenches but were under orders to not follow them any further.

Josh sneaked a look through the periscope and saw hundreds of bodies scattered across the field. As the attack and counterattack let up, Wilms looked behind him and caught sight of a soldier who was shaking all over and had not gotten out of the trench to fight the rebels hand-to-hand. In the absence of a nearby medical orderly, he went over to him to ask him if he was all right.

"When the guy next to me was hit by shrapnel I realized that it could have been me. I don't want to die. I just asked my sweetheart to marry me. We both agreed that when this war is over we are going to get married. I want to be able to live with her and raise a family. I don't want to come home in a box like some of my comrades. When I pictured myself coming home in a box, I started to shake and I couldn't stop it. I just lost control over everything and I wet my pants as well. I'm wondering if maybe I've got malaria, like some of the other soldiers. I was fine during the last attack. I went over the top with everyone else. This time, my knees felt weak and I felt I was going to collapse. I think I need to see a doctor!"

Wilms said, "Maybe you should, but you weren't the only one who started shaking. When the rebels started yelling, there were many others who had the same reaction. Maybe you men ought to talk among yourselves to help figure out what happened to you."

As Josh and Wilms walked away, Wilms whispered softly, "Poor devil. I think that he is never going to be the same after this experience."

They walked back through the communication trench and retraced their steps to meet with some of the sappers, who were ready to start digging the tunnel.

With their work at the front completed, Wilms and Josh walked side by side away from the trenches, eventually finding places on a supply wagon going back to Grant's headquarters. The battle they had just been through had had a strong effect on them. They were both in a very chatty mood, and they continued to process some of the events they just experienced.

In a field outside of Grant's headquarters, they found a few boulders that planters had moved from a field and sat down on two of them. They began to discuss the soldiers' reactions to the battle.

"You know, I studied hypnosis with Doctor Charcot in Paris," Wilms said. "He studied war traumas from the Crimean War, and after years of study he believes that any person who undergoes a war or combat experience is never the same for the rest of their life."

Josh looked Wilms in the eyes and said, "That makes sense to me. The experience in the Mexican War changed me for good. I used to be naive and trusting of the government. Now I am not. I'll never be the person I was again."

"This event that we went through today was a big one. I'm never going to forget what I saw. Doctor Charcot also felt that all soldiers in combat are suffering combat trauma. Some exhibit it at an earlier stage than others. For others, it does not show up until many years after the experience."

"We saw a lot of combat trauma in Mexico," said Josh. "Many soldiers deserted after going through a kind of combat fatigue. It was miserably hot. There was nothing to do but get sick on bad water—and, in between, there were some pretty nasty battles. A person who grows up in a happy family could have a pretty nice life with few traumas—and then they undergo disasters like this."

"Oh, they can win medals and get praised for bravery," said Wilms, "but it's little consolation for what they have done. Something inside of them is always telling them what they did is wrong and *thou shalt not kill.*"

"Then they read in the paper that the war was created by a bunch of fire-eaters that started the conflict just to be able to spread slavery to other areas and take advantage of the natural resources of captured territories," said Josh. "This makes the trauma worse because these soldiers see themselves as dupes for a class of manipulators who have induced them to sacrifice their lives in pursuit of evil goals."

Josh's face turned crimson with emotion as he said, "Now they are not just combat trauma victims—they are angry, radicalized citizens who have an ax to grind against the social order that pushed them into this mess. In my war, it was President Polk who manufactured that conflict for Manifest destiny."

"Anyhow, Charcot," Wilms resumed, "thinks that this anger gets generalized toward social institutions such as schools, churches, and government leaders. Wherever this emotionally scarred individual sees happy, well-adjusted people, he has the deep urge to attack them. Because he cannot be happy, he feels that no one else should be happy."

"I think Charcot's insight is brilliant," answered Josh, "his overall analysis does fit with my life experience. But did he also study the families of these afflicted veterans? What happens to *them*?"

"He did not study the families to any real extent, but living with someone who suffers this way has to have a profound effect on their loved ones. According to Charcot, wars for profit cause social disintegration and deadly anger," said Wilms. "If we consider this war—at least from a northern viewpoint—as a just war, there should be less destabilization among the Union soldiers."

Josh propped his head on his chin, paused for a minute, and answered back, "One would think so, but the individual reactions of the soldiers on one side might also have more complex repercussions for the entire country. Listen to this. Suppose that the Union wins this war, which is bound to happen, and then we are part of one big Union again. What happens to the soldiers who fought for the South after everything they endured?

"Suppose the soldiers read in the paper that the war was started by warmongers and plantation owners for their own needs. If they had any misgivings about what they fought for, they might feel angry with the society that put them in that position."

"Following Charcot's reasoning," Wilms said, "once this war is finished and we are all one people again—and they are free to travel everywhere in the United States—what happens then? They may spit out their vitriol in violent acts in peaceful parts of the United States and cause countless trauma for others."

Josh interjected at this point, "It looks as if Newton's law—that for every action there is an equal and opposite reaction—does not only apply to physics. It can apply to social matters as well. If you damage individuals, that damage remains with them and, at some point, is spit back at society in one negative form or another. Nothing is lost.

"I can't forget the warning of the curandero at Buena Vista fifteen years ago. We can only hope and pray that when this war is completed and the slaves are free, this will help right the heavenly balance sheet so that bad things don't continue to happen to our country."

Wilms answered him back quickly. "At least until the next war comes along and men are used up as cannon fodder. Then the whole cycle could start again."

CHAPTER 64

A COLONY FOR FREEDMEN

Emily and her four former slaves continued to live in the Hurricane Garden Cottage but now under Union protection. Having no more need to act out their previous slave-master roles, they enjoyed the freedom to be themselves for the first time since they had come to the South. Dee Ann continued to live nearby and was granted Union protection as well.

Davis Bend became a nucleus for freedmen. Many of the former slaves were transported by the army to Davis Bend as they were choking up the roads and hindering movements of the Union army. It was easier to keep them fed in one place.

Since there were more and more freedmen running around with no jobs, no food, and no homes—Congress began working on a plan to sustain them. This was the origin of what was later to become the Freedman's Bureau, established to help ameliorate the newly freed slaves' woes. Many of the Union troops recognized the precarious position the freedmen were in, particularly if the Confederate troops should counterattack and recapture any land. Areas like Davis Bend were exposed to cavalry attacks, even if the front lines were many miles away.

In this atmosphere, the Union troops began firearms

training for the freedmen resettled at Davis Bend. They brought a whole consignment of rifles and hand guns there and began firearms instruction in case the rebels came and took back any of this territory. They set up a rifle and pistol range behind the cotton warehouse. Everyone was taught to load and clean guns. The men were taught to use both pistols and rifles, but the women's instruction was limited to pistols.

As few of the former slaves had had any opportunity to handle weapons in the employ of their former masters, to the frustration of their Union army instructors many were slow to learn. Ben Montgomery, the store proprietor from Davis Bend, however, was a marked exception and quite a good shot.

Jackson, Nate, Joan, and Wilma all participated in the training, even though they had been taught it before by Josh. Some of the freedmen were terrible shots because they had no previous training with firearms. Many shots were way wide of the target. The firearms instructor tried to teach them how it was done, but very few got decent scores in marksmanship.

The instructors were laughing at most of the former slaves' performance when they came up to Joan, who was going to get her chance on the pistol. The instructor put his arms around Joan for his own pleasure to show her how to use the gun. The expression on her face showed that she knew very clearly what he was trying to do. She politely squirmed free and began to fire at the target, hitting it dead center six times in rapid succession.

More than mildly surprised, he exclaimed, "Hey little lady, you're a pretty good shot. Can you do that with a rifle as well?" Joan held out her hand for a rifle, which was given to her, and also cut dead center with it. She then asked to reload the pistol and had them throw two candles into the air, proceeding to cut them both in half with well-placed shots.

At that point the instructor told Joan he wanted her to teach the rest of the larger freedman group how to shoot. Nate and Wilma showed good proficiency with the firearms when they took their turns on the range. Even Jackson showed a marked improvement over his past performance in Lowell. The soldiers left a generous supply of ammunition but offered no real military training other than target practice.

During the day, the five spent hours running a makeshift school to teach all the former slaves to read and write on as high a level as possible. This group kept themselves quite busy while waiting for the return of Josh and Wilms from Vicksburg.

Dee Ann came by and helped out as well with the teaching. Communal life was reasonably good for everyone within this enclave, and they all shared what they had, even though they did not have very much. Wilms's hypnoses work with Dee Ann appeared to help ameliorate her trauma, and working productively with the freedmen gave her a new sense of purpose.

In Vicksburg the tunneling had been going on successfully for about three weeks during the month of June. In a separate effort to gain the upper hand, however, several detonations of underground mines under rebel positions had been tried without success. The Union troops had rushed into the crater caused by the mine, only to be ambushed with great loss of life by Confederate troops on the rim of the crater.

Josh and Wilms were feeling downcast at the perversion of the plan they had presented. They requested a meeting with Grant again, but without success. He was not available because he was inspecting another part of the trench line that stretched for miles around the city. Instead, they met with General McPherson to discuss their disappointment at the modification of their original plan.

McPherson spoke apologetically. "Let me preface this discussion by saying that the plan got changed by General McClernand, who was covering for me while I was sick. He thought he could have achieved a spectacular breakthrough by undermining a fort, but it turned into a disaster instead. He took the responsibility on himself to set off the mine, and he alone is responsible for the failure.

"We are ready now to go ahead with the original plan. All we really need is a good diversion for the troops going to the copse of trees."

Raising his finger in the air, Wilms said, "I have an idea. When I was in France, I met students who developed a plan to construct an ancient siege engine called a *trebuchet*, a really long catapult with a counterweight. I helped them build it."

"I'm familiar with the trebuchet," said McPherson. "We had to study it in military history class at West Point."

"We have both key ingredients available here. We can use one of the big telegraph poles just delivered to us and use the solid mortar shot as counterweights," said Wilms. "I am confident that with some carpenters' assistance we can build it fairly quickly.

"The intelligence that we have gathered from captured prisoners tells us that the rebels are starving in Vicksburg. The population and troops are reduced to eating rats if they can still find any. There is just not enough food in the city. If we take a dead goat or other animal carcass and throw it with the trebuchet into a part of the city away from the copse of trees, the rebels will run over to it. It's sure to attract a lot of attention among ravenously hungry people."

"Sure," McPherson said. "A fine thing it is to feed our starving enemies."

"Would you eat food that the rebel army fed you in a situation like that?" asked Josh. "I think not, but it sure will pique their interest and distract them for a while.

If it doesn't work, we can always set off another mine under another redoubt. Then we will start the troops under the tunnel to the copse of trees."

Wilms asked, "When can we begin?"

"Very soon," McPherson said. "Right now, we are negotiating

with General Pemberton. He is refusing our unconditional surrender terms. How long will it take to build the trebuchet?"

"Two days—maybe less," answered Wilms.

"Start on it right away so that we are ready to go if negotiation fails," said McPherson.

The sapper and infantry units had three former carpenters. The engineering unit had good tools. Wilms drew up plans from the machine he had witnessed in France. It rapidly took shape, and they moved it into a position where the communication trench connected with the frontline trench. Both trenches met at right angles, which gave lots of room for the full swing of the trebuchet. To test it out, they carried a nine-inch mortar ball composed of solid shot.

They pulled the telegraph pole with the counterweight back, and let the mortar shell fly. It flew well over the outer ring of trenches, and landed just inside the city limits, not too far from the copse of trees. Just to be sure of the weapon's accuracy, they let two more mortar shells fly with similar results.

Based on this test, they were ready to go the next day. The commissary brought up two goats, and penned them at the long end of the communication trench. At the same time, the troops who were to emerge from the copse of trees moved up to a position near the tunnel. The attack was set for the next morning: July 3, 1863.

The next morning, however, just as the men were lining up to enter the tunnel and the goats were about to be slaughtered, word came through that Grant had accepted Pemberton's offer to surrender the city. The surrender was finalized the next day. The plan never had to be carried out.

Two days later, Josh and Wilms entered Vicksburg and found the city devastated. Grant's troops estimated that they had fired over twenty-two thousand artillery shells at the city, the trenches, and front lines. The gunboats and mortar barges on the river had also fired a huge number of shells into the city.

What was truly amazing was the very low number of casualties among the citizens of Vicksburg, many of whom were able to weather the worst part of the shelling by hiding in underground caves.

CHAPTER 65

COMPLICATIONS ARISE

Wilms and Josh made their way to what had been the telegraph office. All they saw was a bundle of stray wires sticking out of a pile of rubble. After a few sad minutes of staring at the ruin they went over to Feinberg's store to see what had happened there. To their surprise they found Feinberg and his wife in the store with almost no damage. The neighboring buildings were all damaged to some extent, but Feinberg's store was completely intact, except for some broken glass from the windows and a few superficial holes in the lower part of the building.

Josh began talking to Feinberg with a big smile on his face, saying. "You finally did help to make a revolution. You should have seen what it looked like! Tens of thousands of black slaves put down their tools and marched off. This was the biggest labor movement in history. If this happens in other states, then the war is won!"

"I can't believe I have lived to see this moment," said Feinberg. "I have been trapped in the city, so I didn't get to see it with my own eyes. I would like to be able to travel outside Vicksburg to see this for real."

"We will take you down to Davis Bend to see the results of

the revolution," said Wilms. "I wish Cathy could be here to see this."

"Why don't you get her," said Feinberg with a smile.

"I can't, she's dead," said Wilms, his eyes tearing up as he lowered his head.

"I just saw her this morning," said Feinberg. "Do you know something I don't know?"

"We heard from some men who escaped from the siege that the telegraph office took a direct hit and everyone in it was killed, including Cathy and her father."

"That's not true," said Feinberg. At first, we thought she was in there with her father, but only rebel operators ran the office during that day of shelling. We did not realize that Cathy and Ezra were hiding in a cave. The two bodies pulled out of the wreckage were the rebel operators. Still, it took two days to figure out that Cathy and her father were alive.

"General Pemberton did not want civilians operating the telegraph under fire. He said only soldiers should do that job. Those men who told you must have escaped before we all realized they were not dead.

"Why don't you go over to Cathy's house and see for yourself that she is not dead. Her house is still standing, with not too much damage."

Wilms jumped to his feet with a look of shock on his face, his heart pounding, and ran straight over to Cathy's house. He found her with Ezra, busy making repairs to the outside of the house.

He took in the scene for a moment in disbelief and then rushed over to hug her joyously. "You're alive! I can't believe my eyes. I'm so happy! Ezra's alive too! We heard from escapees of the siege that the telegraph office was destroyed, and everyone in it killed."

Cathy's face turned bright red at seeing Wilms after such a

long separation, and with tears running down her face, she kept hugging him and wouldn't let go.

"Yes, we're alive! Our lives were saved by General Pemberton. When he got word that we were operating the telegraph during the shelling, he pulled us out and put army telegraph operators in our place. He saved our lives," said Cathy. "We were very lucky. We are very lucky. We are well, but everyone here is so very hungry."

Wilms hugged her tightly. "You two come with me," he said protectively. "I'll get you fixed up with a good meal. The army has lots of extra food."

After Josh's and Wilms's visit, Feinberg was in an almost euphoric state for the rest of the day despite the chaos that he had been through in the last few months. The news that Josh and Wilms brought him made him feel a sense of accomplishment, although he had done none of the heavy lifting to make it happen.

He decided to write a journal of the events that the slaves had been through. As he began to write, he realized that the responsibility for the destruction of the Confederacy in Mississippi rested squarely on the backs of the black slaves in bondage. They threw off their shackles and pretty much destroyed the underpinnings of the Confederacy in the western part of the state. This occurred even in areas not controlled by northern troops.

Had the slaves not given up on the Confederacy, the Union army would have had a much more difficult time. It could only control a narrow strip of territory for a short period of time. When it left that area, the territory could still have reverted to the rebels.

As Feinberg took stock of what had happened, he realized there was no turning back. When the slaves left there was no economic engine for the Confederacy to run on. Nothing could be done without the slaves wanting it to be done. At this point they held all the economic power.

On the other hand, they did not feel confident, because they had never experienced any great success or independence in their lives and did not really know how to deal with this. It was as though they had just won the lottery on a massive scale but did not know what to do with the winnings.

Feinberg remembered that one of the principles of revolutions was that all revolutions are followed by a period of reaction or counterrevolution. This lack of confidence by the black slaves did not bode well for the future. But then again, this was a moment of joy and celebration at the collapse of the old order. It was too soon to speculate about the future.

Feinberg was still trying to understand why this revolution by the unschooled black slaves had succeeded, while his revolution led by radical theorists like himself had failed. This order collapsed completely with the slaves abandoning the plantations, whereas the European order only partially collapsed, and the old order came right back in a different form.

While mulling over this critical question, an idea came to mind—could the old order come back here, too, in a different form and take back power because the slaves had never held power before and had no experience in participating in a political system?

After his initial euphoria at finding Cathy alive, Wilms was now consumed by guilt about the relationship he had begun with Dee Ann when he thought Cathy was dead. Thoughts kept racing through his mind. "What am I going to do now," he pondered intently, his hands on his temples. "Dee Ann has become quite attached to me. I do have feelings for them both, each in their own way, but I can't marry them both. And Cathy was waiting for us to get married. Why didn't I make more of an effort to verify that she was alive? What am I going to do now?"

He didn't feel fit to talk to either of them until he resolved in his mind what to do. He felt there was no easy way out of the dilemma. If reason told him the best way out of this situation was to tell Dee Ann about Cathy being alive and go back with Cathy—how was he going to tell Cathy what had happened with Dee Ann?

On the other hand, he had to admit in his heart of hearts that the problem was now that he had developed a powerful degree of attraction for Dee Ann. This probably was not going to go away very easily, nor did he want it to go away.

If he told Cathy that he had slept with Dee Ann, she might become insanely jealous or she might reject him and not want to have anything to do with him anymore. Despite his powerful sexual attraction to Dee Ann, he felt he had a deeper connection and need for Cathy in all other respects. This, as well, was not going to go away, nor did he want it to go away. Try as he might, no easy solution would come to his mind.

In his final framing of the problem, he concluded that telling Cathy what happened might cause trouble, but eventually she would understand. Of course, he would have to say goodbye to the sexual relationship with Dee Ann forever, which he was loath to do. Still, he knew that he could not afford to lose Cathy, and he knew how great the pain had been when he thought he had lost her forever.

Just the thought made his knees weak and his heart pound in his chest as he pondered what losing her for a second time would do to him. He went back and forth trying to come up with a plan of action, but all the thinking exhausted him so much that he decided to do nothing for the moment. He would wait out events and see if he might figure out what to do at a later time.

CHAPTER 66

SERVING THE FREEDMEN

It now became more and more obvious to the Union army administration that there were many thousands of former slaves in dire circumstances with no way to feed, clothe, or take care of themselves now that they were no longer slaves. In a desperate attempt to look after these freedmen, the Union army removed many of them to the Davis Plantation. Here, the army hoped that Davis's former slaves would teach the newcomer freedmen skills that they had learned under Davis's tutelage.

The Union army hoped that in doing so, the freedmen could eventually become independent citizens able to make a living and take care of each other. In order to facilitate that process, the army tried to hire former workers and administrators from that same plantation.

It was through this endeavor that Dee Ann found two handsome Union officers knocking at her door one morning.

"Are you Miss Dee Ann McCross?" one asked.

Dee Ann answered the door in her housecoat. "Well, I most certainly am, Captain. Is there anything I can do for you?"

"We would like to bring you to meet with our commanding general in this district. He has some important questions about how the Davis Plantation was managed, and we understand you were Joseph Davis's assistant in many of the management functions. If you're free, the General would like to meet with you now. We can take you over there and bring you back. We came in the wagon outside."

"I would love to be escorted by two of the most handsome officers. I'll just need a few minutes to get ready. If you all will just come in and have a cup of the coffee that I just made, I will get dressed while you drink it."

When Dee Ann returned wearing one of her more fetching dresses, the captain almost knocked over his coffee cup while putting it down, shocked by her complete change of appearance and the sensuality she now exuded. Both officers tried not to make their stares too obvious. Suddenly, their detail seemed anything but routine.

Enjoying the effect she had over the two officers, Dee Ann knew exactly how to manage things, which she felt would seal the deal with the two gentlemen. Facing in their direction, she made sure to bend over really low to the ground while putting on her shoes to give them a good view of her cleavage, which was impossible to miss. By the time she was finished, she felt that she would be able to cajole whatever she needed from them if ever she needed anything.

The officers escorted her with utmost chivalry to meet with General Edward Ord, who had assumed the temporary role as commandant of the district of Warren County, Mississippi.

On the way over, both officers went out of their way to make sure she was comfortable on the ride in the wagon. They were both planning at a later date to come back and see if they could take her for a buggy ride or an outing.

The two escorts led Dee Ann to a courthouse nearby, where a very distinguished looking General with attractive wavy gray hair and a bushy mustache stood out in front, patting down and talking to his horse. His horse, a tall Arabian, looked to her as though it came from one of the plantations nearby.

The two officers saluted Ord and presented Dee Ann to this ruggedly handsome man who was wearing a Union general's uniform. His jacket was double-breasted, navy blue, with three separate tiers of buttons and the shoulder boards of a Major General. Since he was not wearing a hat, Dee Ann had a very good view of the entire geometry of his face. Her escorts saluted and promptly took their leave.

General Ord began by explaining why he was outside patting and talking to his horse. "I've only had this horse for a few weeks. My old mount was killed in the battle at the Black River Bridge."

Dee Ann said, "That horse looks a lot like Hardtack, who came from Quitman's plantation. We used to hunt foxes with the Quitmans, and Hardtack was one of the fastest horses around."

"I believe you're right, but we did not know the horse's name. We rescued him from a burning barn and requisitioned him. Even though we don't know where his owners are–you are right, he is very fast. He will be a good mount for me now that I lost my old one. I was patting him and talking to him because I don't believe in forcing a horse or breaking his spirit. I want to gradually accustom him to me, and also to the noise of battle."

"You probably don't have to worry too much about the noise of battle spooking him," Dee Ann told him, "as all our hunting horses in the area are accustomed to firearms. However, heavy cannonading or exploding shells might be a different story," she conceded.

Then the General abruptly changed the subject. "I wanted to talk to you about working for the army to help us aid the population of freedmen. Let's sit down on those chairs on the porch there so we can have a little chat."

There were two rocking chairs and two colonial-style chairs

arranged on the porch. She wondered why he hadn't suggested his office in the courthouse for the meeting. Then she suddenly realized he was wearing a wedding ring, so perhaps he wanted to stay outside on the porch in full view of everybody to allay any rumors that could be spread about his meeting with her. Having had this thought though, she noted that the general hadn't really seemed to pay much attention to her appearance at all.

"We understand that you were Joseph Davis's assistant and that both of you ran a kind of court to redress grievances among the slave population at Davis Bend. We have moved thousands of freed slaves to the Davis Bend plantation—and frankly, there are frequent disputes and fights among this population now that everyone is living in close quarters."

"You know, General, we also had lots of disputes in the old days before the war."

"We know from what the former slaves have told us," said General Ord, "that you could help us get control and assist this population. We are willing to pay you twenty dollars a week and give you a budget for supplies and assistance for the freedmen to help us do this. We've got to find a way to get these freedmen back to gainful employment. The whole country is going to depend on this. We are willing to consider almost anything to get them back to work."

"General, what do you mean by almost anything? Do you mean corporal punishment?"

"Well no. All we want you to do is what you did before with your uncle. Some of these freedmen are going to be people that you never dealt with before. They are from other plantations. You and your uncle have a good reputation among the black slave population, and for that reason we want to see if you can help all these newly freed individuals. We can promise you backing by the United States army if you choose to undertake this endeavor."

Dee Ann was listening intently to the general, and at this point she absently brushed back a lock of her hair that had gotten in her eyes. "I have one question General. When I worked with my Uncle Joseph we were free to pursue any direction we thought was appropriate. Will we be able to follow the same guidelines that my uncle and I followed?"

At that point the General took out a cigar from his pocket and asked Dee Ann if he could smoke. She quickly assented, and after lighting it, he said, "We want you to succeed and help this population of freedmen so that they can learn to take care of themselves and return to work as quickly as possible. As long as you do nothing to hurt the army, or do anything to help the rebellion, you should have a free hand to operate as you see fit. My office will be open to you to discuss any problems you encounter that you cannot solve easily."

"When can I start?" asked Dee Ann.

"As soon as you can. Tomorrow, if you want to," replied General Ord.

"That suits me fine, General, I'll begin work tomorrow at the big house."

CHAPTER 67

CHANGE OF FOCUS

It was the end of the summer of 1863. The group joined by Wilms was meeting in the sitting room of the Hurricane Garden Cottage, which had served both as their home and base of operations since their earliest days, when Joseph Davis had rented it to them.

"What are we going to do now?" said Jackson. "I've been feeling at loose ends lately.

"When you look at what we just did—we helped pull off the most successful strike since biblical times when the Jews struck against the Pharaoh—everything that's happened to us since seems small in comparison," Jackson went on.

"That's certainly true," Emily interjected forcefully, "but let's not lose sight of the fact that, when we began our mission, we were first and foremost abolitionists. As far as I'm concerned, the work we are doing now in education and reorientation is every bit as important as ending slavery. What good is abolition without learning the skills and self-confidence the former slaves need to fully develop themselves. Remember, they need to become productive members of society."

After a moment of appreciative silence, Joan was the first to speak up. "There is still a war going on outside of Hurricane

Island. We have to judge our potential contributions to that effort in a much larger context."

"Well, you are all not the only ones wondering about the future, I'm wondering about the future too," said Wilms. "After what I've been through in the last year, I don't want to go back to reporting for the Vicksburg newspaper anymore, and even if I did, no one has any money or desire to buy a newspaper. The news is mostly bad these days, and you don't need any more than your own eyes to see it. The infrastructure in the city is in ruins. Survival and hard times have taken over, and there is little interest in anything other than people's immediate needs."

"I'm glad none of us has gotten sick so far," Josh said. "Normally we would want to be out of here during these summer months, but we are stuck here right now. Much of the Union army is stuck here for a while also.

"From what we are all saying, this question has been coming up—what are we to do now that we have succeeded beyond our wildest dreams?"

"I'm for enlisting in the army," said Nate.

"That goes for me too," said Jackson.

"Oh no you're not," said Joan, seconded by Wilma. "We don't want our men going off to war and getting killed."

"There are still large areas of our country under rebel control where slavery is continuing," said Nate.

Jackson banged his fist down on the table emphatically. "We can't stand by and let this happen!"

"I can see where you're all coming from," said Josh. "We all want to do something to continue the battle against slavery. But what we need now is an overall strategy."

"I think we should discuss this with General Sheridan," said Wilms. "He is the temporary military commander here. He knows all about our history here and can give us some good advice. I have worked with him before, and I think he is a good man to discuss our situation with."

Wilms, with his contacts among the generals, was sure he could set up a meeting, so they all agreed to go ahead with the plan. Although the three women went along with it, none of them were very happy about their men going off to war. They also insisted that they be part of the meeting with General Sheridan.

During this period Dee Ann had begun her work continuing on with what her Uncle Joe had started. She ran sessions to adjudicate disputes that the freedmen brought to her.

Some of the situations, however, were much difficult than what she had faced with her Uncle Joe. Many of these freedmen had come from plantations quite a distance away, and some of them were from plantations that did not share the same ethics that Joe Davis believed in.

Some freedmen had been abused in the past and were still angry—and sometimes the anger came out in her meetings with them. All of these freedmen were living on the plantations at Davis Bend under the nominal control of the army.

After the first week of work, Dee Ann met with General Ord to discuss some of the difficulties she was encountering with the population she was working with. They met outside once again, sitting on the porch chairs.

"General, some of the situations are just like the ones I faced with Uncle Joe. Others however, are more difficult to deal with."

"What do you mean exactly by *difficult*?" asked the General.

"Some of these people have just moved here. The housing is inadequate for the new arrivals, and they need work. This population was used to long hours of work in the fields. They need something to do. Idle hands do the devil's work, and they'll soon be at each other's throats.

"Many of the freedmen need medical care. The sanitary conditions for the new arrivals are not sufficient for healthy living. Some of the population has dysentery. We never had bad conditions like this on our plantation.

"One other issue. We did not have that many slaves with serious problems like this in the past. I most definitely could use some other people helping me run these meetings."

The general listened anxiously to what she had to say, but his jaw began to tighten from the stress her words induced. He began to pick apart an old cigar he took out of his pocket, and soon had tobacco all over his pants.

"I have to run an army, and now I have to run a plantation. We've got to get these freedmen back to work, and it is going to be a very big job," said the General.

Sensing the General's increasing level of discomfort, Dee Ann added, "If I can get a few more people to work with me and some assistance in rebuilding the structure of the plantation, I think we will be able to solve these problems, General."

"You shall have it," he replied, "but it may take some time to put all these things in place."

That afternoon the casually but neatly dressed group of seven went to the same courthouse and instead met with General Sheridan in his office. As they were ushered in, they noticed the office was somewhat untidy, with maps and papers scattered all over a huge desk. In contrast, the General was immaculately dressed in his best dress uniform, wearing his shoulder boards and sword.

"We are most pleased to finally meet you, General." Josh began.

"The pleasure is mine," said General Sheridan. "It is a real honor to meet the people who helped to start a revolution among the black slaves. All of you deserve a medal for the work that you did."

"General, it was these black slaves that did the real work in destroying the plantation slave system," Josh added, "which brings us to the reason we came to talk to you. Much of our work here seems to be done. We came to try to destroy the slave system. We have been here more than four years doing our work.

We arrived before the war even started. Much of Mississippi is free now and out of rebel hands, but the rebels are still holding out in a substantial part of the South. There are still large regions where the slaves are not free."

"We have been thinking of how we can best follow up on our original plan. We thought that maybe the four of us men, including John Wilms, would volunteer to serve in the army. This might fit in with what we have done so far.

"The other plan might be to relocate to another part of the South not yet touched by the war and try to do the same thing. For instance, we could go to a state like Georgia and try to raise goober peas instead of cotton. We really don't have a plan yet for our three female members if we join the army. We wanted to have your views on our planning because you have a wider and more comprehensive vision of what is happening in the neighboring regions."

While Josh was speaking, General Sheridan's face went through a number of small grimaces, which gave the appearance that the general was silently assessing their dilemma.

Finally, he ran his hand through his long dark hair and said, "I have some ideas on the subject if you want to consider them. First of all, we believe that your work helped to facilitate the black slaves to revolt, which they did very effectively. This has helped bring the rebels in this state to their knees—not only here, but this has also spread to other states.

"Your efforts and the Emancipation Proclamation are spreading throughout the South every day. It is just a matter of time before they spread to every little corner of the Confederacy.

"You don't need to do any more in another state. The work that you did will precede you. It would be almost impossible for you to start up another plantation as you did before in peacetime. The rest of the South is now wound up tighter than a mainspring in a clock. You could never get started without going through very careful scrutiny.

"As far as the army is concerned, it is an option, but I have another idea. There is a lot involved here, so hear me out on this subject before you comment on it.

"The population of freedmen, whose actual freedom you have helped to set in motion, is having some real difficulties. People are milling around with no work to do. These freedmen need a purpose, a direction, and gainful employment.

"There are needs to rebuild the infrastructure that was destroyed by the war. There are needs for housing and sanitation. If the seven of you could help the army resettle the black population in the Davis Bend area, you would be doing a great service to your country.

"The army has had to take over the administration of the freedmen and protect them. We are now doing both this and fighting a war at the same time. This way you could finish the job that you started. We could put you on the army payroll, and you would be paid just like a soldier."

"What about our women?" asked Nate.

"We also need the women," answered General Sheridan. "They will be paid for their work as well. If you do as good a job at this as you did at destroying the plantation system, we will all be very pleased.

"At General Grant's request we have begun an army bureau that is responsible for assisting these freedmen. If we are successful in Davis Bend, we can use this model program when they are freed from rebel control in other parts of the South. I can't tell you how important this program is.

"These individuals will soon be our newest citizens of the United States, and they are suffering from massive problems, including malnutrition, hunger, lack of medical care, disease, and financial hardship. Please help us see this through to a happy ending. Our Colonel Samuel Thomas is in charge of the program at Davis Bend, but he needs a lot of help. Help us get these freedmen through these crises, and you all can cap your great work with a crowning achievement."

"General, I'm ready to go!" said Jackson, beaming.

"So am I," said Nate.

All of the rest of them, including Wilms, quickly agreed to be part of the project. Wilms, however, did not like the idea of moving to Davis Bend because he wanted to be as near to Cathy as possible. So, he decided that he would need to discuss this plan with her before he got fully involved in the project.

"General," asked Wilms, "is it possible for me to live in Vicksburg and still be part of this undertaking? I'm going to need to discuss this with my fiancée before I can give you my final word on this."

"That's fine with me," General Sheridan said. "You may be able to help out even if you are not staying at Davis Bend all the time. Let me know as fast as you can. One more thing I should tell you–I may be transferred to Tennessee soon, so you will have to deal with General Ord, instead of me. We don't share all the same views, but I think on these issues that shouldn't pose a problem."

"What do you mean exactly, you don't share the same views?" asked Josh.

"He has a different perspective on the freedmen's ability to work than I do," replied the General. "But I think, overall, this situation should work out fine.

"I would like you all to get to know Ben Montgomery. He has been working with us to repair our fleet of boats on the Mississippi over at the Davis Bend plantations. He has run a store as well as a post office over there before the war. Ben is quite an intelligent man who stands out among the backward and impoverished freedmen. Ben has big plans for the Davis Plantation to resume operation. He also has a connection to Joseph Davis, whose land may or may not go back to him at the end of the war."

"Of course, we know Ben," Josh said. "We used to buy merchandise in his store. He is quite a good businessman. He could get you almost anything you needed to run the plantation. If he did not have it, he found a way to get it. He had great relationships with suppliers as far away as Atlanta and all the northern cities."

"I think your relationship with Joseph Davis will get you into his inner circle," the general continued. "If we can build a network of people around this enclave in Davis Bend, we can help nurture it so that it can grow bigger and perhaps help freedmen throughout the South."

"That is consistent with our goals," said Jackson.

Everyone in the group nodded their heads in affirmation.

"All of us as well as the Lincoln administration," the general continued, "know that this is a special and unique colony, and we want it to succeed. It is a great model to build upon. Many within the freedmen populations are refusing to work now that they are free. Right now, there are enormous social, economic, and health problems for the colony to cope with."

"Joseph Davis sure knew how to get every ounce of work out of his slaves," said Josh. "I'll bet, using his methods he could get the freedmen to work just as well."

"I don't doubt it," said General Sheridan. "I just want to say that these problems are not unlike what we are encountering in other parts of the South that were damaged by the war. Here, however, we have an opportunity to build a little homeland for the black population.

"Tomorrow I will come down to the Hurricane Garden Cottage and introduce you to Colonel Thomas, who is responsible for working with all the freedmen in this area."

As the group left the meeting Josh thought, "I hope we're not getting into something over our heads."

CHAPTER 68

RISE OF THE KU KLUX KLAN

At 8:00 a.m. sharp, General Sheridan arrived with Colonel Thomas and introduced him to everyone in the group. After the introductions the General departed, and Colonel Thomas stayed to discuss the beginnings of their work.

"I'm very glad to meet you all. To give you a brief overview of the situation, we have two populations living at Davis Bend now. The first includes many of Joseph and Jefferson Davis's old slaves. The second is made up of freedmen from other plantations. As you probably have noticed, these different groups do not get along that well. The freedmen from the Davis plantations are well-behaved and orderly, but some of the slaves from the other plantations in the area are more prone to thievery, fights, and angry outbursts.

"Ben Montgomery," he went on, "is the real leader of this group at Davis Bend. Frankly I don't have the best relations with him. My responsibility is all the freedmen in the area, not just the old Davis slaves, whom he favors. The fact that the two populations have different needs is causing trouble for us. I feel Ben tries to take better care of the old Davis slaves who appear to swear allegiance to him. I am compelled to take care of all freedmen, regardless of where they came from. In truth, most of them are now very capable of taking care of themselves and are as ready for freedom as the slaves who originated at Davis Bend."

Emily struck a thoughtful pose and then asked, "Are the old Davis slaves really better-behaved than some of the other freedmen from other plantations?"

"You better believe it," the Colonel said. "They almost never commit any crimes. They are calmer and more literate and affluent. Many of them can read, and they take an interest in the affairs of the country and the war. Still, I must say that there are many others who never met Joe Davis or Ben Montgomery, and yet they are wonderful people ready to rise to the challenges of freedom as well.

"Ben feels that many of the freedmen from plantations farther away seem to be completely different. He sees them as angry and sullen. He says that they are more likely to steal things to meet their needs rather than work for food and tools."

"Are some of the freedmen resentful that the Davis freedmen have more material things?" asked Emily.

"I'm sure that's part of the problem," said the Colonel. "I've been trying to equalize resources for everyone in the area, but Ben has been fighting me tooth and nail. He thinks that if I cannot support the higher standard of living at Davis Bend and equalize it to the new freedman, it will destroy the colony.

"He is also terrified of angry, sullen freedmen because he thinks their behavior will incur the wrath of neighboring bands of vengeful whites, of which there are some, and bring civil strife down on the region.

"Who knows, he may be right. But all this has created bad feelings between us. I'm hoping you can help me bridge that gap since you have all worked with Joseph Davis before, and Ben Montgomery knows and respects all of you."

"Do you think it might be a good idea for the seven of us to meet with Ben to see how he views the situation?" asked Nate.

"I'm hoping you will take that initiative–and the sooner, the better," responded the Colonel.

"With the freedmen of various plantations all living in the same spot," said Josh, "the issue of who owns the land of these former plantations is in doubt. Until the courts and government decide, this is going to be a very complex problem. There has been a huge change in a short period of time. It's probably going to take some time to sort things out."

"I'm not so sure we have all the time in the world to work these problems out," said the Colonel. "We contracted with some northerners to come down here and run some of these plantations. Frankly some of them have done a terrible job. They are working the freedmen to death and not paying them a livable wage. It's worse than slavery for the men caught in this trap. Having all these northerners who are seen as surrogate Yankees is also inflaming the local white population. They feel the blacks are taking away some of their power and jobs, and there is a powerful white reaction building against this. All of these factors are helping to destabilize the region."

The seven agreed to pay a visit to Ben Montgomery and get his perspective on how to begin their jobs to help the freedmen in the area.

The next day Josh and Nate dropped by Ben's store to try to set up a meeting with him and the group of seven. Ben quickly agreed to meet with them for breakfast at Briarwood Mansion the next day.

When the seven arrived at Briarwood they were in for a bit of a shock. They knocked at the door, and a black freedman in the role of a servant showed them in. It was just the way Joseph Davis's servants would have showed them in when he was still master.

"We are here to see Ben Montgomery," Josh spoke up as Toby, the doorman, answered the door.

"You all come in and wait in the drawing room. Does you want me to bring you all a cool drink?"

"We'd like that," said Nate who marveled at the similarity of the greeting to that which all the visitors received at the old Davis mansions.

Ben, his wife Mary, and their son Isaiah, greeted them in a most cordial manner. Ben and Mary had many freedmen in the house in the roles of driver, cook, butler, and maid. Irrespective of the presence of these individuals, Ben seemed to do almost all the work. He made all the food and waited on everyone but got a little help from his servants.

Not wanting to rock the boat and damage the relationship, the seven did not comment on the structure of the help in the Montgomery household and its similarity to the Davis's household.

At the breakfast table, Jackson asked Ben, "What do you think about the atmosphere in Mississippi now that many soldiers are being transferred away? Don't you think there is less protection for the black freedmen than in the previous months?

"I have noticed," continued Jackson, "that some of these former rebel soldiers are getting much bolder in transferring their anger toward the black population here. Do you feel this also?"

"Of course, I do," said Ben. "We have to be very careful in this little colony not to ruffle any feathers. The way these former rebels see things is like this: First the Yankees come and take away their livelihood, destroy their homes, and kill their people. Then they put the former slaves in a position of power over them. This is done out of naiveté, stupidity, or anger at the rebels. When the army begins to pull out, as is happening now, a terrible backlash of white anger will come roaring back with a vengeance.

"The vengeance is not towards the Union army, which beat

the crap out of them, but the lowest people on the totem pole, which are the new freedmen. The planters feel that it was the slaves refusing to work and their strike that destroyed the economy of the Confederacy. That is who they are going to blame for the lost war, and there will be hell to pay for it."

"Do you see things getting worse in the future?" Jackson asked.

Ben looked him straight in the eyes and said, "Of course I do. I am as sure of it as the sun rising tomorrow. Just imagine—if you were disenfranchised and your wealth given to someone else—how would you feel?"

"What are we going to do then?" asked Joan. All the women wore a very worried look on their faces.

"We have to be very careful," said Nate.

"Not only careful, but we have to behave the same way we did before, when we were slaves." said Ben. "If we don't, we are asking for trouble. Black slaves who were elected to office or given appointments by the Republican Party are going to be at risk when the army pulls out of here. This will happen soon because the rebels are losing everywhere.

"We have to think a few moves ahead, like in a chess game. If we visualize what our world will be like when the army pulls out, we can make some sound decisions. My biggest concern is our colony of people here. I think we need to concentrate on building a power base among the whites here and say or do whatever is needed to placate them. If we do this right, we can continue the work that Joseph Davis started and make this into a functioning black enterprise."

"But aren't we receiving support from the army?" asked Josh. "Won't that contaminate us with the whites in the area?"

Ben scratched his head and answered. "It could, but we have Joseph working with both the government and the local whites. For all intent and purposes, this is still seen as his land and plantation. So, this is seen as receiving help from the government.

This is well received because he is very popular in the area. We have to keep a very low profile and keep out of politics. Too much notoriety can sink us."

"What about Colonel Thomas?" Josh asked. "How does he fit into the picture with the Davis Bend colony?"

"He does and he doesn't," was Ben's reply. "He wants to help our colony because he sees it as something special, but at the same time he has to help all the freedmen in the area." Then his face showed a look of disgust. "He has been settling many of them here, but many of these folks did not grow up here under Joseph Davis's rules, and they just don't fit in here.

"We would like to help them, but some of them steal things from others, including from us, and start fights. A good deal of them fit in all right, but it only takes a few bad pieces of rotten fruit to spoil the whole bushel. I guess Thomas is okay for what he is doing for the colony, but his focus on *all* the freedmen often puts him at odds with us.

"Our colony bridges two different worlds, the world of the past with the Davis's and the world of the present. We get support from both sides; a few bad moves and mistakes could doom all our work and destroy the colony. Through the army's good graces we receive support in terms of money, hardware, supplies, and farm animals. We are also going to get teachers and workers from up north to help us get started."

"That's why we're here," said Emily. "We want to be able to support you as well."

"So far we have been very lucky," Ben went on. "Through the whites of the old South, we have been allowed to continue with no violence. Much of this support comes to us due to the influence of Joseph Davis. He wants us to succeed and prove the point to others that the black race is as capable as the white race. He also depends on us for economic support in terms of the payments from his land. Yes, this place is going to have to support him as well.

"By the way, please don't mention this to anyone, as it will probably be against state law to allow former slaves to run a plantation. Anyhow, our affiliation with the Davises protects us from the disenfranchised whites' anger at former slaves receiving more power.

"Joe Davis also fights for us politically, just the way he also fought for himself in the past."

"The man I am most concerned about in this whole enterprise is General Ord," said Ben.

"General Ord!" said Josh. "What is wrong with General Ord?"

"I don't trust him," said Ben. "He talks a good game and he praises everyone for the work they have done to free the slaves. It sounds impressive, but I heard him tell an associate that if the former slaves don't go back to work in the fields, the army may need to use force to get them back to work. You all should be wary of him. He is all right as a general and has helped us some already, but inside, he still has some part of him that seems akin to the old South, even though he professes to help the freedmen."

"This has certainly been an eye opener," said Jackson. "Based on what you told us today, I think we can now begin to craft a strategy to help us cope with the changes to come."

CHAPTER 69

IN DEFENSE OF THE COLONY

Shortly after the meeting with Ben Montgomery at the Davis mansion, word came through the Union army commanders that a rebel cavalry detachment had gone on a reconnaissance in force to explore the plantation area in Warren County, Mississippi. Their mission was to explore the possibility of recapturing it now that the Union army was headed deeper into Tennessee and that troop strength was declining in the Vicksburg area.

Upon notification of this unit spotted thirty miles away and headed in their direction, Josh, under Colonel Thomas's direction, called a large group of freedmen who had been trained in firearm use together. They met near the warehouse at Davis Bend. Included in the group were Nate, Jackson, and Wilms. The women–Joan, Wilma and Emily–came along to find out what was going on.

Colonel Thomas began by addressing the group. "We have been acting as if the war is over for this area, but it appears that it is not. A strong force of rebel cavalry is headed this way. The main part of our army is now heavily engaged in Tennessee. We have only a small number of our troops here to maintain order but not enough to engage this enemy. This is primarily a cavalry sortie, but they may have a couple of eight- pounder howitzers with them.

"Since all of you have experience now with firearms, we will need you to help defend the area. If these men succeed and make off with any of you, it will be back to slavery for the duration of the war if they don't kill you instead. For that reason, it is a matter of survival that we stop them."

Josh spoke up, "If we are going to be dealing with a cavalry charge, we need to develop tactics to cope with it. Since many of you are not trained soldiers, our best defense is probably the tried and true hollow square, about five rows deep, with officers in the middle. If Colonel Thomas will let me demonstrate, I can show you how to set it up."

"You may go ahead and demonstrate," said Thomas

Josh lined up everyone in a square several rows deep so that there were reserves to fill the gaps of anyone who was wounded or killed. "When the enemy charges at you, don't shoot until they are less than one hundred feet away."

He had Nate walk about a hundred feet away and make a mark on the ground. "Don't shoot until you are pretty sure of hitting someone. But don't wait until they are too close, or else you may have dead and wounded men and horses intruding on the square. Whatever you do, don't break the square, although a triangle can work if the square is destroyed.

"Cavalrymen and horses that break into the square can be shot from the front, back, and the sides. Mounted riders who ride through the square can be shot on the way in and out. Remember, don't break the square unless we tell you to do it.

"This method has been used since ancient Chinese times, and it has always been the best answer for dealing with cavalry, even when the only weapons in use were bows and arrows. One more thing I want everyone to practice is loading as quickly as you can with the muzzleloaders. Speed in this is the difference between life and death. I'm also glad that we received a good supply of Henry repeating rifles so that we will be able to lay down a good blanket of fire from all sides."

"Well boss, is you goin' to give us enough ammunition?" Joe Green, a freedman, asked?

"Everything we have got," said Colonel Thomas. "We have a day or two till they get here. I want you to practice making this hollow square with Colonel Lawrence until you can get into a fighting square quickly. I want Colonel Lawrence to set up this defensive position. Everyone here must follow his orders because I believe he has the best knowledge of how to stop the enemy."

At that point Josh gave Thomas a peculiar look that said, "I was a Colonel in the *Confederate army*. Why are you calling me Colonel?" He would have to wait until later to find out why.

"I think that they will have to come through the Vicksburg-Port Gibson road," Thomas continued. "It is the best way to get to the plantations. There is a big, muddy clearing along the road where horses will have to go slower because the mud is very deep. They won't have the usual cavalry mobility there, and a slower target is easier to hit. I think we should draw up our square there."

They all agreed to head for that spot as soon as possible. Josh and his group went home to get their supplies and weapons and leave for the field where they were planning on ambushing the rebel cavalry.

'We want to go too," said Joan. When the three women saw what the men were up to, they all decided to go. They felt that if anyone was going to try to enslave free people here, they wanted to stop them.

"I am the best shot around here," said Joan standing tall at her five-foot-five height.

Next, Wilma stood up, throwing her arms and shoulders back to make herself look as big and strong as she could for her imposing height of six feet. "We are all good shots, and Joan is an excellent shot," she said.

"I want to go too," said Emily. "We all have stuck together through everything we have done so far. I don't want us to be separated. We are coming whether you like it or not."

"You women are crazy," said Colonel Thomas, who had accompanied them back to Hurricane Garden Cottage. "This is a rebel cavalry unit. They are the most aggressive unit the rebels have. This unit was trained by Nathan Bedford Forrest himself. He has had a ferocious reputation wherever he's gone."

"That's why we want to go," said Joan.

The women were so insistent on going that the men gave in, hoping to dissuade them before the battle actually took place. In all, a mixture of about five hundred freedmen and about fifty Union soldiers, black and white, headed down to the road where the Confederate cavalry would have to cross in order to reach the plantation area.

What they lacked in regular Union soldiers they made up for in weaponry. They were given one hundred Henry repeating rifles in addition to the standard muzzleloaders issued to everyone. This gave them a considerable firepower advantage because the Confederates only had muzzle-loading carbines and revolvers.

In addition to the rifles, they had a good supply of Colt revolvers. They also had an ample supply of bayonets; however, most freedmen had no experience using them in hand-to-hand combat. Lastly, they had three sharpshooter rifles with telescopic sights, which could be used at long distances.

After a three-hour ride with horses and carts, they reached the spot on the road where the mud had made part of it impassable. Josh laid out a position on the dry ground for a hollow square. All approaches had to traverse this deep muck to reach the position he set up. In addition to the area for the square, he found two hedgerows on either side of the road parallel to the square, where troops could wait in ambush.

Since the women would not be dissuaded from participation in the battle, he decided to station them deep in the hedgerow with a few other skilled shooters. He gave Joan one of the sharpshooter sniper rifles. Emily received a sharpshooter rifle and a revolver. He gave the last rifle to Wilma. Although she was not as good a shot as Joan or Emily, he hoped Joan could teach her a couple of her skills.

The latest scouting reports put the rebels at least twenty miles away, so they had some time to prepare their position. Joan, Wilma, and Emily fired some test shots to zero in the sights on the sniper rifles.

The troops in the hedgerow moved some logs and stumps to set up a defensive position in the thick undergrowth of the hedgerow. They were also given a liberal supply of Henry repeating rifles and several revolvers. The troops who were to form the square also cut logs and moved underbrush to set up a square defensive position in the middle of the road on the part of it that was dry.

Josh looked over the position and made a checklist in his mind to see if he had covered all the possibilities. He was content that there were at least one hundred and fifty yards of deep muck leading up to their position. He felt that this should slow the cavalry down considerably.

He laid out a large square in the middle of the road with hedgerows on each side. Some of his best shots were in the hedgerows. The front, back, and sides of the square in the road were amply equipped with repeating rifles and revolvers. All the troops had a good supply of food and water. There was no way around this position unless the rebels wanted to go thirty miles out of their way on some bad roads amid pockets of Union troops.

Josh thought the sides and back of the square might be

redundant—but, then again, should the cavalry break through, he would have a defense in depth to stop it.

He brought some of the horses down the road to see how well they could walk in the muck and found to his dismay that they were quite able to walk through it, although at a slower pace. Taking in this scene, one of the freedmen shook his head, turned to Josh and said, "Boss, why don't you try coming up at a gallop and see what happens."

Josh galloped into the muck, and the horse taken unawares had a difficult time maintaining its balance, sank into the mud, and almost fell over.

"I think this will work," Josh said to the freedman. "Thanks for the advice."

Next, he sent a group of five soldiers several miles up the road to a makeshift outpost on some heights where they could get a good view with binoculars of comings and goings on the road for about five miles ahead. They were given directions to come galloping back when the rebel cavalry unit was spotted coming up the road.

In the meantime, this hybrid ragtag force of irregulars spent time trying to perfect their improvised defensive structure. After a while they began to cook lunch and pass the food to everyone. They had just finished eating when one of the soldiers on the outpost came galloping back to advise that the cavalry was spotted walking at a leisurely pace down the road.

The other men moved back to a closer position to keep an eye on the rebels. One by one, the returning scouts came back to report the position and speed of the cavalry unit. When the last man came in, everyone got into position blocking the road.

After a while, a lone Confederate cavalryman came cantering down the road and spotted the barricades. He looked over the position with his binoculars, turned, and went back to the others. He did not come far enough to hit the patch of deep muck.

The rebels then brought up their two eight-pounder howitzers, elevated them point blank at the barricades from half a mile away, and began to fire a mix of solid shot and explosive shells at the stumps and branches. This created some disruptions in the defensive line and injured a few of the defenders.

Luckily, no one was killed, and Wilms, who was with the defenders on the front line, quickly took over the role of doctor and gave aid to the wounded. He set broken bones, made splints using wood from the barricades, and treated wounds—all while under fire.

The howitzers then changed to shorter fuses with air bursts over their position. Josh was getting worried about the artillery disrupting his whole line when a shot rang out from a part of the hedgerow much closer to the artillery. It hit the powder bag holding one of the explosive shells that the artilleryman was carrying, detonating it as it was about to be loaded into the gun barrel. The explosion destroyed the gun carriage and killed or injured the whole gun crew.

Two more sniper shots killed two more of the other crew. The remaining gun was hauled back out of range of the snipers but also out of position to fire on the barricades. With their artillery foiled, the cavalry began forming up for a charge. As the unit lined up on the road the bugler blew *forward.* At the bugle's notes, most defenders felt a strong fear course through their veins.

The bugle sounded *charge*, and the horsemen galloped down the road with their sabers in hand. The snipers knocked several horsemen off their horses a long way down from the barricades. As the front ranks of the cavalry hit the deep mud at about one hundred and fifty feet from the front of the square, their rapid deceleration forced all the horses to bunch up and many to collide with each other. This caused some of the riders to be thrown off their mounts and into the mud.

The rapid slowdown of the rebel cavalry offered multiple

targets of opportunity to the improvised army in the square and in the hedgerow. They laid down a withering fire, making good use of the repeating rifles. The front lines of the cavalry were quickly decimated.

A large mass of the rebel cavalry withdrew to the area near one of the hedgerows. At the same time, much of the battlefield smoke drifted over this same area. No longer able to see what was going on, the men became very worried about the fate of the women hiding there.

Nate heard Josh call out, "What about the women! Oh God, let them be all right!" This fear caused them all to fight like demons to protect their women.

During this period of intense fighting Nate was situated in the second line of the front of the square, taking shelter behind a log that he had rolled into the road. He watched the facial expressions of a freedman crouched right in front of him to his right side. When the howitzers opened fire on them, he saw a look of fear course through the freedman's face. Even though he looked terrified, he held his ground and prepared to fire his rifle to repel the attack. Clouds of smoke from the bursting shells drifted over the line of the square. Everyone flinched at the explosions, but no one tried to run away.

When the bugle blew *charge*, Nate was again staring to his right at the same freedman. He noticed the man's jaw tighten up, and he could see vibrations in his jaw muscles when the smoke cleared somewhat during momentary breaks in the action.

"I guess we stopped them this time," Nate heard him mutter.

"They're not going to get through us very easily," replied Nate, but he was not at all sure the freedman heard him in the din of the battle.

Then a second wave of horsemen came on, and the same thing happened again—but this time a few horsemen found a dry patch and were able to gallop up to the front line of the square and jump the barricades. However, soldiers on the sides and back of the square quickly caught them in a crossfire and brought them down.

After the rebels had suffered severe casualties, Josh heard the bugler blow *retreat*, and the cavalry that was left standing quickly galloped back down the road. It looked like the Confederates were at a loss to know what to do next as they languished far back on the road out of range of the snipers. The whole engagement had lasted less than an hour.

Josh, Nate, and Jackson ran over to the hedgerow to see how the women had fared but could not find them. They called out their names but received no response. They were starting to worry whether they had been abducted or killed when Jackson spotted the three walking down the road back to the square. Wilma towered over Joan. They were both walking proudly with their heads held high. They had their rifles slung over their shoulders, military style. Emily was wearing a revolver in a holster around her waist.

"We were worried sick about all of you," Jackson said. "We're sure relieved you're all right."

"We found we could take care of ourselves very well," said Emily.

"Those rebels won't want to mess with us again," said Wilma.

After a while, a white flag appeared, and two men on horseback moved forward. It was obvious that they wanted to talk. Josh, Nate, and Jackson met them at the beginning of the mud.

The rebel captain began by addressing Josh. "Are you in command?" he asked. Josh, Nate, and Jackson all nodded their heads.

"We are the advance guard of a larger army that is coming. We are expecting our troops to arrive tomorrow. You don't have enough men to stand in their way. Their artillery will quickly destroy your position. We will accept your surrender to avoid further bloodshed, and the white troops will be paroled with their sidearms."

"What about the black troops?" asked Nate.

"They will have to go back to their plantations," the captain said. "Anyway, which of you is in charge here?"

"He is," Josh said, pointing to Jackson.

"Let's cut out this hogwash, Captain," said Jackson. "We know you don't have any army. You should be the one surrendering to us. We just gave you a good whipping! We don't believe you when you say slaves must go back to their plantations. If we surrendered, you would hang us all from a tree. Come on–be honest. You're so full of lies that you're probably beginning to believe them. It must be hard on your guys knowing they took a good thrashing from a bunch of no 'count niggers!"

"If you won't surrender," said the captain, "can we at least agree on a truce to pick up the wounded and remove the dead?"

"We don't have any dead, but there are a few wounded," said Jackson. He then looked at Josh, who nodded his head with approval, and he continued, "You can have a truce to bring a score of men down here to remove your wounded and dead. And then clear out of here and don't come back–or we will finish off the rest of you!"

The rebels promptly complied. They picked up their wounded and dead and were quickly on their way.

Josh and his improvised army retained the position for two more days. He sent two men on horseback to shadow the rebel cavalry to make sure they did not double back and force them to fight again from a different and strategically inferior position. Only when Josh was finally satisfied that the rebels had gone away did he give the order for everyone to return to their homes.

During those two days, everyone camped out on the battlefield. It was a beautiful fall evening, cool but not too cold, as they sat on improvised logs having their first dinner there.

Around the different campfires the day's events were recounted from many different points of view. This reflected the diverse positions of the combatants on the battle line.

Now seated along the same road where many soldiers had been killed just a few hours before, these groups of men were bathed in the bluish-white light of the full moon, which illuminated equally the stumps and logs of the defenses. This light gave them the eerie appearance of a surrounding army of ghosts. The atmosphere was completed by the intricate chants of mockingbirds in the nearby trees and the occasional hooting of an owl in the distance.

The group from Hurricane Garden Cottage, joined by Wilms when he finished tending to the wounded, sat around one of the many open fires. A gentle breeze fanned the flames and kept the bugs down. Joseph Davis had purchased a large amount of lemon eucalyptus oil from an Australian merchant several years ago, and everyone had put gobs of it on before the battle. They continued to rub it in, and as a consequence had few problems with bugs.

"Why did you tell that rebel captain that I was in charge here?" Jackson asked.

"Those rebels think the white man is superior to all blacks," Josh answered as the bluish-white light illuminated his face and gave him a ghostly pallor. "I just wanted to rub salt in his wounds and teach him a lesson. I wanted him to think we were taking orders from you."

"I just hope he doesn't take out his anger on other helpless freedmen," Wilma broke in. "But if that was a crack rebel unit, they sure took a drubbing from us."

"If our sharpshooters hadn't hit the ammunition bag with the gunpowder and shell, that battle would have been much more difficult," Josh added. "They could have kept out of range with their cannons and gradually decimated our front line. They also could have destroyed all the defensive works we set up. By the way, does anyone know who fired that shot? They are one of the real heroes of today's battle!"

At that point everyone noticed that Wilma looked at Joan and Joan glanced back at Wilma. There was an understanding between the two of them. Josh took note of the silent communication and asked incredulously, "It wasn't you two, was it?"

"Aren't you glad you brought us along," said Joan. "Actually, it was Wilma who made the shot."

"She coached me through the whole thing," said Wilma. "I was jerking the trigger back too hard, and she showed me how to take a deep breath and squeeze gently. She and Emily hit the other men on the second cannon, and we all hit cavalrymen in the charge."

"If you were in my old unit," said Josh, "I would have recommended you for a medal. Blowing up that powder bag might have won the day for us. I'm going to mention this to Colonel Thomas. If you two were men, you'd probably get a medal—even in this ragtag unit. But I'm not sure the powers that be want to advertise that they are putting women in harm's way deliberately."

"I don't know that we really even needed the square," said Jackson. "We stopped them mostly with our front line. Only a few broke through."

"If Wilma hadn't hit the powder bag," said Josh, "we certainly would have needed it. I just wanted to say, Jackson, that you really did show excellent qualities of leadership when you called that rebel captain's bluff. The lesson from this whole battle is a good defense in depth is an absolute necessity against a cavalry charge."

CHAPTER 70

THE END OF AN ERA

Two weeks after the battle with the rebel cavalry, Josh was called in to General Ord's office and received a battlefield commission of Lieutenant Colonel. This reward was for his work as a Union spy in helping to circumvent the fortifications at Vicksburg. Other factors in the commission were the parts he played in helping the blacks revolt and go on strike, and his role in stopping the advance of the Confederate cavalry.

On receiving the commission, he said, "General Ord, I'm honored to receive this commission for my work, but the real heroes are the black freedmen who went on strike and shut down the plantations and all work in the area. They are also the real heroes of the battle with the rebels as well. They are the ones who ultimately stopped Nathan Bedford Forrest's cavalry."

"That may be so," said General Ord, "but the country is not ready to accept a bunch of untrained niggers bringing the South to her knees and winning an engagement over the best unit of the Confederate cavalry."

At that point Josh understood what Ben Montgomery meant when he said he did not trust General Ord.

There were several very difficult years of work on the plantation following an end to the war. Floods, army worms, and poor growing conditions all contributed to hard times. Finally, conditions began to improve and the plantation began to prosper.

Ben Montgomery had bought even more land from another property right nearby. These were some of the few plantations that were able to get the freedmen to work doing what they did before the war. This took place because the economic conditions were favorable and the freedmen were paid fairly through a sharecrop system that worked here for the benefit of all.

When times got hard, Joe Davis had Ben lighten up on the payments for the mortgage so that everyone shared in both the wealth and the misfortune. The group of six had become seven, and reverted to six again when Wilms returned to Vicksburg to marry Cathy. Next, Dee Ann wedded a Union officer in the army of occupation.

During this period, bad things were beginning to happen to the freedmen in the South outside of Davis Bend. Andrew Johnson, who assumed the presidency after Abraham Lincoln was assassinated, claimed to be carrying on what Lincoln had planned to do with the South but showed little concern for the plight of the freedmen. His sole concern was getting them back to work doing what they had been doing before the war as slaves. He quickly made it possible for many of the former Confederates to return to power, either by amnesty after signing a loyalty oath, or by granting pardons to those with the most property.

As victors after a brutal war, the North could have made proper treatment of the freedmen a condition of being allowed to return to citizenship of the United States.

President Johnson could have tried to get those freedmen the right to vote, which would have protected their newly won freedom. Johnson, however, did not trust the former slaves and felt that they might be in cahoots with their former masters, who were likely to be his political opponents.

He feared that they would vote against him and his policies

if given the chance. It appeared that he had a racially biased view of the potential of the new black citizens. In any case, he bore the responsibility for ordering that all lands in the South be returned to the former owners, effectively disenfranchising any freedmen who had been told that the land would be theirs.

During his tenure in office, a system of contract labor began to appear in the South. Former slaves all over this region were forced to sign these work contracts under pressure from the army. Those who refused to sign could be evicted from the land they no longer had any legal claim to. By and large, the army went from an institution benevolent to the blacks, to one of social control.

While under slavery the black man's entire family had been forced to work. Now under the new South, it was soon discovered that the labor force had been cut down considerably. The labor that hitherto had been unpaid now had to be paid for.

The bottom line now was that the Johnson administration wanted to get the same production out of the South that it had before the war. It tried to use capitalist methods instead of the old feudal system of slavery. But that did not work. Now that they were freedmen, the blacks did not want to work from sunup to sundown in the hot fields that compromised their health and may have shortened their lives. Not at least without adequate remuneration.

President Johnson's United States government tried everything to get the former slaves back to their old production, and since nothing worked, the government began to use force. This force included corporal punishment and enforcement of work contracts. These contracts were enforced from the employer's point of view—and almost never from the worker's, unless they could get the Freedmen's Bureau involved.

Seeing his plans thwarted by the new Freedmen's Bureau, the president tried to emasculate it by firing directors and staff. Lastly, the freedmen had no redress of grievances in the courts.

White employers won almost all the cases brought before them. Due process for the freedmen was effectively circumvented.

While these catastrophic conditions reigned throughout the South, conditions in Davis Bend remained quite a bit better for several reasons. Production of cotton was higher than anywhere else as Ben Montgomery continued the methods of Joseph Davis, who became his mentor and accomplice.

Individuals in power in both the North and the South took note of his success because it was rare in the new South. These people looked to Davis Bend as the model community for blacks that would return the rest of the South to productivity.

Ben Montgomery kept a very low profile so that everyone thought Joe Davis was still in control of the plantation. Most of the local populations thought Davis was simply getting marvelous productivity out of his freedmen, although everyone wondered how he was now able to do it.

The Montgomerys had helped the Union army considerably by running a repair facility on the river for Union vessels, and their son Isaiah had served on one of the ironclads. He therefore had built up considerable goodwill within the army.

The army, in turn, offered protection from hostile forces from the old Confederacy, which had been creating terror elsewhere in the South. Grants and assistance came from the newly formed Freedman's Bureau.

In addition to the six original members of Josh's family, educators and teachers streamed in from up north. To help the colony get a good start, financial forgiveness was also available from Joseph Davis whenever Ben ran into financial trouble from weather, pests, insects, and floods. All these conditions and the backbreaking work the freedmen of the colony put in created a fertile ground for a successful plantation.

It was during this period that Josh ran into Marie Laver as he went out for an early morning walk. As was usual in their interactions, Marie quickly unbalanced the conversation and tried to put Josh on the defensive toward revealing more information than she should know.

"You people sure helped start a revolution," she began. "We know all about what you did to warn the slaves to quit the plantation. You did a good job!" Then Marie gave Josh a sly look. "But guess what we did."

"All right Marie, what did you do?"

"We have voodoo groups everywhere throughout the South," she said, smiling proudly. "We took your warnings and spread them everywhere. We kept spreading them as the Union army moved forward. This was the warning for all the slaves everywhere to quit the plantation and go on strike. We enlarged your plan and made it much bigger. We really won the war and brought the Confederacy to its knees."

"Marie, if you want to take credit for winning the war, be my guest," said Josh.

"I'm glad you see it our way," said Marie. "I'm glad we could work together in a great cause."

When Josh got back, he spoke to the others who were all in the house and getting ready to go out.

"I just spoke to Marie Laver," he said sarcastically, "who advised me that she and her followers won the Civil War by copying our methods and spreading them to plantations in all the territories controlled by the Confederacy."

"Let her take the credit," said Jackson, "but it is a lot of nonsense. I know there are a lot of voodoo people in Mississippi, Louisiana, Alabama, and Georgia—but I never heard about any in Virginia or the Carolinas!"

"I have," said Nate. "Some slaves coming from auctions in New Orleans brought voodoo with them to almost all the Confederate states—but not as much as here."

"I think she has an inflated view of her abilities and her followers—just like a big hot air balloon," Jackson said forcefully.

"She might have helped the revolution as we did. Nobody can take the credit for it except the black slaves who revolted."

"You're right," said Emily.

"We all did our part," Nate went on. "The whole movement was gigantic. We can't even take the credit for it. The rising took place over the whole Confederacy."

"Once a revolution starts, it sets off a reaction like gunpowder," Josh said. "Who knows where it will end up? Black slaves were leaving the plantation and going over to Union troops before they ever reached Mississippi. You are right. Each of us did our part in this movement."

"One can only give credit to the black slaves who revolted," Jackson repeated. "They deserve the full measure of credit. They won the war. I'm not sure they will ever get the credit that they deserve. It is the same story as black soldiers never getting medals for their valor."

CHAPTER 71

REIGN OF TERROR

As the Joseph Davis–Ben Montgomery plantation was struggling but starting to turn a small profit, Joseph Davis arrived at his lawyer's office in Vicksburg. As he was walking up the stairs to the office, he ran into Bob Turner, who had run several plantations in the area before the war.

Turner's first words were an eager question. "How do you do it? I'll give you a hundred dollars if you can show me how to get the niggers who work for me to put in a day's work for a day's pay!" Joe stopped, took off his hat, and made eye contact with Turner.

"I don't know if you're serious or not," said Davis, "but if you are, I'd be willing to talk to you about it. Let's sit down here on these chairs on the landing for a moment; I'm mightily tired of climbing these stairs. The first thing you're going to have to do is stop calling them niggers. That's a pejorative word that implies that they are lazy and shiftless. It then becomes a self-fulfilling prophecy. A person who is accused of something again and again often acts out what people believe they are."

"I don't know if I can do that easily," said Turner. "I get so angry at the workers when they don't produce like they used to. I am also still angry about all these niggers going on strike and leaving their plantations in a time of emergency. I don't know ifn I can ever stop calling them niggers."

"If you don't stop it, you will never get them to work up to their potential. Look, it's like a man who calls his wife a slut or a whore every time she talks to another man. What do you think is going to happen to him?"

At those words Turner cringed as though Davis had kicked him in the balls.

"Well, all I want to say is that how you value a human being is directly related to what you get out of him. That applies to both men and women. If you want me to help, you have to be willing to change some things inside of you. If you are, I might be able to help you."

As Turner walked away, he was thinking two equally disturbing thoughts—could these niggers really be human beings—and—have I been treating my wife wrong all this time?

This same day, Josh and Emily made a trip to Vicksburg to visit Wilms, his old wartime associate and friend. Wilms had bought a house with Cathy, who was now pregnant and soon to give birth.

On the way over to Wilms's house, Josh ran into Joseph Davis leaving his lawyer's office. They shook hands like old friends, and there was not the slightest trace of hostility. Joseph was as warm to him as ever. There had been some rumors circulating that Josh was a turncoat who deserted his post at Vicksburg, but nothing could be proven, and there were many rumors about a lot of people's behavior during the war. Joseph's face lit up when he saw Josh.

"I'm so glad to see you after all we all have gone through. I wish Eliza was still around to see you two. She always had a soft spot for you both."

"We had heard about her passing from Dee Ann," said Josh, "but we did not know where you were, so we could not pay our respects."

Then Emily added, "She was such a good woman. We miss her."

"This was war. I was on the run trying to move my operation to other places away from the war, but as I moved the war came after me. Thank you for paying your respects now, even though a lot of time has passed."

Instead of getting into a discussion of political events, they chose to inquire about Joseph's family.

"What has happened to Jefferson?" Emily asked.

"He is in prison in Fort Belvoir, though he has never been charged with a crime. They have been trying to blame Lincoln's assassination on him but have no evidence at all. They believe he is responsible for the war, so they are vindictive toward him. They have not given him due process of law, so he is still rotting in prison. The full weight of the United States has been turned against him. Some of the Republicans want to hang him. Thank God there are some cooler heads around. It is very significant that they have not charged him with anything yet. I think the prosecutors have a weak case." At this point Joseph's voice cracked with emotion.

"The longer things stretch out," Josh said supportively, "the weaker their case becomes as people just want to forget about the war."

"I hope you're right," said Joseph. "It is a double-edged sword, though. He could rot in prison for a long time, even though their case gets weaker and weaker. A big problem now is that there is a split in the government.

"Many Republicans are accusing President Johnson of trying to restore the Confederacy, and they think that the government should hang Jefferson, even without the evidence or a reason to do it. In this environment I think Johnson is afraid to let him out of prison, lest he be accused of aiding in the restoration of the Confederacy.

"Of course, Jefferson represents a strong symbol of that

Confederacy. They are not simply dealing here with petty officials whom no one knows about."

"When you see him or write to him, give him our best regards and our hope that he gets out soon," said Josh.

"I guess you're not growing much cotton these days," said Joseph.

"It's been very difficult," Josh answered, "with floods, pests and all. We have no money; in fact, nobody has much. The only money we've been able to take in has come from the army, which is paying us to resettle and organize the freedmen. If this works out, maybe we can return to production."

Josh lied here because he had no intention of starting cotton production in any form and was making other plans for his future. This seemed to satisfy Joseph for the moment.

"One other question—how is Dee Ann doing?" Josh asked, changing the subject. We heard she was carrying on the work with the freed slaves that you started, and we also heard she was married."

At that point Emily kicked Josh gently, out of sight of Joseph, to show her displeasure at his bringing up the subject.

"She's doing very well. She married a Yankee colonel, which is not too popular down here. He is, however, a real find. He is intelligent, knowledgeable, and a great addition to our family. Perhaps you will meet him some day. His name is Colonel Ross."

"We also heard that your plantation is doing as well as anyone this year under Ben Montgomery, even though it has been a poor growing year," said Josh.

Joseph's face flushed deep purple and he said, "The floods have been terrible this year, as well as the pests. It's a miracle we have any cotton crop, or any crop at all."

Josh added kindheartedly, "The important thing is that your methods work. You are getting production out of your plantation, when almost no one else is."

"This is true," said Joseph. "In fact, a man just offered me money to show him how to do it. I'm afraid, however, that the real answer to the problem is that many people in the South will have to change the way they manage the former slave population."

Joseph avoided mentioning that he had sold the property to Ben Montgomery, and kept his management of the plantation well-disguised from a legal point of view for a number of reasons. It was illegal to sell property to blacks under the new Mississippi Black Codes. Also, Joseph did not want to give Montgomery a higher profile in the community because it could draw animosity to him and hurt his chances of success. This would also ultimately hurt Joseph's income, which he derived from the plantation. Lastly, Joseph did not want to tarnish his own reputation in the community, which was still raw with the consequences of the war.

He came to the realization that keeping a low profile for both him and his plantation was the best policy for the time being. While the Mississippi Black Codes was an anathema to the Republican Party, many of its tenets would be a force to reckon with for the next hundred years.

After finishing his talk with Joseph, Josh went into town to meet with Wilms and Cathy. He followed Wilms's directions and walked up to his house, which was a medium-size, two-story colonial, more indigenous in style to New England than Mississippi. The house was built on a high point of the bluff looking out over the river. It had a comfortable back porch, where Cathy and John received Josh and Emily after showing them around the house.

"This house has a beautiful view of the river," said Josh. "It is so peaceful here now that the war is over."

"What are you going to do now?" asked Wilms. "You've been working with the freedmen at Davis Bend for many years now. That sure has been a good and useful place to work. The problem is the rest of the South is going back to a stage that seems worse than slavery.

"Negroes are getting beaten, forced to work like slaves, and not getting paid. The Ku Klux Klan is threatening everyone, both white and black. Things still look bad, even though some Negroes have been elected to office and some important legislation has been passed."

"You're right," said Josh. "It's very discouraging. Emily and I were talking about returning to New England."

"We want to raise a family," said Emily, breaking into the conversation abruptly. "We don't want to do it in a place like this, even though Davis Bend is protected from most of the bad things that are happening throughout the South."

"The blacks freed themselves from slavery," said Josh. "They brought the South to its knees, only to lose all they had gained through a reign of terror by reactionary southerners."

They group of six stayed together working with the freedmen for three years while all the plantations in the area suffered calamity after calamity. Davis Bend began to prosper just as the Radical Republicans took over congress and began to push their own version of Reconstruction, which was much more favorable to the black population.

One day, Jackson arrived at breakfast in an ecstatic mood after reading some newspapers from Washington, DC. "It looks like we're finally going to get our freedom," he said. "The Thirteenth and Fourteenth amendments have now passed. Blacks are getting elected in New Orleans. A man named Pinchback was elected Louisiana state senator. It looks like there are opportunities in politics for freedmen and former slaves," he said excitedly. "Good legislation is being proposed by Republicans and blacks. Maybe our ship is finally coming in. Perhaps we should go into politics. There are lots of opportunities around these days."

"Don't do it—it is a trap," said Nate, with a disgusted look on his face. "You heard what Ben Montgomery has said. The only reason we are getting anything is because Union troops are here. When they pull out, everything will go to hell in a hand basket."

Josh agreed strongly with Nate. "This is an artificial situation. As long as the Union troops stay here it looks like we have more freedom. Look what's happening with the Ku Klux Klan in many places. When the army pulls out, all their anger at losing the war is going to be focused on the one population that can't fight back. Please—we have to keep a low profile. We can't get sucked into this trap!"

Jackson was adamant. "I'm not sure I want to stay down here anymore if this is how it's going to be. The Constitution says we all have rights as citizens. Now we have to wait for some jackasses who fought for the rebels to accept us."

Then he stood up tall to his full six-foot-six height, towering over the group like a preacher. "This is like a horse race with two horses racing neck to neck. One horse embodies all that is good for mankind, and the other is pure evil through and through. As long as Reconstruction continues, it looks like the good horse is just barely winning. As disgusted as I am with this violence, we can't really leave now because we don't know who will win this race."

At that point Wilma joined the discussion forcefully. "Did you see what happened in North Carolina? Read this!"

She threw the newspaper down with a loud thump and then thought the better of it and picked up the newspaper to explain the situation. She read them the story about black State Senator Stevens, who was murdered when he came to meet with state Democrats. "They turned him over to Klansmen, who killed him. This in a state with a good governor who couldn't protect him." Wilma shook her head and everyone turned to her, looking somber.

"Trap or no trap," shouted Nate more out of confusion than anger, "we just can't abandon our position now."

"So we've got to stay then," echoed Josh. "But what position do we have by staying here?" He got up and paced back and forth, deep in thought, looking unsure as he faced the group.

"No—we've got to go!" yelled Nate, seemingly reversing his position. "Please hear me out! Please don't stop me or I may lose some of my thoughts." He faced the group squarely, making direct eye contact with everyone. "Remember how we came down here to try to destroy slavery. We felt we would be more effective here than up north, where we were powerless. It's just the opposite now. The whole world has changed dramatically up north since the war ended. From what I am reading in the paper and in letters from my friends in Massachusetts, we might not recognize some parts of the United States now."

"What are you getting at?" asked Josh

"Please let me finish. I am hearing that intelligent people who fought against slavery are now saying that the slaves have had enough help, and the North should give up on Reconstruction now. It is too costly and it is fostering dependence of the freedmen on the government. While this has been going on, the Confederate states are being redeemed and are becoming part of the United States again. This means the return of many old Confederates to power. As quickly as favorable legislation is proposed or passed, these former Confederates are trying to destroy it."

Nate began to break out into a sweat as he spoke with great emotion.

"We need to do something to continue Reconstruction. I think we can do more up north where the real seat of power now rests. We can tell people what it is like down here. We can write articles in the paper and speak to groups. We have got to let people know not to give up on Reconstruction because that could start a bloodbath."

"We have got to move up north. We can't do enough here to affect the outcome of things. We moved south when we felt it would attack slavery, and now we need to move north to try to save Reconstruction!"

"You're absolutely right!" broke in Emily. "We have some other reasons to move north as well. All of us are not getting any younger, and if we don't start soon, we may not be able to raise families, which has been another goal we've all had. Do you want to raise children in an environment where freedmen are being murdered like Senator Stevens was?"

The emotional effect of Senator Stevens's murder stirred up everyone's thinking, and issues that had been under the surface began to come out.

"I think we all need to have a meeting to discuss these events further," said Nate. "The Klan is terrifying all the freedmen. They are looking over their shoulder and afraid to speak their mind. I think we are all feeling like failures after what we felt was one of our greatest accomplishments. We need to come up with a new strategy and plan for our lives."

"Let's do it right now," said Emily, grasping the side of her chair. "This is a crucial decision."

Everyone had an anxious, taut expression as they discussed their different options.

"We have been lucky in Davis Bend so far as many people still think Joe Davis is running the show," said Josh, "and in some ways he is, mentoring Ben Montgomery so that he will succeed with the plantation. Ben is well-liked by most white people in the area," he went on. "It is highly unlikely that he would be a target for the Klan, nor would we be targets because people remember me well–thinking that I fought for the Confederacy when I was walking around in a Confederate colonel's uniform. I think the colony at Davis Bend has been safe from Klan violence because they continue to keep a low profile under Ben's tutelage. At this time, there appears so far to be less Klan violence in this part of Mississippi, around Davis Bend, than in the Carolinas or Georgia. It may be because there are more blacks here and they outnumber the whites in many places. We need to look at more than just Mississippi, if we want to stop the Klan."

"What do we do about the violence in the area," continued Nate, looking intently at Josh. "If we are going to leave, shouldn't we train more freedmen to fight back?"

"We need to be prepared militarily in case things get bad around here," said Josh. "Remember, we are surrounded by thousands of former Confederate soldiers, many of whom gave their all to continue slavery. If we get into a fight with them, we can't win unless Federal troops support us. As we saw from President Johnson's attitude, there are many folks up north who don't want to support Reconstruction. We can offer assistance and protection to people harassed by the Klan. We could offer monetary help from up north as well. I think, however, as Ben Montgomery has pointed out, everyone here needs to keep a low profile at Davis Bend until we have a better understanding of how national politics play out.

"My father has some contacts in the Grant administration. He could get us an audience to discuss our concerns. The government must maintain its vigilance and intervene strongly in the South now, before things get entirely out of hand. If we stay here and become politically active, we could risk destroying the entire colony at Davis Bend.

"I am going to get Seth Feinberg to come down from Vicksburg and discuss this situation with us. It feels like our revolution has been circumvented, and we need to figure out what to do," said Josh.

CHAPTER 72

CONTEMPLATION OF THE FUTURE

A week later Josh convinced Feinberg to take the day off from his now busy store to talk to the group of six. They met in the guesthouse, where they were staying, after greeting Feinberg at the steamboat landing.

Feinberg had aged considerably. All his bushy hair had turned gray, and with his gray beard he now had the distinct appearance of a visiting college professor. The group found his mind as sharp as ever.

"We are all feeling very discouraged. The Klan is wreaking havoc with the freedmen's lives," Nate began. "What did we help to free the slaves for—to lead to this? It looks like the quality of a freedman's life is worse now than it was under slavery."

"Now they are free to be whipped, beaten, or hanged," Josh added, "if they object to these conditions, or try to change them. We don't want to live in a place with lawlessness running rampant like this. The army can't protect anyone any more, and even if it could, many of the people are just waiting for it to leave in order to get even with the freedmen. Many former abolitionists are no longer supporting Reconstruction. This is happening at the same time that previously Confederate states are coming back into the Union. They are electing former Confederates who are trying to undo all the good Republican legislation that has been passed."

"We all dedicated our lives to freeing the slaves," said Joan, her voice quivering with emotion. "We were all prepared to die for this cause if we had to, even though we did not go about things the way John Brown did."

"What was the point of our work?" Wilma added. "I think we all feel like a bunch of fools who were cruelly tricked."

At that point Emily broke in, showing a streak of anger and revulsion. "I just want to get out of here as fast as I can. I hate what the South has become. I hate what these people are doing! They have no moral code."

"We can't let Reconstruction fail," said Josh with a perplexed look on his face. "If it fails, we will still be dealing with the same issues a hundred years from now. You do want to save Reconstruction, don't you Emily?"

"Of course, I do!" answered Emily. "I think we can do much more working up north, which appears to be the prime mover of what takes place down south now."

At that point Feinberg, who had been silently listening and occasionally scratching his head, broke in and began to speak much like a professor talking to a group of students. The last few years of living in America had helped rid him of his need to reverse the subject and verb, but he still had the heavy German accent they all knew.

"These are a part of the lessons of history. From my experience as a revolutionary over the last twenty-five years in Europe and my connection to other revolutionaries, I believe I can tell you some universal truths.

"All revolutions are followed by a period of reaction. This period feels like nothing has happened positively, and things are going backwards or getting worse."

"That's just the way I feel," said Jackson

"Progress is measured over a long period of time, not in tiny parcels of time," said Feinberg. "You all should be proud of what you did. It was part of a mighty move of history. History always moves in the long-term in a direction to resolve these awful situations over time. There will come a time when the offspring of these former black slaves may be running this country."

"As I look at what is going on now, I can't imagine it," said Wilma.

"One of my revolutionary beliefs involves the dialectics of history," said Feinberg. "It involves the interplay of two forces to reach a higher level of solving a problem. The concept is a lot like a disagreement between a husband and wife that is resolved in a positive way for both parties. Men often see solutions one way, and women see it another way. This interplay is usually solved in a positive and creative way if both parties stick with the discussion and agree to work it out. I believe it is the hallmark of a happy marriage.

"While we are talking about some deadly serious things here, and not a happy marriage, I think this dialectic process underlies all of history. Therefore, one can't be discouraged by what appears to be no real progress or a return to an earlier period."

"Sorry, but that whole thing sounds like a pile of highfalutin' gibberish," said Nate. "Freedmen are getting beaten and murdered now. How can we stop this?"

"We can't," said Feinberg. "If the government or the army refuses to intervene, the situation will have to play itself out, and then there will be a reaction back the other way. The government and the people of the United States may need to react to the bad treatment of the former slaves and others in order for it to get rid of the Klan."

"Well, I don't think any of us are willing to wait around here for this to happen. We need to do something to stop this," said Jackson. "I'm for getting out of here as soon as possible and trying to convince northerners to help support Reconstruction."

"That goes for me too," said Nate.

"I think we all feel the same way," Josh said, turning to Joan and Wilma. "Do you agree?"

"Of course, we do!"

"Maybe you all should leave to fight back in a different way," said Feinberg. "I myself would consider leaving, but I can't afford to. I lost almost all my money during the war. I now have a contract selling goods to the US government, which is helping to replenish my losses. When the contract is over, I too may leave—if I can convince my wife to go.

"You all have done enough good work for a lifetime. I can see your point in not remaining here now that the reaction has set in. I still believe that all of this will come right eventually.

"My view of history is an optimistic one. That is why, when I look at all these miserable conditions, I am optimistic for change. It's just that you have to have a long-term horizon when you look at history. This could take a hundred or a hundred and fifty years. We may all be buried in a graveyard when it happens.

"The people who will make change happen will have stood on all of your shoulders and the shoulders of the people who came after you. Nothing is surer than that, one day, change will come. Remember, this is our time, our issue, and our place in history. This is our marker in the parade of generations to come. None of us will probably live to see a resolution of these issues. Nevertheless, history will not forget what all of you did."

EPILOGUE

Joseph Davis died in September 1870, at the age of 86. When the six left to go north there was no one there to hear of their departure other than Ben Montgomery. He was sad to see them leave but was also glad that they were going north to fight for Reconstruction. The six had already said goodbye to their remaining friends, including Wilms and Cathy, and prepared to head north back to Massachusetts.

During their last evening on the plantation, they sat on the porch watching the sun set over the river. They stared out at the fast packet heading for New Orleans rounding the bend in the river.

"I feel like a part of me will be gone when we leave, even though I was only a lowly slave for much of my time here," said Jackson, his voice showing a deeper level of emotion than usual.

"Many of the things we went through may not ever happen again in our lifetime," said Nate thoughtfully. "It is too bad the South has changed and become dangerous now."

"I have mixed feelings about leaving also," said Josh. "But we have to go. Right now, we can be much more effective up north. If we stayed here our only choice would be to keep a low profile in order to protect Ben and the colony. In these violent times, it would have to be even lower than when we began our work."

"It's a special place for me too," said Joan, looking lovingly at Nate. "I fell in love here. There will always be a special place inside of me for this plantation, this river, and the life we led while we were fighting slavery."

"What we did here was the biggest thing in my life," said Josh. "I don't know what life has in store for each of us, but it is probably downhill from here."

"What's downhill about getting married and raising a family?" asked Wilma. "That's what Jackson and I want to do."

"Nothing," said Josh. "Emily and I have been talking about starting a family as well."

"Nate and I are talking about the same thing," said Joan.

"Another thing that's on my mind," said Jackson, "is we've got to figure out a way to make a living when we go north. I could be a blacksmith, but who would hire me?"

"Don't worry about that right now, my father has connections all over New England," said Josh. "He has agreed to help us all get started and reintegrate ourselves back into life in New England."

Emily glanced over with a sad look, and a tear starting to form in the corner of her eye. "I'm sure going to miss this place."

"I think all of us feel the same way about it," said Wilma with a quiver in her lip. "Still, we've got to get out of here while the getting's good. If we can't keep Reconstruction going, things are going to go downhill here very fast."

"With the army pulling out," Nate added, "the Klan is growing rapidly every day. A lot of white folks are going to blame the lost war on the freedmen who deserted their plantations in the middle of a crisis."

"I think you're right," said Josh. "I can't bear to see any of our work unravel in the rest of the state and in other states as well, even if it doesn't effect Davis Bend directly."

They all shared a group hug, as this was their last night on the plantation.

The next morning the six got on the riverboat to Vicksburg where they boarded a train. They retraced the original route they had followed to come south in 1859—this time heading north.

Their departure began in a melancholy mood, but as they traveled into the northeast, their normal fun-loving banter returned as they began to look forward with their old excitement to their new challenges in life.

Once resettled back in Massachusetts, they all began their new lives up north.

The North, they found, had changed markedly since their departure. There were signs of wealth everywhere. Wealthy men with top hats roamed the streets talking about nothing else but making money. Rail lines led everywhere. Everyone wanted to forget about the war because it was a trauma in their minds that they now wanted to lose. Unfortunately, Reconstruction, still connected to the war, was the baby they threw out with the bathwater. This did not bode well for their avowed goal—that of saving Reconstruction.

Nate, having married Joan, got his old job back at the famous Parker Hotel as head chef. With the assistance of Will Lawrence, who cosigned for Nate's mortgage, he and Joan were able to buy a house. They started a family. Nate spent much of his time lecturing and writing on the need to continue Reconstruction, not only for the plight of the freedmen, but for the good of the whole country. He always ended his talks, lectures, and meetings with the words, "If we give up on Reconstruction now, this issue will continue to plague the country for the next two hundred years."

Jackson, after marrying Wilma, set up a blacksmith, veterinarian, and farrier shop in Lowell with Will's financial assistance. He quickly made a success of it. Wilma helped him run the shop after he gave her a quick on-the-job training. As in most things, she proved an apt pupil. He and Wilma raised two boys who both turned out to be gifted athletes. Jackson spent much of his time active in his church and as a social activist in the Boston metropolitan area. He also gave weekly lectures on the need to continue Reconstruction.

Ben Montgomery's cotton plantation prospered until the great depression of 1873 caused major dislocation for farmers everywhere. This was compounded by severe flooding of the Mississippi River. He went bankrupt in 1876 and died a year later. Ten years later, his son Isaiah started a colony based on the Owenistic principles of Joseph Davis at Mound Bayou, Mississippi. He persuaded some of the old veterans from Davis Bend to come to the new colony, which prospered until his death in 1924.

Marie Laver moved to Baton Rouge with many of her followers where she set up a large healing practice, which was still functioning at the beginning of the twentieth century. She continued to claim credit for winning the Civil War

Josh and Emily's adjustment was a bit more difficult than that of the other four members of their former group. Now that Josh had returned, Will wanted him to take over the family business because he was advancing in years. That business had grown greatly during the war.

Josh agreed to do it, thinking it might give him more of a power base to agitate for the continuity of Reconstruction, which he had continued to work and lobby for with all the others. His heart, however, was not really in running a mill. Economic disaster struck in September of 1873. This began the start of a great depression. Hard times, which began during the mid-1870s, saw the rise of unions and much labor unrest.

This was a particularly difficult time for Josh. He found that he sympathized with the working class more than the mill owners and capitalists in the area. This caused an acute role conflict for him as he was now managing a mill. It was actually a mill that had catered more to the workers' needs than did many other mills in the area.

He and his father had difficulty with the local union in their area. The union wanted to show the workers that it could impose demands and get results, even if the bosses they were dealing with were social activists, as were Josh and his father.

This whole experience soured Josh on what he had only undertaken reluctantly in order to help his father. After four unhappy years, he had a long talk with Will and told him that he wanted to leave the mill and move his family out west. He wanted to try his hand at ranching. Josh's cousin also worked in the mill management, and Josh felt he would be a better fit for the role of mill manager. His father reluctantly agreed to Josh's plan.

If the Great Depression of 1873 profoundly changed Josh's personal outlook on the future, it also destroyed most of whatever small interest there was in continuing Reconstruction as people began to pull in their horns and become less interested in the plight of others. In 1874 the depression led to the Democrats taking power in the House of Representatives. To everyone in the know, it meant that for all intent and purposes, Reconstruction would be finished because it was seen by many as an additional economic drain that the country could not afford in hard times. It was in this atmosphere that Josh and Emily decided to shift gears. Nothing the group could do was able to help save Reconstruction, which was brought down by a confluence of many additional adverse forces. In 1875 Reconstruction was overthrown in Mississippi by white supremacists. What was left of it in the South was bargained away in the disputed presidential election of 1876.

Josh and Emily moved out to the Arizona territory, where Emily promptly gave birth to twin daughters. In the first years after their arrival, Josh became a cattle rancher on a large spread not too far from Tucson, Arizona. He thoroughly enjoyed this work and invited his old team to come out west and join him in the business. They did not want to do this since they were well ensconced in their family lives up north.

Josh's parents died in the 1890s, and he received a large inheritance, some of which he used to greatly increase his cattle spread. By 1900 he owned one of the largest cattle operations in the territory.

Despite the distances that separated them, the group continued to meet for yearly reunions, either in the Arizona territory or in Massachusetts, to renew their lifelong friendship. These reunions continued into the early 1900s, when the group was aging but still alive. These gatherings were always joyous events–with families mixing together reliving the past and, as always, looking beyond the present to a better future.

CPSIA information can be obtained
at www.ICGtesting.com
Printed in the USA
LVHW111627130123
736960LV00007B/1527

9 781951 937157